KING ALFR[illegible]

£7.50

8225

WITHDRAWN FROM
THE LIBRARY

UNIVERSITY OF
WINCHESTER

# The Religion of the Heart

# THE RELIGION OF THE HEART

## *Anglican Evangelicalism and the Nineteenth-Century Novel*

ELISABETH JAY

CLARENDON PRESS · OXFORD
1979

*Oxford University Press, Walton Street, Oxford* OX2 6DP

OXFORD LONDON GLASGOW
NEW YORK TORONTO MELBOURNE WELLINGTON
KUALA LUMPUR SINGAPORE JAKARTA HONG KONG TOKYO
DELHI BOMBAY CALCUTTA MADRAS KARACHI
NAIROBI DAR ES SALAAM CAPE TOWN

*Published in the United States by*
*Oxford University Press, New York*

© *Elisabeth Jay 1979*

*All rights reserved. No part of this publication may be reproduced, stored in a retrieval system, or transmitted, in any form or by any means, electronic, mechanical, photocopying, recording, or otherwise, without the prior permission of Oxford University Press*

**British Library Cataloguing in Publication Data**
Jay, Elizabeth
The religion of the heart.
1. English fiction—19th century—History and criticism 2. Evangelicalism—Church of England —Influence 3. Protestantism and literature
I. Title
823'.709' PR830.E/ 79-40391

ISBN 0-19-812092-3

*Printed in Great Britain by*
*Western Printing Services Ltd., Bristol*

*For*
*Richard*

# Preface

IN an avowedly ecumenical age so clear a declaration of interest in the Established church may at first sight seem wilfully retrograde. The academic rationale for illuminating the distinction between Dissenting and Anglican Evangelicalism as practised and recorded by adherents and critics in the nineteenth century will, I hope, emerge in the course of this book. Although I have endeavoured to maintain impartial standards of judgement, the preface is perhaps the correct place to acknowledge an upbringing within the traditions of Anglican Evangelical piety and to thank my parents for, amongst other things, providing me with a subject.

In the process of writing a book which attempts to span, or at least enter, the worlds of church history and literary criticism one inevitably incurs many debts. At various times during my graduate work I was fortunate in receiving supervision from Tony Cockshut, Geoffrey Rowell, and Rachel Trickett. I should also like to thank the following for the help, information and advice they have provided: John Walsh, Valentine Cunningham, Alastair Parker, Peter Toon, and Norman Vance. I am grateful to Anne Bentley, Ian Bradley, Valentine Cunningham, Margaret Doody, Sheridan Gilley, Bryan Hardman, Andrew Kerr, A. G. Newell, S. C. Orchard, Haddon Willmer, John Walsh, and Kathleen Watson for either explicitly or implicitly giving their permission for me to read their theses, and especially to the last two, who entrusted their own copies to me.

St. Anne's College was generous in providing research scholarships and other forms of assistance. The staffs of all the libraries I have used deserve my thanks, but none more so than the staff of Bodley's Upper Reading Room, whose consistent good humour makes it a pleasure to work there.

My most enduring debt of gratitude must, however, be reserved for my first tutor, Dorothy Bednarowska, whose stimulating teaching set me off on the road to more specialized study of the nineteenth century, and whose sustained interest, encouragement, and friendship have been greatly valued.

Finally I must thank my husband who has borne with the numerous disruptions the work entailed, acting as a sounding board for ideas and offering suggestions for improvements in the style.

None of these, of course, can be held responsible for any errors of fact, obstinacies of misinterpretation, or perversities of style which still remain.

*Bladon, 1977* ELISABETH JAY

# Contents

# References

Unless otherwise stated the following editions of these authors have been used.

| | |
|---|---|
| Brontës | *Life and Works of Charlotte Brontë and Her Sisters*, Illustrated Edn. (7 vols., 1872–3); except for *Jane Eyre*, ed. Jane Jack and Margaret Smith (Clarendon edn., Oxford, 1969). |
| Butler, S. | *Shrewsbury Edition*, ed. H. F. Jones and A. J. Bartholomew (20 vols., 1923–6). |
| Dickens, C. | *The New Oxford Illustrated Edition* (21 vols., 1947–1958). |
| Disraeli, B. | *Bradenham Edition* (1926–7). |
| Eliot, G. | *Cabinet Edition* (24 vols., Edinburgh, 1878–18[85]). |
| Thackeray, W. M. | *Oxford Edition*, ed. G. Saintsbury (17 vols., 1908). |
| Yonge, C. M. | *Novels and Tales* (16 vols., 1879–80). |

Unless otherwise stated, books are published in London.

Where the edition of any work to which I refer was published anonymously this is indicated in the first footnote reference and in the Book-list by square brackets.

# Abbreviations

The titles of the following periodicals and reference works have been abbreviated as follows:

| | |
|---|---|
| *AHR* | *American Historical Review* |
| *BST* | *Brontë Society Transactions* |
| *CO* | *Christian Observer* |
| *CQR* | *Church Quarterly Review* |
| *DNB* | *The Dictionary of National Biography* |
| *Edin. Rev.* | *Edinburgh Review* |
| *Fraser's* | *Fraser's Town and Country Magazine* |
| *HMPEC* | *Historical Magazine of the Protestant Episcopal Church* |
| *JBS* | *Journal of British Studies* |
| *JEcH* | *Journal of Economic History* |
| *JEGP* | *Journal of English and Germanic Philology* |
| *JEH* | *Journal of Ecclesiastical History* |
| *JTS* | *Journal of Theological Studies* |
| *MLQ* | *Modern Language Quarterly* |
| *NED* | *A New English Dictionary on Historical Principles* |
| *N & Q* | *Notes and Queries* |
| *NBR* | *North British Review* |
| *NCF* | *Nineteenth Century Fiction* |
| *PMLA* | *Publications of the Modern Language Association* |
| *PP* | *Past and Present* |
| *TLS* | *Times Literary Supplement* |
| *TMSS* | *Transactions of the Manchester Statistical Society* |
| *VN* | *Victorian Newsletter* |
| *VS* | *Victorian Studies* |
| *WR* | *Westminster Review* |

## PART ONE

---

# Introduction

> . . . if history be anything more than a chronological catalogue of facts, if it be concerned with the movements of mind and spirit, then I submit that to read history aright we must know, not only the works of art that each age produced but also their value as works of art.[1]

THE form in which this book is written is dictated by the belief that we cannot fully understand the work of the major English nineteenth-century novelists unless we have some knowledge of the world from which they came. The first part provides this detailed background for the second, which considers individual authors and the tradition of Evangelical portrayal.

The major novelists with whom I am concerned were, for the most part, writing during the early and mid-Victorian period. The notable and consuming interest in themselves manifested by these Victorians was reflected in the novel by the flowering of the great age of domestic realism in English fiction. This study starts with the desire to bring back to the twentieth-century reader the experience and understanding of the nineteenth-century novelists and their audience. A 'classic' may well survive because of the universality of the human emotions it describes or invokes, but to concentrate upon this lowest common denominator, so to speak, is to miss the timbre of the individual voice or the peculiar flavour lent by time and place of composition; it involves a loss of awareness of values and nuances almost commensurate with that experienced in reading literature in translation.

Nowhere is this more apparent than in considering the Victorian

[1] C. Bell, *Art* (1914), p. 97.

novelists' treatment of religion. Today religion is felt to be either too personal or too esoteric a subject to come within the province of the novel. Throughout the Victorian period, however, it was assumed that a man's religious life was so intimately bound up with his social existence and behaviour that to ignore it was to sacrifice a major insight into the influences forming a man's character. Even reviews which deplored the specific treatment accorded to religion in various novels rarely questioned that, rightly understood, religion was native to the novel's sphere,[2] unless, of course, they altogether condemned the fictional mode.

The first part of the book, therefore, attempts to identify the Evangelicals, what they believed, the demands that their faith made upon their everyday life, and the impact they made upon the non-Evangelical world around them. In this endeavour I have not hesitated to use the wealth of material which the novel has to offer. Such a practice necessarily raises the vexed question of using the novel to supplement history.[3] Whilst it must be a tedious and ultimately fruitless process to comb novels for minor examples of facts better documented in primary historical sources, fiction can illuminate historical study by revealing the 'felt' quality of life—contemporary opinion and prejudice. In this respect the treatment of Evangelicalism by novelists who were not doctrinally expert or inspired can be just as useful, in revealing which facets of Evangelical piety made an impact upon the non-Evangelical portion of the population, as can the polemically inspired novel, whose uses and dangers are more easily recognized.

By this arrangement of the material I hope also to be able to show the contribution made by Evangelical ideas and practices to the development and direction of the English novel. Evangelical novels shared in the general contribution made by the religious novel in developing that strain of introspection fostered by Richardson and the sentimentalists, whilst Evangelical literature, in its wider form of religious biographies, tracts, and newspapers, also exerted an in-

[2] e.g. 'Low-Church Novels, and Tendencies', *Christian Remembrancer*, 6 (1843), 518–538; 'Religious Stories', *Fraser's*, 38 (1848), 150–66; 'The Hard Church Novel', *National Review*, 3 (1856), 127–46; [W. Y. Sellars], 'Religious Novels', *NBR* 26 (1856), 209–27; [W. H. Pater], '*Robert Elsmere* by Mrs. Humphry Ward', *Guardian* (28 Mar. 1888), pp. 468–9.

[3] Despite V. Cunningham's survey of the twentieth-century history of this controversy and his defence of the practice (*Everywhere Spoken Against: Dissent in the Victorian Novel* (Oxford, 1975), pp.1–7) reviewers' responses demonstrated that the debate is by no means closed.

fluence upon the secular novel. I shall attempt to demonstrate this latter influence with particular reference to the presentation of death and the emphasis placed upon realism in many Victorian novels.

For the process of literary criticism this method of supplying a historical context for our reading seems equally advantageous. Comparing the reactions of thinking men and women to a religion which they recognized as a pervasive force in the society they sought to portray, helps to throw light upon their relative ability as novelists. Their reaction varied as they attempted to use the provisional and exploratory world of the novel to come to terms with the finality and certainty of the Evangelical dogma which sometimes baffled or angered them in their own lives. A refusal to encounter in fictional terms problems which their letters or articles reveal to have been of some personal concern can serve to highlight or explain certain of their inadequacies as artists.

This method should, then, sharpen rather than blunt our awareness of literary quality. Charlotte Yonge, herself a polemically inspired novelist, provided a *caveat* which anyone attempting to examine the novel's treatment of religion does well to remember: '. . . a "religious tale", overloaded with controversy, and with forced moral, should be carefully distinguished from a tale constructed on a strong basis of religious principle, which attempts to give a picture of life as it really is seen by Christian eyes.'[4]

Her words point to a division, which I have been implying, between minor and major works of fiction—a division based upon the critical belief that novels organized on doctrinal principles fall into the former category when the case they are intended to present proves more important than its imaginative embodiment. J. H. Newman's novel, *Loss and Gain*, for instance, though providing a series of amusing *bons mots* and thumbnail sketches, has rightly been placed by George Levine on 'the boundaries of fiction',[5] since its interest to the reader lies rather in the oblique autobiographical recollections and beliefs of the author than in the intrinsic plot of character interest of the novel. George Eliot's novels frequently owe almost as much to her own memories, and are equally written with a pervasive doctrinal purpose, yet achieve the status of major works because she realized that the most the novel can be expected to do is to dramatize for us the way in which characters live when they fall under the spell of,

[4] 'Children's Literature of the Last Century', *Macmillan's Magazine*, 20 (1869), 310.
[5] G. Levine, *The Boundaries of Fiction* (*Princeton*, 1968).

or consciously adopt, certain beliefs. The temptation to the novelist bent upon polemical victory is to gain a triumph for his beliefs within the short scope of the novel by showing attractive characters living according to the principles he approves and unattractive characters espousing precisely those doctrines under condemnation. George Eliot's recollections of her childhood reading testify to the effect, albeit limited, which this method enjoyed:

> . . . it appears to me that there is unfairness in arbitrarily selecting a train of circumstances, and a set of characters as a development of a class of opinions. In this way we might make atheism appear wonderfully calculated to promote social happiness. I remember, as I dare say you do, a very amiable atheist depicted by Bulwer in Devereux, and for some time after the perusal of that book, which I read 7 or 8 years ago, I was considerably shaken by the impression that religion was not a requisite to moral excellence.[6]

She had been little more than thirteen when she read *Devereux*, and such doctrinally oriented novels were often written with just such a young and impressionable audience in mind. The adult George Eliot did not always herself refrain from another device much favoured by the polemically inclined. Her work is sometimes flawed by the desire to arrange convenient demises or punishments for those who oppose her own codes of doctrine or conduct, thus meeting the novel's need for a greater sense of causality than life itself often presents, but at the expense of the complementary need for verisimilitude.

Authors could of course write intelligently, *in propria persona*, on a doctrinal subject within a novel, and thereby make an impact upon religious opinion, though rarely within the best fictional mode. But then novelists like Hannah More or J. H. Newman, who openly declared that they had seized upon this genre as the most favourable for the promulgation of their doctrine,[7] accorded little of the aesthetic respect to their tool that we might expect from the committed artist. Even Thackeray, who affected to hold novel-writing as a profession and the novel as a genre in low repute,[8] saw cause for satire of the contemporary fashion for the *roman à thèse*, whose con-

[6] *The George Eliot Letters*, ed. G. S. Haight (7 vols., 1954–6), i, 45.

[7] [H. More], *Coelebs in Search of a Wife* (2 vols., 1808), vol. i, pp. vii–viii; J. H. Newman, *Loss and Gain: the Story of a Convert* (1896), p. ix.

[8] *The Letters and Private Papers of William Makepeace Thackeray*, ed. G. N. Ray (4 vols., 1945–6), iii, 13, 287, 294.

tempt for aesthetic integrity he caricatured as a prostitution of art to commercial interest.[9]

Thackeray's own stance as stage-manager of his novels draws attention to the distinction between the author *in propria persona* and the author as omniscient narrator. The 'intrusive' narrator, who fell into disrepute only towards the close of the nineteenth century with the emergence of Henry James as a major figure on the literary scene, enabled the author to comment on the doctrine embraced by his characters. Post-Jamesian criticism has taught us to accept this commentary as long as it is presented with sufficient detachment and tolerant objectivity not to be instantly recognizable as impassioned special pleading: in other words the author's opinions prove acceptable if they serve to illuminate the drama in process, but not if they attempt to replace the drama. Lest this critical approach should seem so dogmatic as to ignore the flexibility of the novel form in the first two-thirds of the nineteenth century, it is worth contemplating the words of Charles Kingsley, a leading exponent of the *roman à thèse* school.

People are too stupid and in too great a hurry, to interpret the most puzzling facts for themselves, and the author must now and then act as showman, and do it for them. Whether it's according to 'Art' or not, I don't care a fig. What's 'Art'? . . . Art ought to mean the art of pleasing and instructing, and, believe me, these passages in which the author speaks in his own person do so . . . Women like them better than any part of a book.[10]

His remarks show how, at worst, the use of the novel as a forum for proselytizing activities stemmed from a contempt for the public's capacity for concentrated thought, and resulted in a devaluation of the form itself.

Yet these minor novels can perform a useful function. Writing at the close of the century Julia Wedgwood, in a review of Mrs. Humphry Ward's novels, expressed it thus:

While the fiction of the day is accessible and intelligible we may gain as much in accounting for that popularity which records the complacency of the crowd in listening to an echo of its own more resonant feelings and

[9] 'A Plan for a Prize Novel', *Miscellaneous Contributions to Punch, 1843–1854* (1908), pp. 175–7.

[10] *Charles Kingsley: His Letters and Memories of His Life, edited by his wife* (4 vols., 1901), iii, 41.

beliefs, as in attending to the accents which will reach posterity. Perhaps in some ways we may gain more. Genius brings in its own individuality to complicate its representative power . . .[11]

Minor novels provide the background against which the greatness of the literary Titans can be clearly recognized, whilst spelling out, for modern readers, threads of argument which were tightly woven into the texture of the greater artists' fictional world but now require underlining to restore them to the clarity of definition they enjoyed in the minds of the artists and their contemporary readers.

## 1. *The importance of Evangelicalism for the nineteenth-century novel*

Major and minor novels alike confirm the historians' acclamation of Evangelicalism as one of the two most important influences in Victorian society. Even those who claim that having 'reached its apogee'[12] in 1833 its 'work was done' and that it had grown 'complacent, fashionable, superior',[13] continue to assert a vaguely defined but powerful influence. Although its contribution to Victorian life is everywhere acknowledged, till recently historians have devoted little attention to studying the evolution of the Evangelical Movement after the advent of Tractarianism.[14] From 1833 to 1845 Oxford and Newman, 'one of the most subtle and attractive minds of the century,'[15] stole the attention of intellectual historians, and Evangelicalism, whose intellectual content had never formed its strongest appeal, was relegated to a peripheral position. It was talked of as a petrified body of reactionary opinion that constituted a drag upon the wheels of intellectual and social progress.

The essentials of Evangelical doctrine were to undergo little modification after 1833, yet the spirit of a movement which laid so great a stress on practical piety was necessarily affected by the way in which it met, or failed to meet, the challenges presented by a

[11] 'Fiction and Faith', *Contemporary Review*, 62 (1892), 217–18.

[12] E. Halévy, *A History of the English People in the Nineteenth Century*, iii, *The Triumph of Reform 1830–1841*, trans. E. I. Watkin (1950), p. 162.

[13] G. M. Young, *Victorian England: Portrait of an Age* (1964), pp. 4–5.

[14] The major work on the period exists in two recent, unpublished theses: B. E. Hardman, 'The Evangelical Party in the Church of England, 1855–1865', D. Phil. thesis. Cambridge 1963. A. Bentley, 'The Transformation of the Evangelical Party in the Church of England in the Later Nineteenth Century', D. Phil. thesis. Durham, 1971.

[15] G. R. S. K. Clark, *The Making of Victorian England* (1962), p. 23, where the historical lacuna to which I refer is noted.

changing society. Evangelicalism, like Romanticism, had offered an alternative to the philosophy on which the new industrial society was founded. Although the precise relation between Evangelicalism and the other dominant philosophy of the age, Utilitarianism, is notoriously difficult to estimate, in theory they were antithetical. Whilst Utilitarianism thought the interests of the individual and of the community should be identical, Evangelicalism asserted the unique importance of the individual. Evangelicalism's emphasis on a personal relationship with God, its rejection of the corporate authority of the Church, and the premium it placed upon the individual's judgement assured a man of a significance frequently denied him in secular society. Utilitarianism's best-informed critic, John Stuart Mill, recognized the Protestant religion as a theoretical champion of the individual, even though like any other religion it might become despotic in practice.[16]

Evangelicalism, as a philosophy, was therefore calculated to appeal to the novelist since it invited him to contemplate characters who recognized no compulsion to conform to the standards of contemporary society. To some novelists this philosophy appeared as little more than a convenient bolster, utilized by the naturally obstinate or arrogant. To a novelist like George Eliot, fascinated by the complex relation between the individual and society, the evangelical spirit served to create characters with a clear sense of their own identity and to throw their conflict with society into more prominent relief.

Evangelicalism was in itself a powerful literary force. In his debate with Gladstone, Lecky drew attention to the popularity of Evangelical literature at the close of the eighteenth century. 'The fact that the greater part of it is almost absolutely destitute of literary merit only strengthens my argument for its representative character, for it shows that it owed its success much more to its substance than to its form.'[17]

The figures compiled by Patrick Scott indicate an increase in the publication of religious books during the first half of the nineteenth century. Between 1801 and 1835 they formed 22·2 per cent of all books published and between 1836 and 1863 33·5 per cent were religious in content.[18] It was the last four decades of the century

[16] *Utilitarianism*, *On Liberty*, *etc.*, ed. H. B. Acton (1972), pp. 71, 119–20.

[17] W. E. H. Lecky, 'The History of the Evangelical Movement', *Nineteenth Century*, 6 (1879), 282.

[18] P. Scott, 'The Business of Belief: The Emergence of Religious Publishing', *Sanctity and Secularity: The Church and The World*, ed. D. Baker (Oxford, 1973), p. 224.

which saw a decrease in religious publishing. A publishing house like Houlstons of Wellington, whose fortune had been built on an exclusively religious list, started to extend its range to secular literature.[19] By 1899 religious books formed only 9·2 per cent of all books published.[20] Although these figures include High, Broad, and Dissenting output, the comparative importance of the Evangelical contribution can be seen in the way that a publishing house's fortune could be affected by the decision to print non-Evangelical religious literature.

In 1835, after the decision to take over the publication of the *Tracts for the Times*, the publishing house of Rivingtons, once much favoured by Evangelical authors, lost the valuable agency of the Society for Promoting Christian Knowledge, by then under Evangelical control.[21] Entrusting Thomas Mozley, an extreme Tractarian, with the editorship of their long established periodical, *The British Critic*, lost the house a readership it never regained, and finally left the house without any periodical.

Many popular Evangelical works may have been bought as gifts which were never read, but the sales figures are still remarkable. The figures for the sale of juvenile literature reflect parental approbation as well as children's reading habits.[22] Mrs. Sherwood's *The Fairchild Family* ran through fourteen editions between 1818 and 1842 when the second part was published.[23] Favell Lee Bevan's *Peep of Day* sold a quarter of a million copies between 1833 and 1867.[24] Catherine Marsh's *Memorials of Captain Hedley Vicars* (1856) which combined the period interest of a Crimean setting, a tale of military heroism and unimpeachable Evangelical doctrine, rivalled even Dickens's

[19] M. N. Cutt, *Mrs. Sherwood and Her Books for Children* (1974), pp. 24, 35.

[20] This sudden fall does not necessarily reflect a commensurate decline in the reading of religious material: religious newspapers took to printing sermons and so decreased the market for the publication of individual sermons. For this and the subsequent information on Rivingtons' affairs, see S. Rivington, *The Publishing Family of Rivington* (1919), p. 154.

[21] For the Evangelical domination of this society's committee after 1833 see *CO* (1833), pp. 428–32, and T. Mozley, *Reminiscences; chiefly of Oriel College and the Oxford Movement* (2 vols., 1882), i, 335–8.

[22] e.g. '. . . at the present time there is nothing that pays so well as an exciting religious novel on evangelical principles. Make all your unbelievers and worldly people villains . . . you will have more readers than Dickens, Bulwer, or Thackeray. Well-meaning mothers will put the book without fear into the hands of their daughters.' C. [E. or H.] Spence, *Mr. Hogarth's Will* (1865), i, 94 ff. quoted by M. F. Brightfield, *Victorian England in its Novels* (4 vols., Los Angeles, 1968), i, 12.

[23] E. Wingfield-Stratford, *The Victorian Tragedy* (1930), p. 65.

[24] R. D. Altick, *The English Common Reader* (Chicago and London, 1967), p. 388.

novels as a publisher's dream. This particular biography sold 78,000 copies in its year of publication, compared with the 35,000 copies of *Bleak House*, sold between 1852 and 1853.[25]

From the first, Evangelical publications received attention from a wider circle than the faithful. In 1809 Jane Austen, who declared that her dislike for the Evangelicals disinclined her to read Hannah More's *Coelebs in Search of a Wife* (1808), nevertheless remarked, 'Of course I shall be delighted, when I read it, like other people.'[26] Both this work and the Revd. J. W. Cunningham's *The Velvet Cushion* (1814) were sufficiently widely read for their detractors to feel that it was worth publishing rejoinders in a similar form to the original.[27]

If the nineteenth-century public liked to read the works of Evangelical authors they also enjoyed the prospect of critical comment upon Evangelicalism in the secular novel.

Although very occasional mention of the Evangelicals had been made in the novel[28] before the publication of Mrs. Trollope's *The Vicar of Wrexhill* (1837), this was the first popular novel, not conceived of in terms of a doctrinal riposte, to confine its attention specifically to Anglican Evangelicals. The absence of comment in this novel upon Evangelicalism's clash with Tractarianism supports the contention that Mrs. Trollope was trading upon the success of Dickens's caricature[29] of Dissent, itself based upon an eighteenth-century tradition, rather than responding to the new stimulus for satire provided by that theological storm. Her sound commercial

[25] P. Scott, op. cit., p. 215.

[26] *Jane Austen's Letters to her Sister Cassandra and Others*, ed. R. W. Chapman (1952), p. 256. A piece of evidence to which insufficient weight is given by P. Garside and E. McDonald in 'Evangelicalism and *Mansfield Park*', *Trivium*, 10 (1975), 34–50. Their biased selection of material is less surprising when it is noted that they rely as a historical source upon the perversely prejudiced work of F. K. Brown, *Fathers of the Victorians* (Cambridge, 1961).

[27] [Anon.] *Coelebs Married: being intended as a Continuation of Coelebs in Search of a Wife* (1814). [H. Corp] *Coelebs Deceived* (1817). [Styles, J.] *The Legend of the Velvet Cushion in a Series of letters to my brother Jonathan who lives in the country* (1815).

[28] For example in Maria Edgeworth's *Ormond: A Tale* (2 vols., 1825), ii, ch. xxiii.

[29] M. Dalziel believes that Cartwright was created 'quite independently of the more famous character', Stiggins. *Popular Fiction One Hundred Years Ago* (1957), p. 161. Dickens's *Pickwick Papers* was published in monthly instalments between April 1836 and November 1837. Mr. Stiggins appeared in Nos. VIII (Nov. 1836), X (Jan. 1837), XII (Mar. 1837), XVI (Aug. 1837), and XVIII (Oct. 1837). *The Vicar of Wrexhill* (3 vols.) was published in the early autumn of 1837, *Publishers' Circular*, No. I (2 Oct. 1837), 1. Her publishing record suggests that she always studied the market carefully. Her first publication, *Domestic Manners of the Americans* (2 vols., 1832) was a conscious attempt to trade upon the recent success of Captain Basil Hall's *Travels in North America* (3 vols., Edinburgh, 1829).

instinct helped her to recognize that the style of religious satire, once directed against the late eighteenth-century Methodists,[30] could now be used against the enthusiastic excesses of contemporary Evangelicals. She seized upon the topic when it was on the point of becoming fashionable. Just as her novels of social concern[31] issue in a line of *romans à thèse* which reach their literary peak in the late 1840s, so *The Vicar of Wrexhill* heralds a succession of popular novels which make use of contemporary interest in religious controversy. Her son, Anthony, whose autobiographical assertions of his business-like attitude to literature were to shock the literary world of the 1880s, was quick to realize how useful the Evangelicals might be to him in his role of chronicler of ecclesiastical society and to recognize their well-attested comic potential. He made open avowal of the parentage of his Evangelical brood, telling T. H. Escott, ' "Dickens gibbeted cant in the person of Dissenters, of whom I never knew anything. I have done so in Mr. Slope, an Anglican, but the unbeneficed descendant of my mother's Vicar of Wrexhill." '[32]

Like his mother before him Trollope was perplexed and irritated by the Evangelicals but was prepared to exploit a personal preoccupation which coincided with a popular interest. 'Readers of the mid-Victorian epoch', Escott claimed, 'saw telling hits and life-like portraits in what may to-day seem not much removed above the level of caricature.'[33] Certainly stereotyped comic figures like the Mrs. Proudie of *Barchester Towers* won greater popularity than the more penetrating study of the intricate relation between dogma and the individual temperament in *John Caldigate*.

Mrs. Proudie was one of the favourites of Victorian literature whom Andrew Lang chose as a subject for his series of pastiches, *Old Friends*.[34] The nostalgic quality behind these reminiscences of

[30] For a detailed study see F. C. Gill, *The Romantic Movement and Methodism* (1937), ch. iv; and A. M. Lyles, *Methodism Mocked: The Satiric Reaction to Methodism in the Eighteenth Century* (1960).

[31] For an analysis of the mixture of genuine concern and commercial acuteness behind *The Life and Adventures of Michael Armstrong, the Factory Boy* (1840) and *Jessie Phillips: A Tale of the Present Day* (1842), see W. H. Chaloner, 'Mrs. Trollope and the Early Factory System', *VS* 4 (Dec. 1969), 159–66.

[32] T. H. Escott, *Anthony Trollope: His Work, Associates and Literary Originals* (1913), pp. 111–12.

[33] Ibid., p. 242.

[34] In two letters to Mrs. Quiverful, Mrs. Proudie first tells of her friendship with the titled convert, Lady Rebecca Crawley, and then of her subsequent disillusionment upon finding Lady Rebecca exercising her wiles upon Bishop Proudie. By introducing Rebecca as a relative of the Revd. Josiah Crawley, Lang draws attention to Trollope's

popular characters reminds us that by 1890, the date of their publication, Evangelicals had ceased to command the eager attention of the secular novelist. There are, of course, exceptions to this generalization. *Catharine Furze*, William Hale White's novel, published in 1893, is partly concerned with the inner life of an Evangelical parson, but the author's evident debt to the tone and content of George Eliot's novels, combined with the placing of the action in the 1840s, gives the work an air of historical reminiscence. Samuel Butler's *The Way of All Flesh* did not appear till 1903, but it had been started thirty years before. The very popularity of this book, I shall suggest in my closing chapter, dealt the death-blow to the tradition of the portrayal of Evangelicals in the novel. Yet this novel again talks of Evangelicalism as a childhood memory and appealed to the same response in its readers.

By the close of the nineteenth century Evangelicalism no longer formed so dominant a feature on the middle-class landscape. It had changed in the nature and therefore the breadth of its impact. The movement had turned away from the world of political and ecclesiastical strife which had obsessed it in mid-century and back to a more single-minded concern with spiritual life.

Just as Evangelicalism was turning away from secular concerns, the novel itself was becoming the vehicle for depicting a world of private values rather than concerning itself with a panoramic vision of society. Wayne C. Booth has warned us of the dangers of being simplistic about the relation between the disintegration of commonly-accepted values and the novelists' retreat to a world of private values.[35] In this context it is difficult to establish whether Evangelicalism in the novel disappeared primarily because as a philosophy it held little relevance for the individual authors or because it no longer formed a central part of the readers' world. One fact clearly emerges. This new fictional world offered little opportunity for the portrayal of Evangelicalism.

## 2. *The selection of the sources*

My subject draws quite naturally to a close at the end of the Victorian era. Even though novelists had by and large ceased to write of

---

odd behaviour in borrowing from Thackeray the name of so famous a character for his own very different creation. *Old Friends: Essays in Epistolary Parody* (1890), pp. 55–63.

[35] *The Rhetoric of Fiction* (Chicago, 1961), p. 393.

Evangelicalism Owen Chadwick's remarks upon the slowness of the secularization process amongst general readers seem apposite: 'Most Victorians held to the framework to the end of the reign. They always read Dickens much more than Hardy and Tennyson much more than Matthew Arnold.'[36]

The first year of Victoria's reign which saw the publication of the first popular novel devoted to the criticism of Evangelicalism might have appeared a suitable place to begin. Yet, as we have seen, Mrs. Trollope is writing of past experience and in an old tradition. Many other Victorian novelists had enjoyed their closest encounter with Evangelicalism in their pre-Victorian childhood or placed the action of their novels in a pre-Victorian era. I have therefore included within the scope of this work the following early nineteenth-century Evangelical writers of fiction whose work might reasonably be assumed to have been readily available to some of the major Victorian novelists: Patrick Brontë (1777–1861), John William Cunningham (1780–1861), Hannah More (1745–1833), Mrs. Mary Martha Sherwood (1775–1851), and 'Charlotte Elizabeth' Browne Phelan Tonna (1790–1846).

Mid-century Evangelical fiction is represented by Lady Caroline Lucy Scott (1784–1857) and the Revd. William Francis Wilkinson (1812–79), and the 1860s and 1870s by Emma Jane Worboise (1825–1887). The remainder of the century is represented by 'Hesba Stretton' (Sarah Smith, 1832–1911) and Mrs. O. F. (her own forenames were Catherine Augusta) Walton (n.d.).

Mrs. Harriet Mozley (*née* Newman, 1803–52), the Revd. Francis Edward Paget (1806–82) and William Sewell (1804–74), their Tractarian-inspired counterparts, all made their significant contribution to fictional polemics in the 1840s. Charlotte Mary Yonge (1823–1901) belongs initially to their band, but her novels span a far longer period.

On the sidelines of this major debate within the Anglican community stand J. A. Froude (1818–94) and John Henry Newman (1801–90) offering agnostic and Roman Catholic views respectively. The liberal position within the Anglican communion, espousing neither Evangelicalism nor Tractarianism, but offering a wide spectrum of comment and solutions to this internecine strife, is represented by the fiction of the Revd. William John Conybeare (1815–

[36] O. Chadwick, *The Victorian Church* (2 vols., 1970, 1972), ii, 464.

1857), Sir Henry Stewart Cunningham (n.d.), and Charles Kingsley (1819–75).

In the case of the Evangelical non-fiction writers I have tried to suggest the diversity of views on dogma and practice current at any one period and to draw attention to the chronology of the changes in attitude. Wherever necessary I have attempted to outline the significant divergences of opinion between Arminian and Calvinist Evangelicals. Eighteenth-century sources which remained influential have been employed. Such a source is Henry Venn's *The Complete Duty of Man* (1763), which, for the Evangelicals, came to replace Richard Allestree's *The Whole Duty of Man* (1658). The next generation of Evangelicals is important both because these men were the fathers of the Victorians and because many of them are referred to in the Victorian novel. In this generation I make particular use of Simeon, the Clapham Sect, and Legh Richmond. As the party grew in the first half of the nineteenth century, selection becomes more difficult. After the disintegration of the Clapham Sect I have concentrated upon those families like the Bickersteths, Marshes, and Venns, who produced Evangelicals 'even unto the third generation', or upon the pronouncements and careers of those men like the Revd. J. W. Cunningham, Shaftesbury and Canon J. C. Ryle, who were commonly regarded as leaders of party opinion.

One example will demonstrate how such major figures are both representative of Evangelical dogma and values, and, through a network of friends and relations, impinge upon the literary world.

John William Cunningham (1780–1861),[37] Vicar of Harrow from 1811 to 1861 gained fame and a nickname from his authorship of *The Velvet Cushion, De Rancé: A Poem* (1815) and numerous occasional sermons. His election to a life governorship of the Church Missionary Society in 1818 confirmed his place in the Evangelical hierarchy and his spell as editor of the *Christian Observer*, from 1850–8, gave him the opportunity to contribute to the formulation of Evangelical opinion. His education in the homes of Evangelical parsons like the Revd. H. Jowett of Little Dunham, Norfolk, and his Cambridge career brought him into contact with many of the leading Evangelicals of two generations. For his second curacy (1805–11) he was fortunate enough to serve under John Venn in the stronghold of the Evangelical leadership at Clapham. Venn, Henry Jowett's great

[37] Unless other references are given the following information is to be found in *DNB*.

friend and his predecessor at Little Dunham,[38] was to become Cunningham's model for Berkely, the kindly elderly Vicar of *The Velvet Cushion*. In pioneer spirit Cunningham left the established haunts of Evangelicalism when his father purchased for him the living of Harrow. He entered a community, whose mainstay, the Drurys of Harrow School, were fervently opposed to Evangelicalism. The fact that it took him thirteen years to establish a local association of the Church Missionary Society is indicative of the uphill battle he was forced to wage.[39] Before this symbolic victory had been attained, Frances Trollope and her family had moved to Harrow. Her social sparring with the persistently equable parson has often been recounted. Her daughter-in-law was to record the Vicar's kindness in promptly offering to take her daughters when Lord Northwick put in an execution upon the house.[40] Cunningham's move to their old house when Frances left for America can only have heaped coals of fire upon her head. Cunningham had probably communicated to his Evangelical brethren his difficulties at Harrow with this most intransigent female member of his flock because, when Frances Trollope published *The Vicar of Wrexhill* ten years after leaving Harrow, Samuel Wilberforce instantly recognized the original intended behind that caricature, Mr. Cartwright.[41]

Gradually, however, Cunningham managed to refashion Harrow into an approved Evangelical community. A succession of curates was to pass through his hands. Amongst them were John Venn (1830–3), the second son of his former Rector at Clapham,[42] and W. F. Wilkinson (1838–44), who published *The Rector in Search of a Curate* (1843), whilst himself holding a curacy under Cunningham.[43]

Through his children Cunningham maintained the intimate link between the literary and the Evangelical world. One son, Sir Henry Cunningham, wrote a novel, *Wheat and Tares*, which depicted, in fictional disguise,[44] the domestic life of Lowestoft Rectory, where John Cunningham's brother Francis, another Evangelical, and his wife, the former Richenda Gurney, had established themselves. One

[38] M. Hennell, *John Venn and the Clapham Sect* (1958).

[39] E. Stock, *History of the Church Missionary Society* (4 vols., 1899–1916), i, 243.

[40] F. E. Trollope, *Frances Trollope, Her Life and Literary Work from George III to Victoria* (2 vols., 1895), i, 204.

[41] A. R. Ashwell and R. G. Wilberforce, *Life of the Right Reverend Samuel Wilberforce* (3 vols., 1880–2), i, 114.

[42] J. Venn, *Annals of a Clerical Family* (1904), pp. 192–3.

[43] J. A. Venn, *Alumni Cantabrigienses*, Part II, 1752–1900 (6 vols., Cambridge, 1940).

[44] So identified by E. Stock, *My Recollections* (1909), pp. 60–1.

of John's daughters, Mary Richenda, married Sir James Fitzjames Stephen, lawyer and literary critic. Sir James Fitzjames, son of a Claphamite father, who had married Jane Venn, sister of Cunningham's former curate, was offered the editorship of the *Christian Observer*, by his uncle Henry Venn, but declined in his father-in-law's favour.[45]

The intricate pattern of relations which has emerged, in the course of this study, as characterizing early and mid-Victorian middle-class society, ensured that few authors can have contrived to escape contact with Evangelicalism. Thackeray, who had striven so hard to mitigate the Evangelical element in his children's education, would have appreciated the irony of his younger daughter's marriage to a renegade son of Clapham, Leslie Stephen, and the relationship she thereby contracted with the Cunninghams and the Gurneys.

[45] L. Stephen, *The Life of Sir James Fitzjames Stephen* (1895), pp. 127–9, 184.

## CHAPTER I

# The Evangelicals

### 1. *A question of definition*

> The opinions expressed and advocated about the matters discussed, are those of an Evangelical Churchman. What THAT means every intelligent Englishman knows, and it is mere affectation to profess ignorance about the point.[1]

> I know what constituted an Evangelical in former times; I have no clear notion what constitutes one now.[2]

'EVANGELICALISM' has frequently been used as an 'umbrella' word to cover a wide range of doctrinal positions and attitudes to church government, embraced variously by Anglicans and Methodists. Although this practice is doctrinally intelligible, in that it reflects beliefs held in common which brought Anglicans closer to their dissenting brethren than to their fellow Anglicans or in that it indicates the breadth of a movement which accommodated both Calvinists and Arminians,[3] it also obscures the divergence between Anglicans and Dissenters upon the matter of church polity and in social status. I hope to show that, since many of the nineteenth-century religious controversies involved the form and authority of the *ecclesia* and since the novelists were primarily concerned to demonstrate religion operating in a social context, it is necessary to isolate the Anglicans, in themselves a sufficiently heterogeneous group from their dissenting brethren. I therefore intend to use the capitalized adjective 'Evangelical' (and its cognate substantives) in a narrowly defined, but historically justifiable, sense to mean those members of the Anglican Church who assented to a group of doc-

[1] J. C. Ryle, *Knots United* (1874), p. vii.

[2] E. Hodder, *The Life and Work of the Seventh Earl of Shaftesbury* (3 vols., 1886), iii, 451.

[3] For the doctrinal divergencies of Arminian and Calvinist Evangelicals see ch. II.

trines, to be specified in my second chapter, commonly denominated evangelical.

The broader use of the term 'Evangelicalism' has tempted both historians, and, following them, literary critics to the erroneous assumption that the two groups shared not only doctrinal sympathies but a common spiritual parentage.[4] R. D. Altick's latest book[5] perpetuates the historical heresy, exposed by Dr. J. D. Walsh's unpublished thesis[6] and his subsequent essay,[7] that Anglican Evangelicalism was an offshoot from the work of the Methodist leaders, Wesley and Whitefield. The confusion in compiling this spiritual genealogy is, however, understandable. Many of the early Evangelicals did sympathize with the aims and methods of Methodism, and accepted the blanket title of 'methodist', though with increasing reluctance. Some parsons like Henry Venn of Huddersfield or William Grimshaw, Patrick Brontë's predecessor at Haworth, went so far as to become 'half-regulars'[8] for a time. They assented to Wesley's belief in the importance of preaching the Gospel wherever it was needed and so, in a manner which allied them with his 'irregular' itinerant preachers, they decided to traverse their own parish boundaries in the search for souls. Yet with the licensing of Methodist preaching houses in 1760 and the extension of the circuit system in 1791, the year of Wesley's death, the fundamental conflict with the parochial system and Church discipline became clear.

Methodists, who had formerly attended some Church services, often ceased to attend when it became possible to receive communion in their own chapels.[9] The French Revolution heightened the

[4] Equally erroneous is the contention lying behind F. K. Brown's *The Fathers of the Victorians* that Evangelicalism had nothing in common with Methodism, which he sees as a disarmingly naïve movement beside the supreme worldliness of Anglican Evangelicalism. Nor does this misguided approach save him from the strange inclusion of Sheridan Le Fanu's *Uncle Silas* as a major example of Evangelicals as depicted in literature. Apart from one very minor figure (the Revd. William Fairfield) the novel is concerned with the purported religion of Silas 'which approached more nearly to the Swedenborg visions than to anything in the Church of England'. *Uncle Silas: A Tale of Bartram-Haugh*, ed. E. Bowen (1947), p. 151.

[5] *Victorian People and Ideas* (1974), p. 167.

[6] 'The Yorkshire Evangelicals in the Eighteenth Century: with special reference to Methodism', D. Phil. thesis Cambridge, 1956.

[7] 'Origins of the Evangelical Revival', *Essays in Modern English Church History in Memory of Norman Sykes*, ed. G. V. Bennett and J. D. Walsh (1966), pp. 132–62.

[8] The use of the term 'regular' to denominate a non-Evangelical Anglican cleric is noted and explained in E. Sidney, *The Life of Sir Richard Hill* (1839), p. 480.

[9] Patrick Brontë's fiancée devoted a portion of one of her letters to the Methodist breakaway. 'Jane [Fennell] had a note from Mr. Morgan last evening, and she desires me

anxiety of the Evangelicals to stress their separateness from Dissent, which frequently bore the taint of Radicalism. This view was apparent in a major apologia for the Evangelicals, *Zeal without Innovation*, published in 1808. The work was warmly praised by Mr. Stanley, one of Hannah More's mouthpieces in *Coelebs*, who further attempted to rationalize the Evangelical attachment to the parochial system. ' "We consider our own parish as our more appropriate field of action, where Providence, by 'fixing the bounds of our habitation', seems to have made us peculiarly responsible for the comfort of those whom he has doubtless placed around us for that purpose." '[10]

Yet despite the firm Evangelical commitment, by the beginning of the nineteenth century, to the principle of Church order, many still felt unable to blame a man for sitting under a Dissenting minister or crossing parish boundaries if this was his only recourse to Gospel preaching. Thackeray's Pitt Crawley attended an Independent chapel in preference to the Parish Church of which his worldly uncle Bute was the incumbent,[11] whilst the occasional Evangelical clergyman who felt himself called rather to a 'congregational than a parochial' ministry continued to defy the Erastian squirearchy.[12] The flavour of High and Dry Erastianism, which could only detect 'disloyalty' to the Establishment in this behaviour, is preserved for us in Mrs. Trollope's *The Vicar of Wrexhill*, where Evangelicalism, though dismissed as hypocritical, is also described as dangerously zealous and, in its readiness to innovate, defiant of the Anglican decorum hallowed by tradition.

The threat of disestablishment, which came to a head in 1833, proved itself a peculiar embarrassment to the Evangelical party. The petitions and meetings for reform, organized by the Protestant Nonconformists, combined with the more violent changes demanded by the Radicals and Catholics, appeared to have found limited government support in plans to suppress Irish bishoprics.[13] This threat

---

to tell you that the Methodists' service in church hours is to commence next Sunday week.' *The Brontës, Their Lives, Friendships and Correspondence*, ed. T. J. Wise and J. A. Symington (4 vols., Oxford, 1932), i, 12. By the close of the century, in parishes where they knew themselves to be safe from the ministrations of an Anglo-Catholic, some Methodists were again attending both their own meetings and a Church service. See C. Mackenzie, *The Altar Steps* (1922), p. 47; and F. Thompson, *Lark Rise to Candleford* (1945), pp. 206, 222.

[10] [ ], *Coelebs* (2 vols., 1808), ii, 66. [11] *Vanity Fair*, p. 100.

[12] See O. Chadwick, *Victorian Miniature* (1960), pp. 49, 80, *et passim.*

[13] For a detailed account see E. Halévy, *The Triumph of Reform* (*1830–1841*), pp. 132–136.

called into question once again the extent to which the Evangelicals were prepared to co-operate with Dissent, and the nature of their loyalty to the Established Church. The question which Newman posed in the first of the *Tracts for the Times*—'. . . on *what* are we to rest our authority, when the State deserts us?'[14]—was particularly directed against the Evangelical belief in the supremacy of the Church Invisible over the Church Visible. The moderate Calvinism which lay behind the thinking of many Evangelical clergy reinforced their allegiance to the body of all true believers or the Elect rather than to the Established Church which included so many purely 'nominal' Christians. The Evangelical view, that membership of the Church of England was not necessary to salvation but expedient,[15] was probably reflected in the average lay mind very much in the manner of Mrs. Bulstrode's conviction that 'while true religion was everywhere saving . . . to be saved in the Church was more respectable'.[16]

The withdrawal of new-style High Churchmen, like Newman and Robert and Samuel Wilberforce, from Protestant interdenominational societies, confirmed the Evangelicals' isolation within the Establishment whilst cementing their close co-operation at the practical level with Dissent. Trollope's description of Mr. Slope—'With Wesleyan-Methodists he has something in common, but his soul trembles in agony at the iniquities of the Puseyites'[17]—must have been true of many less obnoxious Evangelicals.

This fondness for Dissent continued to expose the Evangelicals to attacks from any who posed as good friends of the Established Church. Evangelical defences became particularly vulnerable after the 1851 religious census, which gave the Dissenters a new self-confidence in trying to persuade their allies to leave a Church that could no longer claim to represent the vast majority of the English

[14] 'Thoughts on the Ministerial Commission Respectfully addressed to the Clergy', *Tracts for the Times* (6 vols., London and Oxford, 1834–41), i, 2.

[15] Most succinctly expressed in 1811 by Josiah Pratt. 'The Church may exist under different forms of order and discipline. Nay, the Church may be where there are no outward ordinances and discipline. For we must distinguish between the INVISIBLE CHURCH and the VISIBLE . . . The order and discipline of the Church, therefore, promote the number of the saved, and their advance in holiness. But it is possible to be saved without either . . . But I do not think God appointed Episcopacy as an exclusive form, though it is the most expedient form . . . All that very high churchmen say of the Church is true only of the INVISIBLE CHURCH, but not of the VISIBLE in ANY form.' *Eclectic Notes*, ed. J. H. Pratt (1865), pp. 493–4.

[16] G. Eliot, *Middlemarch* (3 vols.), iii, 124.

[17] *Barchester Towers*, p. 25.

people. Trollope's *Vicar of Bullhampton*, published seven years after the Dissenters' aggressive bicentennial celebrations of the Act of Uniformity, registers the unease experienced by the Evangelicals. The Marquis of Trowbridge, head of a Low Church family, offended by the Anglican parson who holds the living of one of the parishes on his estate, decides to lend his weighty support to the belligerently anti-Anglican Primitive Methodist minister of Bullhampton yet feels nagging twinges of conscience. 'He was a Churchman himself, and he was pricked with remorse as he remembered that he was spiting the Church which was connected with the state, of which he was so eminent a supporter.'[18]

The Marquis's Low Church daughters are out of sympathy with their father. They would have preferred to accuse the parson of High Church practices[19] to seeing their father in open enmity with the Established Church.

As the introduction of this term 'Low Church' might suggest, the historical relation between Evangelicalism and Dissent, which I have outlined, is reflected in the changing terminology applied to the Anglican group. A brief historical guide to the terms which were used at different periods to describe the Evangelicals is necessary to appreciate the type of accusation or defence being made when a nineteenth-century writer chooses one definition rather than another. The word 'Evangelical' came into use as a party term at the time of the Methodist revival, the *OED* of 1897 informs us, though it continues, less justifiably, to assert that 'its earliest associations were rather with the Calvinistic than the Arminian branch of the movement'. By the beginning of the century the historical distinction between Evangelicalism and Methodism to which I have referred was beginning to be reflected linguistically.

'The following,' said Sir Richard Hill, [referring to the Evangelicals at the turn of the century] 'are all now in good fashionable use and tolerable currency—Methodists—Enthusiasts—Schismatics—Evangelical preachers—Disturbers of quiet congregations—Calvinists—Puritans—Canters—Hypocrites—Fanatics, and even Antinomians. The word Methodist, however begins to get rather out of vogue.'

The reason of this was that it was more particularly applied to the Wesleyans. . . . [20]

Though Hannah More's pattern of piety, the Stanleys, might

[18] *The Vicar of Bullhampton* (1924), p. 304. [19] Ibid., p. 114.
[20] E. Sidney, *Life of Sir Richard Hill*, p. 479.

accept the imputation of 'methodism' in its earliest sense—the systematic practice of one's religion—they were well aware that their enemies used it to accuse them of schismatic tendencies.[21] Even their bitterest opponents were angered into an admission of the distinction. It is acknowledged by Sydney Smith in a review of 'the Evangelical and Methodistical Magazines' for 1807, 'which contain the sentiments of Arminian and Calvinistic methodists and of the *evangelical* clergy of the church of England'.

> We shall use the general term of Methodism, to designate these three classes of fanatics, not troubling ourselves to point out the finer shades and nicer discriminations of lunacy, but treating them all as in one general conspiracy against common sense, and rational orthodox christianity.[22]

In the process of endorsing Smith's contention, Southey, in 1809, is driven to the same admission—'the Wesleyans, the Orthodox dissenters of every description, and the Evangelical churchmen may all be comprehended under the generic name of Methodists.'[23] Though the charge of Methodism continued to be levelled against them until the 1830s even authors, like Mrs. Trollope, who violently disapproved of their alleged contempt for Church discipline would make the concession of referring to them as 'Church Methodists'.[24] In *The Vicar of Wrexhill* this term is used in preference to the title 'Evangelical', which is used only once in the caption for the frontispiece to the second volume. By 1852, however, she made grudging use of the latter term. ' "Oh yes!" replied Walter, "she belongs to the Evangelicals as they call themselves, and as they are also called curiously enough, by their opponents, although I presume the latter would not consent to denominate themselves 'anti-evangelists'!" '[25]

This usurpation of the title 'Evangelical' had long been a grievance.[26] The indignation of those Tractarians who had once been Evangelicals resulted in the use of 'x' to denominate the Evangelicals from 'z' to denote the old High and Dry party,[27] or to the nickname 'Peculiars'.[28] One fanatically High Church historian of the Evangelical party, the Revd. W. H. B. Proby, remarked of the term, 'I could

[21] *Coelebs*, ii, 304–5. [22] *Edin. Rev.* 11 (1808), 341–2.
[23] *Quarterly Review*, 1 (1809), 195. [24] *Vicar of Wrexhill*, ii, 261.
[25] *Uncle Walter* (3 vols., 1852), iii, 228.
[26] See [J. Bean] *Zeal without Innovation*, pp. xi, 44.
[27] T. Mozley, *Reminiscences*, i, 137.
[28] E. S. Purcell, *Life of Cardinal Manning* (2 vols., London and New York, 1896), i, 114, 224.

not use it in reference to them without implying that I am *not* evangelical.' He found a line of escape by entitling his two volume work, *Annals of the Low Church Party in England down to the death of Archbishop Tait* (1888).[29]

'Low Church', as the Revd. William Conybeare remarked in 'Church Parties', his widely read article of 1853, was the label applied to Evangelicals by their adversaries.[30] In its original usage, which the *OED* gives as 1702, it had designated the Latitudinarians whose views, doctrinally speaking, could not have been more dissimilar to those of the Evangelicals. Yet the latitudinarian reaction to such issues as Catholic Emancipation, the emergence of the Oxford Movement and the Maynooth debates[31] seems to have drawn them sufficiently close to the Evangelicals on the question of church polity for High Churchmen to have taken malicious delight in confounding the two. The Erastian and conservative bias of these Low Churchmen, whom Shaftesbury, using the phrase in the sense of 'anti-Puseyite', described in 1841 as having 'much political, and personal, and very little spiritual Protestantism',[32] was to lead them to join the Evangelical party in large numbers during the days of such *causes célèbres* as the Gorham Case or the so-called Papal aggression of 1851. The nomenclature they brought with them lent a disrepute very different in character from that which the word 'Evangelical' had formerly implied. If Evangelicalism conveyed fanaticism, Low Churchmanship suggested mere opposition to progressive thinking on matters of doctrine and Church discipline, combined with a lively interest in the rewards available from an increasingly powerful party.

A letter to the *Record* newspaper in 1835, signed 'Low Churchman', deploring the increasingly anti-Establishment tone of the Dissenting mission organizations he once supported, suggests the section of the Evangelical party in which these newcomers felt most at home.[33]

[29] vol. i, p. iii.

[30] *Edin. Rev.* 98 (1853), 273–342. Cf. A. Trollope on the subject of Mr. Stumfold, 'His friends said that he was evangelical, and his enemies said that he was Low Church'. *Miss Mackenzie* (1924), p. 19. According to the Archbishop of Canterbury this distinction still remains. 'He [Dr. Coggan] rejects the common description of himself as a "Low Churchman". "I don't mind being called Evangelical", he says.' *The Times* (20 Jan. 1975), p. 14.

[31] For details of these and ensuing controversies see O. Chadwick, *Victorian Church*. i, 250–309.

[32] E. Hodder, *Life of Shaftesbury*, i, 344.

[33] *Record* (9 Nov. 1835), p. 3.

The publication of the first number of the *Record*, on 1 January 1828, had identified a group within the Evangelical party who felt that they had a policy to offer discernibly different in emphasis from that offered by their colleagues in either the *Christian Observer* or the *Christian Guardian*. The *Christian Observer* had started its life in 1802 as the organ of the Clapham Sect, a number of notable Evangelicals, such as Charles Grant, Zachary Macaulay, James Stephen, Lord Teignmouth, Henry Thornton, John Venn, and William Wilberforce, who derived their collective name from the fact that they and their families lived for a time as a community around Clapham Common. The 'Saints', as they were sometimes also known, were a cultured, wealthy, influential group of upper-middle-class laymen, politically active and socially reforming in disposition. The *Christian Guardian*, started as a London based paper in 1802, by contrast reflected the views of the Evangelical clergy, being aimed at a readership which was characteristically less affluent, more conservative, and above all pietistically rather than politically minded.

The *Record* arose to fill the gap between these two positions. Disturbed by the lukewarm concern for Church reform and the support for Catholic Emancipation displayed by the Saints it voiced an alternative response to the cry of 'Church in danger'. Militantly activist and ultra-Tory politically speaking, 'Recordites' were firm supporters of the Establishment and fanatically anti-Papist. They reflected the views of provincial parishes rather than the urbanity of the capital. Their apocalyptic fervour and zealous espousal of premillenialist doctrine would have been wholly alien to the sensibilities of Low Churchmen, but gradually a coalition was effected so that by 1853 Conybeare was able to detect three elements in the Low Church party: the Evangelicals, the Recordites and a smaller element labelled the 'Low and Slow', who occupied a position analagous to that taken by the High and Dry Churchmen in former days, fearful of innovation in doctrine or church government and committed to an Erastianism more emphatically Protestant in tone.

Conybeare's article further indicates that the term 'Low Church' had by now been adopted as the all embracing term for the new coalition in contradistinction to the High and Broad Church labels.[34]

[34] For serious misunderstandings of this nomenclature see S. Butler, *Way of All Flesh*, ed. J. Cochrane (Penguin edn., 1971), p. 442; and M. F. Brightfield, *Victorian England in its novels*, i, 342. Cochrane refers to 'both Charles Kingsley and Thomas Arnold' as 'of the Low Church party'. Presumably he has been misled, by Samuel Butler's claim that Ernest Pontifex was in some way betraying his High Church principles when he read

The Broad Church combined the Erastian tendencies of the old latitudinarians with a progressive theology.

'Evangelicalism' now began to be used by some writers to conjure up from the past a former purity and unity of doctrinal position from which, it was felt, there had been a sad 'falling off'. In the creation of this myth a roll-call was taken of early Evangelicals, 'men who were in their day "the chariots of Israel and the horsemen thereof" ',[35] which usually included Thomas Scott, Romaine, Newton, Henry and John Venn, Simeon, and Wilberforce, with Milner, Cecil, and Pratt as optional extras, to suggest a unanimity which had never existed. The last of the giants, Simeon and Wilberforce, had conveniently died in the decade which issued in Tractarianism. Occasionally later party leaders like Edward Bickersteth or Lord Shaftesbury were given the dubious honour of inclusion; for with the implied compliment of higher purity went the suggestion that they were the very last of a race doomed to extinction.

By the last third of the nineteenth century 'Evangelical' could be used with equal validity to describe a churchman of firm commitment to the Establishment, a close co-operator with Dissent, or any rabid anti-Ritualist. Yet, however close their sympathy with Nonconformity, there remained the social barrier between Evangelicals and Dissenters.

The principles upon which a church or a sect's polity was decided were theological in origin but became socially divisive in application, in as far as they reflected a desire to ally with or dissociate oneself from the Establishment. Mrs. Worboise, who had allied herself with Dissent, made perfectly clear the Dissenters' pride in the price they paid for their Nonconformity. Speaking of the diversity of Anglican churches in one area, she described some as '*very* Low, so Low that they were *bonâ-fide* Dissenters, only the loaves and fishes, and the *status* of Episcopalianism kept them from open and undisguised secession'.[36]

The Evangelicals were equally clear, on their side, about the

---

*Alton Locke* and Stanley's *Life of Arnold*, into making Kingsley and Arnold into members of a party which, in fact, distrusted them almost as deeply as they did the Tractarians. Brightfield's definition betrays a total misunderstanding of the significance of the word 'Churchmen': 'The term Low Church was applied principally to certain Calvinist, Methodist, or Wesleyan groups—some of them openly seperated from the Church of England . . .'

[35] [W. F. Wilkinson], *The Rector in Search of a Curate*, p. 86.

[36] E. J. Worboise, *The House of Bondage* (1872), p. 12.

nature of the social division. Wilberforce saw his Anglicanism as a special cause for thanking Providence when he considered the jeopardy in which his childhood had been spent. 'If I had staid with my uncle I should probably have been a bigoted despised methodist. . . .[37]

Lord Shaftesbury, whose frequent collaboration with Dissent made him remarkable within his own party, could assume all the hauteur of the born aristocrat and draw upon the traditional repertoire of insults, when wishing to rebuke a Dissenter who had presumed to criticize the Evangelicals. Spurgeon, whom Shaftesbury was later to describe as one of the very few men whose religious views he largely shared,[38] attracted Shaftesbury's publicly announced disdain for an attack upon the position of the Evangelical clergy.

I think that if what we have heard of, had been addressed to me, in my capacity of a layman, I should have taken no notice of it whatever; or, if I had taken any notice of it, I should have merely said to the accuser, 'Sir, I believe you are very ignorant; to say the truth, you are a very saucy fellow, and if you think that you represent the great and good Nonconformists of former days—the Howes, the Bunyans, the Flavels, and Wattses—or even that you have anything akin to the good, sound, and true religious Nonconformists of the present day; you are just as much mistaken as you would be, if you thought you were well versed in history, or had even been initiated in the first elements of good breeding or Christian charity.'[39]

The social gulf between Evangelicalism and Dissent grew throughout the nineteenth century. John Fennell, Patrick Brontë's wife's uncle, had made the transition in 1813 from methodist preacher to ordained deacon of the Church of England with comparative ease.[40] The *Congregational Magazine* for 1820 printed a letter on the subject of 'The Defection of Opulent Dissenters to the Evangelical Church Party'.[41] Yet, in cases where defections reflected an improvement in material circumstances made in one generation the coveted social acceptance could only be achieved by moving one's home. Bulstrode made the leap from Dissent to Anglicanism before his arrival in

[37] R. I. and S. Wilberforce, *The Life of William Wilberforce* (5 vols., 1838), i, 7.
[38] E. Hodder, *Life of Shaftesbury*, iii, 395.
[39] Ibid. iii, 160. Excerpt from an address to Church Pastoral Aid Society, 1862.
[40] *The Brontës, Their Lives*, etc., ed. T. J. Wise and J. A. Symington, i, 6.
[41] *Congregational Magazine*, 3 (Dec. 1820), 464. For this reference I am indebted to K. Watson, 'The Use of Religious Diction in the Nineteenth Century Novel with Special Reference to George Eliot', D. Phil. thesis, Oxford, 1970, p. 29.

Middlemarch.[42] When Catherine Furze's mother decides that it is time to introduce her to more refined society, the transition from chapel to church is accompanied by a removal to the better part of town; but this proves insufficient to secure a position in Church circles and only serves to lose them their former Dissenting friends and trade.[43] The consummate ease with which Ruskin's family moved from Church to chapel emphasizes the hierarchical structure of this religious society.[44]

By the second half of the century it was mere affectation to call 'all people who were at all in earnest about their souls "*Methodists*" ' and claim to be totally oblivious of these distinctions. One of Mrs. Worboise's characters, a lady who has taken up Ritualism as being fashionable, tries to defend her choice by an all-embracing denunciation of the opposing camp, but even this frivolous commentator is clearly aware of a distinction between Evangelicalism and Dissent.

'. . . I assure you it is quite *ton* now to be *very high*! In the best circles there is just a certain clique that is Low Church, but the people who compose it are nobodies, absolute nobodies, I assure you! one may as well be a Methodist or a Plymouth Brother as one of those dreadful vulgar-minded Evangelicals!'[45]

Many of the novelists with whom I am concerned were ill at ease in realms of doctrinal debate but were perfectly capable of distinguishing between Evangelicalism and Dissent in social terms. Moreover since this method involved observation rather than analysis, implication rather than argument, it was more appropriate to the novel.

Dickens showed little interest in the minutiae of sectarian belief which separated the two. He was intent rather upon attacking the evangelical ethos. His pictures of the minister of the Little Bethel which Mrs. Nubbles[46] attended, and of Brother Hawkyard[47] do, however, demonstrate an awareness of the enmity and jealousy felt by the Dissenter for the Anglican. The dividing line between

[42] G. Eliot, *Middlemarch*.

[43] [W. H. White], *Catharine Furze by Mark Rutherford, edited by his friend Reuben Shapcott* (2 vols., 1893).

[44] J. Ruskin, *Praeterita and Dilecta*, ed. E. T. Cook and A. Wedderburn (1908), pp. 71–2.

[45] E. J. Worboise, *Overdale; or, The Story of a Pervert* (1869), pp. 107, 131.

[46] *The Old Curiosity Shop*, ch. xli.

[47] 'George Silverman's Explanation', *The Uncommercial Traveller and Reprinted Pieces*.

Evangelicalism and Dissent as seen by Dickens may not conform to that discerned by ecclesiastical historians, but is nevertheless striking. His Evangelicals, Miss Barbary, the Murdstones, and Mrs. Clennam have a higher social origin than his Dissenters and are more frighteningly powerful. The material greed of a Stiggins or a Chadband differentiates them from the Evangelicals whose interest is in power over others rather than in an exclusive desire for money and creature comforts. The Evangelicals are not comic, but monstrous grotesques, who are shown constricting and crushing, with unremitting zeal, those over whom they enjoy control.

Like Sydney Smith, Thackeray perversely employed his knowledge of the distinction between Dissent and Evangelicalism. He could refer to his Evangelical mother's firm commitment to 'Church-of-Englandism'[48] and then provoke Lord Macaulay's criticism for having 'introduced too much of the Dissenting element into his picture of Clapham in the opening chapters of "The Newcomes"'.[49] His desire to stress the dissenting proclivities of the Hobson family sprang not from Erastian fervour but from the knowledge that this would best serve to undermine their aristocratic pretensions.

Mrs. Oliphant's sensitive appreciation of the social gradations in a small town like Carlingford makes use of religious affiliations to convey itself to her readers. In *Miss Marjoribanks* the Rector, Mr. Bury, lends respectability to Evangelicalism by virtue of his status, but his parishioners are not anxious to attend the tea-parties, given by him and his sister, where 'Dissenters, to whom the Rector gave what he called the right hand of fellowship',[50] were to be met. Lucilla Marjoribanks adopts the veneer of an Evangelical tone, because 'It was the custom of good society in Carlingford to give a respectful assent . . . to Mr. Bury's extreme Low-Churchism.'[51] The arrival of a Broad Church Archdeacon in Carlingford shows how shallow is her commitment. Her spontaneous reaction to a manifestation of embarrassment on the Archdeacon's part demonstrates the real purchase which the traditional social stereotypes hold on her thinking. 'He got up again and made a stride to and fro, and wiped the moisture from his forehead, which, as Lucilla remarked at the moment, had a Low-Church look, which she would not have

[48] *The Letters and Private Papers of W. M. Thackeray*, ed. G. N. Ray (4 vols., 1945–6), i, 466.

[49] G. O. Trevelyan, *The Life and Letters of Lord Macaulay* (2 vols., 1932), i, 57.

[50] [M. Oliphant], *Miss Marjoribanks* (3 vols., Edin. and London, 1866), i, 33.

[51] Ibid. i, 247

expected from him. . . . It was a very Low-Church, not to say Dissenterish, sort of thing to do. . . .'[52]

Since doctrinally unconcerned authors used their awareness of the social difference between Evangelicalism and Dissent creatively it becomes important to note the distortions of interpretation that result from the failure of some modern critics to grasp this distinction. Such misapprehensions are peculiarly fatal when dealing with George Eliot, who combined doctrinal expertise with the capacity for detailed social comment. For the personal knowledge which informed her portraits of Evangelical and Dissenter we have her own word. 'My sketches both of churchmen and dissenters, with whom I am almost equally acquainted, are drawn from close observation of them in real life, and not at all from hearsay or from the descriptions of novelists.'[53]

Her education under the Evangelical Maria Lewis, the Miss Franklins, of Baptist persuasion, and her friendship with the Sibree family, members of an Independent congregation, ensured a wide-ranging, sympathetic knowledge of Dissent. Although she never, despite later rumours of adult baptism,[54] joined any other than the Anglican Church, she joined in the religious worship, leading prayer meetings among the girls,[55] at the school run by Misses Mary and Rebecca Franklin, daughters of the Revd. Francis Franklin, minister of Cow Lane Particular Baptist Chapel. Close acquaintance with Dissent only served to emphasize the nature of the gulf between it and Evangelicalism. Certainly Mary Ann expressed sympathetic understanding of the absolute impossibility of Maria Lewis, 'an attached member of the Establishment', taking a position as governess with any of the wealthy dissenting families.[56] She had, too, expressed a suitably defensive note in recommending an account of missionary activities by a Dissenter, justifying her choice by reference to Bishop Sumner's praise of the book at a Bible Society meeting.[57]

As the book recommendation indicates, Mary Ann had not con-

[52] Ibid. ii, 106–7.

[53] *The George Eliot Letters*, ed. G. S. Haight (7 vols., New Haven, 1954–6), ii, 347–8.

[54] 'George Eliot as a Christian', *Contemporary Pulpit*, 2 (1884), 181. For this reference I am indebted to V. Cunningham, op. cit., p. 146.

[55] J. W. Cross, *George Eliot's Life as Related in Her Letters and Journals* (3 vols., Edin. and London, 1885), i, 27.

[56] *G. Eliot Letters*, i, 91, 115.

[57] Ibid. i, 12.

tented herself with passively observing cultural distinctions but set out to become well versed in the dogmatic basis to sectarianism. She read Professor Hoppus's *Schism as opposed to the Unity of the Church especially in the Present Times*, an essay which won the prize offered by Sir Culling Eardley Smith (future founder of the Evangelical Alliance) and compared this with Joseph Milner's *History of the Church of Christ*, an Evangelical best seller. Her correspondent, Maria Lewis, was provided with the following succinct summary of the different authorial positions.

The former ably expresses the tenets of those who deny that any form of Church government is so clearly dictated in Scripture as to possess a Divine right, and consequently to be binding on Christians. The latter as you know exhibits the views of a moderate evangelical episcopalian on the inferences to be drawn from ecclesiastical remains. . . .[58]

To ignore the fineness of the distinctions George Eliot drew in her novels is to devalue both her aims and achievements. In 1856, the year before her first attempt at fiction, she reviewed Julia Kavanagh's *Rachel Gray: A Tale founded on Fact*. While recognizing the attempt to portray 'that most prosaic stratum of society, the small shop-keeping class' as 'really a new sphere for a great artist', her criticism of the novel makes clear both the area of Miss Kavanagh's failure and her own conviction in the necessity of a careful reproduction of the varieties of flavour abounding in the Evangelical world as she knew it.

It is an abstract piety, made up of humility, resignation, and devotion, feeding on Milton's sonnets, and quite disembodied of sectarian idiom and all other fleshly weaknesses which are beneath Miss Kavanagh's own mind. Our own experience of what piety is amongst the uneducated has not brought us in contact with a Christianity which smacks neither of the Church nor of the meeting-house, with an Evangelicalism which has no *brogue*; and if, when Miss Kavanagh says that her tale is founded on fact, she means that the character of 'Rachel Gray' is a portrait, we are obliged to say that she has failed in making us believe in its likeness to an original.[59]

Presumably Blanche Colton Williams was led into her grossly erroneous assertion that, 'On the non-conformist side, she [George Eliot] created Mr. Tryon [*sic*]',[60] by a misconception of the nature

[58] Ibid. i, 25.
[59] [G. Eliot], 'Rachel Gray', *Leader*, 7 (5 Jan. 1856), 19.
[60] 'George Eliot: Social Pressure on the Individual', *Sewanee Review*, 46 (1938), 238.

of a 'chapel-of-ease'. Chapels-of-ease were semi-private chapels built with the Bishop's permission when an increase or shift in population seemed to render an auxiliary to the parish Church desirable.[61] Miss Williams's own confusion of Anglicanism and Dissent totally deflates the irony directed by George Eliot at the ignorant, bigoted customers in the bar of the Red Lion at Milby.[62]

A similar error concerning Mr. Tryan's ecclesiastical allegiance seems to have been perpetrated by Sumner J. Ferris who maintained that 'not a single Low Churchman is well portrayed in her novels',[63] —a view which it is difficult to reconcile with 'Janet's Repentance'.

Of more concern is the confusion created by Martin Svaglic's article 'Religion in the Novels of George Eliot', which purports to analyse the different varieties of religious experience and denomination found in her novels. He refers to 'Dissent (in the popular sense of the term: Evangelicalism as well as Methodism, Congregationalism, and so forth)',[64] without explaining his use of the word 'popular'. Such a conflation may be a 'popular' twentieth-century error but nineteenth-century readers, if not precisely cognizant of the theological niceties which separated one sect from another, would have been conscious of the social advantages gained by Amos Barton when he left the Independents for the Anglican ministry or of the social gulf traversed by Bulstrode. If Evangelicalism were the same as Dissent Raffles's crude taunt would have lost half its sting for Bulstrode. 'Still in the Dissenting line, eh? Still godly? Or taken to the Church as more genteel?'

It is part of the purpose of this book to provide the information on the changing nature of the Evangelical idiom that is necessary for the appreciation of one author's accurate observation and another's calculated distortion for dogmatic, comic or satirical effect.

[61] The confusion may have arisen because the wealthy Lady Huntingdon, who had been an adept at providing for her Evangelical clergy by building chapels, licensed one of her chapels as a dissenting place of worship. This caused her Evangelical chaplains to resign *en masse*, thus emphasizing that ministry in this type of 'chapel' in no way implied a dissenting connection.

[62] G. Eliot, *Scenes* (2 vols.), ii, 43.

[63] '*Middlemarch*, George Eliot's Masterpiece', *From Jane Austen to Joseph Conrad: Essays Collected in Memory of James T. Hillhouse*, ed. R. C. Rathburn and M. Steinmann, Jr. (Minneapolis, 1958), p. 197.

[64] 'Religion in the Novels of George Eliot', *JEGP* 53 (1954), 150.

## 2. *Evangelical strength and regional distribution*

Although a novel like *Vanity Fair* gives the impression that Evangelicalism was so pervasive a force that it could be encountered amongst the aristocracy, London's merchant classes, in British colonies in French towns, and in military circles,[65] this is more representative of the novel's date of composition (1847–8) than the period it allegedly describes—the period of the Regency and the reign of George IV.

In the opening years of the nineteenth century the Evangelicals were still a small and scattered party, more densely gathered in some areas, such as Yorkshire or Cornwall, where the movement had first appeared. It was of this stage in the movement's development that the Brontës spoke. Patrick Brontë himself belonged to a closely-knit group of Yorkshire Evangelicals but his own memories of previous curacies, together with the experiences of his own curates, would have served to suggest the difficulties encountered by Mr. Weston, who finds himself curate to an unsympathetic member of the High and Dry school,[66] or of St. John Rivers, isolated from intelligent and sympathetic male company.[67] Such conditions gave rise to the formation of eleven clerical societies, between 1750 and 1792, to which members would ride miles, putting up overnight at the host's parsonage.[68] In the next century these societies lost their vitality.[69] Evangelical companionship was no longer so hard to find and, in the aftermath of the Oxford Movement's endeavours to awaken a sense of corporate identity in the Church, clergy of contiguous parishes had been persuaded to overcome their doctrinal differences and meet on a ruridecanal basis. Amos Barton and Archibald Duke attend such a meeting without any sense of being colleagues in a persecuted faction.[70]

Evangelically originated missionary societies provided another cohesive force, with the opportunities that they provided for deputations[71] to make preaching tours, so keeping small, isolated pockets of Evangelicals in the provinces in touch with each other. The

[65] W. M. Thackeray, *Vanity Fair*, pp. 411–12, 782, 818–19, 331.

[66] A. Brontë, *Agnes Grey*. [67] C. Brontë, *Jane Eyre*.

[68] For the best brief account of these societies see M. Hennell, *John Venn and the Clapham Sect*, pp. 276–9.

[69] *CO* (1873), pp. 93–4. [70] G. Eliot, *Scenes*, i.

[71] The word 'deputation', was rather curiously used, as Conybeare noted, to describe one man. *Perversion; or, the Causes and Consequences of Infidelity* (3 vols., 1856), i, 328–9.

acquisition of the Exeter Hall in 1831 as a regular venue for annual May meetings [72] provided the opportunity for gatherings, which, according to the satirically minded, were to the religiously inclined what the London season was for the unregenerate.

The first third of the century had seen a change in the composition and influence of this party, from a minority group within the church, backed by the considerable resources, social, political, and financial of the laymen of the Clapham Sect, to a party with greater clerical support and of broader social composition.

It is not possible to talk in any other than these broad terms of the numerical strength of the Evangelical party. The 1851 religious census, valuable in providing information on sectarian distribution, fails to supply evidence for the factions within the Anglican Church. Any numerical assessments must be based upon informed guess-work and should be consulted with a readiness to allow for uncertainty of definition and personal bias on the reporter's part. Estimating the numbers of Evangelical clergymen at any one time has been the method most frequently employed. Although modern historians have felt that Gladstone was inclined to minimize the influence of a party from which he had grown apart,[73] his estimate of an increase from one in twenty to one in eight between 1820 and 1830 seems to tally reasonably well with the guess hazarded in 1839 by James Grant, a devout Calvinist, when one allows for the intervening nine years' growth: 'I should suppose there could not have been [twenty years before] one Evangelical clergyman for fifteen or twenty of an opposite class. Now, perhaps, the Evangelical clergy may be in the proportion of one to five of those who are merely moral preachers.'[74]

By 1853 Conybeare, working on a sample of 500 clergy, claimed that Low and High Church clergy, in equal numbers, accounted for 80 per cent of the Anglican ministry. Examination both of subscription rates to missionary societies, noted for their party affiliation, and of the sales figures of party newspapers serves to confirm Conybeare's general contention that the early 1850s saw a marked expansion in Evangelical numerical strength.[75]

The greater numerical strength of the party did not, however,

[72] For a detailed history see F. M. Holmes, *Exeter Hall and Its Associations* (1881); also L. W. Cowie, 'Exeter Hall', *History Today*, 18 (1968), 390–7.

[73] D. Newsome, *The Parting of Friends* (1966), p. 8.

[74] Quoted by E. Halévy, *The Triumph of Reform*, p. 162.

[75] See O. Chadwick, *Victorian Church*, i, 446.

indicate a commensurate unified influence. Against the numbers recruited by the fight against Tractarianism and Neology one has to set the divisions created by the issues of millenarianism and the apostolic purity of the Church. Three novels, written within the space of ten years, illustrate even more sharply the scope which existed for a wide range of estimates of the Evangelical influence.[76] In 'Janet's Repentance', published in 1857, George Eliot describes the Revd. Edgar Tryan's advent in Milby in the mid-1830s as a belated instance of a 'new movement', whose tide was already on the turn.[77] Her tendency was to judge the strength of a movement in terms of its spiritual efficacy and to secure her own position in the line of historical progress by dating the movement's decline from the moment of her own disenchantment.

Mrs. Oliphant, on the other hand, writing only a decade later, attributes social, political and financial power to the Evangelicals. A wealthy Evangelical patroness takes comfort when her High Church nephew is appointed to another parish, after she has denied him the living at her disposal. ' "I daresay he's bold enough to take a bishopric", she said to herself; "but fortunately we've got *that* in our own hands as long as Lord Shaftesbury lives;" and Miss Leonora smiled grimly over the prerogatives of her party.'[78]

Trollope, who had written *Barchester Towers* in the same year as George Eliot's *Scenes of Clerical Life*, was alert to the importance of the change of ministries for Evangelical hopes of clerical preferment. Despite Lord Shaftesbury's gloomy predictions when his step-father-in-law became Prime Minister,[79] the first Palmerston ministry witnessed the Evangelicals' first accession to power in the matter of important appointments. The deaths in swift succession of both the Bishop and the Dean of Barchester suggest the almost unprecedented number of appointments which were to fall to Palmerston, or Lord Shaftesbury, his bishop-maker, to fill. In the space of ten years he had the nomination of 19 English sees, 6 Irish sees and 13 English deaneries at his disposal. Despite Shaftesbury's

[76] Each of the several methods of estimation employed suffers from severe limitations. Conybeare tried three: taking a sample of five hundred clergy, examining subscription rates to missionary societies noted for their party affiliation, and looking at the circulation figures of extremist newspapers. *Edin. Rev.* 98 (1853), 273–342. The most that the historian can hope to do is to guage the expansion or contraction of the party.

[77] *Scenes*, ii, 66.

[78] *The Perpetual Curate* (3 vols., Edin. and London, 1864), iii, 290.

[79] E. Hodder, *Life of Shaftesbury*, ii, 490, 505.

high Tory reputation Palmerston's first appointments were suspected of being selected in the usual tradition, for their political sympathies, to be expressed in Whig votes in the House of Lords. Bishop Proudie is pre-eminently a Whig,[80] but has made clear his Evangelical sympathies in his choice of a wife. It seems in fact more likely that Palmerston's political interest was served by selecting men whose keen pastoral vocation would prevent them from playing much part in secular government. Proudie certainly enjoyed the reputation for lack of learning and incompetence levelled at the Palmerston appointments and the effect made by him and his entourage upon the diocese of Barchester would justify Chadwick's judgement that 'those ten years of Palmerston continued to raise the authority and lower the prestige of the evangelical party'.[81]

This apparent gain in ecclesiastical power accords ill with Samuel Butler's claim that in 1858, with the exception of a small and persecuted group, 'the Evangelical movement . . . had become almost a matter of ancient history'.[82] Butler, writing with the hindsight of twenty years further observation, had the benefit of a series of articles in newspapers and magazines, which, in pronouncing death by misadventure upon the Evangelical party, had located the origins of dissolution in the period when Evangelicalism changed from a missionary force to an aggressively self-defensive combination of Protestants.[83] Butler's philosophy, like George Eliot's, encouraged him to espouse a view which could represent vital Evangelicalism as a spent force, clung to only by those who were no longer involved in the main line of human progress.

Novels also provide an impression of Evangelical distribution throughout the country. Personal experience occasionally entered into the choice of locality for the Evangelical drama to be enacted. Trollope chooses South West England for the setting of *Rachel Ray* and much of *The Belton Estate*. In *Miss Mackenzie* Mr. Maguire is given an interim curacy in the tin mining area of Cornwall. Trollope had known a family of Evangelicals in Exeter during his youth[84] and

[80] A. Trollope, *Barchester Towers*, pp. 17, 295.

[81] *Victorian Church*, i, 469.

[82] *Way of All Flesh*, p. 205.

[83] e.g. M. Pattison, 'Learning in the Church of England', *National Review*, 16 (1863), 187–220; E .H. Plumptre, 'Church Parties, Past, Present, and Future', *Contemporary Review*, 7 (1868), 321–46; A. W. Thorold, 'The Evangelicals of 1868', *Contemporary Review*, 8 (1868), 569–94; *CO* (1873), pp. 83–96; *The Times* (31 Jan. 1879), p. 9, (6 Feb. 1879), pp. 9, 10; R. E. Bartlett, 'The Church of England and the Evangelical Party', *Contemporary Review*, 47 (1885), 65–81.

[84] T. A. Trollope, *What I Remember* (2 vols., 1887), i, 39–40.

his acquaintance with this region was resumed in 1851 at a time when events such as the Exeter surplice riots or the Gorham case confirmed the appropriateness of this choice.[85] His knowledge of this area, often regarded as a stronghold of dissenting evangelicalism and High Church Anglicans, may well have led to the valuable indications we receive from *Barchester Towers* of the Evangelical plight. The Gorham Case had suggested that a High Church bishop did not necessarily imply the absence of Evangelical clergy in that diocese, but equally clearly showed that the Evangelical cause would not be augmented by appointments within that bishop's presentation. The arrival of the Proudies and their entourage showed how such a power base could give their party an illusion of strength not representative of their true influence in the diocese at large. Compton Mackenzie, also drawing his conclusions from personal experience,[86] suggests that by the close of the century the battles waged against dissent, on the one hand, and Ritualism, on the other, made the remote south-west the home of isolated and eccentric Evangelical parsons.[87]

The most popular fictional choice for an Evangelical abode, or coterie, continued to be one of the watering-places, since these places found favour in Evangelical eyes from the beginning of the century. Bath, Tonbridge, and Brighton had been amongst the places chosen by Selina, Countess of Huntingdon, as suitable centres for the work of converting the aristocracy to Methodism. Wilberforce and his Regency contemporaries needed to take their wives and families to the fashionable southern resorts and suitable churches and chapels were required. Nothern merchants, like the Gladstones, would have secured similar northern livings. One such was 'F . . . a village about two miles distant from A', the fashionable watering-place, where Anne Brontë's Mr. Weston became incumbent.[88] Of the southern resorts Cheltenham comes immediately to Mr. Bulstrode's mind as an appropriate place for him to retreat with Harriet.[89] Cheltenham and Bath offered congenial surroundings to the lonely, wealthy, and religiously-minded, such as Lady McLeod,[90] Miss Mackenzie[91] or Miss Baker.[92] They also provided a convenient hunting-ground for fortune-hunters prepared to don an Evangelical mask. Obadiah

[85] T. H. Escott, *Anthony Trollope*, p. 229.
[86] *My Life and Times: Octave Four, 1907–15* (1965).
[87] *The Parson's Progress* (1923), ch. xxii; *The Heavenly Ladder* (1924), ch. ii.
[88] *Agnes Grey*, pp. 480, 454.
[89] G. Eliot, *Middlemarch*, iii, 293.
[90] A. Trollope, *Can You Forgive Her?* (2 vols., 1938), i, 190.
[91] A. Trollope, *Miss Mackenzie.*
[92] A. Trollope, *The Bertrams* (3 vols., 1859).

Boodle proceeds from the seaside resort, where he met the Duffs and the Wards, to Cheltenham where he discovers a wealthy Evangelical widow.[93] The Revd. Panurgus O'Blareaway marries the rich Mrs. Lavington to become religious leader of 'Steaming-bath'.[94] The widow Barnaby finds that in order to join the highest circles there an Evangelical deportment is necessary.[95] Becky Sharp settles at the end of her career amongst the religious circles of Bath and Cheltenham.[96]

The picture presented by these novels is supported by such figures as are readily available for the general trends in regional growth. In 1820 the Yorkshire subscriptions to the Church Missionary Society were larger even than those from the combined London parishes. York still led the provinces during the year 1847 to 1848, contributing 12 per cent of the whole, but by the close of the century there had been an increase of 150 per cent in the southern Canterbury province, compared with an 85 per cent increase in the York province. In the accounts for 1820 Bath, Cheltenham, and three other southern watering-places had been recorded as contributing centres. By the close of the century there were twenty-four such centres recorded, by now contributing 12 per cent of the society's entire income.[97]

The novelists subscribed to the belief that Cambridge rather than Oxford was the University home of the Evangelicals.[98] Newman, ignoring the sons of wealthy and cultivated Evangelicals, like the Wilberforce brothers, who had been sent to Oxford, writes of the Evangelicals of the 1830s as a minority set congregated in the poorest of halls.[99] Mrs. Sherwood sends her hero, Henry Milner, to Oxford[100] at the same period presumably because of family connections.[101] By 1837 Mrs. Trollope was able to assure her readers

[93] H. Mozley, *The Lost Brooch*.

[94] C. Kingsley, *Yeast: a problem* (1902), ch. xviii.

[95] F. Trollope, *The Widow Barnaby* (3 vols., 1839), ii, ch. xii.

[96] W. M. Thackeray, *Vanity Fair*, ch. lxvii.

[97] E. Stock, *History of the Church Missionary Society*, i, 477–9.

[98] A popular fallacy challenged by B. E. Hardman, op. cit., p. 372. J. S. Reynolds, *The Evangelicals at Oxford, 1735–1871. A Record of an Unchronicled Movement* (Oxford, 1953).

[99] J. H. Newman, *Loss and Gain: The Story of a Convert* (1896), pp. 53, 146.

[100] M. M. Sherwood, *The History of Henry Milner, Pt. IV* (1837).

[101] Her brother, Marten Butt, was at Oxford, and she had visited him there. N. R. Smith, *The State of Mind of Mrs Sherwood* (1946), p. 4. Her son, Henry, was at The Queen's College, Oxford contemporaneously with his fictional namesake. J. Foster, *Alumni Oxonienses, 1715–1886* (4 vols., 1887).

that 'the thing does not take at Oxford', where ideas like 'elective grace' are 'famously quizzed';[102] but *The Vicar of Wrexhill* displayed no awareness of Oxford as the centre of Tractarianism. Six years later, however, Cunningham's curate at Harrow was voicing the fears of Evangelical parents when he depicted Charles Spencer, an Evangelical parson's son, coming down to his father's parish, intent upon defending the new Tractarian ideas he has imbibed at Oxford.[103]

Though initially no more welcome than at Oxford, the Evangelicals achieved a continuity of tradition at Cambridge, which, of the two universities, had been the more inclined to favour Nonconformity since the late sixteenth century. Sympathetic fellows facilitated the entry of men like Patrick Brontë, and security was provided when Simeon obtained the living of Holy Trinity, Cambridge, thus providing a foothold outside the ever changing college communities. Sir James Stephen's opinion that 'Charles Simeon is worth a legion of Newmans',[104] was true, if only in respect of the continuous influence exercised over fifty-four years' ministry in a university church. By Simeon's death in 1836 a tradition had been established. Bishop H. C. G. Moule recollected that in the early 1860s 'Sim' was still current usage for describing a Cambridge Evangelical.[105] His memories receive confirmation in Butler's *The Way of All Flesh*.[106] Amongst fictional Evangelical clerics Amos Barton[107] and Theophilus Cardew[108] shared a Cambridge background. Trollope's Evangelical pastors, if fortunate enough to have been to one of the universities, have been undergraduates at Cambridge. Slope, the sizar from Cambridge,[109] has sufficient presumption to consider himself an Oxford fellow's equal in the competition for a deanery.

## 3. '*All Sorts and Conditions of Men*'

### i. *The clergy*

Though Anglican orders conferred a certain assured social position

[102] *Vicar of Wrexhill*, ii, 11–12.

[103] W. F. Wilkinson, *The Rector in Search of a Curate.*

[104] Quoted by D. Newsome, 'Justification and Sanctification: Newman and the Evangelicals', *JTS* 15 (1964), 40.

[105] *Charles Simeon* (1892), p. 74.

[106] See below, Chapter VI.

[107] G. Eliot, *Scenes*, i, 39.

[108] W. H. White, *Catharine Furze*, ii, 7.

[109] A. Trollope, *Barchester Towers*, pp. 22, 304.

on their recipients, the Evangelicals in the ministry were often regarded as likely to be socially inferior to their Broad Church or Tractarian colleagues. Evangelical attitudes to the pursuit of knowledge, combined with the financial and educational poverty of the social class from which men like Slope or Barton appeared, led the novelists to depict many an Evangelical parson as little better educated than many of his parishioners. The hardening of Evangelical opposition to all advances in the field of Biblical criticism confirmed the image of a party which rejoiced in appropriating the Pauline description of the Corinthian Christians 'not many wise men after the flesh, not many mighty, not many noble'.[110]

Some of the most famous forefathers of the movement, such as Thomas Scott and John Newton, and in the next century Edward Bickersteth, had not been to Oxford or Cambridge before their ordination in an age when ordination for a non-graduate was exceptional. Evangelicals led the way in training non-graduates for the ministry; St. Bees, Cumberland, being founded in 1816, the Islington Church Missionary Society Institution, for the training of missionaries, in 1825, and St. Aidan's Birkenhead in 1846.[111] Trollope calls upon these names to suggest the social and educational inferiority to their brother clergy of some of the Evangelical clergy. Mr. Frigidy, a would-be cleric, who considers all three, fears that the entrance tests of 'even the initionary gates of Islington' might be too forbidding for him.[112] Rachel Ray, in her contempt for her sister's suitor, 'declared that Mr. Prong had been educated at Islington, and that sometimes he forgot his "h's" '.[113] The outside world's scepticism at the level of attainment derived from these colleges is scarcely surprising in view of the opinion expressed by Bishop Robert Bickersteth, Edward's nephew, of a comparable establishment at Lichfield.

> ... the standard of attainment which secures the usual certificate of Lichfield is, so far as I can judge, not high ...

[110] 1 Cor. 1: 26. The Revd. D. D. Stewart, proudly quoting this text, footnoted the final phrase as follows: 'A pious member of the British nobility recently expressed thankfulness for the *m* in this word.' *Evangelical Opinion in the Nineteenth Century* (1879), p. 10.

[111] F. W. B. Bullock, *A History of Training for the Ministry of the Church of England in England and Wales from 598 to 1799* (St. Leonard's-on-Sea, 1969); and *A History of Training for the Ministry of the Church of England in England and Wales from 1800 to 1874* (St. Leonards-on-Sea, 1955).

[112] *Miss Mackenzie*, p. 46.

[113] *Rachel Ray*, p. 52.

I think you will sympathise in my desire to obtain candidates who have a degree, and to make the admission of candidates from Theological Colleges who are non-graduates, the exception. Of course all this relates to an intellectual training; but I would infinitely prefer a man from a Theological College of high spiritual qualifications, though of inferior mental culture, to a man of the highest intellectual attainment, with a low standard of piety, whatever his academic distinction.[114]

Robert Bickersteth's position was derived from the views of the Clapham Sect generation, whose attitude to the intellect could be seen as a rejection of the dilettanteism which had sometimes accompanied the Enlightenment. Hannah More, a former member of the Blue Stocking circle, has a wise country parson in *Coelebs* express his opinion that 'the younger part of a clergyman's life should be in a good measure devoted to learning', so 'that he may afterwards discover its comparative vanity'. This observation is followed by the acid remark that ,'It would have been a less difficult sacrifice for St. Paul to profess that he renounced all things for religion, if he had had nothing to renounce.'[115] Simeon found it necessary to remind his young disciples that there was no inherent harm in gaining academic distinctions,[116] since many of them were receiving letters from their zealous relations like that received by John Bickersteth, from his brother Edward, congratulating him on a lower degree than anticipated since only a 'carnal' heart would desire one higher than God appointed.[117] The insidious nature of this non-material ambition was adverted to by Mrs. Sherwood during the course of Henry Milner's Oxford career.[118] Mrs. Oliphant taking her cue from this lively fear for the intellectual's soul depicts a dying Evangelical fanatic warning his young companion. 'You once spoke eagerly about going to Oxford, and taking honours. My dear friend, trust a dying man. There are no honours worth thinking of but the crown and the palm, which Christ bestows on them that love Him.'[119]

A generation of Tractarian-influenced novelists perpetuated the myth that Evangelicals believed that piety was necessarily found in

[114] M. C. Bickersteth, *A Sketch of the Life and Episcopate of the Right Reverend Robert Bickersteth* (1887), pp. 164–5. Cf. W. F. Wilkinson, *Rector in Search of a Curate*, p. 152.

[115] i, 302–3.

[116] A. W. Brown, *Recollections of Simeon*, p. 126.

[117] T. R. Birks, *A Memoir of the Rev. Edward Bickersteth*, i, 159.

[118] M. M. Sherwood, *A History of Henry Milner, Pt. IV* (1837), p. 258.

[119] *A Son of the Soil*, ii, 80.

inverse ratio to learning. Constance Duff is worried about her brother's Oxford career, not because of its profligate nature, but because he is coming to put his trust in learning.[120] Though Newman discounted reason as the primary basis of Christian belief, seeing it rather as a means by which to approve faith,[121] he deplored the lack of 'intellectual basis' in the Evangelical religion.[122] He characterized the position he believed them to hold in Freeborn, who regards the reason of the unconverted as a carnal weapon to be eschewed, and faith as a gift of grace which altered the constitution of the convert, so that only he might know its presence. Faith as practised by Freeborn had no basis in reason and could not be detected by it.[123]

Shaftesbury's simple dichotomy, 'Satan reigns in the intellect, God in the heart of man',[124] was the result of teaching which presented Evangelicalism as exclusively the religion of the heart, easily to be comprehended by the simplest of mortals on an individual basis, rather than through the accumulated wisdom of tradition. His appointment of pastoral workers, rather than scholars, to the Palmerstonian bishoprics cemented, in popular opinion, the belief that Evangelicals were constitutionally unable to provide men of academic distinction.[125] The young Gerard Manley Hopkins remarked as if having discovered the habitat of *rara avis*, 'At Hampstead lives almost the only learned Evangelical going, T. R. Birks.'[126]

Ordination was only the first step in a ministerial career. Evangelicals had early found difficulty in obtaining livings or curacies, when few bishops were sympathetic to the cause and many livings were held by wealthy latitudinarian clerics. Only a few of the early Evangelical clergy, such as Henry Venn Elliott and Cadogan, had themselves come from the social class used to exercise patronage and occasionally, like Grimshaw, experienced conversion only after their installation. In order to rescue eloquent but indigent converts, whom they had been losing to Dissent, Evangelical societies

[120] H. Mozley, *Lost Brooch*, i, 135–6.

[121] 'Faith and Reason, contrasted as habits of mind', *Sermons and Discourses, 1825–39*, ed. C. F. Harrold (1949), 306–25.

[122] *Apologia pro Vita Sua*, ed. M. Svaglic (Oxford, 1967), p. 98.

[123] *Loss and Gain*, p. 141.

[124] E. Hodder, *Life of Shaftesbury*, iii, 19.

[125] e.g. M. M. Bevington, *The Saturday Review 1855–68; Representative Educated Opinion in Victorian England* (New York, 1941), p. 84; and Joseph Romilly Diaries, 29 Nov. 1856.

[126] *Further letters of Gerard Manley Hopkins*, ed. C. C. Abbott (1956), p. 18.

sponsored the training of men like Patrick Brontë.[127] Simeon and his colleagues so successfully pursued a policy of buying the patronage of available livings that writers were gradually able to indicate the complexion of a church's religion by mere reference to the patron.[128] Jokes upon the ease with which Simeon's name could be allied with the concept of simony were not lacking. The suspicion and resentment his policy met is understandable only in terms of the complete revolution in patronage practice that he effected. It was his boast that he listened to none but his own conscience. 'In these matters', he wrote ,'*I know none but God.* I would not know my own father, or my son . . .'[129] One of Mrs. Oliphant's novels conveys perfectly the indignation of a generation accustomed to the old practices. Mr. Wentworth, a squire of the old High and Dry school, is appalled by his sister's determination to appoint a 'gospel' minister to a living in her gift, regardless of the available family candidate.

'I think it's a man's bounden duty, when there is a living in the family, to educate one of his sons for it. In my opinion, it's one of the duties of property. You have no right to live off your estate, and spend your money elsewhere; and no more have you any right to give less than—than your own flesh and blood to the people you have the charge of.'[130]

Worse than this, patronage exercised upon a principle of 'spiritual meritocracy' produced social turmoil. Mrs. Farebrother, contemplating her son's career, remarks, 'It was not so in my youth: a Churchman was a Churchman, and a clergyman, you might be pretty sure, was a gentleman, if nothing else. But now he may be no better than a Dissenter, and want to push aside my son on pretence of doctrine.'[131]

George Eliot did not subscribe to the belief that social gentility should be taken into account in patronage, but Trollope did. From the standpoint of the American Senator, in the novel of that name, he outlines the apparent injustice and folly of the old system, but finally he allies himself with the Anglican Rector who dismisses the criticisms as those of an ignorant outsider, who, moreover, is no

[127] For examples of this policy in operation see J. D. Walsh, 'The Magdalene Evangelicals', *CQR* 159 (1958), 499–511.

[128] [C. S. C. Bowen], 'The English Evangelical Clergy', *Macmillan's Magazine*, 3 (Dec. 1860), 117; F. E. Paget, *The Warden of Berkingholt* (1843), p. 293; W. H. White, *Catharine Furze*, i, 101; S. Kaye-Smith, *Anglo-Catholicism* (1925), ch. v; A. L. Rowse, *Autobiography of a Cornishman: a Cornish Childhood* (1942), p. 146.

[129] W. Carus, *Memoirs of the Life of the Rev. Charles Simeon* (1847), p. 747.

[130] *The Perpetual Curate*, iii, 126.

[131] G. Eliot, *Middlemarch*, i, 259.

gentleman.[132] Though he was aware that 'the word is one the use of which almost subjects one to ignominy', he felt that there existed certain positions, amongst which he numbered Church livings, 'which can hardly be well filled except by "Gentlemen" '.[133]

Accusations of social climbing via an Evangelical ministry were made on all sides. Sydney Smith seems to have given birth to a tradition by referring to Methodist ministers (under which heading, it will be remembered, he includes the Evangelicals) as a 'nest of consecrated cobblers'.[134] His sneer was presumably based upon the fact that the first Baptist minister to India, William Carey, had been by trade a cobbler,[135] it being difficult to find candidates from the higher classes ready to accept the discomforts and dangers the vocation demanded. Cobbling, too, was a trade which gained a particular reputation for the radicalism with which Dissent, and by extension Evangelicalism, was tainted. From then on the novel was full of clergymen with this illustrious origin. George Eliot's comment that Amos Barton's father had been a cabinet-maker, rather than was frequently supposed a cobbler, is a jibe at this tradition.[136] Once a living had been obtained, or, as in the case of Charles Honeyman,[137] a chapel-of-ease purchased, the social adventurer was at liberty to add wealth to his social status. In many novels the time-serving Evangelical minister devotes himself to securing the financial rewards of the care of the fatherless and widowed. Mrs. Trollope,[138] Thackeray,[139] Conybeare,[140] Kingsley,[141] and Anthony Trollope[142] all depict Evangelical ministers in pursuit, or in triumphant enjoyment, of such prizes. Usually their spouses came from the rich merchant classes, but the occasional cleric decided for rank as well as money and contrived to worm his way into the aristocracy.[143]

[132] *The American Senator* (1931), ch. xlii. [133] *An Autobiography* (1968), p. 34.

[134] *Edin. Rev.* 14 (1809), 40.

[135] E. Stock, *History of the Church Missionary Society*, i, 59.

[136] *Scenes*, i, 13–14. Cf. Mr. Dempster's obscure remark 'I knew we had nothing to expect in these days, when the Church is infested by a set of men who are only fit to give out hymns from an empty cask, to tunes set by a journeyman cobbler', *Scenes*, ii, 118. [137] W. M. Thackeray, *The Newcomes.*

[138] *Vicar of Wrexhill; The Lottery of Marriage: A Novel* (3 vols., 1849).

[139] *The Newcomes.* [140] *Perversion*, i, 326. [141] *Yeast*, ch. xviii.

[142] *Barchester Towers; Rachel Ray; Miss Mackenzie; The Eustace Diamonds.*

[143] e.g. Trollope's Mr. Emilius, *The Eustace Diamonds;* and Conybeare's Mr. Mooney, *Perversion*, i, 326: in the one case a convert Jew, in the other a Millenialist. Joseph Wolff, a famous Evangelical who was both, married Lady Georgiana Walpole and declined to accept her personal fortune from fear of the scandal this might create. S. C. Orchard, 'English Evangelical Eschatology, 1790–1850', D. Phil. thesis, Cambridge, 1968, p. 149.

## ii. *The laity*

The great strength of the Evangelical party, as High Churchmen were fond of emphasizing, was its lay support. The pronouncements of Hannah More, William Wilberforce, or Lord Shaftesbury commanded as much authority for the Evangelicals as did any clerical teaching. This fact goes far in explaining the interest, shared by novelist and reader alike, in exploring the Evangelical ethos, for although a man might with ease avoid his local church and clergyman, a movement which had agents in so great a cross-section of society could not be ignored and might be a potentially dangerous influence.

Active minorities wielded great power and attracted the persecuting tendencies which accompany any such minority. A man like Wilberforce who enjoyed the Prime Minister's confidence, and offended so many by his agitation for the abolition of slavery and its associated commercial interests, naturally drew suspicion upon the political independence which he and his colleagues asserted. Whilst *Vanity Fair*'s famous cartoonist, Spy, openly proclaimed that the Tory Shaftesbury operated as a non-partisan in politics, the covert suspicion still remained that he could at any time act as the leader of a potentially vast political force.[144] Since voting according to conscience was compatible with either a Tory or a Whig complexion,[145] novelists could either, like Trollope, distribute the honours evenly, or, like his mother, choose to see them as probable supporters of whichever party they most disliked.

Very rarely, if ever, did the novelists suggest that the Evangelicals were a socially disruptive force in the way that the Methodists had been. Sir Gilbert Scott recalled, as an exception, how in his grandfather's parish 'community of religious feeling was allowed to override difference of worldly position',[146] and, how, on occasion, labourers had sat at table with this clergyman, who had originally been a grazier. Men from superior social backgrounds easily rejected the temptation of social egalitarianism to which their spiritual principles might have inclined them. In the confidence that God had appointed his social station in life, Simeon reflected, 'I might live as

[144] *Vanity Fair*, 2 (13 Nov. 1869), 274.

[145] See I. Bradley, 'The Politics of Godliness: Evangelicals in Parliament 1784–1832', D. Phil. thesis, Oxford, 1974.

[146] *Personal and Professional Recollections*, ed. G. G. Scott (1879), p. 28.

my servants do, but I should be wrong.'[147] Yet the fact remained that Evangelicalism created strange bed-fellows. Trollope's Marquis of Trowbridge, who is mortally offended if his family is in any way compared with lesser beings, is yet prepared to consort with the uneducated Primitive Methodist minister because they share Evangelical sympathies.[148]

Though Evangelicalism may have started its missionary activities in small Yorkshire and Cornish villages, towards the close of the eighteenth-century advocates were found for the belief that the English upper classes were equally in need of the good news, as Cowper's poem 'Truth' suggests:

> Envy, ye great, the dull unletter'd small:
> Ye have much cause for envy—but not all.
> We boast some rich ones whom the Gospel sways;
> And one who wears a coronet, and prays;
> Like the gleanings of an olive-tree, they show
> Here and there one upon the topmost bough.[149]

The Evangelicals fully realized the advantages to be gained from such a display case. A tract, entitled *A Coronet laid at the feet of Jesus; as illustrated by the conversion of the late Lord Bloomfield*,[150] was published by George Scott—an enterprise distinguishing him from his egalitarian namesake in the family of Thomas Scott, the grazier. The nobility were found useful for assuming the vice-presidencies of the great missionary societies, not so much for their financial contributions as for their social prestige. Samuel Butler's notebooks gleefully record an incident which showed that the Evangelicals sometimes lost sight of the fundamental distinction between converted and unconverted when worldly influence was badly needed.

In 1824 Lord Orford was invited to become President of the Norwich Bible Society. His reply was as follows:

'Sir—I am surprised and annoyed by the contents of your letter—surprised, because my well-known character should have exempted me from

[147] A. W. Brown, *Recollections of Simeon*, p. 124.

[148] *The Vicar of Bullhampton*. Cf. Shaftesbury's plight in this respect. 'Shaftesbury had always been an isolated figure. Those who shared his personal memories and upbringing did not share his interests; those who shared his interests did not fit into the background of his private life . . . ' G. Battiscombe, *Shaftesbury* (1974), pp. 321–2.

[149] 'Truth'. *ll*, 375–80.

[150] George Scott (1866).

such an application; and annoyed, because it compels me to have even this communication with you.

I have long been addicted to the gaming table; I have lately taken to the turf; I fear I frequently blaspheme; but I have never distributed religious tracts. All this was known to you and your society, notwithstanding which you think me a fit person to be your president. God forgive your hypocrisy.

I would rather live in the land of sinners than with such saints.'[151]

In a sense this incident validated Hannah More's contention that religious hypocrisy was rare amongst the upper classes, since they gained no credit by assuming a religious guise.[152]

It was rather from the middle classes that men and women emerged who discovered that a reputation for piety could be gained from appearing on the subscription lists of such societies. The character who hoped to disguise his or her activities in the financial or social demi-monde by such means became a favourite literary figure.[153] Becky Sharp was perhaps the most famous of them all. Thackeray takes his leave of Becky when her name is on all the charity lists and she has found acceptance in the religious world. The depth of the irony employed here is only appreciated when we remember how, before Becky had induced Jos to disgorge all his money, her efforts to regain social status by good works came to nothing.[154] The Evangelical world, Thackeray implies, is like the rest of Vanity Fair in knowing the precise value of the social coinage, which it will not allow an unsuccessful social adventuress to depreciate.

The merchants and bankers of Clapham retained sufficient worldly common sense to realize the gain to be made in demonstrating that Evangelicalism was not necessarily the prerogative of the poor Dissenting classes.[155] They were always subject to attack

[151] *Further Extracts from the Note-Books of Samuel Butler*, ed. A. J. Bartholomew (1934), p. 298.

[152] *Coelebs*, ii, 402.

[153] *Inter alia*, Godfrey Ablewhite in W. Collins, *The Moonstone;* [J. F. D. Maurice], *Eustace Conway; or, The Brother and Sister* (3 vols., 1834).

[154] *Vanity Fair*, chs. lxiv, lxvii.

[155] Sir James Stephen explained that Wilberforce's 'public usefulness is promoted by having so respectable a mansion, so much in the eye of the public . . . Constituted as the world is, example and influence will be the more efficacious, the more personal consequence is attached to them . . .' R. I. and S. Wilberforce, *Life of William Wilberforce*, iii, 390–1. Cf. a letter from William to his son Samuel Wilberforce, outlining the rationale for a careful choice of acquaintance and explaining the Evangelical attitude to 'singularity', quoted by D. Newsome, *The Parting of Friends*, pp. 54–5.

from those who, assuming that evangelicalism implied enthusiasm, treated any sign of moderation as a cardinal sin against the command of separateness. In fact the Anglican Evangelical tradition consistently maintained a strong awareness of the difficult course to be steered between the Scylla of conformity to the world and the Charybdis of wilful singularity. A recognizable symptom of imminent secession, whether to Rome or Dissent, came to be a rejection of the *via media* position, symbolized by Wilberforce's *Practical View*, in favour of a greater apostolic purity.

Part of Evangelicalism's success in infiltrating society so widely throughout the upper and middle classes, by the time of Victoria's accession, was the result of the business-like approach to the dissemination of the Gospel,[156] adopted by the group most often attacked for having 'their conversation in heaven, without renouncing the society of man'.[157] Clapham, their headquarters, therefore became the focus for a complex reaction of jealousy and contempt. Much of this reaction is explicable in social terms. Thackeray and Disraeli both produced fairly lengthy sketches of this community in *The Newcomes* and *Falconet* respectively. Their dislike for Clapham stemmed from a natural resentment of those who had stood out against and destroyed the standards of Regency society which both had aspired to in their youth, and who had yet created a new aristocratic milieu in which the pious sons of merchants found themselves welcomed. Surely, they argued, there must have been hypocrisy to be condemned in an other-worldly piety which resulted in marked material success. Both authors reacted by attempting to belittle that social respectability which at one time they had most coveted, but which they also came partly to despise.

In this endeavour they chose to ignore the entrée to the best society which Wilberforce had always enjoyed,[158] but their criticisms aptly suggest the social snobbery in which some of the sons of Clapham indulged.

The Wilberforce sons, particularly Sam, thought of themselves as members of the upper classes and despised the more obviously lower-middle-class friends of their parents, such as Legh Richmond, a physician's son. A letter from Elizabeth Wilberforce to Robert

[156] D. Spring, 'The Clapham Sect: Some Social and Political Aspects', VS 5 (1961), pp. 35–48.

[157] R. I. and S. Wilberforce, op. cit. iii, 392.

[158] Madame de Staël described him as 'L'homme le plus aimé, et le plus consideré de toute l'Angleterre.' R. I. and S. Wilberforce, op. cit. iv, 158.

makes it clear that this trait had manifested itself before their Oxford days.

I sometimes wish you and dear Sam, where there is real piety, were more disposed to get over manner and not as I fear to prefer a man for his elegant and gentlemanlike manners to one who has more piety. Not that I would wish you at all to keep company below yourselves for I think that has a very prejudicial effect on people and prejudices others against religion, but that in some instances you should get over a disagreeable manner for the sake of religion. Oh when I think of our name—what is expected from us and what religious advantages we have had—I tremble . . .[159]

Sir James Stephen, another second generation Claphamite, lights upon an interesting choice of phrase to express his regret for Newman's separation from the Evangelical party. Newman behaved, he said, 'as if the dread of being vulgar was to pursue us in religious just as much as in social matters'.[160] He later explained to Newman that he brought his own family up in the system 'which, to fastidious persons like myself, has perhaps the least attraction',[161] but this did not prevent him from publicly animadverting on the 'coxcombry' and 'affectation' of Charles Simeon, the attorney's son.[162]

In origin many of the Claphamites were merchants or bankers, but, as Disraeli acidly observed, of a respectable heaviness not to be found amongst the new railway magnates.[163] In *The Newcomes*, which describes the progress of the Hobson family, whose money had been made in banking, Thackeray claimed to be writing *The History of a Respectable Family*. It was remarked, in an article in *Tinsley's Magazine*, describing the requisite composition of an Evangelical Drawing room of the 1870s, 'A banker who is supposed to be as safe in this world as in the next', was always one of 'the professional men of eminent piety', in attendance.[164] The sight of worldliness hand-in-hand with other-worldliness was one which fascinated the novelists. Examples of the service of God through an understanding of the ways of Mammon, such as that provided by Sir James Stephen's career, must have been rare, but he won for

[159] Quoted by D. Newsome, *The Parting of Friends*, p. 72.

[160] Quoted by D. Newsome, 'Justification and Sanctification: Newman and the Evangelicals', *JTS* 15 (1964), 40.

[161] Ibid., p. 47.

[162] *Essays in Ecclesiastical Biography* (2 vols., 1849), ii, 368.

[163] *Falconet*, p. 471.

[164] 'Evangelical Drawing-Rooms', *Tinsley's Magazine*, 9 (1871–2), p. 114.

himself the sneering title of Mr. Over-secretary Stephen for his determined assumption of power at the Colonial Office. How could the unconverted understand the zeal which might motivate a successful barrister to become a less well-paid civil servant, except in terms of power seeking—an interpretation apparently justified by his indefatigable industry in pursuit of policies which he approved. Yet even at his office he was capable of reflecting, amidst the excitement of the Reform Bill, 'Well—"the lord God omipotent reigneth", and it does not really much matter what may occur in this short life; if all be bravely encountered, patiently endured, and wisely improved . . .'[165]

The Middlemarchers came to explain the phenomenon of their Evangelical banker, Mr. Bulstrode's considerable secular power, ostensibly obtained 'for the glory of God', as 'a sort of vampire's feast in the sense of mastery'.[166] The feeling was more bluntly expressed by the banker's brother-in-law who accused him of trying to play both bishop and banker.[167] Though studied with more sympathy and in greater detail than other fictional bankers, Bulstrode shares many surface similarities with them. Since love of money was at the root of all evil, the handling of money, went the novelists' reasoning, must lay a man open to greater temptations than other men. The frequency with which banks crashed in the nineteenth century made the appearance of respectability important for bankers, whilst making clients exceptionally wary. The fineness of the distinction made between financial speculation and the gambling, of which Evangelicals so notoriously disapproved, was in the minds of many novelists mere casuistry. Trollope's Banker Bolton and his wife brand their prospective son-in-law as a gambler because he has gained an income from the harsh life and sudden pieces of fortune of a gold prospector rather than 'in a gradual, industrious manner, and in accordance with recognised forms'.[168]

There were many studies of the man 'who stands high among us, and who implores his God every Sunday to write that law on his heart, [and] spends every hour of his daily toil in a system of fraud, and is regarded as a pattern of the national commerce'.[169] Mr. Meredith, father of the young Evangelical fanatic in Mrs. Oliphant's

[165] C. B. Stephen, *The First Sir James Stephen: Letters with Biographical Notes* (Gloucester, 1906), p. 23.

[166] G. Eliot, *Middlemarch*, i, 235.

[167] Ibid. i, 197. [168] *John Caldigate* (1946), 121–2.

[169] A. Trollope, *Phineas Finn* (2 vols., 1937), ii., 221

*Son of the Soil*, combined Evangelicalism with being a swindler in a joint-stock company. Mrs. Oliphant's observations upon public reaction to his declared insolvency suggest the popularity of the theme which the novelists were handling.

He was a pious man, who subscribed to all the societies, and had, of course, since these unpleasant accidents occurred, been held up to public admiration by half the newspapers of Great Britain as an instance of the natural effect produced upon the human mind by an assumption of superior piety; and more than one clever leading article, intended to prove that lavish subscriptions to benevolent purposes, and attendance at prayer meetings, were the natural evidences of a mind disposed to prey on its fellow-creatures, had been made pointed and emphatic by his name.[170]

*The Old Grey Church*,[171] one of a number of novels categorized by George Eliot, in her days as a reviewer, as belonging to 'the *white neck-cloth* species'[172] of silly novels, contains a major figure to whom Bulstrode bears certain marked resemblances. Lushington's rise to wealth and prominence owes its origin, as does Bulstrode's, to his promotion from being a mere bank clerk to a major force in a friend's firm. Like Bulstrode he is an Evangelical whose religious principles become subordinated to his compulsive interest in financial affairs. He too defrauds the heir of his former partner by failing to disclose the inheritance due to him, but adds to this offence the more heinous and unconnected crimes of fraudulent conversion and forgery, which in the days of the novel's setting were offences punishable by death. Poetic justice is meted out in this novel by the hangman's rope rather than by the social oblivion into which the Bulstrodes melt away.

Bank clerkdom or the lower echelons of the civil service[173] form the lowest classes from which the Anglican Evangelicals are selected in the nineteenth-century novel. Fictional and non-fictional sources alike suffer from the same drawback of being written by and for the articulate literate portion of the population. From these Evangelicalism emerges as mainly the religion of the leisured or professional classes, and perforce of their servants, but not of the urban proletariat. The 1851 religious census certainly revealed that workers

[170] *Son of the Soil*, ii, 68.

[171] [C. Scott], *The Old Grey Church* (3 vols., 1856).

[172] 'Silly Novels by Lady Novelists', *Essays of George Eliot*, ed. T. Pinney (1963), p. 317.

[173] See Mr. Snape in A. Trollope, *The Three Clerks* (1959), p. 16.

in larger towns remained untouched by Anglicanism and subsequent efforts for the mass evangelization of the artisan classes were bedevilled by the reputation which lower-middle-class support for the missions gave them. Only in country towns or villages, where a more integrated community might still exist, could the church expect to influence a wider cross-section, and the evidence provided by the novel leads one to imagine that this was a feature of the first rather than the second half of the century. Mr. Cartwright can still ruin the life of a poor schoolmaster for refusal to attend Evangelical parish services,[174] and Mr. Budd threaten to dismiss any of his workmen who do attend an Evangelical evening lecture[175] in the 1830s. Barchester, though an old-fashioned country town, is large enough for Mrs. Proudie's policy of confining her trade to the regenerate to be a totally ineffectual economic sanction.[176] The poorer classes appear throughout the period, both in the secular novel and in Evangelical propaganda, as recipients of patronage, or examples to their social peers, as pawns in a middle-class game. The eponymous hero of the immensely popular *Christie's Old Organ* is still in 1873 only a stereotyped penniless orphan who through generous patronage is enabled to become 'a Scripture reader amongst the lowest class of the people' in his town.[177] Only in the Dissenting world do the poor begin to attain real individuality.

[174] F. Trollope, *Vicar of Wrexhill*, iii, 73.
[175] G. Eliot, *Scenes*, ii, 119–20.
[176] A. Trollope, *The Last Chronicle of Barset* (1932), ii, 289.
[177] O. F. Walton, *Christie's Old Organ* (1882), p. 21.

CHAPTER II

# Evangelical Doctrine

> . . . there never was a religious persecution in which some odious crime was not, justly or unjustly, said to be obviously deducible from the doctrines of the persecuted party.[1]

WHEN Gladstone, normally a precise and careful writer, came to define the doctrine of the Evangelical movement he was forced to generalize in these vague phrases: 'It aimed at bringing back, on a large scale, and by an aggressive movement, the Cross, and all that the Cross essentially implies . . .'[2]

Evangelical religion is founded upon a personal apprehension of God. No human mediator is admitted to distance the relation between God and man. The onus of interpreting God's Word therefore rests firmly upon the individual and there is no appeal to any authoritative body for dogmatic pronouncements beyond the Thirty-nine Articles, whose very breadth of possible interpretation made them inadequate foundations for a theological system. Attempts to impose doctrinal uniformity, on any but the broadest framework, were and are doomed to failure.[3] Any discussion of Evangelical doctrine can only presume to deal with a consensus of beliefs held by different individuals over the time span of a couple of centuries.

The mixture of Arminians and Calvinists within the Evangelical body creates a further difficulty in giving an accurate picture of the school's doctrine.[4] It is not easy to assess the balance between these two doctrinal approaches at any one time in the party, and the assessment tends to depend upon the prejudices of the critic in

[1] T. B. Macaulay, *Critical and Historical Essays contributed to the Edinburgh Review* (3 vols., 1843), i, 121.

[2] *Gleanings from Past Years*, vii, 207.

[3] See *A History of the Ecumenical Movement, 1517–1948*, ed. R. Rouse and S. C. Neill (1967), pp. 318–24, for the history of the Evangelical Alliance.

[4] The best account is to be found in J. D, Walsh, thesis cit., especially pp. 66–84.

question.[5] Novelists, by and large, tend to portray Anglican Evangelicals as Calvinist in persuasion, partly because Arminianism was particularly associated with dissenting Methodism and partly because the hard logic of true Calvinism provided both a clarity of definition and an intellectual position which could easily be shown to be at odds with natural human sympathies.[6] For instance, although Mrs. Trollope's foe, the Revd. J. W. Cunningham, was an Evangelical of Arminian persuasion, as any reader of *The Velvet Cushion* would soon have realized,[7] her fictional target for abuse, Mr. Cartwright, is described as an ultra-Calvinist, thus enabling her to present a stronger case against the divisiveness fomented by Evangelicalism. The Calvinist tenets of predestination and Particular Redemption, which, most Evangelicals were agreed, usually formed an abstract personal belief rather than a prominent part of the teaching of Moderate Calvinist clergy,[8] provided a useful platform for a villainous parson bent upon dividing families into the sheep, who might be fleeced, and the goats, anxious to afford 'worldly' protection to the flock upon whom he preyed. Unfortunately Mrs. Trollope's desire to amass all the possible charges against Evangelicals led her to a grand disregard for consistency. Cartwright is abused as a 'Church Methodist',[9] presumably an allusion to his sectarian rather than his doctrinal tendencies, although this remains unclear, described repeatedly as a Calvinist[10] but also mocked for his verbal reliance upon the doctrine of Assurance,[11] one much favoured by Arminians but scarcely mentioned by Calvinists. Rather than feeling that Cartwright's utter contempt for consistent doctrine is being condemned, the reader comes to suspect that Mrs. Trollope had only the very vaguest notion of the very real differences existing within the bosom of the Evangelical party. For her the very name of Evangelical was anathema and anything implied by this

[5] e.g. F. K. Brown seems to have based his assertion that Evangelicals were predominantly Arminian upon a belief that Calvinism was a less worldly philosophy. *Fathers of the Victorians*, p. 49.

[6] The second reason seems to have led the Brontë's biographer, Winifred Gérin, into transforming Aunt Branwell from an Arminian to a Calvinist.

[7] *Velvet Cushion*, pp. 118–19.

[8] See J. Bean, *Zeal without Innovation*, pp. 45–56; J. Scott, *The Life of the Rev. Thomas Scott*, 5th edn. (1823), p. 446; *The Life of the Late Rev. Henry Venn*, ed. H. Venn (1834), p. 31.

[9] *Vicar of Wrexhill*, ii, 261.

[10] Ibid. i, 282, ii, 312.

[11] Ibid. ii, 317. The concept of Assurance is explained below, pp. 103–4.

word sufficient to damn a person without requiring any internal consistency.

Hardy employs a curious anachronism in *Tess of the D'Urbervilles* which has the ring of doctrinal confusion. Alec d'Urberville is described variously as 'a ranter'[12] and 'a Methodist'[13] according to the resources of the individual's vocabulary, though Hardy, as narrator, supports the latter description.[14] He also tells us that Alec's doctrine 'was a vehement form of the views of Angel's father',[15] who was known to be a Calvinist. Although he could of course have been a Calvinistic Methodist, a follower of Whitefield or of the Countess of Huntingdon's Connexion, by this stage he would probably have been described as such or as an Independent. Henry Moule claimed that there were fewer than twenty Dissenters in his entire parish of 2,200 souls at Fordington, and no chapel,[16] but Hardy must have come into contact with Methodism in Dorset even if only through the history of the Tolpuddle Martyrs. It seems more likely that Hardy, like Mrs. Trollope, is using the term 'Methodist' in the manner popular in the first forty years of the century to imply carelessness or contempt for the claims of the Establishment, since Alec claims to differ only on 'the question of Church and State'[17] from Mr. Clare. The uncertainty at this critical point in the story is one more indicator of the weak artistic grasp that Hardy had upon his melodramatic villain.

Generally speaking the nineteenth-century Evangelicals themselves seemed to agree with the tolerant position adopted by Cunningham's fictional Vicar, reserving condemnation only for ultra-Calvinism; but their very reluctance to speak out firmly upon what had been a divisive controversy led their critics to infer support for whatever doctrine they most disliked, as we shall see when examining in turn the constituent parts of the Evangelical doctrine.

[12] *Tess of the D'Urbervilles* (1912), pp. 385, 417. F. Pilkington's assertion that 'The seducer of Tess for a time was an aggressive Plymouth Brother', seems altogether too specific an interpretation of the term 'ranter'. 'Religion in Hardy's Novels', *Contemporary Review*, 188 (1955), 34.

[13] *Tess of the D'Urbervilles*, p. 406. [14] Ibid., p. 392. [15] Ibid., p. 385.

[16] J. E. Orr, *The Second Evangelical Awakening in Britain* (1949), p. 109. For Hardy's intimate knowledge of Moule see below, pp. 118–20.

[17] *Tess of the D'Urbervilles*, p. 393. Hardy may well have been reminded of this usage by Henry Moule's obituary. *The Vicar of Fordington: Sketches of the Work of the late Rev. Henry Moule, M.A.* (Dorchester: 1880), where it is remarked of Moule's arrival in Fordington, 'the new Vicar was found to be what was called in those days a "Methodist" '. I came across this obituary in vol. v (1877–83), p. 82, of the scrapbooks compiled by H. J. Moule (11 vols.), kept at Dorchester County Museum.

## 1. *The essential doctrines*

### i. *Original sin*

The concept of Original Sin, or for the Calvinist, the conviction of Total Depravity, was the linchpin of the Evangelical creed. Mrs. Sherwood clearly did not think that William Wilberforce had gone 'too far' in asserting, 'that it lies at the very root of all true Religion, and still more, that it is eminently the basis and ground-work of Christianity'.[18] Before Mr. and Mrs. Fairchild teach their children the doctrine of the Trinity, they first affirm their conviction of total depravity.[19] The children's active illustration of this principle lent them an interest and attraction comparable to that felt by many readers for Milton's Satan. Yet, however damaging to didactic intentions, the doctrine's potential utility for the novelist can be seen when her fictional children are compared with the pallid juvenile protagonists of later nineteenth-century 'Evangelical style' fiction, whose appeal relied merely on a winsome and wholly incredible goodness.[20]

George Eliot's belief that we are all born into moral stupidity, rather than into Arcadian innocence, lends her work the same type of strength. The possible derivation of her humanist belief from the Christian doctrine of original sin is suggested by the consequent importance it throws upon the actions and love of a personal saviour figure in the redemptive process.

The significance of sin in the divine plan was to stay with another author who fell away from the Evangelicalism of his youth. Indeed, according to Froude, it was the inadequacy of the Evangelical system to cope with the consequences of their first tenet of faith which led Newman to 'a religion where sacraments were numerous and constant, and absolution more than a name, and confession possible'.

And sin with Newman was real; not a misfortune to be pitied and allowed for; to be talked of gravely in the pulpit, and forgotten when out of it; not

[18] *A Practical View*, 2nd. edn. (1797), p. 24.

[19] *The Fairchild Family*, i, 2, 17. Cf. Mrs. Sherwood's children's version of *Pilgrim's Progress* which introduces a character not found in Bunyan's *dramatis personae*—'. . . one who had been brought up under the same roof with them, as ill favoured and ill conditioned an urchin as one could see, whose name was *Inbred* or *Original Sin*'. *The Infant's Progress from the Valley of Destruction to Everlasting Glory* (Wellington, 1814), p. 5.

[20] e.g. in the works of Amy Le Feuvre, Hesba Stretton and Mrs. O. F. Walton.

a thing to be sentimentally sighed over at the evening tea-party, with complacent feeling that we were pleasing Heaven by calling ourselves children of hell, but in very truth a dreadful monster, a real child of a real devil, so dreadful that at its first appearance among mankind it had convulsed the infinite universe, and that nothing less than a sacrifice, so tremendous that the mind sinks crushed before the contemplation of it, could restore the deranged balance.[21]

Lady Caroline Scott's *The Old Grey Church* demonstrates the sentimental debasement of the concept of original sin which occurs when novelists start to wish to entertain in a manner compatible with Evangelicalism rather than being fired with converting zeal. Although perfunctory acknowledgement of sin and God's redeeming power are made, in careless moments the authoress refers to the heroine's 'innocent smile' and 'innocent laugh' contriving to portray a child of innocence tempted rather than innately corrupt,[22] and the tenor of the story suggests that men succumb to temptation because they find themselves in unfortunate circumstances, not because they have failed in the never-ceasing battle with the evil within their own flawed natures.

The phrase, 'Child of innocence', serves as a reminder of a fundamental conflict between Evangelical dogma and Romantic philosophy. The idea of the human pilgrimage from the Innocence of childhood to the Experience of adult life, which received its finest expression in Wordsworth's 'Ode: Intimations of Immortality from Recollections of Early Childhood', was totally incompatible with the Evangelical's vision of the child, who was to be taught to lisp from its earliest years the confession 'Lord, I am vile, conceiv'd in sin.'[23] Although by merely moral standards, Wordsworth's poetry became acceptable to Evangelicals his religious precepts required admonition. The *Christian Observer* for 1850 pinpointed the crucial error in his desire for a 'oneness with nature'. 'He must remember, that he speaks of fallen man, and of a "creation made subject to vanity", and that the ruin is altogether too great to be repaired by any influence of man upon creation, or of creation upon man.'[24]

In Dickens's pictures of young children who die only to be swept

[21] J. A. Froude, *The Nemesis of Faith* (1849), pp. 160–1. Newman's retention of this conviction can be seen in 'Moral Consequences of Single Sins', *Parochial and Plain Sermons* (1868), iv, 42.

[22] *Old Grey Church*, i, 196, ii, 42, 147.

[23] M. M. Sherwood, *The Fairchild Family*, i, 44.

[24] *CO* (1850), p. 313.

immediately back to heaven, their natural home, where they achieve an angelic status, we can see his debt to the Romantic tradition which resulted in an incapacity to comprehend the 'unnaturalness' of Evangelical doctrine.[25] He saw people not in the light of the theological division between the saved and the damned, but as innocent or corrupt. A passage from 'Two Views of a Cheap Theatre' makes clear Dickens's failure to grasp the significance of the doctrine of original sin in the Evangelical scheme.

Is it necessary or advisable to address such an audience continually as 'fellow-sinners'? Is it not enough to be fellow-creatures, born yesterday, suffering and striving to-day, dying to-morrow? . . . by our common aspiration to reach something better than ourselves, by our common tendency to believe in something good . . .—by these, Hear me!—Surely, it is enough to be fellow-creatures.[26]

For the Evangelical, the phrase 'fellow sinners' did not serve as a mere religious equivalent for 'dear friends' but as a reminder of their common inheritance of sin. Dickens's sympathies with Unitarianism[27] may well have reinforced his debt to the Romantic tradition at this point. Coleridge felt that he had only achieved a true understanding of sin when he rejected Unitarianism as being too morally easy.[28]

Few novelists were so absolute in their dismissal of the doctrine as Dickens, but objections could swiftly be lodged to the practice even if the theory proved acceptable. The difficulty in distinguishing original sin from individual sin provided the chink in the Evangelical armour where confusion and self-deception could appear. 'Now to be a sinner in the gross and a saint in the detail; that is, to have all sins, and no faults', remarks Coelebs, 'is a thing I do not quite comprehend.'[29] Hazlitt showed no such reticence and took pains to spell out the rationale for such an attitude.

Religious people often pray very heartily for the forgiveness of a 'multitude of trespasses and sins', as a mark of their humility, but we never knew them admit any one fault in particular, or acknowledge themselves in the wrong in any instance whatever. The natural jealousy of self-love is in

[25] See *The Letters of Charles Dickens*, ed. W. Dexter (3 vols., 1938), i, 221.

[26] *The Uncommercial Traveller and Reprinted Pieces*, p. 36.

[27] E. Johnson, *Charles Dickens: His Tragedy and Triumph* (2 vols., 1953), i, 464.

[28] See *The Collected Letters of Samuel Taylor Coleridge*, ed. E. L. Griggs (6 vols., Oxford, 1956–71), iii, 498.

[29] H. More, *Coelebs*, i, 62.

them heightened by the fear of damnation, and they plead *Not Guilty* to every charge brought against them, with all the conscious terrors of a criminal at the bar. It is for this reason that the greatest hypocrites in the world are religious hypocrites.[30]

Such mental processes had characterized Bulstrode's spiritual life until that moment when the memory of personal sin 'sends an inevitable glare over that long-unvisited past which has been habitually recalled only in general phrases'.[31] Charlotte Yonge's Angela Underwood is brought to realize, similarly, that she has only embraced Evangelicalism as a narcotic to soothe her sense of personal guilt.[32] This tendency was sufficiently familiar for Henry Thornton to make specific mention of it in his immensely popular *Family Prayers*. 'Open Thou our eyes, that we may perceive ourselves to be sinners in Thy sight,—partakers of a fallen nature, as well as actual transgressors against Thee . . .'[33]

Even this confession of two distinct varieties of sin could lead to a pride and complacency in the 'redeemed', as Trollope underlined in his portrait of St. Stumfolda.

. . . Living, as she did, in an atmosphere of flattery and toadying, it was wonderful how well she preserved her equanimity, and how she would talk and perhaps think of herself, as a poor, erring human being. When, however, she insisted much upon this fact of her humanity, the coachmaker's wife would shake her head, and at last stamp her foot in anger, swearing that though everybody was of course dust, and grass, and worms; and though, of course, Mrs. Stumfold must, by nature, be included in that everybody; yet dust, and grass, and worms nowhere exhibited themselves with so few of the stains of humanity as they did within the bosom of Mrs. Stumfold.[34]

This heavy-handed, but amusing, parody of the language of Evangelical confession also points to the understandable habit of ranking sinners which took place amongst some of the converted. A certain superiority, it was felt, must accrue to the regenerate, and so the specific individual sins, which the converted so frequently camouflaged under the generic title 'original sin', in their own case, became added on to the sum of inherited iniquity in the case of the unconverted. Mrs. Bolton's firm conviction that all men are worms

[30] 'On Religious Hypocrisy', *The Complete Works of William Hazlitt*, ed. P. P. Howe (21 vols., 1930–4), iv, 129.

[31] G. Eliot, *Middlemarch*, iii, 126.

[32] *Pillars of the House*, ii, 635.

[33] *Family Prayers* (1834), p. 52.

[34] *Miss Mackenzie*, pp. 115–16.

and dust does not prevent her from applying severer standards to her daughter's husband and his chief witness.[35]

Three authors, Trollope, Dickens, and Mrs. Gaskell, indirectly revealed the essentially anti-Christian nature of such a habit of mind, when they directed their attention to society's attitude to the fallen woman and the illegitimate child.

In each case they use a professing Christian of Evangelical proclivities to act as spokesman for a view which does not satisfactorily distinguish between Christian standards and social condemnation. The Revd. Harry Fenwick reminds his Methodist colleague, Mr. Puddleham, of the story of Mary Magdalene, in the context of a discussion about his fallen parishioner, Carry Brattle.

> 'And isn't my case very bad, and yours? Are we not in a bad way,—unless we believe and repent? Have we not all so sinned as to deserve eternal punishment?'
>
> 'Certainly, Mr. Fenwick.'
>
> 'Then there can't be much difference between her and us. She can't deserve more than eternal punishment. If she believes and repents, all her sins will be white as snow.'[36]

Miss Barbary, who has curiously elected to suffer for her sister's lapse, determines that another shall feel the seal of misery and shame. 'You are different from other children, Esther, because you were not born, like them, in common sinfulness and wrath. You are set apart.'[37]

When Mr. Bradshaw, a prominent member of a Dissenting community, discovers that his employee, Ruth Denbigh, has had an illegitimate child, he feels he may have earned the world's scorn for taking her in, and in his anger is stung to describe Leonard as a bastard, asking, 'Do you suppose that he is ever to rank with other boys, who are not stained and marked with sin from their births?[38]

These authors, as I have suggested, were correct in inferring a flaw in Evangelical logic. Their sympathy with those who challenge the Evangelical characters led them further—to questioning the very concept of sin and judgement. Dickens's *Life of Our Lord*, written for his own children, shows his anxiety to present Christ as 'Gentle Jesus meek and mild', while ignoring completely the

[35] A. Trollope, *John Caldigate*, p. 540.
[36] A. Trollope, *The Vicar of Bullhampton*, p. 124.
[37] C. Dickens, *Bleak House*, p. 18.
[38] E. C. Gaskell, *Ruth* (1906), pp. 336–7.

elements of stern judgement in His nature. Mrs. Gaskell's sympathies in *Ruth* are with the Dissenting minister, Thurstan Benson, who like the Unitarian authoress, dismisses the concept of 'original sin'.[39] The theological gulf between such authors and the Evangelicals they sought to criticize can perhaps best be appreciated by reference to an entry in Shaftesbury's diary, after he had heard religious teaching which did not appear to be firmly based upon a heartfelt conviction of sin.

. . . is falling rapidly into the errors of the day. He preaches very smooth things. In a long sermon about forgiveness and God's mercy, he only mentioned 'sin' once. 'It is not,' he said, 'that I intend to suppress God's hatred of sin. God forbid.' And there it ended. Then, at the close of his sermon, in order to magnify the mercy of God, he exclaimed, 'There is no one in this congregation who, having come to the service an unbeliever, may not leave it justified before God.' That is true, no doubt, but is it truly stated? What is belief? What does it contain? What does it demand? Does it demand conviction of sin, confession of sin, repentance and faith? All these things, except faith, are dropped now-a-days, and people are led to believe that to accept Christ as a Saviour, and to wish for His salvation, is the sum and substance of a heart turned to God. It requires no self-abasement, no confession of the justice of the Divine wrath, no acknowledgement of inherited corruption; and, disguise it as the preacher may, no sense of demerit, and no sense of deserved condemnation. It is, in fact, reduced to an easy, agreeable acceptance of a pleasant invitation, to be had at any time that is convenient to you. Herein lies the seed of an incipient Antinomianism.[40]

Shaftesbury would have seen nothing to criticise in the opinion 'placed' in the mouth of Mrs. Mozley's unsympathetic character, Constance Duff: 'We may see amiable, moral, and talented persons, and admire them; we may even in a certain degree sympathise in their pursuits and views; but we must never forget there are but two characters in the world—those who are born again, and those who are still at enmity with God.'[41]

ii *Conversion*

Constance's refusal to acknowledge to Grace, her significantly named playmate, the possibility of a gradual growth into Gospel Christianity is an interesting reminder of the period at which the

[39] E. C. Gaskell, op. cit., pp. 94, 119. [40] E. Hodder, *Life of Shaftesbury*, iii, 22–3.
[41] *Lost Brooch*, i, 136.

book was written. There had always been a few Evangelicals to the left of the party who insisted on sudden conversion, and amongst these Edward Irving's emotional preaching had made its greatest impact in the late 1820s and early 1830s. The desire of the majority of Evangelicals to play down any suggestion of the necessity of a sudden and violent conversion experience stemmed partly from embarrassment at the memory of the excesses which had undoubtedly accompanied some of the early Methodist conversions.[42] Patrick Brontë's friend, William Morgan, writing in the early years of the Tractarian Movement, was anxious to stress the orthodox Anglican Evangelical attitude to the conversion experience:

The relations of conversions are very frequently misunderstood and misrepresented. It is not *one* solitary circumstance which takes place in a moment, that generally brings a soul to God. A variety of facts, means, events or causes, in succession, like links in a chain, may give light to the understanding, a bias to the will, conviction to the conscience, and rectitude to the affections. Sudden and great terror experienced at times by many unconverted men, is not a sure sign and proof of genuine repentance and true faith. Felix trembled, and Agrippa was almost persuaded to be a Christian, under St. Paul's powerful address, but we have no certainty that they ever became real converts. The question, therefore, as to the *means* by which any soul is converted, is not of that importance as the *evidence* of it, in the subsequent life of a good man.[43]

George Eliot stood apart from the majority of Victorian novelists in her understanding of, and ability to use, the long-drawn-out pattern of Anglican Evangelical conversion. She clearly distinguished between the Methodist and Anglican modes. Dinah Morris's preaching on the green at Hayslope in *Adam Bede* is part of a Methodist open-air ministry embarked upon partly because the local church pulpit remained closed to a lay preacher and partly for the immediacy of the impact it might make upon the local population. The threat to Anglican decency implied by the freedom from the restraint of a consecrated building or a formal liturgy is epitomized by the reaction of Joshua Rann, the parish clerk and sexton, who 'was inwardly maintaining the dignity of the Church' by repeating to himself a quotation from the psalm he had read the last Sunday afternoon. Dinah's preaching enjoys immediate and

[42] *CO* (1802), p. 669; (1804), pp. 55–6, 372, 519–20, 568, 640–1.

[43] *The Parish Priest, Pourtrayed in the Life, Character, and Ministry of the Rev. John Crosse* (1841), pp. 2–3.

visible results: she draws forth 'many a responsive sigh and groan from her fellow-Methodists', and reduces Bessy Cranage to wild sobbing, but no lasting effects are recorded.[44]

The short-lived nature of some conversions effected at revivals where spiritual activity was felt to be worked up rather than prayed down was a major factor in Evangelical distrust of revivalism.[45] George Eliot's interest in the use of 'awakening' sermons may have been stimulated by reports of the American Revival of the late 1850s. The conversion of the schoolgirl heroine of Mrs. Worboise's *Thornycroft Hall* is of particular interest in this respect. She owes her conversion to hearing Charlotte Elliott's hymn, 'Just as I am', written in 1836, which became extremely popular in the revivalist era at the close of the 1850s. Mrs. Worboise's knowledge of the hymn's contemporary use and appeal is apparent in the implicit warning offered to her readers when she stresses the essential restraint and solitary nature of the experience: 'If there had been ecstasy, it might have passed; but there was only calm trust, simple rest, peace and joy in believing.'[46]

George Eliot's fiction repeatedly paid tribute to the greater efficacy of the quieter but no less emotionally intense aids to conversion employed by Anglican Evangelicals. Of her own conversion we hear nothing, and the silence in her letters as to any specific day being celebrated as an anniversary of the event would suggest that like Simeon she might declare, 'to specify *the day* that I was *renatus*, is beyond my power'.[47] She was well versed in Evangelical biographies that stressed the lengthy and painful process of soul-searching and development that characterized the conversion experience.[48]

In 'Janet's Repentance' George Eliot had depicted the double conversion process which frequently took place before a man became converted from 'nominal' to 'sincere and serious Christianity'. Like

[44] *Adam Bede*, ch. i. [45] See below, pp. 117–21, 267.

[46] *Thornycroft Hall* (1864), p. 186. It is difficult to reconcile this with Mrs. M. Maison's assertion that 'Miss Worboise, and her readers, preferred St Paul's road to Newman's, and rejected conversions characterized by slow, almost imperceptible growth in favour of conversions characterized by the sudden shock and the blinding flash—this in itself perhaps a typical Evangelical tendency.' *Search Your Soul, Eustace* (1961), p. 112.

[47] W. Carus, *Memoirs of the Life of the Rev. Charles Simeon*, p. 711.

[48] *G. Eliot Letters*, i, 38 refer to her reading E. Sidney, *Life of Sir Richard Hill*, in which Hill is recorded as saying that it was not an 'easy matter for me to ascertain the time when the first dawnings of divine light began to break in upon my soul': p. 15.

Thomas Scott, whose autobiographical work is mentioned in this tale, Janet at the outset is a 'nominal' Christian whose highest vision of the Christian life is expressed in small deeds of charity which in no way differentiate her from the philanthropic atheist. She receives her first new impressions of the 'Methodism' she had helped to persecute from the quiet parochial work done by the Evangelical curate, the Revd. Edgar Tryan, as Scott does from the Revd. John Newton, better known to posterity in the more colourful role of 'the old African blasphemer'.[49] Janet, again like Scott, was reluctant to come to terms with her new impressions because they might involve 'a reversal of the past which was as little accordant with her inclination as her circumstances'. Scott was aware that an honest reappraisal might result in loss of preferment and social prestige; Janet too could foresee an aggravation of her domestic burden and the mockery of the town for such a change of allegiance. Other agents, however, were at work to bring such people to the 'legal' stage of conversion, when a man realized his moral failings and endeavoured to lead a life of strict obedience to God's law. The moralistic works of High Church piety that served as an awakening agent in Scott's conversion obtained their correlative for Janet in Mrs. Raynor's simple version of this tradition.

The period between becoming a 'legal' Christian and the time when one was able personally to appropriate the merits of Christ produced the real drama of conversion since the period involved might be a matter of months or, in some cases, years. Patrick Brontë's recognition of this led him to contribute a dramatic monologue in prose form to William Morgan's monthly magazine, the *Pastoral Visitor*, in which he tried to give 'a just representation of the views and feelings of an awakened sinner, before he has got proper notions of the all-sufficiency of Christ'. Its publication in serial form over two numbers underlined the dramatic tension created by articulating the thoughts of a palpitating conscience against the ever present consciousness of eternal salvation or condemnation.[50]

Janet Dempster's brief attempt at fulfilling her duties is doomed to failure because she relies upon her own strength and expects recognition and reward for her endeavours from her unjust husband. The morning after she has been thrown out of her home her own

[49] *Scenes*, ii, 180–3. T. Scott, *The force of Truth an Authentic Narrative* 5th edn. (1836), pp. 21–2.

[50] *Pastoral Visitor*, No. 7 (July 1815), 52–4, and No. 9 (Sept. 1815), 78–9.

insufficiency is revealed to her and the first glimmerings of the promise of the Gospel dawn upon her. She then appeals to Tryan for help and receives it in the form of verbal testimony. One of the reasons that Tryan's story seems to derive from literature rather than life is that he is providing Janet with a prototype for the experience she is to undergo in much the same way that Wesley sent out questionnaires for the stories of his assistant preachers and then 'edited' them so that they should provide a normative path by which new members could check their symptoms. George Eliot's own predilection for moral symmetry found ample scope in this tradition. Tryan is able to convince Janet that a period of blasphemous rebellion, a mind 'at war with itself and with God', followed by months of desperate searching had before been the prelude to 'hope and trust, which is strength'. The clue to the sense of a pattern had been provided for him not by written accounts of fights with blasphemous thoughts like those recorded by William Grimshaw but by another man whose experiences led him to 'understand the different wants of different minds'.[51]

True to her Feuerbach-inspired concept of the Incarnation George Eliot then raises Tryan from a mere Evangelical guide and counsellor to a man whose practice of self-transcending love has made him one with God and, at the very close of the tale, we are shown Janet witnessing for Tryan rather than God. Yet, anxious not to give offence, George Eliot provided for precisely that leap of faith which she denied herself but wished to leave open for others: 'The act of confiding in human sympathy, the consciousness that a fellow-being was listening to her with patient pity, prepared her soul for that stronger leap by which faith grasps the idea of the Divine sympathy.'[52]

In the history of Maggie Tulliver's conversion George Eliot depicts another variety of the Evangelical experience. Like the early Evangelicals hers is essentially a solitary awakening, originating in a sense of spiritual insufficiency in the face of new tasks and burdens, and stimulated by a course of private study. Like those men in isolated Yorkshire and Cornish villages she found herself suddenly cut off from companions of her own age and social class and thrown back upon her own resources. She then began 'making out a faith for herself without the aid of established authorities and appointed guides'. Her feelings are awakened, as many another Evangelical's

[51] *Scenes*, ii, 227–33. [52] *Scenes*, ii, 292.

had been, by reading Thomas à Kempis, and manifest themselves in a striving for self-renunciation and a zealous endeavour at the moral life characteristic of the 'legal' period of conversion.[53] Slowly it is borne in upon Maggie that her own strength is insufficient to enable her to do what she knows to be right, but at the moment when she comes to learn a true dependence on God and a resignation to His will her prayer of dedication is cut off by the flood, and as with Janet the difficulty of reconciling the daily life and devotion of the sincere Christian with the practice of the Religion of Humanity is avoided.

George Eliot had been able to use Evangelical conversion patterns to express an individual psychological drama but for the most part Victorian novelists anxious to criticize the uncontrolled emotionalism and physical excitement which they felt had become a conventional sign of an inner change confined themselves to representing this taking place in the Dissenting world. The one major exception was Mrs. Trollope who transplanted the scenes of frenzied worship she had witnessed at a five day revivalist Camp meeting in Indiana to the house and grounds of an English upper class family in England. In *Domestic Manners of the Americans* she had recorded the programme of a public sermon followed by appeals for the penitents to come forward to the 'pen' where they appeared to have 'fits'. 'The preachers moved about among them, at once exciting and soothing their agonies. I heard the muttered "sister! dear sister!", I saw the insidious lips approach the cheeks of the unhappy girls . . .'[54] Next morning, however, she says that they were all '. . . eagerly employed in preparing and devouring their most substantial breakfasts . . . The preaching saint and the howling sinner seemed alike to relish this mode of recruiting their strength.'[55]

Although it has for centuries been an effective deflationary argument that in the excess of mystical experience the subject was partially able to forget the body, but when the fit had passed physical needs reasserted themselves, Mrs. Trollope undermines the force of her serious criticism of a mode of religious experience

[53] Professor Haight ignores this tradition when he writes that Maggie 'found her solace not in evangelical tracts but in Thomas à Kempis's *Imitation of Christ* and in the *Christian Year* of John Keble, the "true and primary author" of the Oxford Movement'. (*George Eliot: a Biography* (1969), p. 18.) Keble's hymn-book, published in 1827, six years before the Oxford Movement began, was read with approval by many an Evangelical.

[54] *Domestic Manners of the Americans*, i, 239.

[55] Ibid. i, 241–2.

that offended her notions of propriety by her suggestion that the preachers were mainly motivated by sexual desires. Suggestion becomes firm accusation in *The Vicar of Wrexhill.* Fanny Mowbray is an impressionable adolescent and as such a likely candidate for religious experience which depends upon a disturbed emotional and physical equilibrium for its most intense effects. When Lady Harrington speaks of Evangelicals always 'selecting' young girls first for their conversion preaching we have been prepared by the frontispiece to the second volume for the conscious hypocrite, Cartwright, stimulating and manipulating emotional frenzy. The picture shows the parson stooping over the kneeling Fanny,[56] and lest we should be left in any doubt of the sexual motivation of this 'awakener', by the end of the book one of his flock, a widow, has become pregnant. In the process of transferring the setting to England Mrs. Trollope has contrived to make the Anglican version seem far more dangerous by virtue of the very privacy in which it operates. Cartwright as a parson has free access to the homes of the wealthy and can seclude his dupes in locked libraries and dressing rooms or lead them into the more remote parts of the grounds. Mrs. Trollope had based her novel on a mocking interpretation of the description of Evangelicalism as 'the religion of the heart'.

### iii. *Justification by faith*

It was easy to dismiss Evangelicalism as an outlet for hysteria or as the refuge of hypocrites when regeneracy seemed to require so little objective proof. Repeatedly Newman and his sister, Mrs. Mozley, circle back upon the problem of what the Evangelicals meant by 'true faith'. Newman's fictional hero, Reding, dissatisfied with the Evangelical Freeborn's assertion that faith 'is seated in the heart and affections' presses for a means to distinguish false faith from true faith.[57] Cornered, Freeborn supplies the test which William Wilberforce had formulated: 'The tree is to be known by its fruits; and there is too much reason to fear that there is no principle of faith, when it does not decidedly evince itself by the fruits of holiness.'[58]

Yet though the fruits may be important they are quite distinct from justification itself, Freeborn insists. No wonder Newman gave this interchange a prominent part in his novel since it reflected one

[56] *Vicar of Wrexhill*, ii, 40; and Frontispiece by Auguste Hervieu, Mrs. Trollope's close friend.

[57] *Loss and Gain*, p. 141.

[58] *Practical View*, p. 126.

of his earliest divergences of opinion from the Evangelicals.[59] A letter on the subject written to Samuel Wilberforce in 1835 indicates that Newman shared the widespread feeling that millenialist teaching had encouraged a large number of Evangelicals of this period to undervalue the process of Sanctification—the continuous action of the Holy Ghost in making the believer holy. 'My reasons for dwelling on the latter subject [sanctification] was my conviction *that we required the Law* not the Gospel in this age. We want rousing —we want the chains of duty and the details of obedience set before us strongly . . . In truth men *do* think that a saving state is one, where the mind looks to Christ—a virtual antinomianism.'[60]

If the perceptive Newman saw the consequences in terms of 'virtual antinomianism' it is scarcely surprising that Lawyer Dempster should have gained a reputation for far-sightedness, and successfully worked up popular prejudice against the new Evangelical incumbent when he remarked, '. . . he preaches against good works; says good works are not necessary to salvation—a sectarian, antinomian, anabaptist doctrine. Tell a man he is not to be saved by his works, and you open the flood-gates of all immorality.'[61]

Moderate Calvinist Evangelicalism did not provide a fertile field for the belief that predetermination to election or damnation made it possible to disregard all moral laws. Edmund Gosse recorded the true story of a dissenting Antinomian, an impecunious retired solicitor who forged the signature of a wealthy boarder who died in his house. Even after sentence the criminal retained his conviction in his freedom from the confines of the moral law, and 'made the final statement that at that very moment he was conscious of his Lord's presence in the dock at his side, whispering to him, "Well done, thou good and faithful servant" '.[61a] I include this illustration to indicate by contrast how far away Calvinists like Mrs. Clennam or Bulstrode were from Antinomianism. Although Newman might feel that the line which divided the Antinomian who 'actually holds that he may break the law' from the 'spiritual believer' who 'only holds that he is not bound to keep it' was so thin as to be invisible, in practice both these characters were aware of the moral wrongs they had committed and endeavoured to hide them.

[59] See D. Newsome, 'Justification and Sanctification: Newman and the Evangelicals', *JTS* 15 (1964), 32–53; and the debate Newman entered into in the *Christian Oberver* (1837), pp. 63, 114–26, 141–98, 243–63, 317–52.

[60] Quoted by D. Newsome, *JTS* 15 (1964), 43.

[61] G. Eliot, *Scenes*, ii, 47.

[61a] *Father and Son* (1966), p. 145.

James Hogg's *The Private Memoirs and Confessions of a Justified Sinner* (1824) is the most powerful nineteenth-century exposure of the evils resulting from the Calvinist conviction of an assured position amongst the elect; but the fanatical adherent, with his ruthless logic, is alien to the realms of English Protestantism. As Newman discovered, 'it is not at all easy . . . to wind up an Englishman to a dogmatic level'.[62] Yet the fear of excess was often present. The Arminian Vicar of *The Velvet Cushion* explains that he has chosen this strain of Evangelicalism not because Calvinism necessarily leads to Antinomianism 'but that very high Calvinism easily admits of, and not unfrequently suffers such a perversion . . .'[63] Wesley, the leading exponent of Arminianism in eighteenth-century England, aware of the Antinomianism that solifidianism might produce, estimated the place of 'works' higher than Calvinists. His espousal of Free Will necessitated a belief that a man might always slip back into a state of perdition and conversely led him to embrace the doctrine of Perfection.[64] Sanctification, taught in so positive a manner, seemed unbiblical, or even heretical to Calvinists, who believed that life, even after conversion, was a state of continuous warfare with sin in which the final victory only was assured, and that the very idea of linear progress to perfection would necessarily elevate 'works' and devalue the Atonement.

Sarah Lane and a fellow parishioner, Calvinist Evangelicals of the most rabid variety, are satisfied with their attack upon their mild and benevolent Rector, Dr. Bethell, only when they have been able to attach a label to his heresy. ' "He's legal; he preaches up works and morality", continued Mrs. Kettle; "he's an Arminian, that's what he is!" '[65] These doctrinal divergences become important to the novel reader in picking up the clues to a character's position on the theological spectrum, so carefully planted for us by the more doctrinally aware of the novelists. Constance Duff spells out her position.

. . . I am *sanctified* or *made holy* by faith in Christ; my sins are washed away by His blood, and my heart renewed by His spirit; I renounce my own righteousness, and His righteousness is imputed to me. These

[62] *Apologia Pro Vita Sua*, ed. M. J. Svaglic (Oxford, 1967), p. 185.

[63] J. W. Cunningham, *Velvet Cushion*, p. 117.

[64] *A Plain Account of Christian Perfection as Believed and Taught by the Rev. Mr. John Wesley from the Year 1725 to 1765* (Bristol, 1766).

[65] E. J. Worboise, *House of Bondage*, p. 50.

benefits are given me, not for any merit of my own, but simply by believing in all Christ has done and suffered to procure my salvation. Thus it is that my soul is freed from guilt—by faith. It actually cleanses me from sin. . . .[66]

It is the type of testimony liable to be 'skipped' or at most briefly skimmed by the modern reader who then finds it difficult to see why such apparently harmless 'piety' should be given to the unpleasant Constance to expound, or why Mrs. Mozley's own hackles clearly rise at such doctrine. The key word for contemporaries with any knowledge of current debate would have been 'imputed'. An allusion to 'imputed' righteousness would immediately have placed Constance with Calvinists who wished to minimize the human contribution to justification, whereas the use of the word 'imparted' would just as clearly have placed her with those who assumed that the process of sanctification was important.[67] This elucidation of a minor point in a book which, though popular in its own day, is now considered of period interest only, may seem of merely academic interest, but it serves to give us a detailed background to a short scene in a major novel of the Victorian era, *Middlemarch*. When George Eliot makes Mr. Tyke 'an apostolic man' who preaches about 'imputed righteousness and the prophecies in the Apocalypse',[68] she is partly adding to the authenticity of historical detail by depicting the interests of the type of man on the left wing of the Evangelical party who would have read the *Morning Watch* or the *Record*, and closely defining his doctrinal position as Calvinist. An understanding of the implications of the phrase 'imputed righteousness' helps us more fully to perceive the nature of the choice Dorothea makes in choosing Farebrother as the new Lowick incumbent. Farebrother's concern is the totally opposite one of practical concern for the process of sanctification, living as 'a parson among parishioners whose lives he has to try and make better'. Dorothea's subsequent remark, having considered Tyke's interests and doctrinal position, 'I have always been thinking of the different ways in which Christianity is taught, and whenever I find one way that makes it a wider blessing than any other I cling to that as the truest—I mean that which takes in the most good of all kinds, and

[66] H. Mozley, *Lost Brooch*, i, 143.

[67] For a contemporary explanation of Anglican Arminian objections to the theological implications of 'imputed' see W. F. Wilkinson, *Rector in Search of a Curate*, p. 100. See also H. A. Hodges, *The Pattern of Atonement* (1955), pp. 69–73.

[68] *Middlemarch*, ii, 338.

brings in the most people as sharers in it', can then be seen as more than a vague statement of benevolent disposition, and as a rejection of the narrow selectivity of Calvinism.[69] This episode serves to underline George Eliot's eminence as a novelist interested in religion. The subtle way in which she extracts the maximum effect from a few briefly given doctrinal details, both to convey necessary information about minor figures and to aid our understanding of the attitudes of the major characters who discuss them, distinguishes her work from the minor apologetic novels where information works at only the simplest level of polemic. The passage also serves to distinguish her from many contemporary novelists who lacked sufficient sense of the religious to grasp the import of the distinction that Legh Richmond's biographer is making when he says, of his conversion, 'This change was not a conversion from immorality to morality; for he was strictly moral, in the usual acceptation of the term.'[70] For the most part they showed little understanding of a system of theology which did not regard the Victorian ethical code as its highest court of appeal. They judged a man by his effective social benevolence, believing this to be the point at which humanitarian standards and the New Testament moral code they mainly embraced, met. Although George Eliot chose not to depict the quality of a man's relation with his God, finally electing to show how a man's beliefs affected his fellow creatures, her novels take into account the strength and quality of a man's intentions, the intensity of the spiritual struggle or soul-searching which produced the decision to do either good or evil, and that not necessarily as the world defines it. It is this finer appreciation of the religious life which distinguished her character Bulstrode from the multitude of religious hypocrites skulking through the pages of other Vicrtoian novels.

### iv. *The authority of the Word*

Again, most novelists found it easier to concentrate on the way in which Evangelicals 'used' the Bible rather than dealing with the thorny topic of Biblical inspiration. The 'guidance' that men purported to receive from the Word could be judged by moral and practical criteria whereas the latter subject demanded a theological turn of mind and a willingness to display to one's readers possibly

[69] See below, p. 238.

[70] T. S. Grimshawe, *A Memoir of the Rev. Legh Richmond* (1828), p. 23.

unorthodox opinions. The Bible, Evangelicals agreed, was the means whereby God revealed His purposes to man. It contained the whole truth necessary for a man's salvation. Anything which detracted from its central position, whether the sensory impressions much employed by Roman Catholics,[71] or the arrogance of a man like Edward Irving who complained that 'so much store is set in these times by the circulating and translating of the word and so little to the stout and able preaching of the word',[72] was to be deprecated. But, the Fairchilds assured their children, Bible-reading was a profitless activity without the gift of the Holy Spirit to enable a man to interpret it aright.[73] Edward Bickersteth, indeed, claimed that converted Christians had a monopoly in this field. 'But depend upon it the great reason why men do not understand their bible, is because their hearts are unrenewed by divine grace. How can an earthly, sensual, wordly-minded man, enter into the meaning of the pure, holy, and heavenly truths of the gospel?'[74]

It is not far from this position to the negative corollary illustrated by Mrs. Trollope. Fanny Mowbray tells her brother, when she finds herself unable to confute the texts he produces,[75] that it is a sin for her to listen to one numbered amongst the unregenerate quoting the Bible.

Yet the devious interpretations of the prophetic books of the Bible current in the 1820s confirmed orthodox suspicions that it was not easy for the Evangelicals to obey Simeon's precept, 'endeavour always to get at the plain honest meaning of your passage'.[76] Constance Duff having delivered a homily upon the dangers of the imagination makes one concession: ' "Well, then, if you will employ it", continued Constance, "use it on the Bible, and on religious subjects; there you are safe." "And some of those subjects are just what I would starve it upon", remarked Campbell.'[77]

The recurrent bitter theological controversies raging around the British and Foreign Bible Society's avowed intention of circulating the Authorized Version without doctrinal comment were rehearsed fictionally only in the pages of sectarian novelists such as Patrick

[71] See C. Scott, *Old Grey Church*, i, 181, where this habit is denounced.
[72] H. C. Whitley, *Blinded Eagle* (1955), p. 115.
[73] M. M. Sherwood, *Fairchild Family*, i, 29.
[74] *A Help to the Study of the Scriptures* (Norwich, 1815), p. 45.
[75] *Vicar of Wrexhill*, ii, 182.
[76] A. W. Brown, *Recollections of Simeon*, p. 134.
[77] H. Mozley, *Lost Brooch*, i, 296.

Brontë, J. A. Froude, F. E. Paget, J. H. Newman, and W. F. Wilkinson,[78] who were led into digressions which must have been tedious to all but the most partisan of readers.

In Newman's case the fictional airing of this dispute illustrates how certain beliefs can be positively disadvantageous to work as a novelist. His involvement with the Evangelicals had taught him to distrust argument based upon individual judgement as a means of arriving at doctrinal truths, but his consequent refusal to allow Reding to enter into debate puts him on a par with the Evangelicals who decline to argue with the 'carnal' minds of the unconverted. Newman's uncritical presentation of his hero's intellectual arrogance prepares us for the dramatization of the argument in favour of the appeal to authority. The satirical picture of the prolonged dissension to which private judgement leads is intended by the author to induce in us a silent contempt for the tenet and a conviction that all superior minds will ally in the recognition of the Catholic tradition.[79] Where Newman attempted to transplant theological polemic to the unreceptive ground of the novel, Charlotte Yonge showed herself ultimately a better novelist and a more persuasive teacher. Her novels serve to remind us of Conrad's dictum that the appeal of fiction 'to be effective must be an impression conveyed through the senses; and, in fact, it cannot be made in any other way, because temperament, whether individual or collective, is not amenable to persuasion'.[80] Her novels taught people to refer to authority rather than the Bible by frequently repeated example, not by any systematic attack upon the use of the Bible, which might encourage a reader to compare the two approaches.

Many a prominent novelist also maintained silence on the controversial subject of verbal inspiration. Before the 1830s many Evangelicals would have agreed with Simeon in avoiding argument concerning disputed passages, such as possible later interpolations, for fear of weakening the belief of 'tender consciences'.[81] Not until the neologists joined forces with the geologists in questioning the

[78] P. Bronte, *The Maid of Killarney; or, Albion and Flora: A Modern Tale* (1818), pp. 72–3; J. A. Froude, *Nemesis of Faith*, pp. 60–7; F. E. Paget, *The Warden of Berkingholt* (Oxford, 1843), ch. xi.; W. F. Wilkinson, *Rector in Search of a Curate*, pp. 306–7.

[79] *Loss and Gain*. For the role of the intellect in Catholic theology, as only one of the God-given faculties which, if overemphasized, may serve to separate us from God see J. P. de Caussade, *Self-Abandonment to Divine Providence*, trans. A. Thorold, ed. J. Joyce (Ill., 1962), pp. 8–10.

[80] J. Conrad, Preface to *The Nigger of the Narcissus* (1950), p. ix.

[81] A. W. Brown, *Recollections of Simeon*, p. 369.

status to be accorded to certain portions of the Bible did the Evangelical line harden into a dogmatic assertion of verbal inspiration. Samuel Butler showed historical sensitivity in referring to Theobald's sermons in the 1830s being concerned with 'the subject of geology—then coming to the fore as a theological bugbear',[82] yet it is a mark, both of Butler's own complete rejection of verbal inspiration, and of the period at which he wrote, that he felt able to mention the controversy so openly in the pages of a novel. The reasons for the restraint in choosing this aspect of Evangelicalism for critical comment are complex and vary from author to author. It would be fair to say that the full implications of the 'heroic age' of geology, beginning in about 1790 and culminating in the publication of Lyell's *Principles of Geology* (1830), which set out the evidence for the prolonged and natural origins of the earth, were slow in being realized and in gaining general currency. To the popular mind these discoveries seemed perhaps to exclude the Old Testament from 'the view . . . that every book, and chapter, and verse, and syllable of the Bible was given by inspiration of God.'[83] The tendency to discard the teaching of the Old Testament in order to preserve the prime importance of the New Testament teaching is perhaps more understandable when seen as a reaction to the sort of obstinate defence of verbal inspiration employed by Shaftesbury.

I have heard with my own ears a master in Israel remark in a public assembly, that to say that the Book of Chronicles and the Gospel of St. Luke stood on the same ground of inspiration was to utter an untenable proposition. I say that to make such a declaration is to concede the whole question. Moreover, men contend that one part of the Bible is inspired, and that another is not, or that there are differences in the degrees of inspiration. The whole authority of the Bible is thus cut up from the beginning to end. Depend upon it, my friends, that there is no security whatever except in standing upon the faith of our fathers, and saying with them that the blessed old Book is 'God's Word written', from the very first syllable down to the very last, and from the last back to the first.[84]

Shaftesbury was right in detecting that the doctrine of verbal inspiration could not be held with moderation, for it then offered no protection against the Higher Criticism which had begun to assail the New Testament. The inroads Shaftesbury had feared were swiftly

[82] *Way of All Flesh*, p. 40.
[83] J. C. Ryle, *Bible Inspiration: Its Reality and Nature* (1877), p. 41.
[84] E. Hodder, *Life of Shaftesbury*, iii, 7.

made. By 1872 Mrs. Worboise, though clinging firmly to evangelicalism herself, felt it safe to mock the blind obscurantism of some Evangelicals. If Shaftesbury read *The House of Bondage* he would doubtless have considered the liberal Evangelical Rector, 'a master in Israel' sadly gone astray, and taken his stand with a congregation, who, when asked 'What is it to believe rightly?', replied, 'To believe what is *written*, just as it stands. I believe that the entire world was drowned, that the whale swallowed Jonah, and vomited him up again in three days; and if the Bible told me Jonah swallowed the whale, I should believe it just the same.'[85]

Charles Hennell, originally a Unitarian and latterly a Freethinker, had published his *Inquiry concerning the Origin of Christianity* in 1838—a book which had proved a catalyst in the development of the young Mary Ann Evans's religious thought. The Higher Criticism, originating in Germany, was given currency in England only with the appearance of such translations as George Eliot's of Strauss's *Leben Jesu*, published in 1846.[86] A further time lag might well be expected before the creative writer felt sure enough of his own position on these disputed matters to assimilate the material within the framework of his fictional world.

Thackeray, for instance, had drunk from the source of neological criticism early in his career. On a visit to Germany in 1830 he had been sufficiently struck by the different religious atmosphere to write to his mother, 'The doctrine here is not near so strict as in England—many of the dogmas by w$^{h}$. we hold are here disregarded as allegories or parables—or I fear by most people as fictions altogether.'[87]

Thackeray soon developed a lasting dislike of the Old Testament and of the narrow intolerance he believed that some Evangelicals derived from its teaching. This attitude brought him into conflict with his mother, a devout Evangelical. Over the years Thackeray was forced to clarify his position in a manner which comes as a surprise to readers of his novels accustomed to the almost studied ambivalence of attitude that pervades them. His devotion to, and respect

[85] *House of Bondage*, p. 98.

[86] H. R. Murphy provides no evidence for his claim that much German criticism was available in the 1820s and 1830s in Britain and only seized upon in the 1840s when a sufficient number of people were disgusted 'with the ethical implications of Christian orthodoxy'. 'The Ethical Revolt against Christian Orthodoxy in Early Victorian England', *AHS* 55 (1955), pp. 800–17.

[87] *Thackeray Letters*, i, 140.

for, his mother led him to entrust his children to her after his marriage crumbled, yet his reunion with them in 1846, to which G. N. Ray has attributed his 'change of heart' as an author from a savagely destructive artist to an ethically concerned commentator,[88] served to bring a new seriousness to his religious thought as he recognized his responsibility for his children's eternal welfare. He was forced to become personally engaged and yet to temper his naturally acerbic argumentative manner with the realization that he and his mother, though their attitudes were irreconcilable, were equally sincere. In a long letter to his fifteen-year-old daughter, Anne, who had been using her father's known opposition to the Evangelical belief in verbal inspiration as grounds on which to resist the reading specified by her grandmother, he first advises obedience in this instance and then sets out his own views on Biblical inspiration.

To my mind Scripture only means a writing and Bible means a Book. It contains Divine Truths: and the history of a Divine Character: but imperfect but not containing a thousandth part of Him—and it would be an untruth before God were I to hide my feelings from my dearest children: as it would be a sin, if having other opinions and believing literally in the Mosaic writings, in the 6 days cosmogony, in the serpent and apple and consequent damnation of the human race, I should hide them; and not try to make those I loved best adopt opinions of such immense importance to them.[89]

Such personal involvement combined with a fair-minded appreciation of the integrity of the opposition's motives are alien to the atmosphere of his novels. In these he can maintain a pose of Olympian justice, or hide his irresolution in irony, or descend to sneering derision, because he does not permit his characters to interact so as to produce dilemmas in which moral good varies according to the eye of the beholder. To have introduced such issues into his novels would have altered their texture. Sentimental pathos which Thackeray could handle so well as he manipulated those characters without heroic status, might have had to give way to tragic nobility. So Thackeray softens the edge of his Evangelical portraits, portraying those like Sir Pitt who fall away from their

[88] 'Vanity Fair: One Version of the Novelist's Responsibility', *Essays by Divers Hands, being the Transactions of the Royal Society of Literature of the United Kingdom*, ed. E. Marsh, N.S. 25 (1950), 87–101.
[89] *Thackeray Letters*, iii, 95–6.

first loyalties, or, avoiding the heart of the conflict, separates Sophia Alethea Newcome from her stepson, at the very age when Thackeray himself had begun to realize what fundamental differences would separate him from his mother. In Thackeray's case the refusal to deal with doctrinal matters in the novel sprang partly from a reluctance to broadcast opinions which he knew hurt his mother, partly from a disinclination to disseminate views unpopular with his public,[90] but mainly from the impossibility of combining the emotional perceptions and irresolutions, to which they gave rise, with his favourite pose of debonair ironist.

In Dickens's novels we do not expect to hear of intellectual controversy, but his letters confirm that his inclination to rest his Christianity upon the Gospels made him sympathize with the liberal school, whilst the witch hunts organized by the fundamentalists augmented his dislike of the Evangelicals.[91] Perhaps his anxiety to impress the sophisticated, unorthodox coterie whom Lady Blessington gathered around her prompted him to choose the topic of the Word's central importance for a satirical poem for her Annual. The poem, entitled 'A Word in Season', in itself an allusion to Evangelical jargon, makes play with the contrast between this 'highly civilised and thinking nation' and the barbarian East where the strife between a thinly disguised Evangelicalism and Tractarianism is enacted.

> They have a superstition in the East,
> That Allah, written on a piece of paper
> Is better unction than can come of priest,
> Of rolling incense, and of lighted taper;
> Holding that any scrap which bears that name
> In any other characters its front impress'd on,
> Shall help the finder thro' the purging flame,
> And give his toasted feet a place to rest on.

Dickens does not trouble himself to come to grips with the reasons behind religious warfare only regretting that, '. . . they who should have oped the door / Of charity and light, for all mens' finding, /

[90] This judgment is based upon Thackeray's open avowals. *Thackeray Letters*, ii, 204; and G. S. Haight, *George Eliot and John Chapman* (New Haven, 1940), p. 179. For the very real possibility of martyrdom as a consequence of publishing unorthodox views see W. H. Dunn, *James Anthony Froude: A Biography, 1818–1856* (Oxford, 1961), pp. 135–7.

[91] *Dickens Letters*, ii, 818; iii, 352, 402.

Squabbled for words upon the altar-floor, / And rent The Book, in struggles for the binding.'[92]

His reference in later years to 'the Colenso and Jowett matter'[93] does not suggest that Dickens had read either Colenso's *The Pentateuch and the Book of Joshua Critically Examined*, or *Essays and Reviews* in which Jowett's 'On the Interpretation of Scripture' appeared. The point which he picked out for sympathetic agreement, namely a belief in progressive revelation, more specifically pleaded for in C. W. Goodwin's essay 'On the Mosaic Cosmogony', could have been culled from any newspaper report of the time. Although he gave it as his opinion that only an acceptance of the new scholarship could retain men's allegiance to Christianity he is interested in a retention of Christ-like virtues rather than a complete Christ-centred theology.

Trollope shared neither Thackeray's carefully defined personal position nor Dickens's doctrinal unconcern. Although Trollope makes it clear to his readers that he is concerned with the social attitudes and life of the clergy rather than with their doctrinal position we might have expected to have heard more of the changing atmosphere of doctrinal controversy. In the political novels we do not look for a systematic explanation of Conservative or Liberal doctrine but we are given a sense of the factors that contribute to the decline of Liberalism and of the new social phenomena which force men slowly to reconsider their position on certain key issues. Amongst his novels, as A. O. J. Cockshut remarks,[94] only *The Bertrams* makes any attempt to refer to the question of the challenge to faith presented by the new critical scholarship. George Bertram, who had once thought of becoming a clergyman, undergoes a crisis of faith. He writes a book called 'The Romance of Scripture', whose title is sufficient to shock the Evangelical circles of Littlebath. He explains that he sees the Bible as specifically the product of oriental language and thought.

'A book is given to us, not over well translated from various languages, part of which is history hyperbolically told— . . . part of which is prophecy, the very meaning of which is lost to us by the loss of those things which are intended to be imaged out; and part of which is thanksgiving uttered

[92] J. Forster, *The Life of Charles Dickens*, ed. J. W. T. Ley (1928), pp. 294–5.
[93] *Dickens Letters*, iii, 352.
[94] A. O. J. Cockshut, *Anthony Trollope: A Critical Study* (1955), p. 78.

in the language of men who knew nothing, and could understand nothing of those rules by which we are to be governed.'[95]

The flutter amongst the Evangelical dovecots that this attitude could be counted upon to produce can be gauged by the pronouncement of Canon Ryle, a leading Evangelical polemicist, upon attempts to treat the Bible as comparable with other revered texts.

To talk of comparing the Bible with other 'sacred books' so-called, such as the Koran, the Shasters, or the book of Mormon, is positively absurd. You might as well compare the sun with a rushlight,—or Skiddaw with a mole hill,—or St. Paul's with an Irish hovel,—or the Portland vase with a garden pot, or the Koh-i-noor diamond with a bit of glass. . . . To talk of the inspiration of the Bible, as only differing in *degree* from that of such writings as the works of Homer, Plato, Shakespeare [,] Dante, and Milton, is simply a piece of blasphemous folly.[96]

Bertram also made the accusation, which was frequently levelled against the Evangelicals—that they held to the verbal inspiration of the Authorized Version, a belief lent credence by their early opposition to the Revised Version. 'It seemed to him that the generality of his country men were of opinion that the inspired writers had themselves written in English.'[97]

Trollope gives us a tantalizing glimpse of the state of mind of the younger generation in the year before the publication of *Essays and Reviews*; Bertram is given a *cri de coeur* that crystallizes his generation's dilemma over the fundamentals of faith, just as Tancred had voiced the previous generation's desire for a direction to their endeavours.[98] 'What is vital, and what is not? If I could only learn that! But you always argue in a circle. I am to have faith because of the Bible; but I am to take the Bible through faith.'[99]

Yet Trollope ducks the central issue, by implying that the fault lies more with Bertram than in the circumstances of the age. His dilemma of faith is seen merely as a projection of his own weakness, not as a reflection of the crisis of belief by which an entire generation of men of intellectual pretension felt themselves threatened. An authorial comment in the course of this novel suggests that Trollope by no means found the nature of Bertram's doubts wildly alarming.

[95] *The Bertrams* (3 vols., 1859), ii, 249.

[96] *Bible Inspiration*, p. 22.

[97] *The Bertrams*, ii, 46.

[98] B. Disraeli, *Tancred*, p. 56. '. . . What is DUTY, and what is FAITH? What ought I to DO, and what ought I to BELIEVE?'

[99] *The Bertrams*, ii, 250–1.

It is the spirit with which Bertram confronts his doubts that Trollope criticizes. 'Men may be firm believers and yet doubt some Bible statements—doubt the letter of such statements. But men who are firm believers will not be those to put forth their doubts with all their eloquence.'[100]

Trollope is careful both in *The Bertrams* and in his article 'A Clergyman who subscribes for Colenso' not to specify, other than in the most general terms, the precise Biblical statements which were subject to doubt. In the latter, he acknowledges that he has been disturbed by 'the incompatibility of the teaching of Old Testament records with the new teaching of the rocks and stones', but he makes no attempt to say whether it is only fundamentalist beliefs which must suffer or whether his whole concept of God has been troubled by the moral implications of natural selection. Perhaps this is the most revealing sentence in the article:

> Most men who call themselves Christians would say that they believed the Bible, not knowing what they meant, never having attempted,—and very wisely having refrained from attempting amidst the multiplicity of their worldly concerns,—to separate historical record from inspired teaching.[101]

Trollope, one suspects, avoids these contemporary issues in the novels, not from fear of disturbing his readers' faith, but because he is reluctant to come to grips with the problems they raise for himself.[102] The problem of natural selection and its implications might well have been particularly acute for him, founded as his religion was upon a moral sense of the relation between God and His creation. His emotional desire for the untroubled waters of the old doctrine and his intellectual conviction of the necessity of launching forth upon the uncharted and dangerous stretches of the new are clearly stated in the closing stages of this article. 'If one could stay, if one could only have a choice in the matter, if one could really believe that the old shore is best, who would leave it? Who would not wish to be secure if he knew where security lay?'[103]

And so when he came to speak of the Evangelical approach to liberal theology, like Bertram 'He was angry with himself for not

[100] *The Bertrams*, ii, 49.

[101] *Clergymen of the Church of England* (1866), 119–28.

[102] Cf. *The Letters of Anthony Trollope*, ed. B.A. Booth (1951), p. 385; 'I am afraid of the subject of Darwin. I am myself so ignorant on it, that I should fear to be in the position of editing a paper on the subject.'

[103] *Clergymen of the Church of England*, p. 128.

believing, and angry with others that they did believe.'[104] Though he recognized that as a theologically ill-equipped layman he should refrain from close analysis of the problems involved he resented the intellectual dishonesty, as he saw it, of the Evangelical party's decision to pretend that these problems did not exist. This complaint was at the centre of what had been envisaged as the first of a series of reports upon the Exeter Hall May Meetings for the *Pall Mall Gazette*. The letter purporting to come from a Zulu friend of Bishop Colenso takes great exception to the 'star turn' of the annual meeting of the Society for the Propagation of Christianity among the Jews, a 'beautiful silver-white haired canon', whose speech was devoted to an attack on Colenso. The arguments, such as they were, were felt to be unjust for 'no discussion was allowed in the Hall of Exeter, and . . . the audience there assembled would listen to no arguments opposed to their own established modes of believing'. Trollope, in his Zulu guise, summarizes the Revd. Canon McNeile's teaching, picking out for criticism precisely those elements which had troubled Bertram.

> Our SAVIOUR had said that the Scriptures cannot be broken, and therefore, declared the canon, every word in the Old Testament, as translated into English, must be true. The moon did stand still, and by inference the sun did ordinarily, in the days of JOSHUA, move round the earth, seeing that it is declared to have stood still miraculously upon one special occasion only. But the canon went into none of these little difficulties . . .

Under the guise of disliking an approach which appeared to treat the female intellect with contempt Trollope proceeds to describe with sarcastic force words spoken by the Canon, which in another context might well have formed the text of Trollope's own writing: ' ". . . and do not", said he, "do not, I implore you, vex with such reasonings the minds of these poor ignorant ones whom it is your duty to guide in the 'right way' ". Then he waved his right hand gracefully over the heads of the ladies . . .'[105]

Mingled with his resentment of the easy dismissal of complex problems can be detected an accompanying dislike of the easy familiarity and proprietary air with which the 'righteous' referred to the Scriptures. The same jocose complacency that characterized Mr. Stumfold may well have been directed at Trollope himself

[104] *The Bertrams*, ii, 249.
[105] 'The Zulu in London', *Pall Mall Gazette* (10 May 1865), pp. 3–4.

during this meeting. An incident in McNeile's speech, reported in *The Record*, is omitted from Trollope's list of indictments: '. . . we must have the hardihood—I was going to say the blasphemous hardihood;—but you see that would injure what I am saying . . . Now (addressing the reporter) don't write "blasphemous". (A laugh.)'[106]

Trollope was sufficiently well known a literary figure to be recognized and singled out as 'the reporter' which can only have caused so socially gauche a man extreme discomfort and embarrassment.

From his contemporary, George Eliot, we might perhaps have anticipated a moving account of the personal crisis brought about by her reading of Hennell and Strauss, but no overt mention of the challenge to Evangelicalism presented by neology occurs in her novels. As I shall suggest in a later chapter George Eliot was not anxious to spread the unease she had personally experienced. The need is avoided by locating the novels which deal with Evangelicalism in provincial backwaters or the Great Reform Bill era or earlier. The Revd. Amos Barton, for instance, would have been at Cambridge a full ten years earlier than Theobald Pontifex and his own intellectual limitations would not have inclined him to take up 'the geological issue'.

With Samuel Butler we leave the world of the highbrow Victorian agnostic and encounter an author whose restraint in publishing *The Way of All Flesh* seemed to stem more from a reluctance to offend the living with barely disguised caricatures than from high-minded concern for the faith of his fellow men. Butler's obsessive interest in what seemed the wilful obscurantism of the Evangelicals led him to explore time and again the clash which he felt should have resulted from the old beliefs with the new scholarship. In the way he treats this clash we can perhaps detect an attempt to rationalize and give intellectual status to his own falling away from Christianity, which seems to have had no such origin.[107]

In 1865 he published the fruits of his Biblical studies in New Zealand in an anonymous pamphlet entitled *The Evidence for the Resurrection of Jesus Christ as given by the Four Evangelists critically*

[106] *Record* (8 May, 1865), p. 3. It is from this report that I have identified the unnamed Canon of Trollope's account as Canon McNeile.

[107] Similarly in *The Way of All Flesh* Ernest adopts Darwinian views only after his faith has 'dropped off him', perhaps because of the shock in 'the change in his surroundings'.

*examined*. This passed unnoticed by the general reading public. This pamphlet probably formed the core for *Fair Haven*, which he published in 1873. In this complicated private joke he set out to mock both the Evangelicals and the liberal school of theology. Of the two, Butler had more sympathy with the Broad Church theologians, because they openly gloried in the irreconcilability of certain portions of the Bible. He could not forgive the Evangelicals for purporting to advocate 'the duty of independent research, and . . . the necessity of giving up everything rather than assent to things which our conscience did not assent to',[108] and then refusing to confront the evidence before them.

Goaded by the lack of understanding which met his obscure attack Butler reverted to the problem once again in a series of letters to the *Examiner* in 1879, reprinted under the collective title *A Clergyman's Doubts*. He was able to devote his contempt to the Broad Church position in these articles because he had fully exploited the Evangelical attitudes in *The Way of All Flesh*, which was by now almost completed. Indeed the opening letter of this series, detailing the Evangelical upbringing and the intellectual climate of the late 1850s, is reproduced almost verbatim from *The Way of All Flesh*, chapter forty-seven.[109] Theobald Pontifex's intellectual career symbolizes what Butler believed to be the inevitable overthrow of all Evangelicals who were unable to support unquestioningly the doctrine of biblical authority.[110] Christina and Charlotte retain power because they have been able to perceive the advantages of an assumption of higher vision from which the unregenerate are excluded. They appeal to the 'inner light of conscience' as a defence for their interpretation of the Word and their consequent actions. Christina has indeed been outmanoeuvred by one of her own family, probably Charlotte, who has been 'vouchsafed direct and visible angelic visits',[111] both as a testimony to her superior righteousness and as a bolster to the absolute authority which will then have to be accorded to her judgement.

Butler's parody of the appeal to the 'inner light' is the product of a logical escalation of tactics applied to a situation which by its very nature defies the laws of reason. It took a man of Shaftesbury's intellectual and moral calibre to admit the problems which an

[108] *Fair Haven*, p. 14.
[109] Cf. *Collected Essays*, i, 56 and *Way of All Flesh*, pp. 205–6.
[110] See below, pp. 265–6. [111] *Way of All Flesh*, pp. 379–80.

individual interpretation of the Bible raised when inference alone might have to suffice as a guide for action.

> I sometimes pause to reflect whether I can be right, whether I have followed the true course, whether—when so many 'pious' people either thwart or discourage me—I must not be altogether in error. They read and study the Bible; they pray for guidance and light; they ask, and surely obtain, God's grace to judge aright; they surely, too, must make (is it so in fact?) their conduct the subject and consequence of fervent supplication before and after they have resolved to weaken my efforts? What can *I* do which *they* do not do? If I say with fervour before I act, 'Prevent us, O Lord, in all our doings', &c., so do they, doubtless, when they prepare a resistance to me. They implore Almighty God that all their 'works may be begun, continued, and ended in Him!' Is it so? If it be, I am indeed gravelled.[112]

Edmund Gosse's amusing anecdote about his discovery that two could play at the game of calling divine guidance to the support of a personal decision[113] finds a fictional equivalent in an encounter between Trollope's Mrs. Bolton and Hester. Mrs. Bolton had intended 'to speak burning words of reproof', but found herself 'gravelled' when Hester countered her advice from the Lord with the assertion that her actions were based upon an appeal to the same source. The obvious answer, to Mrs. Bolton's mind, was that Hester had not asked aright, but she 'hardly knew how to mount to higher ground, so as to seem to speak from a more exalted eminence.'[114]

It was in this area, where personal desires could be shown to have been fused with religious beliefs and duties, that the novelists were most at ease. Here, without giving offence by direct denial of the primary tenets of the faith, they could give free rein to criticism of a system which apparently encouraged certain results which by merely 'moral' standards could be seen to be reprehensible.

## 2. *The non-essential doctrines*

### i. *Eternal punishment*

> 'I cannot believe that man placed here by God shall receive or not receive future happiness as he may chance to agree or not to agree with certain doctors

[112] E. Hodder, *Life of Shaftesbury*, ii, 2.
[113] *Father and Son*, pp. 154–6. [114] *John Caldigate*, p. 443.

> who, somewhere about the fourth century, or perhaps later, had themselves so much difficulty in coming to any agreement on the disputed subject.'
>
> 'I think, Bertram, that you are going into matters which you know are not vital to faith in the Christian religion.'[115]

This exchange between Bertram and a clerical friend in *The Bertrams* neatly demonstrates Trollope's capacity for recognizing the distinction between a debating point useful for an attack upon one aspect of Evangelical dogma and a sound basis for a devastating critique of Christian religion as a whole. In alluding to the doctrine of eternal punishment novelists not only found themselves free from charges of irreligion but could exploit to the full the divisions in Evangelical thinking on tenets which, though not central to the Evangelical canon, might reasonably be assumed to be implied by it.

Something of the heat generated by the discussion of eternal punishment is conveyed by the language Canon Ryle saw fit to employ when considering the views propounded by Canon Farrar in his work *Eternal Hope*. 'What does it amount to but telling God, that you, a poor short-lived worm, know what is good for you better than He? It will not do; it will not do. . . . You must read it all, and believe it all.'[116]

Any suggestion that punishment might be other than co-extensive with eternity was felt to belittle the importance of the Atonement and would lead the doubter on to embrace Roman Catholic purgatorial doctrines in full.

These fears motivated the *Christian Observer* in 1837 to warn parents, who had previously relied upon Mrs. Sherwood's books as a suitable medium for their children's instruction, of her new heretical views.[117] This year saw the publication of Part IV of *The History of Henry Milner* in which Henry's guardian explains to his ward, now an undergraduate, his changed attitudes to the millenium and eternal punishment. He now envisages that after death all men will be given the chance to purge their sins through suffering, so that they may all be admitted to the New Jerusalem. This Universalist philosophy is juxtaposed in the novel, not, as one might expect, with Calvinism, but with Arminianism.[118]

[115] *The Bertrams*, ii, 250.

[116] *Eternity: being thoughts on 2 Cor. iv. 18* (1877), p. 30.

[117] *CO* (1837), pp. 306–7.

[118] *History of Henry Milner* (1837), iv, 370–4.

The Arminians, though not emphasizing how few were chosen, still retained a belief in eternal punishment, though they varied in the use they made of the doctrine. In a series of Rules for Lay Assistants that Wesley prepared he posed the question, 'What inconvenience is there in speaking much of the wrath and little of the love of God?' and, as was his habit, provided his own answer, 'It generally hardens them that believe not and discourages them that do.'[119] Patrick Brontë, an Arminian, made known the impossibility of his being comfortable with a coadjutor 'who would deem it his duty to preach the appalling doctrines of personal Election and Reprobation'.[120] His personal distaste for emphasis upon eternal perdition is apparent in his serialized tract on conversion. His fictitious 'awakened sinner, before he has got proper notions of the all sufficiency of Christ', is represented as saying, '. . . I think I hear the sentence of eternal condemnation thunder in mine ears—But yet, there must be mercy in heaven: the groans of the dying Saviour loudly proclaim there is.'[121]

Like Helen Huntingdon, the heroine of Anne Brontë's *The Tenant of Wildfell Hall*, he refuses to dismiss hell as fabulous because this might teach some 'poor wretch . . . to presume upon it to his own destruction',[122] but, whenever he mentions it, tempers the reference by simultaneously offering hope. The effects of Patrick's reticence may well be seen in the young Jane Eyre's pagan response to Brocklehurst's menaces,[123] in Helen Burn's eschatological reflections or in Anne's unorthodoxy. Just as Anne's hopes for her dissolute brother Branwell resided in the eventual salvation which she looked for in the afterlife, so Helen Huntingdon's return to her husband and her subsequent sufferings are justified:

'How could I endure to think that poor trembling soul was hurried away to everlasting torment? it would drive me mad. But, thank God, I have hope—not only from a vague dependence on the possibility that penitence and pardon might have reached him at the last, but from the blessed con-

[119] *John Wesley*, ed. A. C. Outler, p. 163.

[120] J. Lock and W. T. Dixon, *A Man of Sorrows* (1965), p. 292.

[121] *The Pastoral Visitor*, No. 7 (Bradford, July 1815), 54.

[122] A. Brontë, *Tenant of Wildfell Hall*, p. 166.

[123] The monthly magazine, *The Children's Friend*, edited by Carus Wilson, Brocklehurst's 'original', provides numerous examples. The increasing liberalism of the 1850s had no effect on him. His obituary records that he was so moved by the debauchery of the southern port town, where he had retired for his health, that he was soon busy writing and circulating tracts with such titles as 'Portsmouth in Flames'. *CO* (1860), p. 153.

fidence that, through whatever purging fires the erring spirit may be doomed to pass—whatever fate awaits it, still it is not lost, and God, who hateth nothing that He hath made, will bless it in the end!'[124]

She had given earlier expression to her purgatorial theories in a poem entitled 'A Word to the Elect', which as this title, and even more clearly its first title, 'A Word to the Calvinists', indicated, was directed against those Evangelicals who wished to restrict heaven even further by their theories of predestination:

> I ask not how remote the day,
> Nor what the sinner's woe,
> Before the dross is purged away;
> Enough for me to know
> That when the cup of wrath is drained,
> The metal purified,
> They'll cling to what they once disdained,
> And live by Him that died.[125]

The Calvinist, Richard Cecil, openly declared how useful men of his persuasion found the doctrine, particularly in preaching to the young: 'I generally have recourse to terrible images. I explain salvation by a house on fire; for I remember, when I was a child, and learned from bad companions to curse and lead a wicked life, I thought I would keep on, if I could but escape hell.'[126]

The damaging effects of presenting a small child with 'a horrible tract which commenced business with the poor child by asking him in its title, why he was going to Perdition? . . .' are captured for us by Dickens in his picture of Arthur Clennam returning to those surroundings which his childish imagination had suffused with spectral horrors: 'Arthur opened the long low window, and looked out upon the old blasted and blackened forest of chimneys, and the old red glare in the sky which had seemed to him once upon a time but a nightly reflection of the fiery environment that was presented to his childish fancy in all directions, let it look where it would.'[127]

Much criticism was levelled at a method of teaching which emphasized the retributive function of the divinity to the detriment of a God of Love and Mercy. Dickens and Thackeray, however, fell into the trap of tipping the scales just as far in the other direction,

[124] *Tenant of Wildfell Hall*, p. 421.

[125] *The Poems of Emily Jane Brontë and Anne Brontë*, ed. T. J. Wise and J. A. Symington (Oxford, 1934), p. 221.

[126] *Eclectic Notes*, ed. J. H. Pratt, p. 6.

[127] *Little Dorrit*, pp. 29, 38.

and were forced to be as selective as the Evangelicals in the portions of the Bible to which they lent credence. Some Evangelicals did find it difficult to hold in tension the concept of a God of love and of wrath. Mrs. Oliphant's picture, in *A Son of the Soil*, of a hell-dominated Evangelical theology is interesting in that it shows how, far from a belief in hell being the linchpin for the doctrine of Atonement, it could undermine redemption.

The name of the Redeemer was named a great many times therein, but the spirit of it was as if no Redeemer had ever come. A world, dark, confused, and full of judgements and punishments—a world in which men would not believe though one rose from the grave—was the world into which he looked, and for which he was working.[128]

From Mrs. Worboise's novels it appears that some Evangelicals had solved the problem by effectively denying the Trinity and referring to 'God out of Christ' as 'a consuming fire'.[129] The separation can be seen in a novel by a convert to Anglican Evangelicalism, the Revd. G. Macdonald. In *David Elginbrod* we are subjected to teaching 'out of the mouths of babes and sucklings'. A young boy's dream of a court scene where Jesus rescues him from a vindictive God reduces Christ to a schoolboy hero, subjected to some peculiarly unfortunate physical as well as spiritual adulation (after his rescue little Harry lays hidden from the general view kissing His feet), and God to a Satanic figure.[130] As Velvet Cunningham had suggested this teaching served merely to create a Christian mythology almost indistinguishable from the classical. 'What painter who has sketched a portrait of Christ, ever thought of arming him with thunders. No—love was his weapon; and I feel sure, that this is the weapon his ministers should chiefly employ.'[131] The reactions of J. A. Froude[132] and Charles Kingsley[133] demonstrate the dangers inherent in painting God as a Christian Zeus. God had been reduced to the level of an anthropomorphic force by this teaching. Both writers implied that the only manly reaction to such a figure would be to offer resistance. If His dire threats were effective as a deterrent then they should not have been, was their theme. Thackeray, who inclined towards the theory that evil would

[128] *Son of the Soil*, i, 287.

[129] *House of Bondage*, pp. 46, 148. For her further comment see *Oliver Westwood: or, Overcoming the World* (1878), pp. 5–6.

[130] *David Elginbrod* (3 vols., 1863), iii, 186–8.

[131] *Velvet Cushion*, p. 108.

[132] *Nemesis of Faith*, pp. 11–13.

[133] *Alton Locke* (1902), i, 114.

be annihilated in the afterlife, went further and informed his mother that, as visions of hell did not prevent sin, the only conceivable use for the Lazarus and Dives story was as an exemplum for children, 'persons that is who had but indistinct notions of morals'.[134] Butler took perverse pleasure in intimating that the thought of hell alone maintained men's loyalty to Christianity.[135]

Perhaps the realization of its dubious utility in the missionary field was one of the many reasons for Evangelicals slowly dropping their insistence upon this part of the creed. Their attitude in the Athanasian Creed dispute[136] or the Church Missionary Society's refusal to endorse the hard line Calvinism of Carus Wilson's son-in-law[137] are indicative of the growing humanitarianism and sensitivity of public opinion being reflected amongst the more liberal Evangelical circles. Utilitarian theories of penal reform which concentrated upon deterrent and reformatory purposes perhaps had their effect in minimizing the belief in the efficacy of the retributive aspects of hell. An interesting example of the way that Utilitarian theory became absorbed by the Evangelical consciousness appears in Mrs. Sherwood's *Henry Milner* where the very language in which she defends the fall and consequent punishment suggests the influence of Evangelicalism's most powerful nineteenth-century rival. 'Might it not be possible that it was necessary, for the greater good of the mass of created being—in short, for producing the utmost possible quantum of felicity, that some examples should be made?'[138]

Since it was commonly held that the doctrine of eternal punishment was likely to be of most use in training the young, it is perhaps not surprising that one of the best guides to the slow quiet change in the Evangelical climate of belief is to be found in a comparison of various editions of Mrs. F. L. Mortimer's children's best-seller *Peep of Day*[139] (1833)—which had been used, without reference to its changing forms, to illustrate the peculiar horrors of the Evangelical hell and their God 'that blend of Peeping Tom and the

[134] *Thackeray Letters*, i, 402–4. [135] *Erewhon*, pp. 112–13.

[136] In this controversy the Evangelicals joined forces with the Broad Church, against the High Church, in favour of relegating the Athanasian Creed to the back of the Prayer Book and making its inclusion in services non-compulsory.

[137] C. C. Lowndes, *Unevangelized Heathen, Everlasting Torments, and Church Missions* (London and Windermere, 1866), pp. 5, 22.

[138] *History of Henry Milner*, iii, 240.

[139] 250,000 copies had been sold by 1867. R. D. Altick, *The Common Reader*, p. 388.

Marquis de Sade whom pious Evangelists dared to cast for the divine role'.[140] By the time of the 1909 version, which received Evangelical sanction in the form of a preface by Bishop H. C. G. Moule, the God who appears in the chapter entitled, 'Judgement Day', is cast in the role of a winning estate agent, enticing men to heaven with promises of all conceivable delights and comforts, and the problem of the ultimate fate of the wicked is quietly ignored.[141]

The Evangelicals made no public renunciation of this doctrine but withdrew it from prominence. As a correspondent of Dean Farrar remarked, many an Evangelical had within the confines of his own heart become an Universalist as death approached either for himself or his dearest relations.[142]

ii. *Millenarianism*

Intimately linked with views upon eternal punishment or Eternal Bliss after Judgement were one's views upon the Second Coming. As Mr. Dalben, Mrs. Sherwood's mouthpiece, observed it made little sense to talk of a God who might arrange an opportunity for purgatorial preparation for heaven whilst concurrently envisaging the Millenuim as being introduced by a Christ who would enter in upon His reign by destroying the unregenerate.[143]

The increased interest in eschatological studies manifested in the 1820s seems to have been partly a product of England's rapid economic growth and increasing power. England's successful emergence from the Napoleonic Wars coincided with the height of Evangelical activity in founding missionary societies; these combined factors led to a conviction that England might become God's instrument for gathering in the nations to the establishment of His Kingdom upon earth. Napoleon's defeat, as Thomas Mozley explained, had a direct significance in the realms of prophetical

[140] E. Wingfield-Stratford, *Victorian Tragedy*, p. 184.

[141] Only one metaphor changed between the 1849 and the 1873 versions, published during the author's lifetime. In 1891 a 'new edition, carefully revised' retained the 1873 emendation and the references to the Biblical texts upon eternal punishment at the foot of the page, but cut the detailed description of torment by about half, making its threats more abstract. The 1909 version removed the passage altogether. Editions compared: F. L. Mortimer, *The Peep of Day; or, a Series of the earliest religious instruction the infant mind is capable of receiving, with verses illustrative of the subjects* (1849), pp. 297–300; (1873), pp. 173–6; (1891), pp. 164–5; (1909), p. 216.

[142] Letter from C. J. Young to Farrar, 27 Sept. 1880, quoted by G. Rowell, *Hell and the Victorians* (Oxford, 1974), p. 149.

[143] *History of Henry Milner*, iv, 371–2.

speculation. Mozley records the setting up of a twice weekly study group in Oxford in 1829 to which Newman belonged.

The choice of the subject for our meetings belonged rather to the time than to the men that made it. Prophecy was much preached and written upon in those days. For years before it had been debated all over the land whether Napoleon or the Pope were Antichrist, for one of them it must be, and the downfall of the former had decided the question for, that is against, the latter.[144]

This interest in prophecy was also an aspect of the apocalyptic mood of late Romanticism, reflecting the feeling of an hiatus as men became conscious of the ending of one era and were still unsure of what the future might hold. An impact was made even upon the least intellectual of men. It is an argument that Mr. Vincy grasps at, as a drowning man clutches at straws, to delay a decision on his daughter's wedding. 'We may all be ruined for what I know—the country's in that state! Some say it's the end of the world, and be hanged if I don't think it looks like it!'[145]

The literature and art of that period gave evidence of that symbolic sense of extremity and terror felt by men of imagination. Byron's *Heaven and Earth* (1822), Thomas Campbell's *The Last Man* (1823), the apocalyptic paintings of John Martin, found their Evangelical equivalent in poetry such as Robert Pollok's *The Course of Time* (1827), Robert Montgomery's *The Messiah* (1832), or Heraud's *The Descent into Hell* (1830), and *The Judgement of the Flood* (1834), which was suffused with a sense of the latter days being at hand.

By 1838 the young Mary Ann Evans was sufficiently moved by this sense of imminent apocalypse to think 'that a sober and prayerful consideration of the mighty revolutions ere long to take place in our world would by God's blessing serve to make us less grovelling, more devoted and energetic in the service of God'.[146]

The concept of an imminent Millenium served then to provide a theological perspective for this sense of transition, lent to the Evangelicals a sense of their own importance, and provided an opportunity to formulate an Evangelical Utopia. The last point is well illustrated by Mr. Dalben's sketch of the Millenium, where Christ was to come to set up a 'pure theocracy', which the elect

[144] *Reminiscences*, i, 176.
[145] G. Eliot, *Middlemarch*, ii, 122.
[146] *G. Eliot Letters*, i, 11–12.

would participate in running for a thousand years before the final Judgement, whilst the unregenerate would become a subject race in a purgatorial state.

Although the details of her millenial vision changed,[147] Mrs. Sherwood was always a member of the pre-millenial school of thought. The post-millenial school believed that Christ would arrive in judgement at the conclusion of the thousand years, but as the initial enthusiasm, that gave rise to multitudinous societies, began to be somewhat dampened, when men realized that one decade and then two had passed without the wholesale conversions they had anticipated, the idea of labouring patiently for the allotted period gave insufficient excitement and did not seem in keeping with those strange and troubled times. The pre-millenialists sought a more immediate divine sanction and believed that Christ would issue in the thousand years, Himself effecting the restoration of the Jews and the conversion of the heathen.

Since prophetical study was subject to the individual's responsibility of interpreting the Word in accordance with the signs and types he perceived around him these visions were often highly idiosyncratic. Men like the famous Baptist Noel had originally become interested in millenarianism because they saw it as an accumulative force, yet, as individual theories were developed as to the best mode of restoring the Church to an apostolic state fit to welcome the Lord, they found that Millenial debate was fissiparous in effect.

Mozley recalled[148] and Newman dramatized the concern, which prevailed in the early days of Tractarianism, over the tendency to secessions amongst those interested in prophecy. A chapter near the end of *Loss and Gain* introduces Reding to a procession of seceders from Anglicanism, their common denominator being Evangelical zeal in search of a truly apostolic church. First to appear are 'Jack, the kitchen-boy at St. Saviour's', together with the Revd. Alexander Highfly, members of the Holy Catholic Church of Huggermugger Lane, being, respectively, 'next to an Angel', and an Apostle, in

[147] They changed between 1829 and 1837, when Part IV of *The History of Henry Milner* appeared. In 1829 she believed that only the saints would survive the millenium, whilst, at its advent, the wicked would enter 'one long night, one terrible despair'. *The Millenium: or, Twelve Stories designed to explain to Young Bible Readers the Scripture and Prophecies concerning the Glory of the Latter Days* (London, Derby, Glasgow and Worcester, 1829), p. 133.

[148] *Reminiscences*, i, 175.

rank. This extraordinary combination suggests the contempt that Newman felt for the odd assortment of upper-middle-class intelligentsia and uneducated lower classes that Irvingism had attracted. Underlying the caricaturist's humour, however, is a strain of sober criticism comparable to the complaints of disillusioned Evangelicals that millenialists were diverting their message from preaching Christ crucified to Christ and his disciples glorified on earth.[149] The truth of this accusation may be assessed from this passage from Mrs. Sherwood's book, *The Millenium.*

'In the four gospels we find the account of our Saviour's abode with us, in his state of suffering and humiliation, but it is in the books of the prophets, that we find the history and description of his second coming, and it is my great delight, my dear children, to turn from the account of his sufferings and his cruel death, to the view of those lovely passages in scripture, whereby I am led to the assurance of seeing him in glory, and finding myself united with him for ever.'[150]

Yet the millenialists' naïve integrity of purpose won from Newman a sympathy not extended to the right wing of the Evangelical party, who had mounted a witch-hunt, in the millenialist societies and through their newspapers. Having dismissed those 'furious Exeter-Hall beasts',[151] Reding is next visited by a young lady whose quest for 'a pure religion' had taken her from Anglicanism to the New Connexion to the Plymouth Brethren and had brought her to enlist Reding as the leader of a new sect. What to modern eyes seems little more than a comment upon the vagaries of the religiously inclined female should, I think, suggest to us the volatile state of religious emotions in the twenties and thirties and the fluid nature of Dissent before the mid-century process of 'group hardening'[152] had occurred. Newman was after all familiar with the subsequent history[153] of the Revd. H. B. Bulteel, Curate of St. Ebbe's, with whom he had served on the Oxford branch committee of the Church Missionary Society.[154] After a period of High Calvinism Bulteel

[149] See W. Carus, *Memoirs of the Life of the Rev. Charles Simeon*, pp. 657–8.

[150] *The Millenium*, p. 21.

[151] *Loss and Gain*, p. 395.

[152] The term employed by Professor W. R. Ward to describe the process of the emergence of the modern denominational system. 'The Last Chronicle of Barset: or, The Early Victorian Church Revived', *JEH* 18 (Apr. 1967), 69.

[153] See *Letters and Diaries of John Henry Newman*, ed. C. S. Dessain (vols. xi–xxvi, 1961–74), xii, 292.

[154] T. C. F. Stunt, 'John Henry Newman and the Evangelicals', *JEH* 21 (Jan. 1970), 65–74.

embarked in 1831 upon a Wesleyan style itinerant preaching tour. Then, in a period of strong anti-Calvinist reaction, he fell under Irving's spell in London. Relieved of his licence by the Bishop he nevertheless returned to Oxford to start a ministry, operating in his own house and garden until a chapel was built for him by the 'Bulteelers'.[155] Two years before Newman wrote *Loss and Gain* Bulteel left Oxford to become associated with the Plymouth Brethren in Plymouth, many of whom had been harvested as converts from that preaching tour of his Calvinist phase fifteen years before.

Though prophetical lectures continued under Evangelical auspices and the work of interpretation was carried on by men such as Edward Bishop Elliott, whose *Horae Apocalypticae* (1844) devoted some thousand pages to identifying Antichrist with Rome, the next generation of Evangelicals displayed some embarrassment in alluding to the enthusiasm of their spiritual fathers.[156]

Novelists seized this chance to satirize the excesses of a previous generation. Disraeli's sensitivity to changing fashion enabled him to indicate the puritanical seclusion and other-worldly pursuits of the Anglo-Irish nobility from whom Tancred's mother came by reference to their ardent interest in the millenium.[157] In the very year of *Tancred*'s publication another such aristocrat, Lord Shaftesbury, to whom personally millenial belief was of such central importance that he had the inscription, 'Even so come, Lord Jesus', engraved in Greek upon the flaps of his envelopes, showed himself aware, in his diary, of the apparent eccentricity of his views:

> Sept. 17th. [1847] . . . Dear old Duchess of Beaufort here; talked much with her on the Second Advent; we both agree and delight in the belief of the personal reign of our blessed Lord on earth. I cannot understand the Scriptures in any other way; it is, however, a doctrine much abhorred by certain people, and greatly ridiculed and persecuted in those who profess it; the adversaries argue and revile as fiercely as though they attacked or maintained the fundamentals of the Christian religion, whereas the reception of this text, however comfortable, is no matter of faith.[158]

[155] For further details see J. S. Reynolds, *The Evangelicals at Oxford*, pp. 97–9; and H. H. Rowdon, *The Origins of the Brethren* (1967), pp. 66–9.

[156] e.g. W. F. Wilkinson, *Rector in Search of a Curate*, pp. 225–7 and the *CO* review of this novel (1843), pp. 631–7, 663–94.

[157] *Tancred*, pp. 13, 70–1.

[158] E. Hodder, *Life of Shaftesbury*, ii, 10; ii, 226–7.

Shaftesbury was himself an outstanding answer to those who argued that the expectation of an imminent Millenium militated against social concern and missionary activity. Edward Bickersteth's resignation from the secretaryship of the Church Missionary Society on becoming a pre-millenialist lent fuel to the fire, since he had begun his prophetical studies in an effort to dispel the notions of those men who could not believe that missionary agencies would secure the gradual conversion of the world.[159] Samuel Butler frequently inveighs against millenialists like William Bickersteth Owen's mother who learnt to regard the earth as 'but a place of pilgrimage—only so far important as it was a possible road to heaven'.[160] Young Victoria Buxton spoke slightingly of a millenialist acquaintance who found the belief appealing precisely because it provided a convenient mask for her own lethargy: 'She is not at all like us—teaching and visiting is an immense effort to her—indeed even dressing to go out to tea, or writing a letter, is rather burdensome, and she looks forward to the Millenium as a time when such toils shall cease! She would be very sorry to think that it was *not* to begin in 1867'.[161]

George Eliot feared that the doctrine produced 'no really holy, spiritual effect'.[162] Rufus Lyon's obsession with prophetical interpretation is seen as an outdated but harmless peccadillo, though it does cause him to neglect minor domestic concerns.[163] Dorothea feels that Mr. Tyke's sermons about 'the prophecies in the Apocalypse' will 'be of no use at Lowick'.[164] In *Middlemarch* George Eliot also makes a brief allusion to the tenuous link between Millenarianism and revolutionary chiliasm, observed as a working-class phenomenon by E. P. Thompson.[165] 'Even the rumour of Reform', she wrote, 'had not yet excited any millenial expectations in Frick', since these stolid countrymen were 'less given to fanaticism than to a strong muscular suspicion'.[166] Confusions inevitably occurred when men spelt out in metaphorical terms their vision of Utopia; the unorthodox pre-millenialist, Millenial Marsh, Vicar of

[159] T. R. Birks, *Memoir of the Rev. Edward Bickersteth*, ii, 61.
[160] *Fair Haven*, p. 14.
[161] G. W. E. Russell, *Lady Victoria Buxton* (1919), p. 26.
[162] *The Essays of George Eliot*, ed. T. Pinney (1963), p. 181.
[163] *Felix Holt the Radical*, ch. xli.
[164] *Middlemarch*, ii, 338.
[165] E. P. Thompson, *The Making of the English Working Class* (1968), pp. 52–6.
[166] *Middlemarch*, iii, 32.

a Birmingham Church, was wrongly understood by working-class Radicals and Chartists of the Great Reform Bill era to be referring to the secular Golden Age for which they were working.[167] Little was made of this apparent connection in the Victorian novel, since a clear division had arisen by mid-century between the working-class dissenting attachment to politically-inclined chiliastic religion and the Anglican non-temporal involvement. Indeed the jibe was more frequently made that Anglican representatives of millenarian societies were attracted to the faith by the easy money to be had from gulling wealthy zealots. Well-informed critics like Conybeare and Wilkinson were probably aware how much of the financial support came first from Henry Drummond, the impresario responsible for Irving's rise to fame, or Lewis Way, who ensured the financial solvency of the Jew Society. Those foolish enough to believe in the wilder millenarian theories, it was argued, could almost certainly be duped to more immediate material advantage.

The conversion and restoration of the Jews to Israel was intimately linked with millenarianism, for it was held that the recreation of the state of Israel would either immediately precede, or coincide with, the beginning of the millenium. The unsettled situation which prevailed in the Middle East throughout the nineteenth century was seen as an opportunity for hastening the Lord's work. Conybeare even suggested in his novel *Perversion*, that the Millenarian Society was capable of supporting Jewish Emancipation Acts or new laws of usury so that the Jews would both become increasingly unpopular and be deprived of their major means of livelihood, so being forced to hurry back to their homeland.[168] Indeed the devious means of conversion sometimes employed by the London Society for Promoting Christianity amongst the Jews helps to explain why convert Jews were a favourite target for satire. Straight bribery was employed to attract converts and then a total renunciation of the Jewish community was required as evidence of conversion, which sometimes resulted in the convert having to be kept by his new brothers in the faith since he was alienated from his former sources

[167] [C. Marsh], *Life of William Marsh* (1867), p. 146. For Marsh's exact position on millenialism see S. C. Orchard, op. cit., p. 74.

[168] *Perversion*, i, 342. Despite the provocation such ideas offer to read the title in accordance with modern usage the word 'perversion' is used here, and in other nineteenth-century novels, in the religious context as the opposite of 'conversion' to imply a change to error in belief.

of income.[169] Undoubtedly a certain amount of personal anti-Semitism accounts for the prominence of convert Jews in Trollope's satire. The endless procession from Mr. Emilius to Mr. Groschut combined for him the vulgarity of Evangelicalism with the characteristics of a race whose values and financial powers jeopardized the existence of an English gentleman.[170]

As their resistance to the entry of Jews to Parliament[171] demonstrated, most Evangelicals in fact remained clear about the distinction, which their critics claimed they had failed to make, between a converted Jew and a Jew still under the old dispensation. Wilkinson's caustic remark that the leading society should be renamed The Society for Promoting Judaism among Christians[172] was an idea that received fuller treatment from Newman. After receiving visitors from seceders to Protestant Dissent Reding is visited by Zerubbabel, a deacon of the Church of England who had become a convert to Judaism and prophesied that he would soon be joined by his former colleagues now that the Jerusalem Bishopric had been established.[173] This caricature carries in its inspiration Newman's knowledge that the Jerusalem appointment had been 'the beginning of the end' for his own attachment to Anglicanism,[174] since the Tractarians were scandalized by the 'double sin'[175] of the symbol of the Establishment's willingness to ally itself in the project with Lutheran Protestantism and so to set aside the authority of the Prayer Book and the Articles.

[169] H. H. Norris, *The Origin, Progress and Existing Circumstances of the London Society for Promoting Christianity amongst the Jews* (London, 1825). This book also recounts a scandal, current in London, which very probably formed the basis for Mrs. Trollope's *Vicar of Wrexhill*. Christian Friedrich Frey, a convert Jew, was a founder member and full-time agent of this society. After protracted negotiations for an Anglican ordination he left hurriedly for America. He had been found guilty of adultery with the wives of several prominent Evangelical ministers connected with the society. Mrs. Trollope always insisted that her tale was founded upon the facts with which Henrietta Skerrett her 'very intimate friend' furnished her—'of course on the condition of their being modified, as facts need to be before they are acceptable in any work of art'. Her acquaintance with the Skerrett sisters dated from the early years of the century and survived at least until 1837. One of the sisters held a position at court and would therefore have been well placed to hear scandal of a society which enjoyed the active patronage of the Duke of Kent. F. E. Trollope, *Frances Trollope*, i, 49, 256.

[170] See *Phineas Finn*, *The Eustace Diamonds*, *Is He Popenjoy?* and also 'The Zulu in London', *Pall Mall Gazette* (10 May 1865), pp. 3–4.

[171] T. R. Birks, *Memoir of the Rev. Edward Bickersteth*, ii, 388; E. Hodder, *Life of Shaftesbury*, i, 330–1; ii, 231.

[172] *Rector in Search of a Curate*, p. 280.

[173] *Loss and Gain*, Part III, ch. vii.

[174] *Apologia*, p. 136.

[175] W. F. Wilkinson, *Rector in Search of a Curate*, p. 309.

By the 1870s, Mrs. Worboise implies, those who retained the enthusiasm of the thirties and forties had seceded from the lukewarm Society for the Propagation of Christianity among the Jews and formed Zion societies,[176] where they met to read works from the early period such as *Judah's Lion* (1843). In this popular work Charlotte Elizabeth had sought to dramatize her personal belief that the restoration of the Jews and the overthrow of the Papacy would together introduce the Millenium.

It took Samuel Butler, with his detailed knowledge of Evangelical vagaries, to derive his own exquisite amusement from such refinements upon the millenarian restoration theme as the controversy over the identity and whereabouts of the lost Ten Tribes of Israel. When Higgs alights upon the Erewhonians he is temporarily exhilarated by the thought that 'they might be the lost ten tribes of Israel, of whom I had heard both my grandfather and father make mention' and that he had perhaps 'been designed by Providence as the instrument of their conversion'.[177] Typically, Butler, rather than merely enjoying the fantastic element in this belief or taking pains to demonstrate its unsound theological basis, debases the theory by sneering at the profiteering spirit which accompanies Higgs's missionary inclination.

In criticizing Millenialist doctrines there were two methods employed by the doctrinally concerned and caricaturist alike. The confident predictions with which the chronology of the Millenium was forecast could easily be undermined by the relevant spokesman in the novel postulating a date which antedated the novel's publication. Although the failure of the millenium to commence on a particular date in no way served to destroy the theory as a whole, since the symbolic figures used as a basis could be recalculated and manipulated at will, this method served to pour scorn upon the combative tenacity with which each eschatologically inclined Evangelical clung to his own interpretation. By extension, if so many individuals involved in the dissemination of this belief could be made to appear foolish, the belief itself might be thrown into disrepute.

Secondly the recondite terms which the millenarians employed and their habit of describing contemporary events and signs in the most obscure of biblical language gave opportunity for verbal

[176] *House of Bondage*, p. 348.
[177] S. Butler, *Erewhon*, pp. 41–2.

humour. Few of the novelists' inventions could in fact hope to rival the risible inventions of the millenialists themselves, such as McNeile's sermon, 'EVERY EYE SHALL SEE HIM, or *Prince Albert's visit to Liverpool used in an illustration of the second coming of Christ*',[178] or the prayer used by Haldane Stewart after the return of 500 of his parishioners from seeing the Great Exhibition, 'May the sight of the Crystal Palace lead to a desire to enter the new Jerusalem.'[179] Once one had embarked upon the intriguing pastime of trying to equate contemporary events with biblical symbols there was a strong likelihood of Millenarianism becoming a self-confirming belief. An entry in Edward Bickersteth's diary amply illustrates this point.

February 22, 1835. Everything in Providence and Prophecy calls me to watchfulness, and preparedness for the day of Christ. The return of Sir R. Peel to power, and his inability to stand, seen by the first division in the house, and then, if he fails, the apparent inlet of the overthrowers of our national institutions, may well fill the Christian patriot with fears for his country, and these must be greatly increased by the predictions of God's word.[180]

### iii. *Special Providence*

Bickersteth's reflections remind us of that third disputed area of Evangelical dogma, the role of Providence. Eighteenth-century Evangelicalism relied heavily upon the evidence of Nature to prepare men's souls and confirm them in the Gospel truth, finding this at the same time a useful means by which to counteract the Deist concept of a remote figure uninterested in the world He had set in motion.[181] This method of instruction received what was, in theory, a shattering blow from the growing evidence for evolution based upon a process of natural selection. Tennyson was swift to take the point that the moral and theological implications of this theory presented for men 'Who trusted God was love indeed / And love Creation's final law'. If Nature ,'careless of the single life', could be seen in control this minimized the possibility of a benevolent God's interference and brought men dangerously close again to a Deist philosophy, in which the God who had created a self-sustaining

[178] *Edin. Rev.* 98 (1853), 292 n.
[179] D. D. Stewart, *Memoir of the Life of the Rev. James Haldane Stewart* (1856), p. 341.
[180] T. R. Birks, *Memoir of the Rev. Edward Bickersteth*, ii, 71.
[181] e.g. H. Venn, *Complete Duty*, p. 41.

universe became a near irrelevance to modern man. Evangelicals however continued to preach the doctrine of a Provident and all-powerful God.

Providence is rarely challenged in the novel as directly as in Hardy's works. In *Tess of the D'Urbervilles* his vision of an amoral force is placed in direct opposition to specifically Evangelical beliefs. Tess, parroting Angel's teaching, demands of Alec the Methodist preacher, 'How can I pray for you . . . when I am forbidden to believe that the great Power who moves the world would alter His plans on my account?' With this 'merciless polemical syllogism' Tess overthrows Alec's Methodist conviction just as Angel had rejected his parent's firm Evangelicalism with its aid.[182] Most mid-Victorian novelists tended to confine themselves to exploring the doctrine's moral effects. Thackeray, whose letters revert to the issue more than once, might express his dislike of those 'who are forever dragging the Awful Divinity into a participation with their private concerns' and claim that he himself could not 'request any special change in my behalf from the ordinary processes, or see any special Divine *animus* superintending my illnesses or wellnesses',[183] but showed no enthusiasm to make this belief public in his novels.

When it came to tracing the workings of Providence in detail there was considerable disagreement among Evangelicals over the extent to which one should expect God to override natural order and interfere directly in everyday life. Many early Evangelicals seemed to have shared Wesley's view of the absolute necessity of belief in Special Providence,[184] a variety of minor miracle worked by God for those who were his servants. Their letters and biographies abound in striking instances of preservation from accidents, but the second generation occasionally showed an awareness of the spiritual dangers of fostering collections of these incidents.[185]

Yet an Evangelical best seller of the period, Hannah More, included an entire chapter on 'The Hand of God to be acknowledged in the daily Circumstances of Life' in her work on *Practical Piety*, in which she advocated this detailed recording of events.

[182] *Tess of the D'Urbervilles*, pp. 408–9.

[183] *Thackeray Letters*, iv, 128–9.

[184] *The Journal of the Rev. John Wesley*, ed. N. Curnock (8 vols., 1909–16), vi, 326.

[185] A. B. Brown, *Recollections of Simeon*, pp. 327–8; M. Hennell, *John Venn and the Clapham Sect*, pp. 264–5; *CO* (1808), p. 316.

We may also trace marks of his hand, not only in the awful visitations of life, not only in the severer dispensations of his Providence, but in vexations so trivial that we should hesitate to suspect that they are providential appointments, did we not know that our daily life is made up of unimportant circumstances rather than of great events. As they are, however, of sufficient importance to exercise the Christian tempers and affections, we may trace the hand of our heavenly Father in those daily little disappointments and hourly vexations which occur even in the most prosperous state. . . .[186]

The narrative written by Miss Clack in Wilkie Collins's *The Moonstone* thrives upon the habit of ejaculatory prayer fostered by a consciousness of a special mission and consequent special protection. From the persistency with which Collins levelled his satire against this particular habit we might have been led to suspect a personal animus. A venomous letter to Charles Ward concerning a trusteeship he had to administer for a certain Mrs. Jones might provide some hint of the source of his dislike.

Is the Jones-fund (may 'the Lord' soon take her!) paid into *my* account regularly? . . . If it only rests with *me* to decide the matter, pay this pious bitch the two quarters together—so that we may be the longer rid of her. . . . Tell me whether (by the help of the Lord) Mrs. Jones's dividends are now regularly paid into my account only. I don't want to pay Mrs. Jones (and the Lord) out of my own pocket.[187]

The freedom Collins permits himself in alluding to the habit suggests that he found it irritating rather than blasphemous. Mrs. Trollope's distaste for the exclamatory religious style, which sprang from a sense of religious decorum alien to Collins, found vent in mockery as open and high-pitched as his. It was, in part, her inability to see that good taste required silence rather than a caricaturing reproduction of the original offences that led Thackeray to compare *The Vicar of Wrexhill* to certain Roman Catholic theological textbooks written for devout purposes yet 'so ingeniously obscene as to render them quite dangerous for common eyes'.[188] Mrs. Trollope's dislike of references to Providence had, however, a moral undertone also. It is not merely the choice of words that Sir Gilbert Harrington, an essentially eighteenth-century figure, is

[186] *Practical Piety*, p. 136.
[187] K. Robinson, *Wilkie Collins: A Biography* (1951), p. 222.
[188] 'Our Batch of Novels for Christmas, 1837', *Fraser's*, 17 (1838), 81.

taking exception to when he remarks, on finding a copy of an important letter, 'had such a thing happened to Mr. Cartwright, he would have declared it providential—but I in my modesty only call it lucky'.[189] Mr. Cartwright conspires to elevate his own designs and desires into the express will of God. In argument with the refractory Rosalind he explains that 'it is in order to combat and overthrow such notions as you now express, that God hath vouchsafed, by an act of his special providence, to send upon earth in these later days my humble self, and some others who think like me . . .'[190] Perhaps the tendency Sydney Smith observed,[191] for the espousal of this doctrine to lead to the self-adulatory belief that the successful man is necessarily the righteous man, made Dickens associate the doctrine with such a man as Pecksniff. In one of those asides sometimes introduced by Dickens, as though he has suddenly seen the opportunity for exploring in his fiction a problem that has vaguely yet persistently perplexed him in life, he makes Pecksniff's allusion to Providence, 'perhaps I may be permitted to say a special Providence', the excuse for considering 'a question of philosophy'. He recalls the text upon which the doctrine was based[192] and pauses to ponder the point which must have recurred to him every occasion that a National Day of Thanksgiving had been held. 'That many undertakings, national as well as individual—but especially the former—are held to be specially brought to a glorious and successful issue, which could never be so regarded on any other process of reasoning, must be clear to all men.'[193]

Perhaps the finest literary portrait of a man whose undertakings are a source of self-congratulation, conducted as they are under the consciousness of a benevolent Providence, is George Eliot's Bulstrode, whose portrait forms part of a wider critique of the doctrine in *Middlemarch*.[194]

Mrs. Oliphant, like Dickens, had been troubled by the implications of this doctrine. The measure of her concern can be seen in the way that she attributes faith in it not to fanatics or thoroughgoing hypocrites but to characters who do not concern themselves with

[189] *Vicar of Wrexhill*, ii, 45.
[190] *Vicar of Wrexhill*, i, 319.
[191] ('B. D. Hatchard'), 'On the Causes of the Increase of Methodism', *Edin. Rev.* 22 (1808), 316.
[192] Luke, 12: 6, 7.
[193] *Martin Chuzzlewit*, p. 329.
[194] See below pp. 240–3.

thinking out the problems it raises. Lucilla Marjoribanks is too protected by a cocoon of self-satisfaction to start querying apparent injustices in the universal scheme of things which do not directly affect her.

'It is a special providence', said Lucilla to herself, with her usual piety; and then she folded up the paper in a little square, with the announcement in the middle which had struck her so much. . . . Lucilla, for her part, felt no difficulty in discerning the leadings of Providence, and she could not but appreciate the readiness with which her desires were attended to, and the prompt clearing-up of her difficulties. There are people whose inclinations Providence does not seem to superintend with such pains-taking watchfulness; but then, no doubt, that must be their own fault.[195]

Lucilla's essentially pagan sense of immediate rewards and punishments easily accommodates itself to the doctrinal formula acceptable in Low Church Carlingford. But with Lucilla's paganism goes a warm-hearted concern for those mortals in whose lives she deigns to act the part of Providence. With this character Mrs. Oliphant can indulge in amused reflections on the way in which men mould their pictures of Providence to reflect their own personality, but it is the sterner thought, suggested in the last sentence of the quotation, that she ponders in *A Son of the Soil.* Here we are shown the totally passive acquiescent Evangelicalism of a young girl who accepts all that life has to offer her as a grand example of the text 'All things work together for good to them that love him.' Whilst she would never indulge in the manipulations of a Lucilla or a Bulstrode and then sanction her own deeds by reference to Providence, nor willingly injure another mortal, this is largely because she lacks their dynamism. The Providential dispensation which she accepts and praises, when it brings her the husband for whom she has longed, has involved the death of her step-mother and children. Perhaps, Mrs. Oliphant implies, her passivity may be true faith but if so it rests upon a naïveté which may be construed as childlike saintliness but appears to others as mere childishness. The active hero of the book accepts the burden allotted to him in the shape of this utterly dependent devotion but does so only with a struggle in which he realizes that 'personal content or dissatisfaction has a great deal to do with the way in which a man regards the tenor of Providence'.[196] Throughout this novel Mrs. Oliphant

[195] *Miss Marjoribanks*, iii, 266–7.
[196] *Son of the Soil*, ii, 272.

has criticized an Evangelical thought pattern which inclines man to accept all life's events as orderings of Providence. The series of domestic disasters and tragedies with which Mrs. Oliphant's private life was strewn and the endless labour she had taken upon herself, to no apparent avail, may well have given her cause either to wonder with what personality she would have had to have been endowed to accept these disasters with saintlike composure, or to question the entire doctrine of Special Providence. How could one accept a Providence who, in order to effect minor personal triumphs, would allow or even contrive so much suffering for others? No wonder that she embraced Tennyson's *In Memoriam*, as did her most attractive heroine, Lucy Wodehouse, when confronted with the death of those she loved rather than the pious consolations proffered by those whose advocacy of Special Providence never seemed to have confronted the issue of pain and disease in the world.[197]

Perhaps, after all, only a very deep sense of the all-pervasive evil in this world could lead a painstakingly sincere and not unintelligent man to search anxiously for any sign of the Lord's hand at work. Shaftesbury, regarded by some as 'the raven, the disheartened and dispirited Jeremiah of the Church—a pessimist, who sees and fears the worst',[198] spent his holidays collecting page after page of examples of Special Providences.[199] Yet he was abruptly reminded that 'the mass', even of the Evangelical 'world were all erect against the admission of Special Providence', when he was forced sorrowfully to record the reaction of his beloved wife Minny to his own praises of God's providential guidance in the matter of the Jerusalem Bishopric. ' "You din this perpetually in my ears, and it sets my back up against it, always talking of how wonderful, how wonderful" . . . (—mocking the manner—) . . .'[200]

By this small domestic incident we are reminded how easy it was for contemporaries to satirize the Evangelical. The whole-hearted earnestness of their individual commitment did not incline them to embrace with equal fervour the text 'Let your moderation be known to all men.'

[197] *The Autobiography and Letters of Mrs. M. O. W. Oliphant*, ed. Mrs. H. Coghill, 3rd edn. (1899), p. 315; *Perpetual Curate*, ii, 248.

[198] H. B. Macartney, *England, Home, and Beauty: Sketches of Christian Life and Work in 1878* (1882), p. 34.

[199] E. Hodder, *Life of Shaftesbury*, ii, 273.

[200] G. F. A. Best, *Shaftesbury* (1964), p. 31.

iv. *Assurance*

A personal and absolute conviction of salvation, entirely independent of the evidence of Sanctification, was occasionally elevated into the doctrine of Assurance. Wesley and his early Arminian Anglican associates, who appealed to their own experience, for a time taught that Assurance was an integral part of the faith,[201] but most moderate Calvinist Evangelicals tended, like Henry Venn, to avoid even the word Assurance, preferring to replace it with the phrase 'affiance in Christ'.[202] It was the intrinsically personal nature of this doctrine and its emotional bias that aroused distrust. As Legh Richmond's Dairyman's Daughter expressed it, 'When I ask my own heart a question, I am afraid to trust it, for it is treacherous, and has often deceived me.'[203] George Eliot's delicate awareness of sectarian differences led her to place her attack upon the doctrine of Assurance in the primitive, extremist, dissenting community of Lantern Yard. Whereas William Dane's Assurance is based upon a vision vouchsafed to him, Silas Marner, constantly in a state of 'hope mingled with fear',[204] is too self-doubting to elevate his cataleptic fits into evidence of Assurance. Not only does this example suggest how dangerous it had been to universalize a particular experience into a fundamental doctrine but calls into question the strong possibilities for hypocrisy the belief provides, since there is no objective test to which such a profession can be subjected.

Positive teaching concerning the concept of Assurance continued to be generally avoided by nineteenth-century Evangelicals, preachers and novelists alike. To insist upon it as a necessary condition of salvation could only be discouraging, whilst to deny its existence as a state of mind could scarcely be helpful to those intent on conveying the sense of certainty, of absolute joy and peace, which the wandering soul would instantly recognize upon conversion to true Christianity. That being said, it is clear from the writings of the Newman family that the doctrine received a brief resurrection in the Evangelical circles of the late 1820s. It seems probable that they encountered the doctrine through the medium of those Oxford Evangelicals who were influenced by Edward Irving.[205]

[201] *John Wesley*, ed. A. C. Outler (New York, 1964), p. 205.

[202] *Complete Duty*, pp. 92, 402.

[203] *The Dairyman's Daughter* (Otley, 1816), p. 36.

[204] *Silas Marner*, p. 12.

[205] E. Irving, 'Signs of the Times, and the Characteristics of the Church', *Morning Watch*, 1 (1829), 641–66.

Mrs. Mozley introduces the concept when, in response to her heroine's innocent inquiry as to how a man might be sure that he did not deceive himself in the matter of his conversion, Constance asserts 'he has the witness in himself, which assures him that he believes in Jesus.'[206] Francis Newman, in the process of describing the vagaries of his own spiritual pilgrimage, alludes to the doctrine as one of especial use as a weapon against apostasizers: 'I know that many Evangelicals will reply, that I never can have had "the true" faith; else I could never have lost it . . .'[207]

So keen was John Henry Newman to destroy everything that encouraged assurance and security, feeling that this would necessarily lead to Antinomianism, and yet so urgent was his personal need for certainty that he worked out a solution recounted to us in *Loss and Gain*. When Reding joins the Roman Catholic Church it is explained to us that this conversion process differs from the Evangelical formula in that it is possible to have habitual moral certainty before conversion, the certainty that the Roman Church is the true church, and that absolute certainty is the reward of conversion.[208]

The 'religion of the heart', which, in origin had been a reaction against the intellectual deism of the eighteenth century, became outflanked on its emotional side by the secular Romantic movement and was increasingly felt to be an anti-intellectual force. The Evangelicals whose opinions I have cited have been literate and, for the most part, educated men, and yet, from their pronouncements, it becomes clear how a doctrine, which at first attracted men by its vital simplicity and consequent flexibility for the individual conscience, grew increasingly rigid without gaining a commensurate intellectual clarity, when men were trapped in an extremist position by the onslaughts of Neology and Ritualism. It was in these extreme, and often undignified, positions that the novelists caught the Evangelicals.

Yet a doctrine which placed so much emphasis upon good works as being 'those outward actions which manifest the inward disposition of the mind' should perhaps be judged also upon its practical piety. For in the observance of this, Lord Ashley assured

[206] *The Lost Brooch*, i, 144.

[207] F. W. Newman, *Phases of Faith: or, Passages from the History of my Creed* (Leicester, 1970), p. 133.

[208] *Loss and Gain*, p. 384.

an assembly of young men, lay the security of one's doctrinal purity.

Nothing is more likely to keep you from mischief of all kinds, from mischief of action, of speculation—from every mischief that you can devise, than to be everlastingly engaged in some great practical work of good. Christianity is not a state of opinion and speculation. Christianity is essentially practical, and I will maintain this, that practical Christianity is the great curer of corrupt speculative Christianity. No man, depend upon it, can persist from the beginning of his life to the end of it in a course of self-denial, in a course of generosity, in a course of virtue, in a course of piety, and in a course of prayer, unless he draws from his well-spring, unless he is drawing from the fountain of our Lord Himself. Therefore, I say to you, again and again, let your Christianity be practical.[209]

[209] E. Hodder, *Life of Shaftesbury*, i, 327–8.

## CHAPTER III

# Practical Piety

### 1. *Liturgical piety*

> Who was he, and where did he come from? Was he young or old? High, Low, or Broad? Would he go in for choral services and intoning, or would he offer up extempore prayer before the sermon, and encourage 'tea-fights'? Would he preach the 'Real Presence', or would he denounce Baptismal Regeneration—although he proclaimed it *nolens volens* at the font?[1]

SINCE the effective essentials of Evangelical doctrine often brought Anglicans closer in thought to converted Dissenters than to other members of the Established Church, they were frequently charged with undervaluing the Liturgical practices of their own Church. Yet, despite doctrinal emphasis on the individual's experience and right to judgement, early Evangelicalism reinfused a moribund church with new zeal for the old corporate acts of worship. Evangelical piety began to mark out for itself a pattern of worship, involving certain services, or parts of services, on which they placed an emphasis that distinguished them from their Anglican contemporaries, at first the High and Dry remnants of eighteenth-century orthodoxy and later the Tractarians and Ritualists. Victorian novelists were able, therefore, to use a shorthand system to enable their readers to discover a man's exact flavour of churchmanship. For the modern reader, however, with the change in religious observances, this notation has become obscure, and what served as a signpost to our forefathers has become a vague indication of religiosity to us. Very occasionally the modern reading makes more sense. Dickens's position on the outskirts of formal religion is indicated by the apparent carelessness with which he turns Mrs. Pardiggle into an extreme High Churchwoman or Tractarian, by her attendance at early matins,[2] whilst depicting her as involved in

[1] E. J. Worboise, *House of Bondage*, p. 14.
[2] *Bleak House*, ch. viii.

an interference masquerading as philanthropy which normally characterizes some form of Evangelical activity for him. He is more concerned with secular traits of character that manifest themselves in the religious world as well as in any other than with making a serious criticism of a particular variety of churchmanship.[3]

For many authors, however, Evangelical interpretation of the duties and pleasures of corporate worship, the war with Ritualism, or the rivalry with Dissent, presented a fine drama which could be treated in secular terms. That passage in *Barchester Towers* where Archdeacon Grantly considers the weapons at his disposal in the war with the Slope and Proudie contingent, without regard to his own religious convictions, conveys exactly the tactical use made of such devices by authors like Trollope.

Dr. Proudie and his crew were of the lowest possible order of Church of England clergymen, and therefore it behoved him, Dr. Grantly, to be of the very highest. Dr. Proudie would abolish all forms and ceremonies, and therefore Dr. Grantly felt the sudden necessity of multiplying them. Dr. Proudie would consent to deprive the church of all collective authority and rule, and therefore Dr. Grantly would stand up for the full power of convocation, and the renewal of all its ancient privileges.

It was true that he could not himself intone the service, but he could procure the co-operation of any number of gentlemanlike curates well trained in the mystery of doing so. He would not willingly alter his own fashion of dress, but he could people Barchester with young clergymen dressed in the longest frocks, and in the highest-breasted silk waistcoats. He certainly was not prepared to cross himself, or to advocate the real presence; but, without going this length, there were various observances, by adopting which he could plainly show his antipathy to such men as Dr. Proudie and Mr. Slope.[4]

Mrs. Arabin's change of allegiance is symbolized by 'a handsome subscription towards certain very heavy ecclesiastical legal expenses which have lately been incurred in Bath'[5]—a reference to the prosecution of Archdeacon Denison for his extreme views on the doctrine of the Real Presence of Christ, and upon the nature of that reality regardless of the state of the recipient.

[3] Mr. Nicodemus Dumps, the misanthropist, acts with a fine disregard for sectarian concern, to further human misery. He subscribes to the Society for the Suppression of Vice, and to the support of two itinerant methodist ministers, as well as agreeing to stand as godfather in an Anglican baptismal ceremony. 'The Bloomsbury Christening', *Sketches by Boz*, pp. 467–83.

[4] *Barchester Towers*, pp. 41–2.

[5] Ibid., p. 505.

As might be expected only those novelists with a declared doctrinal commitment saw fit to discuss at greater length the Evangelical attitude to this sacrament. Tractarian-influenced criticism usually reflected Charlotte Yonge's verdict that 'they did not always dwell enough on the Sacraments or on the oneness of the Church. When they talked of Faith, they meant chiefly our trust in Our Lord's Merits, rather than belief in all the other articles of the Christian faith.'[6] Yet in her novels, anxious as always to stress practical good rather than theoretical controversy, she pays homage to the early work of the Evangelicals in introducing monthly rather than quarterly celebrations of communion.[7]

Only after the advent of Tractarianism were the Evangelicals forced into the position where their definition of the nature of the presence of Christ in the Eucharist compelled them to hold a lower doctrinal estimate of this Sacrament. Mrs. Worboise makes a sweeping attack on Anglo-Catholics and Evangelicals who, by remaining within the Establishment, tacitly endorse the doctrine of transubstantiation by obeying the Prayer Book's injunction for ministers to consume the remnant of the consecrated bread and wine. She concludes her criticism in verse designed to convey a low estimate of the elements.

> Oh! presumptuous undertaker,
> Never bread could bake its baker,
> Yet a man can make his Maker![8]

The celebration of the second Anglican sacrament, Baptism, achieved a prominence in the mid-Victorian public conscience scarcely credible by modern standards. The average educated nineteenth-century layman's awareness of the doctrinal and legal significance of the Gorham case forces us to recognize a wholly unfamilar intellectual atmosphere.[9]

High Churchmen might suspect Evangelicals of denying the language of the Prayer Book, which implied that infants were regenerated in baptism, because they would wish to insist on the need for subsequent conversion, but, in fact, the Evangelicals were

[6] *English Church History* (1883), p. 201.

[7] See M. Mare and A. C. Percival, *Victorian Best-Seller* (1947), p. 108.

[8] *Overdale*, p. 474.

[9] e.g. C. Bronte, *Shirley*, p. 2; F. Trollope, *Uncle Walter*, ii, 204; *Thackeray Letters*, ii, 663. For a rehearsal of the case and its precise significance see O. Chadwick, *Victorian Church*, i, 250–71.

themselves divided upon this issue.[10] We can gain an insight into the spectrum of Evangelical opinion from the works of three apologetic novelists, Butler, Newman, and Mrs. Worboise. Samuel Butler's wholesale opposition to Christianity enabled him to suggest the diversity of Evangelical opinion in a manner not possible for the other two authors, anxious as they were to gain support for a particular doctrinal slant.

In the late 1850s Theodore Pontifex, by now Low Church rather than Evangelical, finds himself unprepared 'for the almost contempt with which Ernest now regarded the doctrines of baptismal regeneration'.[11] Only if we are aware of the presence within the Evangelical party of men like Henry Venn Elliott,[12] Henry Moule, the parson Thomas Hardy regarded as his parish priest,[13] and presumably Theodore, who believed that a child entered into 'covenanted privileges' at Baptism and that God visited the child with the life and light of His Holy Spirit, does Samuel Butler's personal shock[14] at the apparent inefficacy of Baptism become intelligible. Ernest in his ultra-Evangelical phase agreed with an Evangelical like William Marsh, who saw it merely as a proleptic sign of the appropriation of God's grace.[15] In *The Fair Haven* Butler traced another reaction to the discovery.[16] Like Samuel Butler himself John Pickard Owen was surprised to find that there was no correlation between baptism and good conduct in the members of his Sunday School class. Instead of accommodating his arguments to the belief sanctioned by the Gorham judgement, that baptism need be no more than a sign of one's acceptance into the Visible Church of God, Owen, like his creator, concluded that if the words were not susceptible to the extremest possible interpretation of the view he had held then they

[10] Best seen in W. Goode, *The Doctrine of the Church of England as to the effects of Baptism in the case of Infants* (3 vols., 1849); or W. F. Wilkinson, *Rector in Search of a Curate*, pp. 118–42.

[11] *Way of All Flesh*, p. 228.

[12] J. Bateman, *Life of the Rev. Henry Venn Elliott* (1868), pp. 233–5.

[13] It would seem that Hardy more nearly captured the half superstitious regard felt by countryfolk for the rite of Baptism in *Tess of the D'Urbervilles*, pp. 118–23, than had Henry Moule in his *Two Conversations between a Clergyman and One of his Parishioners, on the Service for the Public* (1843) where the parishioner displays a quick understanding of his parson's high evaluation of the sacrament. For the connection between Hardy and Moule see below p. 118.

[14] H. F. Jones, *Samuel Butler: Author of Erewhon (1835–1902): A Memoir* (2 vols., 1920), i, 61.

[15] C. Marsh, *Life of William Marsh*, pp. 130–3.

[16] *Fair Haven*, pp. 15–17.

were worthless. Owen decided to determine the truth of the doctrine, in its highest sense, by consulting the parish register—a course which William Marsh had declared untypical of any but the most bigoted. 'I never met with anyone but a clergyman, and an extreme party man, who really did say, "When I doubt my regeneration, I go to my baptismal register and am satisfied." '[17]

As is made clear in the chapter entitled 'British Formulae', in *Erewhon*,[18] any doctrine that relied on compromise necessarily partook of insincerity for Butler. Owen seceded to join the Baptists, a pattern legitimated by the secession of ultra-Calvinists like J. C. Philpot who believed that the celebration of Baptism was incompatible with his belief in Particular Redemption;[19] but Owen's subsequent swift secession to Rome suggests the more deeply unsettling effect such a revelation had had for Butler himself.

Although Newman the theologian must have been aware of the diversity of Evangelical opinion on the subject, Newman the polemical novelist quickly perceived the advantage to be gained by restricting their spokesmen to voicing the extreme view that the sign of Baptism in no way implied the receipt of grace. Such a devaluation led Freeborn, Newman ensured, to a position where he was forced to admit himself an Anglican in name only.[20]

At the opposite end of the ecclesiastical spectrum Mrs. Worboise's advocacy of the Universal Church led her to ensure that any Anglican Evangelicals granted her approval would share Freeborn's view.[21] Newman's fears are, of course, confirmed when Mrs. Worboise's most favoured characters become Dissenters rather than remain on the horns of a dilemma highlighted by Spurgeon in his most controversial sermon preached in 1864, where he attacked Evangelicals for pleading an interpretation of baptism in the light of the Articles as distinguishing them from the Dissenters, but also, in their internal war with the High Church, propounding theories shared by the Baptists.[22]

Confirmation, the Church's follow-up to Baptism, though an

[17] Marsh, op. cit., p. 289.

[18] *Erewhon*, ch. xviii.

[19] J. H. Philpot, *The Seceders: The Story of J. C. Philpot and William Tiptaft* (1964), pp. 94, 117.

[20] *Loss and Gain*, p. 37.

[21] *Thornycroft Hall*, p. 267; *Overdale*, p. 28; *Heart's Ease in the Family* (1874), pp. 42–44.

[22] C. Ray, *Life of Charles Haddon Spurgeon* (1903), p. 301.

affecting ceremony, was seen by Mrs. Worboise as divisive, both because it was the means of giving effect to the status of Anglican communicant, which served as a barrier to inter-communion,[23] and because preparation for communion was made the excuse for sectarian teaching. Evangelicals had been responsible for the restoration of this service to its rightful dignity but, with the advent of the Oxford Movement, found it increasingly necessary to stress Simeon's teaching that it was not an ordinance of God, nor an apostolic creation, but merely a useful means to ensure that one's flock was adequately prepared to receive Communion.[24]

The practical achievement in this field of Henry Ryder, the first Evangelical bishop, received literary support from Mrs. Sherwood in the form of a work entitled, *The Lady of the Manor: being a series of conversations on the subject of Confirmation intended for the use of the Middle and Higher Ranks of Young Females.*[25] The conversations were to last for seven volumes in all—a fact which helps to explain the misery of George Eliot's Mary Dunn when she finds that it is necessary for her, coming of Evangelical parents, to receive preparation from Mr. Tryan over and above that given to Miss Townley's pupils by Mr. Crewe.[26] Mrs. Worboise contrives to introduce a sectarian note when she makes the learning of the Thirty Nine Articles the heaviest of such preparatory tasks in *Thornycroft Hall.*[27] For the Tractarian, confirmation was a means to Grace, as illustrated by Charlotte Yonge's novel *The Castle Builders: or, the Deferred Confirmation*, where the rite receives almost sacramental significance.[28] In *Chantry House* Miss Yonge spelt out for her readers the nature of the mistake she believed Evangelicals to have made about this ceremony. The young candidates felt themselves incapable of attaining 'the feelings in the Confirmation poem in the *Christian Year*', because 'the evangelical belief that dejection ought to be followed by a full sense of pardon and assurance of salvation somewhat perplexed and dimmed our Easter Communion'.[29] The error

[23] *Thornycroft Hall*, p. 41; *House of Bondage*, ch. xl, which is entitled, 'Why Nora was not confirmed'.

[24] A. W. Brown, *Recollections of Simeon*, p. 239.

[25] Ruskin gave a copy of the fifth edition (1841) to a young friend. M. N. Cutt, *Mrs. Sherwood and Her Books for Children* (1974), p. 122.

[26] *Scenes*, ii, 107.

[27] *Thornycroft Hall*, p. 40.

[28] *Castle Builders* (1854), p. 145.

[29] *Chantry House* (2 vols., 1886), i, 54–5.

of confusing confirmation with conversion is one that Mrs. Worboise's young spokesmen for Evangelical theology would never have made but one, which, given the ardent serious nature of Miss Yonge's children, has a psychological plausibility suggesting a picture rooted in experience.

If the Evangelicals were accused of treating Confirmation merely as an excuse for doctrinal education they were conversely attacked for neglecting their responsibility as catechists. Yet here again early Evangelicals had been responsible for reviving the organized practice of hearing children repeating their catechism to the parson or Sunday School teacher. Charlotte Yonge paid tribute to Hannah More's work in this field in *The Cunning Woman's Grandson.*[30] Mrs. Sherwood produced *Stories Explanatory of the Church Catechism* (1817) and *A Series of Questions and Answers, illustrative of the Church Catechism* (1827). Charlotte Brontë assumes that St. John Rivers will devote an hour each day to catechizing the infants at the village school,[31] or that Mr. Hall will catechize the children during his visits to needy cottagers in his parish[32]—a practice validated for her by her father or his old friend, John Crosse, the blind Vicar of Bradford, whose biography devoted an entire chapter to 'Mr Crosse as a Catechiser'.[33] By the mid-1840s, however, the practice of hearing the catechism at Sunday School had become 'a badge of party', a symbol of Tractarian allegiance, according to the Evangelical Misses Shaw in *The Castle Builders*, who are anxious to attract the children of Dissenters to a Sunday School run by a committee and not under the parson's authority.[34]

The Evangelical change in direction, or emphasis, in their teaching on these services was attributable to their being frightened by the Oxford Movement and its aftermath into becoming Low Churchmen. Their reluctance to allow men to 'put their trust in forms and ordinances' laid them open to the accusation of wilful opposition, arising from jealousy at the effectiveness of Tractarianism, and consequently of treacherous alliance with Dissent.[35]

[30] *The Cunning Woman's Grandson*, p. 82.

[31] *Jane Eyre*, p. 469.

[32] *Shirley*, p. 126.

[33] W. Morgan, *The Parish Priest*, ch. viii. See ibid., p. 8, for Patrick Brontë's intimacy with the author.

[34] *Castle Builders*, pp. 107–11.

[35] See the reaction of the Evangelical Miss Hepburns to their new Tractarian parson in C. M. Yonge, *Pillars of the House*, ii, ch. xxxv.

In their campaign against the Tractarian revival of private confession, the Evangelicals themselves suffered from no divided impulse and were able to gain the support of many Protestants, whom in other contexts they would have referred to as 'nominal Christians'. In 1858 there were two much-publicized prosecutions of curates who were accused of asking improper questions with reference to the seventh commandment.[36] An Evangelical witch-hunt was prompted by the second case, dealing with Alfred Poole, curate of St. Barnabas, Pimlico. Protestant hysteria is captured by Trollope in that passage in *The Last Chronicle of Barset* where Mrs. Proudie immediately assumes that her husband's episcopal advice to Mr. Crawley, 'to make such amends as may come from immediate acknowledgement and confession', will necessarily be seen as an advocacy of 'auricular confession'.[37] The fascinated horror with which the inquisitorial persecution was carried out is reflected in this piece of suggestive writing in the pages of the *Christian Observer*.

It was, then, on a Friday, at four o'clock, in the autumn, when light was dim in London, and in the vestry of St. Barnabas there was almost total darkness, that this young dissolute woman called by appointment, on Mr. Poole. She called on him at the Parsonage; she was taken into the vestry. The vestry, which looks into a gloomy court, is even in sunlight obscure; at such a season and such an hour, it was nearly dark. It is, however, as Mr. Poole naïvely says, *the place where confessions are wont to be made*. The door was locked, or, as Mr. Poole puts it, was secured, and then proceeded the ceremonial.[38]

The chance of combining doctrinal instruction with the sensational possibilities involved in examining priestly practices was not one to be missed by Mrs. Worboise. In *Overdale; or the Story of a Pervert*, in which she undertook to dramatize the disintegration of family life, a wife dies estranged from her clerical husband, whose confidence in his confessor has led him, and one of his sons, into a Jesuit seminary, whilst his eldest daughter is immured in a French nunnery. We are assured in the concluding chapter that 'the same story is being told daily in every county of England'[39] but we cannot escape the feeling that the novelist has seen it as her duty to

[36] *The Times* (27 Sept. 1858), p. 8, commenting on the case involving West, the curate of Boyn Hill, near Maidenhead, who was finally acquitted, reflects the strength of popular anti-Papist feeling.

[37] *Last Chronicle of Barset*, i, 111–13.

[38] *CO* (1859), 245–55.

[39] *Overdale*, p. 496.

'heighten' these true experiences that she describes. Since she is anxious to stress the tragedy which engulfs the innocent who are brought to believe in confession, the broad hints of the depravity of the confessional liaison, open to the *Christian Observer's* reporter, are not available to her. The essential innocence of a foolish girl who agrees to meet her confessor late at night in church can only be preserved by endangering the reader's purity of mind. We are told that when her confessor, a Jesuit in disguise,[40] demands the details of a proposal for marriage that she has just received, '. . . he asked her questions which no mother would have asked—strange questions, of which she could not clearly see the import, but which drove the blood from her heart, and coloured her cheeks with burning blushes . . .'[41]

The exercise of the imagination, often regarded as a dangerous habit, seems to receive encouragement when it involves calculating the enormities committed by one's enemies.

If the Evangelicals accused the Tractarians of reviving parts of the Liturgy whose administration the Anglican Church had, in its wisdom, allowed to lapse, they were in turn upbraided for undermining the entire Anglican Liturgy by the emphasis they placed on more spontaneous forms of expression. Simeon had been anxious to clear his colleagues from this charge. When appointed, in 1811, as preacher for the University of Cambridge, he chose to deliver a course of sermons at St. Mary's entitled, 'The Excellency of the Liturgy',[42] and on another occasion told his undergraduate audience that 'The finest sight short of heaven would be a whole congregation using the prayers of the Liturgy in the true spirit of them.'[43] Yet in their anxiety to replace dead forms with meaningful acts of devotion and instruction many Evangelicals were replacing the regular daily reading of services with 'services' of their own composition.[44] The

[40] The reader is helped to penetrate this disguise with the standard test applied by Victorian novelists to crypto-Jesuits. Herbert Vallance, the confessor, cannot look his interlocutors straight in the eye. Cf. M. O. W. Oliphant, *Perpetual Curate*, ii, 317–8; iii, 111, where Gerald Wentworth displays the same inability once he has decided to leave his wife and family and secede to Rome. A fiercely anti-Catholic book of the day provides a possible explanation. W. Hogan, *Auricular Confession and Popish Nunneries*, 3rd edn. (Liverpool, 1847), p. 97, cites the Institutum Soc. Jes. ii, 114 ed. Prag., in folio, where, he asserts, the Jesuits are instructed to look lower than the person they address at all times.

[41] *Overdale*, pp. 378–9.

[42] W. Carus, *Memoirs of the Life of Charles Simeon*, p. 293.

[43] A. W. Brown, *Recollections of Simeon*, p. 221.

[44] C. Smyth, *Simeon and Church Order* (Cambridge, 1940), p. 229.

Revd. W. F. Wilkinson's fictional Rector defends the holding of an evening lecture in the school-room thus: ' "I think", said the Rector, "that it is desirable for a minister of the Church of England to maintain a lecture of this description, as a kind of testimony against formalism—a witness that he does not deem forms essential to worship, or absolutely necessary." '[45]

Mrs. Trollope, brought up in the old school of orthodoxy, is likely to have encountered this type of attitude at Harrow, where Wilkinson served as a curate. In *The Vicar of Wrexhill*, Freeman, the significantly named landlord of the local inn, and his 'God-fearing' family refuse to attend the Evangelical parson's Tuesday evening expositions and his Thursday and Sunday evening lectures on the grounds that these are not in the ordinances of the Anglican Liturgy.[46] The local schoolmaster is however financially dependent upon the parson and, despite his scrupulous Church attendance, prayer and Bible reading with his pupils, is virtually excommunicated by the parson for refusing to allow his boys to attend the evening lectures.[47] The schoolmaster not only objects to unwarranted additions to the Liturgy, but voices a second objection to the evening gatherings: '. . . these late meetings, which break up quite in the dark, do bring together a great disorderly people. 'Tis an excuse, sir, for every boy and girl that is in service to get out just when they ought to be at home, and altogether it is not quite the sort of thing I approve for my boys.'[48]

Although this type of accusation is clearly related to the tradition, stemming from the early days of the church,[49] of portraying minority religious groups as clandestine orgiasts, Mrs. Trollope had personal experience of Methodist meetings being used by servants as a pretext for illicit rendezvous. Yet from her account of the notorious Nancy Fletcher, whom she temporarily employed as a domestic servant in Cincinnati, it would appear that she made little effort to dissociate the hypocritical excuse of attendance at a

[45] *Rector in Search of a Curate*, p. 48.

[46] *Vicar of Wrexhill*, ii, 322.

[47] Ibid. iii, 67–73.

[48] Ibid. iii, 68.

[49] See A. N. Sherwin-White, 'Why were the Early Christians Persecuted?—An Amendment', *PP*, No. 27 (Apr. 1964). An interesting nineteenth-century example of this desire to stigmatize the unfamiliar religious sect in a universally comprehensible manner occurs in Dickens's *American Notes*, p. 218, where he says of the celibate Shakers, '. . . let them for me, stand openly revealed among the ribald and licentious; the very idiots know that *they* are not on the Immortal road, and will despise them and avoid them readily'.

Methodist meeting from the hint that Methodists actually countenanced prostitution at their evening meetings.[50]

So widespread did this practice of holding week-day lectures become that attendance at them became for the novelist a readily recognizable hallmark of Evangelicalism.[51] In his novels Trollope contrives not only to use the practice as a symbol of Evangelical allegiance, but also to make the manner of its observance a mode of differentiating the earnest and sincere Evangelical from those loud in their protestations but lax in conduct.[52] In *Miss Mackenzie* Mr. Stumfold's respect for his wealthier clientele has led him to convert the parish evening lecture into a social event open by formal invitation only. This type of entertainment, *Tinsley's Magazine* informed its readers, 'is designated by the polite as an "evangelical drawing room", and by the more profane as a "talkee-talkee" '.[53]

If amongst the middle classes evangelicalism became increasingly secular in its practice, the mid-century census on attendance at a place of religious worship reminded Evangelicals that amongst the working classes it was scarcely practised at all. New methods and forms were needed, and so, with episcopal support, they turned to open-air preaching and then to mission services, at first in the Exeter Hall and then in more secular buildings, where the poor, whom they were trying to attract, would not feel debarred from entrance by social discrimination. This 'phase of what might be called the New Evangelical Movement',[54] received little attention from novelists. Sir Henry Cunningham made passing reference to Evangelical optimism on this front.[55] Charlotte Yonge takes a side swipe at open air preaching in her picture of the Ranter, who later turns out to be an 'offshoot of a great revival which the Plymouth Brethren were organising'.[56] His activities embarrass the Evangelicals of the village in *Pillars of the House* and thus lend evidential

[50] *Domestic Manners of the Americans*, i, 77–81. Cf. T. A. Trollope, *What I Remember*, i, 93, where Mrs. Trollope's inclination to discredit religious teaching of which she disapproved, in a manner not dissimilar from Dickens, is revealed in an anecdote related by her son.

[51] e.g. C. Dickens, *Bleak House*, p. 15; G. Eliot, *Scenes*, ii, 167; H. Mozley, *The Fairy Bower*, pp. 128–9; F. Trollope, *Uncle Walter*, iii, 129; A. Trollope, *The Belton Estate*, p. 88; E. J. Worboise, *Thornycroft Hall*, p. 13.

[52] *The Bertrams*, ii, 243; *Last Chronicle of Barset*, i, 172; *Miss Mackenzie*, ch. iv.

[53] 'Evangelical Drawing-Rooms', *Tinsley's Magazine*, 9 (1871–2), p. 111.

[54] E. Stock, *History of the Church Missionary Society*, ii, 30.

[55] *Wheat and Tares*, p. 254.

[56] *Pillars of the House*, ii, 580.

support to the old High Church arguments, used by Miss Yonge, that such a manifestation of the Evangelical impulse demonstrates the dangers of sympathy and co-operation with Dissent. Dickens devoted an article to the theatre services, puncturing the illusion that they were reaching the working classes for whom they were intended, and criticizing the preacher who patronized his audience.[57] In the decade or so following Dickens's article, some of the Anglican Evangelicals had become aware of the truth of the High Church premonitions of danger and the validity of Dickens's portrait of the histrionics of popular preachers.[58]

If this aspect of the renewed interest in spiritual life and in mission received little attention from the novelists the so-called 'Second Evangelical Awakening' received even less. This comparative absence of comment is interesting, both because of the light it throws upon historical speculation and from what it tells us of the province of the novel. J. Edwin Orr, whose research is chiefly responsible for the creation of the concept of a coherent revival movement,[59] seems to have confused the use of new techniques of mass evangelism, such as theatre services, with the spread of the 'revival' emanating from the United States and reaching Britain through Ireland.[60] His reliance upon a paper entitled *The Revival*, which was produced with the sole aim of fostering the belief that a Revival of mammoth proportions and vast interdenominational scope was taking place, led him to elevate sporadic outbursts of spiritual fervour in a Dorsetshire village or a Liverpool penitentiary into a movement comparable with that immense growth of popular religion amongst the lower and upper classes in the latter portion of the eighteenth century. The very few references which occur in the novels[61] suggest a movement primarily inspired and effected by Dissenters, confirming the impression gained from Evangelical pamphlets and newspapers that the Anglican Evangelical clergy held back from a movement which they felt to be tainted with

[57] *All the Year Round*, 2 (25 Feb. 1860), 416–21. Later republished under the title 'Two views of a Cheap Theatre', in the series 'The Uncommercial Traveller', for which it had been written.

[58] E. Hodder, *Life of Shaftesbury*, iii, 354.

[59] *The Second Evangelical Awakening in Britain.*

[60] The involvement of the Evangelical Alliance, which had strong links with America, in both movements does serve to complicate the issue.

[61] H. Cunningham, *Wheat and Tares*, p. 119 which refers to the revival in Dumfriesshire, and Mrs. Humphry Ward, *David Grieve* (3 vols., 1892), i, chs. ix and x, which again refers to revivalism in Scotland.

Methodist 'enthusiasm'.[62] For the novelists to have depicted Evangelicals as hysterical 'irregular' preachers, would, however convenient for the unsympathetic novelist, have been palpably untrue. The picture provided by Trollope and his contemporaries supports Eugene Stock's contention[63] that the clergy were too involved in the bitter controversies with 'Rationalism, Ritualism, and Radicalism' to devote time to harvesting the fruits of any revival in the late 1850s.

The only novel which captures the flavour of this period of spiritual excitement was written thirty years later. It is likely that the picture of Mr. Clare of Emminster and the temporary conversion he wrought in Alec d'Urberville, Alec's subsequent itinerant preaching as a Methodist and the employment, by Alec and his co-evangelists, of the text-painter, reflect Hardy's memories of one of the centres of this sporadic revival, Fordington, a village on the outskirts of Dorchester. The Revd. Henry Moule, Vicar of Fordington, and his family were close friends of Hardy throughout his life. Hardy and his mother[64] had attended Moule's services and, on Henry Moule's death, Hardy wrote to one of his sons, Handley Carr Glynn Moule, Bishop of Durham, to say that he had always regarded himself as Moule's parishioner.[65] The impact that Moule had made on him is conveyed in his report of a lengthy discussion he had had with Matthew Arnold in which Arnold had produced a fitting tribute for the dead man. 'His words "energy is genius" express your father very happily',[66] Hardy wrote to the bereaved family. The Revd. Henry Moule, together with at least two of his sons,[67] was an Evangelical of the old school, of Calvinist persuasion[68]

[62] See *CO* (1859), pp. 725–31; and below, p. 267.

[63] *History of the Church Missionary Society*, ii, 336–8.

[64] H. C. G. Moule, *Memories of a Vicarage*, p. 56.

[65] 'Though not, topographically, a parishioner of your father's I virtually stood in that relation to him, and his home generally, during many years of my life, and I always feel precisely as if I had been one' (11 Feb. 1880). F. E. Hardy, *The Early Life of Thomas Hardy 1840–91* (1928), p. 176.

[66] Loc. cit.

[67] Handley Carr Glynn Moule and Henry Moule, on whose death Hardy wrote, 'I have just lost an old friend down here, of forty-seven years' standing. A man whose opinions differed almost entirely from my own on most subjects, and yet he was a good and sincere friend—the brother of the present Bishop of Durham, and like him in old-fashioned views of the Evangelical school.' F. E. Hardy, *The Later Years of Thomas Hardy 1892–1928* (1930), p. 105.

[68] See H. Moule, *'Hope against Hope' illustrated in the case of the convict Edwin Preedy who was hanged for murder at Dorchester, March 27, 1863* (1863), p. 17, where he expresses his conviction that a man can be totally reprobate.

like Angel Clare's father, and Hardy, like Angel Clare, continued to admire his practical, unselfish exertions for his parishioners. The second generation of the Clare family bear certain resemblances, in occupation, if not in character, to the Moules. One of the Moule brothers, George Evans Moule, curate to his father during Hardy's adolescent years,[69] became a missionary. Two of the younger brothers also became clergymen.[70] Hardy was perhaps closest to the two classicists of the family, Horace and Charles Moule. With Horace Moule he was in the habit of walking in the fields around Dorchester discussing his Greek studies and recently published theological works such as *Essays and Reviews*,[71] rather as the Clare brothers discussed *A Counterblast to Agnosticism* on their walking tour.[72] Charles, like Cuthbert Clare,[73] was a Fellow of Corpus Christi College, Cambridge, and later President of the same college, and continued to enjoy visits from and walks with Hardy to the end of his life.[74] Hardy himself said that Angel Clare was partly drawn from Charles Moule,[75] though perhaps he might have included himself as another progenitor. Angel, like Hardy, rejected the idea of Holy Orders,[76] accepted the necessity of another career when a University education seemed impossible—and yet, throughout the subsequent changes of philosophy, still admired and respected the all-embracing love of the older Clares, combined though it was with a narrow dogmatism which he found personally unsatisfying.

As a picture of the revivalism of this period the account of Mr. Clare's earnest preaching for missionary societies,[77] taking the regular opportunities of occupying another's pulpit rather than

[69] 1851–7, *DNB*. Angel's sister has married a missionary. *Tess of the D'Urbervilles*, p. 202.

[70] As we know from the title page of the issue of funeral sermons preached on the Revd. H. Moule's death. The first makes reference to his temperance beliefs *Doctrine, Manner of Life, Purpose: Sermons on the occasion of the death of the Rev. Henry Moule by three of his sons*, p. 9. He had practised temperance at a stage when this was unusual amongst Calvinist Evangelicals—and this may explain the rather forced passage in *Tess* where Angel has to be reminded by his father that 'we never drink spirits at this table, on principle.' *Tess*, p. 207.

[71] F. E. Hardy, *The Early Life of Thomas Hardy*, p. 43. Horace, who committed suicide, was apparently one of those alluded to in Hardy's poem 'The Five Students'. *The Later Years of Thomas Hardy*, p. 212.

[72] *Tess*, p. 15.

[73] Ibid., p. 202.

[74] F. E. Hardy, *The Early Life*, p. 160; *The Later Years*, p. 159, describes him as 'the oldest friend of Hardy's in Cambridge, or for that matter anywhere'.

[75] F. B. Pinion, *A Guide to the works of Thomas Hardy and their Background* (1968), p. 281.

[76] F. E. Hardy, *The Later Years*, p. 176.

[77] *Tess*, pp. 102, 393.

organising revivalist meetings, confirms H. C. G. Moule's assertion of the spontaneity of the awakening. 'No artificial means of excitement were dreamt of; my Father's whole genius was against it. No powerful personality, no Moody or Aitken, came to us.'[78]

Hardy credits Mr. Clare with an integrity of purpose and sufficient intelligence both to recognize his limited instrumentality and to accept that not all his spiritual ducklings will turn out to be swans.[79] The text painter and Alec d'Urberville are interesting studies of revivalist converts, usually more dogmatic and intolerant than their teachers, and inclined to schism. Hardy's picture of this movement is a refreshing change from early pictures of the revivalist spirit, in that he invests the originator with a dignity and integrity lacking from the framework of a Mrs. Trollope or a Dickens, but this springs from a combination of personal respect and the implicit assumption that it is safe to pay respect to a set of beliefs and practices which are now outdated. The 'old-style' Evangelicalism attracts none of the Clare sons, nor for that matter the converts—a curious piece of wish-fulfilment on Hardy's part, given his awareness of the unchanged allegiance of those Moules who were his contemporaries.

With Alec and his conversion testimony we return nearer to the world of Dickens or Mrs. Trollope,[80] where sexual excitement is never far away from displays of abnormal religious fervour. Yet Hardy's diagnosis induces a sense of pathos in the reader rather than the prurient laughter evoked by the other two authors. By means of Tess's recollection of the teaching of Christian history that 'the greater the sinner the greater the saint',[81] Hardy removes himself from the general smear campaign tactics usually employed. Even in Alec's case, though this phase in his career only represents a sublimation of his driving physical lust, he turns to revivalist theology, not as a means of prosecuting his desires, but as a way of conquering his animal instincts.

Contemporary attacks on the hysterical symptoms accompanying the revival and the short-lived nature of the conversions were confined to magazine articles rather than appearing in the novel. John Chapman devoted a lengthy review,[82] wrongly attributed by

[78] *Memories of a Vicarage*, p. 49. [79] *Tess*, p. 213.

[80] See particularly Mrs. Trollope's account of a Camp Meeting in Indiana, *Domestic Manners of the Americans*, i, ch. xv. [81] *Tess*, p. 390.

[82] [J. Chapman], 'Christian Revivals', *WR*, N.S. 17 (1860), 167–217.

many at the time to George Eliot's hand,[83] to a fairly balanced account of the history and phenomenology of revivals. *Once a Week*[84] and *All the Year Round*[85] confined themselves to inveighing against the revival as it had so far manifested itself in the United States and Ireland but shared the antagonistic attitudes displayed in this attack on British manifestations of the movement by the *Saturday Review*: 'We only want devotees to cut themselves with knives and lancets, and to fling themselves under the wheels of Lord Shaftesbury's carriage, while the Traviatas of the midnight meetings will be quite ready to revive the worship of Ashtoreth or Baal-peor at a moment's notice.'[86]

Nor did the advent of Moody and Sankey and their big business organization, fifteen years later, stir the novelists to take up the subject.[87] The possible reasons for the novelists' reticence are various. Some novelists were deprived of the forum for comment which the novel might have provided by the way in which they set their novels back in time. Dickens and Mrs. Trollope may well have been thought to have worked dry the vein of satirical humour at the expense of the disturbed equilibrium of ranting preachers. Amongst the less sympathetic novelists there may have been a dislike of giving publicity, however unfavourable, to a phenomenon which, if neglected, might die a natural death, especially as these outbursts accorded ill with the usual picture of Evangelicalism brought to its death throes by the spiritual laxity of its worldly exponents. Finally the flavour of the social novel with its domestic concerns was at odds with the technique and material needed to paint mass meetings. It was only by reintroducing the picaresque novel form that Sinclair Lewis was able to depict the character and fortunes of the revivalist preacher, Elmer Gantry, and to give us a glimpse of revivalist meetings.[88]

[83] G. S. Haight, *George Eliot and John Chapman*, p. 223.

[84] *Once a Week*, 1 (15 Oct. 1859), 312–13.

[85] 'Hysteria and Devotion', *All the Year Round*, 2 (5 Nov. 1859), 31–5.

[86] Quoted by M. M. Bevington, *The Saturday Review, 1855–1868*, pp. 87–8.

[87] Although again periodicals devoted space to the movement. *Punch* in particular printed a long comic poem one week and an apology the next. *Punch*, 68 (1875), 123, 139.

[88] For the considerable research which went into Lewis's picture of American Revivalism see M. Schorer, *Sinclair Lewis: An American Life* (1961), pp. 448–51, 460. See also Lewis's attempt to portray the mid-nineteenth-century revivalist Charles Grandison Finney in a poor late historical novel, *The God-Seeker* (1949). Comparison with Finney's posthumously published autobiography, which Lewis clearly used, reveals how the novelist consciously cheapened the original with hints of vulgar theatricality.

Evangelicals could be distinguished from their fellow Anglicans not only by the services they encouraged or disapproved of but by the manner in which they conducted their worship. In the Evangelical emphasis upon the sermon, critics claimed, could be seen precisely that undervaluing of the Liturgy, that tendency to set vital preaching above the Sacrament without the word of God, which had led to the schismatic tendencies of Methodism. The Oxford Movement's endeavour to replace the Sacraments at the centre of the Church's worship jolted some Evangelicals and their sons into an awareness that they had 'attached a somewhat excessive importance to this part of the service'. Many Evangelicals continued, like Sir Henry Cunningham's Mrs. Ashe, to ask first of a new minister, 'And [is he] a good preacher?'[89]

'The preacher may be praised', but only at the expense of the impersonal tradition of the Liturgy was the burden of Thackeray's 'wild onslaught upon sermons and preachers' in the *Irish Sketch-book*. The strength of feeling displayed here could easily lead one to attribute the words to a clergyman at the centre of liturgical debate and serves to acquaint us with the genuine concern for the decency and formality of the Anglican tradition, as much as the sheer facility for verbal parody, that lay behind the vicious attacks on extempore preaching in the work of Thackeray, Mrs. Trollope, or her son Anthony.

> And it need not be said here, that a church is not a sermon-house—that it is devoted to a purpose much more lofty and sacred, for which has been set apart the noblest service, every single word of the latter has previously been weighed with the most scrupulous and thoughtful reverence.
>
> And after this sublime work of genius, learning, and piety is concluded, is it not a shame that a man should mount a desk, who has not taken the trouble to arrange his words beforehand. . .?
>
> And it comes to this,—it is the preacher the people follow, not the prayers; or why is this church more frequented than any other?[90]

In *The Newcomes* Thackeray returned to the attack with a portrait of the Revd. Charles Honeyman, whose 'ideal of clerical usefulness', like a certain class of Evangelical ministers described by Conybeare,

[89] H. Cunningham, *Wheat and Tares*, p. 85. See also W. Morgan, *The Parish Priest*, p. 4. n. 'When the word of the Lord was *scarce*, it was highly *esteemed*, I do not know but that we make *preaching* now too common, and neglect *praying*, *reading*, and *meditation* in secret.'

[90] *Irish Sketchbook*, pp. 264–5.

was the 'possession of a chapel in a large town, which he may fill with his own disciples'[91] and where his duties were confined to preaching to an uncritical and adoring audience. Thackeray's suggestion that such power without responsibility soon led to a dilution of the doctrine and the growth of the cult of the individual minister receives some corroboration from the career of the most popular of early nineteenth-century preachers, Edward Irving.

Yet those ministers who remained faithful to the Evangelical message were not beyond criticism. Its very theological simplicity and its insistence upon preaching 'Jesus Christ and Him crucified' led to a certain meagreness of content. Even the most devoted of biographers was forced to recognize this limitation. Recalling John Crosse's preaching, William Morgan wrote, 'Though he might appear to some fastidious hearers to have a sameness in his sermons, yet the oftener any one heard him, the more he was liked and revered.'[92]

Simeon had done his best to remedy the situation with his publication of *Horae Homileticae* in 21 volumes, containing 2,536 sermon outlines. These 'dry and marrowless "Skeletons" ', as J. C. Philpot described them, continued to provide 'patent crutches' for many clergy well into the second half of the century.[93]

The anxiety to concentrate upon the one thing needful gave rise to a periphrastic style which sought variety in the manner of presentation rather than from the development of the subject. From the artistic point of view, peculiarities of phrase and intonation are particularly useful to the novelist for the purpose of differentiating one man, or one group, from another, and it was at this point that Evangelical ministers became susceptible to attack. As Mrs. Worboise noted through her mouthpiece, Nora:

'. . . preaching is not of much account among the Ritualists; the service—or performance, rather—is everything. And really for a man who is in orders, and can't preach, or won't take the trouble to preach, the High Church is a harbour of refuge. . . . Now the Evangelicals, though their

[91] *Edin. Rev.* 98 (1853), 293; *Perversion*, i, 349–51. The *Record's* advertisement column offers some corroboration, e.g. 'COLLEAGUE WANTED early. Graduate, and single preferred, Evangelical, Spiritually-minded (Rom. i. 16). Evening communion. Pleasant sphere. Few poor. Lay Helper kept. Stipend 160*l.* Address Rev. C. Bradshaw Foy, St. Mary's Vicarage, 54 Brook Green, West Kensington S.W.' (8 Jan. 1904), p. 33.

[92] *The Parish Priest*, p. 67.

[93] J. H. Philpot, *The Seceders*, p. 195; [S. L. Breakey], 'A Few Words about Sermons', *Cornhill Magazine*, 3 (1861), 551.

discourses are chiefly what N. P. Willis calls "inspiration and water", must get up a sort of eloquence. . . .'[94]

Novelists, by virtue of the trade in words they themselves plied, were acutely sensitive to the obscurities of metaphor and grammar, the rhetorical redundancies, the vacuity of their professional ecclesiastical colleagues and were frequently prone to label it all as 'cant'. Once an author like Dickens had learnt to secularize the content of the preacher's address, so as to minimize the offence offered to his readers,[95] he had found an amusing field for satire, in which he could make full use of his mimic abilities.[96] Perhaps the novelists themselves were the ultimate beneficiaries of the Evangelical devotion to the homiletic tradition. A generation accustomed to listening to, buying, reading, or having read to them, the lengthy discourses so frequently published by ministers more or less eminent, made a sympathetic market for the prolix style and content of the three-decker novel.

If lengthy sermons were felt to be one characteristic of Evangelical services, fervent hymn-singing was also recognized as a specifically Evangelical practice during the first half of the nineteenth century: so much so that on the publication of *The Christian Year* Hurrell Froude remarked, 'People will take Keble for a Methodist.'[97]

Hymn-singing was felt to have a dissenting origin. Indeed John Venn openly declared that by introducing the practice at Clapham he had hit upon a plan to snatch the wind from the sails of the Dissenters and increase his own congregation at their expense:

I attribute it . . . in part to the improved state of our singing which has been the means of keeping many from the meetings who were allured to go by the excellence of the music. . . I am persuaded that the singing has been a great instrument in the Dissenters' hands of drawing away persons from the church, and why should not we take that instrument out of their hands?[98]

[94] *House of Bondage*, p. 515.

[95] E. Wagenknecht, *Harriet Beecher Stowe: The Known and The Unknown* (New York, 1965), p. 150.

[96] Dickens's contention that 'it must be within everybody's experience that the Chadband style of oratory is widely received and much admired' (*Bleak House*, p. 264) received confirmation in independent witness to the peculiar pronunciation and style employed by leading Evangelical clergy. *CO* (1865), p. 393; and C. M. Davies, *Orthodox London*, p. 170.

[97] *The Autobiography of Isaac Williams*, ed. G. Prevost (1892), p. 22.

[98] M. Hennell, *John Venn and the Clapham Sect*, p. 267.

Dr. Isaac Watts had after all been a Nonconformist and John Wesley's popular hymns were 'in effect, a little body of experimental and practical divinity'. The dogmatic nature of Wesleyan hymns often rendered some alteration necessary before moderate Calvinists could sing them whole-heartedly—a practice which Wesley referred to disapprovingly.[99] Orthodox churchmen still felt that, even after emendations, too little effort had been made to accommodate these new hymns to the framework of the Church's calendar.[100] As the spokesman for orthodoxy in the 1830s says, in Charlotte Yonge's *Chantry House*, 'We thought everything but the New and Old Versions smacked of dissent, except the hymns at the end of the Prayer-Book . . .'[101] The advent of the Oxford Movement finally rectified this and challenged Evangelical leadership in the field. Evangelicals saw the polished translations which began to be made from the Roman and Paris breviaries in the 1840s as integrally linked with the Tractarian ethos. The doctrinal warfare that was waged over the hymn-book is suggested in *Pillars of the House* where the Evangelical schoolteachers complain that the Tractarian parson took from the children 'that precious hymn:

> Till to Redemption's work you cling,
> By a simple faith,
> "Doing" is a deadly thing,
> "Doing" ends in death.'

Charlotte Yonge's own involvement in this battle is indicated by her footnote to the word 'Redemption', 'The real word is too sacred for quotation.'[102]

Evangelical families quickly saw the educational value inherent in getting children to learn the hymns by heart. Three generations of the Bickersteth family pursued the habit, adopted from the Clapham Sect, of repeating favourite hymns on Sunday night.[103] The domestic scene has been vividly imprinted on our minds by Samuel Butler's

[99] J. Wesley, *A Collection of Hymns for the Use of the People called Methodists*, 3rd edn. (1782), pp. iv, vi.

[100] An early attempt had been made to remedy this deficiency by Reginald Heber, who published a series of hymns for use at festivals, the first four of which were published under the signature D. R. (the last letters of his Christian and surname) in *CO* (1811), pp. 630–1.

[101] *Chantry House*, ii, 123.

[102] *Pillars of the House*, ii, 351.

[103] M. C. Bickersteth, *Life of the Right Rev. Robert Bickersteth*, p. 129.

picture of Theobald concentrating on pronunciation rather than dogma.[104]

George Eliot's authorial reminiscences in Shepperton Church[105] show how, with the disappearance of the set piece anthems, so much disapproved of by Wesley as excluding most of the congregation, and the replacement of Sternhold and Hopkins (1562) or Tate and Brady's metrical versions of the psalms (1696) by hymn-books, went the dominance of the church gallery minstrels over the musical part of the service. Yet the Evangelicals recognized music as at best a handmaid to worship and at worst a snare. Henry Venn Elliott, himself a hymn-writer and brother of Charlotte Elliott, one of the most renowned of Evangelical hymnodists, saw the Revival hymns of the 1860s, with their repetitious versification and popular music, as an indication of the misdirected emphasis of the movement: 'I cannot think', he said, '. . . that souls get to heaven by exciting or marching music'.[106]

The words rather than the quality of the music were important to Evangelicals but the Oxford Movement served to awaken a generation, including names such as Sir Henry Cunningham, Charlotte Brontë and Mrs. Worboise, to the possible aesthetic pleasures to be found in the hymn-singing practice of their Evangelical youth.[107]

Though the Evangelicals slowly reconciled themselves to the need for improvement in musical standards,[108] chanting proved unacceptable to them. Mr. Slope's sermon in *Barchester Towers*, in which he alluded 'with heavy denunciations to the practice of intoning in parish churches' because 'the meaning of the words was lost when they were produced with all the meretricious charms of melody',[109] captures the thread of this argument.

Slope was caught on the horns of a dilemma which became an increasing embarrassment to the Evangelicals. Had he preached against chanting in cathedral services he would 'have overshot his mark' by criticizing an old Anglican tradition, but he was anxious to fire warning shots in a popular battle against the enemy of Ritualism, which did not as yet exist in Barchester. In their conviction that 'Ritualism is the Colorado beetle of ecclesiasticism—you cannot

[104] *Way of All Flesh*, pp. 95–6. [105] *Scenes*, i, ch. i.
[106] J. Bateman. *Life of the Rev. Henry Venn Elliott*, p. 248.
[107] H. Cunningham, *Wheat and Tares*, p. 8; Charlotte Brontë, *Shirley*, p. 131; E. J. Worboise, *House of Bondage*, p. 122.
[108] *CO* (1860), 417–27. [109] *Barchester Towers*, p. 46.

keep it out',[110] Shaftesbury and those Evangelicals who gained for the Church Association the reputation of a 'persecution society' came to employ methods more appropriate to the treatment of vermin than to brothers in Christ. In this way they alienated their natural supporters, the old orthodox High Churchmen, and taught men initially only interested in improving the decency of worship to see themselves as martyrs to a doctrinal cause. Mrs. Oliphant's *Perpetual Curate* provides a particularly perceptive account of the process. Frank Wentworth, the curate referred to in the title, receives an unheralded visit from three Evangelical aunts at Eastertide. His aunts have in their hands the patronage of an old family living, but feel it important that the next incumbent shall be a Gospel minister. Frank's obstinate integrity forces him to leave the decorations in his chapel untouched, although he is aware that this act of defiant independence will probably lose him the living in their gift. Yet the honesty, which sometimes displayed itself as stubbornness, also caused him to reflect, as he knelt to pray before delivering his sermon on Church ordinances and rubrics, that his martyrdom was self-induced and that perhaps 'surplices and lilies' were scarcely worthy of this stand of principle.[111]

The flavour of churchmanship symbolized by the wearing of a surplice in which to preach the sermon is another of those devices frequently used by the Victorian novelists,[112] the significance of which has become opaque to modern readers. The importance attached by the Evangelicals to a part of the service which was non-sacramental and non-liturgical was illustrated by the removal of the surplice before the sermon, signifying that the preacher did not speak under or with the authority of the Church.[113] In *The Newcomes* Thackeray alludes to the move by Blomfield, Bishop of London, which was to provide fuel for the flames of a fire that raged far beyond the confines of his own diocese. Although he opened his fourth Diocesan Visitation Charge of 1842 with a condemnation of Tract XC he then directed his clergymen to adhere precisely to the Prayer Book's rubrics on ritual, himself providing working definitions of the more contentious.[114] Charles Honeyman who followed

[110] E. Hodder, *Life of Shaftesbury*, iii, 452.
[111] *Perpetual Curate*, i, 56.
[112] e.g. C. Brontë, *Shirley*, p. 2; S. Butler, *Way of All Flesh*, p. 383.
[113] W. W. Berry, *A Few Words in Favour of the Black Gown for Preaching at Morning Service* (1843), pp. 8, 11.
[114] O. Chadwick, *Victorian Church*, i, 214–15.

implicitly the orders of 'the high priest of his diocese' was typical of many a parson who became alienated from his parishioners. Their conservative Protestantism Thackeray illustrated both verbally and pictorially in the image of Mrs. Hobson Newcome who 'shuddered out of the chapel where she had a pew, because the clergyman there, for a very brief season, appeared to preach in a surplice'.[115]

The 'surplice riots' of 1845 and 1849[116] that occurred in the Exeter diocese kept the controversy fresh in the public mind. Although the Evangelicals found themselves hoist with their own petard when in 1871 the Purchas Judgement declared the practice to be in keeping with Anglicanism,[117] the details of these widely publicized[118] court cases lingered long in the lay mind. Compton Mackenzie's choice of Elphinstone as the middle name of a Victorian Evangelical parson in *The Altar Steps* presumably alludes to the name of the plaintiff involved in the case which gave rise to the Purchas Judgement, for his novels frequently display a Butlerian disposition to transpose fact into fiction.

Mackenzie was a schoolboy at a time when 'religion offered a great partisan fight' and became deeply interested in this Indian summer stage of the Ritualist controversy which was partly stirred up by that militant, fanatic Protestant, Kensit. He recalls, in his autobiography, that the Bishop refrained from wearing cope and mitre at his Confirmation service from fear of exacerbating the Ritualist crisis.[119] The whole issue became increasingly vivid for him because he became involved in a live melodrama that reached the national press. He helped in the temporary escape of a schoolboy friend from his Evangelical parents, the Revd. A. R. Cavalier and his wife, who beat their son and called him 'a dirty Rit' when they discovered his involvement with the priests belonging to the Society of the Holy Cross.[120]

The abusive language and grotesque accusations levelled against the Ritualists by those who regarded themselves as educated

[115] *The Newcomes*, p. 56.

[116] These riots bear a marked similarity to the displeasure manifested by the Elizabethan Puritan laity against the wearing of the surplice and square cap by their clergy. P. Collinson, *The Elizabethan Puritan Movement* (1967), pp. 94–5.

[117] See M. C. Bickersteth, *Life of the Right Rev. Bickersteth*, p. 213.

[118] Public greed for details is reflected in the *Rock's* increased circulation which the newspaper attributed to their discovery of the Ritualist Conspiracy. *Rock* (1 Jan. 1875).

[119] *My Life and Times: Octave II, 1891–1900* (1964), pp. 198, 217–9.

[120] *My Life and Times: Octave II, 1891–1900* (1964), pp. 243–6.

gentlemen frequently comes as a shock to the modern reader. It is worth remembering, at this point, that the Evangelicals were supported in their vituperative attacks by Broad Churchmen, anti-Evangelical papers like *Punch*,[121] and even by T. H. Huxley, who expressed the belief that *The Priest in Absolution*, a book published in two parts by the Society of the Holy Cross, must have been the product of a diseased mind.[122] If the secular mind could be so roused it was no wonder that Evangelicals, who saw themselves as the guardians of the Protestant tradition in the Anglican Church, should feel impelled to speak out boldly. Francis Close, who had outdone Kingsley in the insults he had offered to Newman,[123] was not the man to allow the dignity of his office as Dean of Carlisle to cause him to take a back seat in the renewed fight against this new manifestation of disguised Romanism. In a letter of encouragement to the new, militantly Evangelical, paper, the *Rock*, he wrote:

> Don't be afraid of speaking out, Mr. Editor. We cannot too much avoid the scandalous personalities of many of the ritualistic journals, but we must not be mealy-mouthed, we must call things by their right names. . . I believe that the THING called RITUALISM is nothing more nor less than a part of the 'Mystery of Iniquity', of 'the Man of Sin', of 'the Roman Antichrist'. [124]

Mrs. Worboise's *House of Bondage* is a fine example of the Evangelical literary attack on Ritualism. The matter is serious enough for her to drop the mask of impartial narrator and append doctrinal footnotes to the heavily didactic conversations.[125] Remembering her profession as a novelist, she next attempts to dramatize the peculiar horrors of Romanism. The Revd. Charles Pettifer, who has traversed the path from Evangelicalism to Ritualism, has, at his wife's expense, refurnished the rooms attached to his church. His wife, searching for evidence of his supposed marital infidelity, decides to inspect these in a chapter enticingly headed 'What they found in the Den.'[126] In order to reach his den they have to pass through a vestry littered with the discarded symbols of his Evangelical phase, a collection of tracts, and now made gaudy with Ritualist trappings such as illuminated texts. 'I dare say', Mrs.

[121] *Punch*, 59 (1870), pp. 7, 220. [122] *Nineteenth Century*, 2 (1877), p. 337.

[123] After the publication of Tract XC Close remarked 'I would not trust the author of that Tract with my purse.' G. Berwick, 'Close of Cheltenham: Parish Pope—I', *Theology*, 39 (1939), 197. [124] *Rock* (7 Feb. 1868), p. 3.

[125] *House of Bondage*, p. 524. [126] Ibid., ch. xlvi.

Pettifer tartly remarks, 'the Puseyities, like their examplars, the Papists, think a little dirt promotes sanctity.'[127] This patently absurd remark relies for its intended effect on an allusion to a reversal of the proverb concerning cleanliness, on the tawdry gaiety of popular Catholic festivals, and the poverty and filth of the Papal states, a scandal much publicized by English travellers. Pettifer's inner sanctum reveals heights of self-indulgence in its furnishing, repugnant to Evangelical austerity and suggestive of spiritual debauchery. All this prepares us for the chapter entitled, 'Mr. Pettifer spends Christmas in Rome',[128] in which he 'topples over into the cesspit of Rome',[129] the automatic fate of fictional Ritualist moths who hover around the Roman candle. As if still in fear of being considered too 'mealy-mouthed', Mrs. Worboise produces one more tactic from the anti-Ritualist repertoire. A Ritualist curate, one Cyril de Grey, is introduced and undergoes the humiliation of a rejection by the novel's heroine.

'I could not love a man of such inferior capacity as to find pleasure in robes, and candles, and genuflections, and banners, and male millinery, and tinsel generally. And as for your dogmas, they seem to me just intolerable nonsense! You insult me when you ask me to believe that a piece of bread is my God!'[130]

As if the accusation of unmanliness or the doctrinal revulsion were insufficient, Nora, who has been brought up in France, flings one final taunt. She asserts that the Ritualists are only feeble imitators of the Roman Catholics who handle ritual with true mastery. The Victorian regard for honesty as the cardinal virtue nowhere manifests itself more strangely than in the grudging admiration accorded by vehement Evangelicals to Roman Catholic ritual, in comparison with the utter contempt they expressed for the excesses of the Ritualist Judases.

The sheer ornateness, the theatricality, of Ritualist 'performances' was so alien to the Puritan tradition that authors usually unsympathetic to Evangelicalism expressed their disquiet. One recalls Balin bursting into the chapel of King Pellam, where 'he stared about the shrine, / In which he scarce could spy the Christ for

[127] Ibid., p. 447. [128] *House of Bondage*, ch. liv.

[129] Trollope had caught her imagination with his description of Dean Arabin, who had all 'but toppled over into the cesspool of Rome'. *Barchester Towers*, p. 114. She uses it again, this time citing its source, in *Overdale*, p. 132.

[130] *House of Bondage*, pp. 461–2.

Saints'.[131] Not only, Tennyson suggests, has Pellam's obsessive study of Saints' lives and the collecting of relics unfitted him for normal social contact and monarchical rule, but it has paved the way for subversion and the rebellion of the realm against Arthur, that truly Protestant hero. Colonel Newcome, who had revolted against the severities of Evangelicalism in his youth, is nevertheless shocked to detect the resemblance of one of the singers in Charles Honeyman's chapel to a famous professional bass. 'There are some chapels in London', Thackeray reflects, 'where, the function over, one almost expects to see the sextons put brown hollands over the pews and galleries, as they do at the Theatre Royal, Covent Garden.'[132] The advice proffered by Mrs. Worboise, in *Overdale*, was that where the parish church had been commandeered by a Ritualist incumbent, the congregation would be well advised to inform him that they intend to read the weekday prayers and Sunday services at home until they were assured of the return of 'the good old, simple Evangelical Church of England, which teaches and preaches the plain, unmingled Gospel of the Lord Jesus Christ'.[133] The reappearances of 'false prophets' within the Anglican Church, now Ritualists rather than the unenlightened parsons of former days, reinforced the Evangelicals' attachment to the family unit as a medium for the practice of corporate piety and a symbol of their Protestantism.

## 2. *The family and the home*

The idealization of home life in the nineteenth century has been variously attributed to the decrease in infant mortality and the consequent appearance of larger families,[134] the spread of the male's possessive instincts from business to family life[135] or, conversely, the need for a domestic haven where the businessman could retreat from growing economic pressures upon his physical and moral state.[136] Yet none of these observations explains why the home should

[131] A. Tennyson, 'Balin and Balan', *Idylls of the King*, *ll.* 402–3.

[132] *The Newcomes*, p. 150. The same novel exhibits admiration for 'the beautiful parts of the great Mother Church', as seen at St. Peters's, Rome during the Christmas celebrations, p. 466.

[133] *Overdale*, p. 296.

[134] H. V. Routh, *Money, Morals and Manners as Revealed in Modern Literature* (1935), p. 144.

[135] N. Mitchison, *The Home and a Changing Civilization* (1934), pp. 5–6.

[136] H. V. Routh, op. cit., pp. 146–7.

have become the synonym for moral virtue rather than physical comfort. It is perhaps to Evangelicalism that we should look as a decisive factor in that 'silent revolution' in manners and morals to which Thackeray referred in speaking of the gap between the gambling, duelling, swearing buck of George IV's reign and the gentlemen of thirty years later 'so exquisitely polite with ladies in a drawing room'.[137] For in 1784, in George III's reign, Cowper was already presenting as an ideal a picture of domestic bliss and the ritual of family life which we associate with the more liberal Evangelicalism of mid-Victorian times.[138]

In *The Velvet Cushion*, the Revd. J. W. Cunningham clarified the essentially Protestant nature of the attachment to family life, when he wrote, 'Popery is the religion of Cathedrals—Protestantism of houses—Dissenterism of barns.'[139] The last phrase, deleted in later editions, underlines Cunningham's identification of 'Protestantism' with 'Anglicanism', for in Methodist homes ministerial duties often imposed an itinerant life on the head of the family so that home life suffered from the absence of clear paternal direction. Tractarianism teaching men to set a higher value upon the Church as the focal point of the religious community crystallized the Evangelical commitment to the home. The comparative remoteness of the influence of the Church on one of Evangelical upbringing is perversely reflected in Samuel Butler's jotting, 'It is not the church in a village that is the source of the mischief, but the rectory. I would not touch a church from one end of England to the other.'[140]

The family provided the most immediate sphere for the exercise of the sense of accountability for one's fellow mortals: '. . . my father or mother, husband or wife, children or servants', wrote Henry Venn, 'are the very persons, with whom as I have the most to do, so shall I have the most to answer for!'[141] Concern for others could act as a kind of thermometer by which to record one's spiritual temperature, or as Bickersteth expressed it for his wife's edification, 'When we become cool about our own souls, we cease to be anxious about the souls of others.'[142] When manifested positively, this concern was denounced as interference by novelists like Trollope, and, when practised with an eye to the calibrations of one's own

[137] 'George the Fourth', *The Four Georges*, p. 792.
[138] *The Task*, Bk.IV. [139] *Velvet Cushion*, p. 17. [140] *Notebooks*, p. 341.
[141] J. Venn, *The Life and a selection of letters of the late Rev. Henry Venn*, ed. H. Venn (1834), p. 206.
[142] T. R. Birks, *Memoir of the Rev. Edward Bickersteth*, ii, 53.

spiritual temperature, led to the sanctimonious unpleasantness of a Mrs. Clennam or a Christina Pontifex. Even clergymen saw their families as the sphere in which they must prove themselves faithful over little before ministering to the greater needs of the parish. Cunningham's elderly Vicar in the *Velvet Cushion* regarded his parish as a large family but 'felt that his first duties were at home; that this was the little garden which his God expected him, first, to rescue, and fence in from the waste'.[143] The imagery in which Cunningham chose to depict his duties illuminates for us that episode in Trollope's *John Caldigate* where Mrs. Bolton, who has lavished all her possessive love upon her only daughter Hester, feels that the only means to save her daughter's soul is to prevent her from rejoining her possibly bigamous husband. She imprisons Hester in Puritan Grange, literally 'fencing' her in with the aid of the family gardener. Mrs. Bolton had ensured, during Hester's childhood, that the conditions inside the 'garden' had been attractive, even mitigating the 'theological hardness of the literature of the house' so that Wordsworth and Thomson were admitted.[144] Yet when Hester reached maturity her mother 'was so afraid of the world, the flesh, and the devil, that she would fain shut up her child so as to keep her from the reach of all evil'.[145] Trollope then explores the tension which operates between her possessive love and the dogma she embraces—a tension which, given her illogical nature, warps both elements.

The Evangelicals took seriously the first 'cause for which Matrimony was ordained', feeling themselves called upon to preserve this peculiarly Protestant part of their heritage. William Marsh spoke for many, novelists included, when he said, 'God made the family . . . priests made the nunnery.'[146] Robert Bolton had carefully calculated the effects in remarking to his father, 'Give a girl good looks, and good sense, and good health, and she is sure to wish to be some man's wife,—unless she be deterred by some conventual superstition.'[147]

Even more perverse than a conventual desire was the inclination toward celibacy. Not only might the celibate state make it more easy for a clergyman to secede to Roman Catholicism but it unfitted him for pastoral duties. The rumours set afloat by the Evangelical Miss Hepburns in Charlotte Yonge's *The Pillars of the House* indicate the mixture of fears which led to the distrust of celibacy.

[143] *Velvet Cushion*, p. 177. [144] *John Caldigate*, p. 428. [145] Ibid., p. 172.
[146] *Life of William Marsh*, p. 498. [147] *John Caldigate*, p. 171.

The natural antipathy these ladies feel for a new clergyman who takes from them their exclusive supervision of the Sunday school is reinforced by his Tractarian principles, his celibate state and his association with a group of young curates in London, whose appearance on the pastoral scene, to help Clement with his duties, is taken to herald the formation of a monastery.[148]

Newman's establishment at Littlemore had probably intensified the fear that celibacy would lead to the monastic rule. Newman's personal predilection for the celibate state is perhaps most fully voiced in *Loss and Gain*. In the second part of the book two chapters are devoted to a discussion between the hero Charles Reding and his friend Carlton on the expediency and possible spiritual superiority of the celibate state,[149] a point more logically dealt with in the first section of the Appendix to the *Apologia*. Reding notices that his friends and family are upset by any reference to celibacy,[150] but it is seen as being most specifically at odds with Evangelical theory and practice when Carlton jokingly alludes to the premature nature of Reding's worries. ' "Not a very practical difficulty to you at the moment", said Carlton; "no one is asking you to go about on Coelebs' mission just now, with Aristotle in hand and the class-list in view." '[151]

In her novel *Coelebs in Search of a Wife* Hannah More had epitomized the ideal Evangelical marriage. It is understood by the hero himself that it is his duty to seek out a partner for life and in his travels he is given ample opportunity to contemplate the best manner in which to fulfil the duty of raising a family. The principle of Evangelical selection of a wife is outlined by the authoress in the Preface: 'Love itself appears in these pages, not as an ungovernable impulse, but as a sentiment arising out of qualities calculated to inspire attachment in persons under the dominion of reason and religion; brought together by the ordinary course of occurrences, in a private family party.'[152]

Lest romantic impulses should get the better of Coelebs his

[148] *Pillars of the House*, ii, chs. xxxv and xxxvii.

[149] *Loss and Gain*, Pt. II, chs. iv, v.

[150] Cf. H. Mozley, *The Lost Brooch*, ii, 29–30, where Newman's own sister expresses the view that it is wrong for a young man to talk of his desire for celibacy. This brief and condemnatory comment clearly had its impact on young readers. Charlotte Yonge recorded a discussion of this passage she and her young friends at Ottery held. C. Coleridge, *Charlotte Mary Yonge: Her Life and Letters* (1903), p. 375.

[151] *Loss and Gain*, pp. 193–4.

[152] *Coelebs*, p. vii.

mother reminds him, 'Remember that the fairest creature is a fallen creature.' [153]Actually Hannah More does herself an injustice in suggesting that Coelebs and his wife-to-be meet in 'the ordinary course of circumstances', for Coelebs has promised his parents that he will defer his choice of a spouse until he has travelled to see the daughter of an old friend of theirs, brought up under an Evangelical regime. In this she is faithfully recording the practice of her contemporaries in the Clapham Sect in the days when the Evangelicals were a small and scattered party. Indeed the frequency with which these men sought their wives in Yorkshire is reminiscent of Abraham's insistence that Isaac's wife should not be chosen from the Canaanites amongst whom they lived, but from his own kindred in Mesopotamia.

Equal circumspection was needed in the choice of servants. Advertisements for 'serious' footmen became a standard literary joke. One has only to recall the establishment at the Clapham 'Hermitage', depicted by Thackeray, where 'the lodge-keeper was serious', 'the head-gardener was a Scotch Calvinist' and the housekeeper a Southcottian to recognize the practice, which, though grotesquely parodied in this instance, prevailed amongst Evangelicals.[154] It is a mark of Mrs. Proudie's essential worldliness that she is prepared to tolerate 'occasional drunkenness in the week' amongst her footmen provided only that they shall be strict in their Sabbath observance.[155] Yet more than an outward parade of family conformity was involved when the Evangelicals embraced, as their own, Joshua's vow—'As for me and my house, we will serve the Lord'. This was the burden of Hannah More's *Thoughts on the Importance of the Manners of the Great to General Society* in which she upbraided the wealthy for causing their servants to sin in telling social lies for their employers, working on Sunday, and indulging in careless conversation in front of them. In many of the upper-middle-class families in which Evangelicalism took root, servants often saw more of the children than did their parents so that it became important for them to share their employers' views if they were expected to uphold godly values in disciplining the children.[156]

[153] Ibid., p. 13.
[154] *The Newcomes*, p. 22.
[155] A. Trollope, *Barchester Towers*, p. 22.
[156] See *Eclectic Notes*, ed. J. H. Pratt, p. 73. 'Care should be taken that what parents do should not be undone by servants. Servants speaking evil of the master or mistress of the house must have a mischievous effect. It is the duty of mothers to be as Sarah was—*much in the tent*'.

When weighed against the child's possible eternal perdition, 'Mrs. Newcome's own serious maid' would have felt justified in laying information against Nurse Sarah 'for telling Tommy stories of Lancashire witches and believing in the same'.[157] Charlotte Yonge and Harriet Mozley alike testify to the influence exercised by an Evangelical governess true to her calling.[158] They had shared an upbringing flavoured with Evangelicalism and an adult life of moderate Tractarianism. The doctrine of reserve in the communication of religious matters came to appeal to them and disposed them to disapprove of the possibly dangerous effects of a governess who herself spoke freely of the most serious matters and encouraged her pupils to do so before they were of an age to appreciate these mysteries.

Victorian novelists have contrived to portray 'truly Christian' homes as the dark places of the world. This was partly because the home became in miniature the battlefield on which the Evangelical cause must be won or lost. Although Trollope does not make Calvinism wholly responsible for Mrs. Bolton's attitudes he does underline the danger of practising, in the home, a religious philosophy whose tenets are so at odds with the natural order of emotions. The firmness required militates against natural warmth and love. Mrs. Sherwood's popular *History of the Fairchild Family* was, as the sub-title declared, 'calculated to shew the importance and effects of a religious education'. Despite the attempt to create an atmosphere of parental love by distributing the phrase, 'My dear', liberally throughout the sermonizing passages, each declaration of love is accompanied either by some 'merciful' punishment or by verbal qualification such as Mrs. Fairchild's teaching to little Henry, who is jealous of his sister, Lucy. 'I love you, my child: notwithstanding which, I know that you have a wicked heart, and that your wicked heart will often make you unhappy where there is nothing else to make you so.'[159]

In *Little Dorrit* Dickens produced an imaginative evocation of the grimmer aspect of family life, when dictated by Calvinist Evangelicalism, as compelling and perceptive in its way as the more subtly portrayed psychological warfare of Mrs. Bolton and her daughter in Trollope's *John Caldigate* and superior to Butler's

[157] W. M. Thackeray, *The Newcomes*, p. 25.
[158] See C. Yonge, *Chantry House*, i, 122; H. Mozley, *The Fairy Bower*.
[159] M. M. Sherwood, *Fairchild Family*, i, 48.

portrayal of Battersby, because less marred by personally vindictive jibes. In the third chapter, ironically entitled 'Home', we see the adult Arthur Clennam return to his mother's house, where she has by now created around herself a cocoon of darkness and coldness, unaffected by the natural cycle of the seasons as it is apparently untouched by the human emotion which her son's 'hopeful yearnings' momentarily betray.[160] At the conclusion of the book Mrs. Clennam explains to Little Dorrit the system which she applied to Arthur's education.

'For his good. Not for the satisfaction of my injury. . . I have seen that child grow up; not to be pious in a chosen way (his mother's offence lay too heavy on him for that), but still to be just and upright, and to be submissive to me. He never loved me, as I once half-hoped he might—so frail we are, and so do the corrupt affections of the flesh war with our trusts and tasks; but he always respected me and ordered himself dutifully to me.'[161]

In this scene Dickens has illuminated a keenly felt Evangelical dilemma which the Revd. J. C. Ryle determined to resolve for his parishioners.

Precious, no doubt, are these little ones in your eyes; but if you love them, think often of their souls. No interest should weigh with you so much as their eternal interests. No part of them should be so dear to you as that part which will never die. . . To pet and pamper, and indulge your child, as if this world was all he had to look to, and this life the only season for happiness; to do this is not true love but cruelty.[162]

Mrs. Clennam's disclosure also reflects how far her real, though thwarted and perverted love had, in her own mind, led her away from the principles of her religion to admit that Arthur might become 'just and upright' without being 'pious in a chosen way'. In the first part of *The New Machiavelli* H. G. Wells offers his reasons for the 'enormous toll of human love and happiness' taken by the practice of Evangelicalism.

It is their exclusive claim that sends them wrong, the vain ambition that inspires them all to teach a uniform one-sided God and be the one and only gateway to salvation. Deprecation of all outside the household of

[160] *Little Dorrit*, p. 32. [161] Ibid., p. 791.

[162] J. C. Ryle, 'Train up a Child in the Way he should go,' *A Sermon for Parents preached in Helmingham Church*, 2nd Thousand (1846), pp. 14–15.

faith, an organized under-valuation of heretical goodness and lovableness, follows necessarily. Every petty difference is exaggerated to the quality of a saving grace or a damning defect.[163]

Underneath the scurrilous accusations of Mrs. Trollope's *Vicar of Wrexhill* lies the consistent and serious criticism that Evangelicalism in its initial and most ardent stages is a divisive force in the family. She illustrates 'the schism which has unhappily entered so many English houses under the semblance of superior piety'[164] in the break-up of the Mowbray family, consequent upon the Vicar teaching two members of the family to separate themselves from the unregenerate, and underlines her message by repeating the pattern in all the families of the parish to whom we are introduced. Mrs. Trollope, her son, Anthony, together with Dickens and Thackeray attributed the denunciatory teaching, which led to division within the family, to the Old Testament teaching they had discarded. For them natural affection was superior to a state of Grace if that Grace came into conflict with the demands of love. Apart from Thackeray,[165] they all forgot, or conveniently ignored, the fact that the same Gospels, to which they were inclined to confine theological authority, presented their God of Love uttering the stern words,

> Suppose ye that I am come to give peace on earth? I tell you, Nay; but rather division:
>
> For from henceforth there shall be five in one house divided, three against two, and two against three.[166]

That certain converts strove officiously to fulfil Christ's prediction is, however, suggested by the fact that Simeon found it necessary to advise his young hearers that if they were already engaged when they became converted they were under an obligation to stand by their plighted word, though they could but hope that their partner might break the tie as unsuitable.[167]

Even if married to a partner about whose regeneracy one was unsure, as were Mrs. Bolton and Mrs. Clennam, one could start afresh with the raw material provided by children. Of course a strict adherence to Calvinist tenets would teach the parents that no amount

[163] *New Machiavelli* (1925), p. 62. [164] *Vicar of Wrexhill*, ii, 15.

[165] Thackeray quoted the comparable passage from Matthew 10: 34. *Thackeray Letters*, iii, 169.

[166] Luke 12: 51–2.

[167] A. W. Brown, *Recollections of Simeon*, p. 248.

of effort could affect their children's predestined election or damnation,[168] but one suspects that the novelists were psychologically perceptive in portraying parents praying for their children's election against any hope afforded them by their doctrine. Not all Evangelicals were committed to the extreme Calvinist position as is shown by Hannah More's overt criticism of the Ranbys of Hampstead, who left their daughters' education to God,[169] and by the popularity in Evangelical circles of her works such as *Strictures on the Modern System of Female Education* or *Hints towards forming the Character of a Young Princess*. The seriousness with which the Evangelicals took their responsibility to educate their children can be seen in the fictional retreat of the Stanleys, the family which raises Coelebs's bride, into the country where they can oversee their children's education without fear of social distraction, or in Wilberforce's decision in 1812 to abandon his Parliamentary seat for Yorkshire that he might devote the time to his family.

Evangelicals were united in the belief that a good Christian home presented the best educational environment. Clapham, as Disraeli observed,[170] displayed a marked fear of the training ground for the British élite, the Public School. James Fitzjames and his brother, Leslie Stephen, were only permitted to attend Eton as day-boys.[171] The Wilberforce children, according to Thomas Mozley,[172] grew to resent their education at home under a series of vulgar ignorant tutors, whose piety displayed itself in parochial duties rather than in educational zeal.

The employment of a respected tutor was one of the alternatives Cowper had suggested in his vehement attack upon the Public Schools in *Tirocinium*. If such an arrangement proved impracticable, or the home influence was detrimental, he recommended sending boys to 'some pious pastor's humble cot'. George Eliot's Tom Tulliver enjoys, in the nominally Evangelical Mr. Stelling's home, a second-rate version of the education that many of Clapham's sons experienced.

Mrs. Sherwood, who had herself, in unregenerate days, attended the school in Reading where Jane and Cassandra Austen had been educated, knew that parents sometimes had to leave their children

[168] See J. H. Philpot, *The Seceders*, pp. 160–1.

[169] *Coelebs*, i, 51. [170] *Falconet*, p. 474.

[171] This was the only form of attendance at Public School which the Revd. W. F. Wilkinson was prepared to countenance. *Rector in Search of a Curate*, p. 221.

[172] *Reminiscences*, p. 101.

at non-Evangelical schools, when their career or their health forced them abroad. Mr. Dalben, guardian of Henry Milner, 'a little boy, who was not brought up according to the fashions of this world', was forced to do just this. Mrs. Sherwood, anxious to prove the adequacy of home education, ensures that Henry immediately takes his place in the top form. He justifies her liberal concession to the necessity of classical studies by managing to retain a pure imagination. His exemplary behaviour (he 'made it a matter of principle, never to join in a jest which seemed to bear against his masters')[173] wins the unconvincingly pious confession of a fellow schoolboy that 'we have allowed ourselves to injure each other by improper communications'.[174] Yet even Henry cannot, single-handed, reform such an institution. In the following volume Henry receives the small consolation Mrs. Sherwood feels able to offer parents for whom school is the only solution: '. . . it may have been an advantage to you to have had such a little peep into the world and its ways, as you have obtained at Clent Green. A large school, where the masters are not pious, is a world in miniature . . .'[175]

For Samuel Butler, or his fictional counterpart Ernest Pontifex, attendance at a non-Evangelical school provided 'a little peep into the world and its ways', that came as a welcome relief from an Evangelical home. For Charlotte Brontë, education at an Evangelical establishment, Cowan Bridge, was sufficient to confirm that systematized Evangelicalism could be administered with a harshness undreamt of in the most devout of Evangelical homes.

The Evangelical attempt to curb and oppress the natural vitality of childhood became a favourite theme for critical novelists. The very place names chosen by Samuel Butler—Crampsford, Christina's home, and Battersby where Ernest is brought up—tell their own story.

When the remarks of certain leading Evangelicals are laid side by side with the supposed caricatures of the novelists it is sometimes difficult to tell one from the other. Even in the second volume of the *Fairchild Family*, whose fierceness was softened by Mrs. Sherwood's gradual change in theology, one detects the attitudes that rightly disturbed the novelists. Speaking of twin girls, aged seven, Mrs. Sherwood says, 'They did not make any noise; in all their behaviour

[173] *The History of Henry Milner*, Pt. II, 5th edn. (1835), p. 395.
[174] *The History of Henry Milner*, Pt. II, 5th edn., p. 367.
[175] *The History of Henry Milner*, Pt. III (1831), p. 6.

they showed that they had been well brought up, and that the blessing of God was with them.'[176] Dickens himself could not have imagined a statement such as that given by the Revd. G. Pattrick at a meeting of the Eclectic Society in 1798 to discuss 'the treatment of Children's Depravity'. 'I contended once a whole night with a child when seven months old. And it has left a permanent effect to this day.'[177]

When a father could say as Mr. Fairchild did, 'I stand in the place of God to you, whilst you are a child',[178] and combined this belief with a personal vision of a God of firm justice and dreadful retribution, he would clearly perceive it as his duty to break down stiff-necked opposition. Samuel Butler's realization of this led him to reject a God who could in any way be seen to resemble his earthly father. Similar standards and practices had of course prevailed before the advent of Evangelicalism. By publishing a letter of hers Wesley gave evangelical endorsement to the system in which his mother had educated him:

> Break their wills betimes; begin this great work before they can run alone, before they can speak plain, or perhaps speak at all. Whatever pains it cost, conquer their stubborness; break the will, if you would not damn the child. I conjure you not to neglect, not to delay this! Therefore (1) Let a child, from a year old, be taught to fear the rod and to cry softly. In order to do this, (2) Let him have nothing he cries for; absolutely nothing, great or small; else you undo your own work. (3) At all events, from that age, make him do as he is bid, if you whip him ten times running to effect it. Let none persuade you it is cruelty to do this; it is cruelty not to do it. Break his will now, and his soul will live, and he will probably bless you to all eternity.[179]

At the verbal level there is very little to distinguish this from the sanctimonious sadism indulged in by Dickens's Mr. Murdstone.[180] In Dickens's view such training could only produce hypocrisy.

The strain upon the offspring of prominent Evangelicals was considerable, especially if their father held, as did Basil Woodd, that 'they should know more than others'.[181] It is upon the duty following

[176] *History of the Fairchild Family*, Pt. II, p. 27.

[177] *Eclectic Notes*, ed. J. H. Pratt, p. 74.

[178] *History of the Fairchild Family*, Pt. I, p. 269.

[179] Quoted by P. Sangster, *Pity My Simplicity*, p. 30.

[180] Cf. *David Copperfield*, p. 46. A conversation between David and Mr. Chillip, later in the book, makes explicit Murdstone's use of the religious mask. Ibid., p. 834.

[181] *Eclectic Notes*, ed. J. H. Pratt, p. 390.

from the immense privileges they have enjoyed, in the shape of 'a father and a grandfather of whom to show yourselves worthy', that Christina,[182] and Fanny Butler,[183] become so emphatic. Thackeray's Newcome brothers present a paradigm of the kind of reaction Dickens anticipated from such an upbringing. Young Tom's behaviour was so at odds with the family code that he was dispatched to the army in India. Legh Richmond's son, Nugent, had to be sent to sea for similar reasons, making sufficient of a moral recovery to justify the inclusion of his life when Edward Bickersteth came to write, *Domestic Portraiture, or the Successful Application of Religious Principles in the education of a family, exemplified in the memoirs of three of the deceased children of the Rev. Legh Richmond.* As for the Hobson twins, 'though at home they were mum as Quakers at a meeting, used to go out on the sly, sir, and be off to the play, sir, and sowed their wild oats like any other young men. . . .'[184] The records of hypocrisy are less frequent, necessarily so if it proved effective, but Samuel Butler's behaviour on his occasional visits home seemed to have conformed to parental, or sisterly, requirements and his acts of rebellion were mental rather than practical. A remark made by a vicar in Charlotte M. Yonge's *The Pillars of the House* when the faith of her upbringing fails a girl at a moment of crisis, throws some light upon such notable failures of the evangelical system as Grimshaw's sons, Charles Wesley's sons, or Branwell Brontë: 'People who have been led out of something like Egypt, are apt to think those secure who have never been from under the shadow of the Cloud, and have known no bread but manna. We forget how much depends on being "mixed with faith in the hearers".'[185]

The Evangelical view of the family as a unit particularly favoured by God received its symbolic expression in the ritual of Family Prayers. The practice of praying in a family unit was not an Evangelical innovation.[186] In *The Cunning Woman's Grandson* Charlotte M. Yonge shows a family of 'good Churchmen' in the Cheddar area who hold family prayers as an old Puritan tradition before they come

[182] S. Butler, *Way of all Flesh*, p. 105.

[183] *The Family Letters of Samuel Butler 1841–1886*, ed. A. Silver (1962), p. 41.

[184] W. M. Thackeray, *The Newcomes*, p. 60.

[185] *Pillars of the House*, ii, 520–1.

[186] A domestic chaplain had frequently read daily prayers to wealthy families. See J. Austen, *Mansfield Park*, ed. R. W. Chapman (1970) ch. ix. In any attempt to revive this practice the Evangelicals were inclined to see a threat of the 'priestly authority' they associated with Jesuitical powers employed against the interests of a united family. See C. L. Scott, *Old Grey Church*, i, 59–61.

into contact with Hannah More and her sisters.[187] They perhaps used something such as Benjamin Jenks's *Prayers and Offices of Devotion for Families* (1697) whose Calvinist assumptions attracted Thomas Scott as his views became increasingly Evangelical.[188] The Evangelicals were, however, responsible for popularizing Family Prayers among the middle-class laity. Initially it had been a spontaneous decision on the part of men like Simeon and Wilberforce to use daily worship to share with their family the benefits they had received in the assurance of salvation. When writing of the first four decades of the century, novelists seemed to think that they could use the observance of family prayers as a badge of Evangelicalism, unless otherwise clearly stated. Pitt Crawley is shown haranguing the family at Queen's Crawley before 1815[189] and in the 1830s in which *Middlemarch* takes place, it is still a matter for remark that Bulstrode 'goes the length in family prayers'.[190] By the 1860s the practice has clearly become widespread and no longer served to distinguish the Evangelical from the nominal or liberal Christian. Archdeacon Grantly, it will be remembered, abandons family worship on the day that the news of Mrs. Proudie's death reached him.[191] Here evidence from works of fiction convincingly establishes the spread of this habit at a period earlier than that for which those ecclesiastical historians who have not used this source are able to do.[192]

It is indicative of the formalism that typified Theobald Pontifex's religion that, long as Overton found them, his family prayers lasted only ten minutes. The ceremony could stretch to 'a full hour' of devotions at rectories such as Thomas Scott's at Aston Sandford,[193] and, lest it should be objected that a later generation would temper their father's practice, it can be noted that Samuel Wilberforce learnt nothing from the restraint practised by his parents. It is recorded that on one occasion he rose and gave a sermon lasting an hour at the conclusion of the prayers.[194]

If, as has been claimed, Evangelicalism fostered a patriarchal

[187] *The Cunning Woman's Grandson* (1890), pp. 126, 156.
[188] J. Scott, *Life of the Rev. T. Scott* (1823), p. 72.
[189] W. M. Thackeray, *Vanity Fair*, p. 94.
[190] G. Eliot, *Middlemarch*, i, 197.
[191] A. Trollope, *Last Chronicle of Barset*, ii, 292.
[192] e.g. see C. Smyth, *Simeon and Church Order*, p. 20.
[193] G. G. Scott, *Personal and Professional Recollections*, ed. G. G. Scott, p. 28.
[194] E. Olivier, *Without knowing Mr. Walkley* (1938), p. 64.

family, the conduct of family prayers could be used as an example by which to discern the structure of any particular family.[195] The service was usually conducted by the head of the family and in his absence the wife or eldest son might assume the responsibility. A visiting clergyman could, however, pre-empt all other claims. This last alternative, it is hinted, was the device employed at the Clapham 'Hermitage' so that no further tussles for domestic power took place between the 'bishopess of Clapham' and 'the man whom she had placed at the head of her house'.[196] If, in the presence of the male head of the household, the wife or daughter assumed the responsibility, this provided an economical image with which novelists could indicate the dominant force in a particular household.[197] These women found support for their longing for power in a religion that inclined them to anticipate on earth the superior position in the after life to which the elect looked as their right. Such a religion, it was felt, might encourage the subversion of the conventional family structure.

The contents of the ceremony as well as its manner of conduct came in for criticism. The Biblical passages cited by novelists are usually taken from the Old Testament. The previously mentioned tendency of many novelists to confine the canon to the four Gospels partly explains this, but it was also a reflection of practice. Conybeare attributed the Judaical character of the 'Recordite' party partly to the practice of reading the Bible straight through—a habit which led to doctrinal imbalance since four Old Testament pages were read for every one from the New Testament.[198] Exposition and prayer followed. It was this rather than the Bible-reading that aroused adverse comment, especially if the individual conducting prayers chose to exercise his talents as an extempore speaker. Some families saw the family circle as a suitable arena for the development of this facility. One such family known to G. W. E. Russell decided to allow their servants the opportunity. The result was not in every

[195] D. Spring, 'The Clapham Sect: Some Social and Political Aspects', *VS* 5 (1961), 46–7. Corroboration for such a view is offered by the Revd. J. Goode's proposition, 'A man must be both Priest and King in his family, and Prophet too!' *Eclectic Notes*, ed. J. H. Pratt, p. 74; or by E. J. Worboise, '. . . I do not believe that any family really prospers, or can be in a morally healthy state, where the true head renounces his prerogatives . . .' *Overdale*, p. 219.

[196] W. M. Thackeray, *The Newcomes*, pp. 28, 40.

[197] See H. Mozley, *The Lost Brooch*, i, 92–3; A. Trollope, *John Caldigate*, p. 149; E. J. Worboise, *Thornycroft Hall*, p. 21.

[198] *Edin. Rev.* 98 (1853), 288.

respect encouraging. The kitchen maid's eloquence may have been found acceptable unto the Lord but certainly did not find favour on earth: ' "And we pray for Sir Thomas and her Ladyship too. Oh, may they have new hearts given to them!" The bare idea that there was room for such renovation caused a prompt return to the lively oracles of Henry Thornton.'[199]

The use of Thornton's posthumously collected *Family Prayers* became for the Victorians 'the distinctive sign of true Evangelism'.[200] Between its publication in 1834 and 1854 thirty-one editions appeared. Its unmannered simplicity of style, the notable absence of strained metaphorical language, so often associated with Evangelical prayer, and its clear relation to a specifically Anglican liturgy help to explain its continued use. These prayers, as E. M. Forster remarked, evoke 'daily gatherings of piety and plenty'.[201] They were written for middle-class usage and their emphasis on prayer for the able guidance and well-being of servants committed to one's care explains the disuse into which they fell as society itself changed.

By the close of the century the family ideal was weakening. Middle-class parents had been the first to enjoy the advantages of lower mortality and, it has been argued, found their relative living standards declining,[202] so that it became more difficult for them to support, and therefore exercise some degree of authority over, dependent sons and daughters for some years past childhood. Increased educational opportunities began to teach women to look beyond the domestic confines for spheres in which to expend their energy and ability. The Great War acted as a catalyst, speeding up these processes and, by removing so many men from the community, prevented many women from finding in marriage what they had been taught to think of as the natural and highest means of personal fulfilment.

As long as the ideal of the family survived, Evangelicalism retained its importance as a subject for the social novelist. Paradoxically Evangelicalism came to be denounced as inimical to the family when its teachings had provided the most coherent religious justification for the ideal. Victorians had taken to their hearts the

[199] *Household of Faith* (1902), p. 241.

[200] E. M. Forster, 'Henry Thornton', *Two Cheers for Democracy* (1951), p. 198.

[201] *Two Cheers for Democracy*, p. 199.

[202] For a review of the various interpretations of the changes in middle-class fertility at this period see H. J. Habakkuk, *Population growth and economic development since 1750* (Leicester, 1971), ch. iii.

emotional and social results of the ideal without necessarily accepting the religious philosophy from which this phenomenon was a mere outcrop. The paradox may perhaps be explained by the influence on Evangelical attitudes of eighteenth-century pragmatism. The founders of nineteenth-century Evangelicalism, and, indeed, most of the Evangelical writers who are referred to in this analysis of attitudes to family life, themselves received an eighteenth-century education. Hannah More, Mrs Sherwood or the Eclectic Society members formed their ideas in an age which, when it considered the role of the family, thought of it in terms of moral and legal duty, or of social utility. It was proper that 'a man of family' should be respected, Dr. Johnson told Boswell, because this was conducive to a respect for authority which was the mainspring of their society.[203] The right of parents to contract marriages of convenience for their offspring went largely unquestioned; primogeniture was regarded as both necessary and natural, and consequently 'the chastity of women' was 'of the utmost importance, as all property depends upon it'.[204]

By the time that Evangelicalism had secured a wide influence the Romantic Movement had generated attitudes of mind unsympathetic to such prudent ordering of human passions. The Romantic movement as such had passed the Evangelicals by, and the change in direction stimulated by the apocalyptic mood of late Romanticism was not fertile in the field of practical piety. Indeed, the tendency to regard the 1830s as the 'latter days' worked directly against an interest in such mundane matters as the process chosen to educate the coming race. The energy of the Evangelical party was taken up for another fifty years in waging a series of wars with the seceding apostolical movements, the Tractarians, the Ritualists and the neologists: there was no time left to devote to rethinking their teaching on family life. It is indicative that Bishop Ryle, 'the Prince of Tract writers',[205] whose tract circulation figures numbered 12,000,000, published only one tract directly relating to this topic, *Train up a child in the way he should go—A Sermon for Parents*. This was preached near the beginning of his parochial ministry in his first living at Helmingham in 1846 and re-published unchanged in 1886. The publication in the last decade of the century of two tracts

[203] J. Boswell, *The Life of Johnson*, ed. G. B. Hill, revised L. F. Powell (6 vols., Oxford, 1934), ii, 153. [204] Ibid., ii, 457.

[205] The title conferred upon him by a fellow tract writer, [Anon]., *Bishop Ryle: The Prince of Tract Writers* (Stirling, 1890).

entitled *The Whole Family* (1897) and *Our Home* (1898) reflect his belated awakening to the appeal of the human family used as a metaphor for the universal church. Perhaps the subtitle, '*Home, Sweet Home*', to that immensely popular work *Christie's Old Organ*, had alerted the Bishop to the fact that ' "Home" is a word that touches the hearts of English people with peculiar power.'[206] With an air of discovery he remarked,

> Community of blood is a most powerful tie. I have often observed that people will stand up for their relations, merely because they *are* their relations—and refuse to hear a word against them,—even when they have no sympathy with their tastes and ways. Anything that helps to keep up family feeling ought to be commended.[207]

The picture of the Cratchit family in Dickens's *A Christmas Carol* suggests how Romanticism had stimulated the awareness of the family unit as a natural organism which could serve to protect the weak, and by its loyalty, preserve the self-respect of the bread-winner in a society where the employer's interest in his labourers was entirely bounded by the cash-nexus.[208] Romanticism too had been responsible for fostering the notion of the child as a natural innocent who should be given the opportunity and freedom to develop his own individuality. It is this feeling which lies behind the revulsion of a Dickens or a Thackeray at the concept of a child as a depraved creature who needs coercing into a state of Grace.

A final curious aspect of the literary attack on this facet of Evangelicalism was that those who were most virulent in their criticisms were precisely those who had not themselves enjoyed what they saw as an increasingly widely-accepted vision of bliss. A secure home life for novelists like Trollope and Dickens became sacrosanct in an inverse proportion to their own early experience of it. Trollope's own early life, committed to the indifferent care of his depressive, irascible father and apparently an outcast from his mother's affection, and the consequent intensity of the pleasure he must have derived

[206] *Our Home* (Stirling, 1898), p. 7. Or again cf. 'Hesba Stretton', [Sarah Smith] *No Place Like Home* (n.d.)

[207] *The Whole Family* (Stirling, 1897), p. 4.

[208] A modern sociologist has noted that the self-conscious articulation of fears concerning the fate of the family unit 'seems to be markedly a feature of adaption to a modern industrial type of life'. Raymond Firth, 'Family and Kinship in Industrial Society', *The Sociological Review*, *Monograph No. 8*. (Oct. 1964), p. 68. Less happily he sees in 'the silent communion of the family round the TV screen', a possible 'modern analogue of family prayers'. Ibid., p. 77.

from his own happy marriage, resulted in the elevation, within his novels, of the family group against those great evils, loneliness and morally paralysing self-devotion. The frequently observed sentimentality of Dickens's pictures of family life in the early novels must also be seen against the instability of his home in childhood and his inability to realize in his adult life the literary image that he had painted. Dickens never ceased to identify himself with the outcast orphan figure, but as he experienced, in adult life, the bonds which his own family inevitably laid upon him, those fictional pictures of happy families, in natural organic groupings, disappeared. Evangelicalism became the synonym for those forces the individual most feared as subversive of the ideal family unit, so that for Dickens, Butler,[209] or Trollope it was seen as an instrument for the suppression of individuality, whereas for Charlotte M. Yonge Evangelicalism encouraged that reliance on individual judgement that threatened the authority of the adult members of those vast cohesive families that peopled her imagination.[210]

### 3. *The instruments of personal piety*

Corporate worship could never take the place of personal devotions. Here too the Bible retained its central position. Lay visitors, like Agnes Grey,[211] and clergymen alike recognized it as part of their duty to help the illiterate to a personal apprehension of the Bible. The intimate knowledge of the Bible gained in this regular reading and study is reflected in Victorian writing of every variety. If belief in verbal inspiration waned in later life, the rhythms and language of the Authorized Version remained. Ruskin grew to regard his systematic learning of the Bible as the most valuable part of his education.[212] Nowhere is the use of the Bible as a vehicle for the expression of personal feeling more startling to the twentieth-century mind than in the pages of the Evangelicals' private diaries.

The early Evangelicals followed or revived the Puritan practice of keeping a diary as a record of, and means to, the spiritual life.

[209] For further analysis of Butler's attitude to the family see below pp. 274–7. ff.

[210] Cf. C. M. Yonge's objections to Mrs. Sherwood's tales. 'Little children amaze their elders, and sometimes perfect strangers, by sudden inquiries whether they are Christians . . . they judge their superiors and utter sentiments which are too apt to pass for practice . . .' *Macmillan's Magazine*, 20 (1869), 309.

[211] A. Brontë, *Agnes Grey*, p. 386.

[212] *Works*, xxxv, 14, 40–1.

Wesley attributed the spiritual pedigree of his Journal to 'advice given by Bishop Taylor in his *Rules for Holy Living and Dying*'.[213] Wesley began his diaries in the Holy Club days at Oxford; Henry Venn and Wilberforce began theirs in their 'legalist' phases as a record of attempts to live up to the high demands of their faith. For them, as for the Puritans, the diary became a 'substitute for the confessional'.[214] This disciplined aid to recollection and self-examination could not be acquired too early. At age nine and a half Lucy Fairchild is equipped with a diary and instructions to 'write in it every day the naughty things which pass in your heart'.[215] Harriet Mozley who must have been familiar with the curiously immature heart-searchings of the anti-Evangelical Hurrell Froude nevertheless portrays the diary-keeping habit as an Evangelical practice. Like Charlotte Elizabeth, who distinctly disapproved of the habit since 'she had long been persuaded that there is no such thing as an honest private journal',[216] Mrs. Mozley took pains to show how valueless such an exercise becomes if the diary is to be subjected to the scrutiny of mamma and the governess every Saturday night. For Constance Duff, the most pious of her fictional family, the diary becomes a mode for self-congratulation; for the governess the diaries are a source of information not accorded the privacy of the confessional.[217] In *The Lost Brooch* Mrs. Mozley returned to the attack. Mary Anne, the most deceitful and foolish of the children, is the apologist for a practice which she claims to be an easy pastime and a necessary qualification for the name of Christian.

'Why it seems the easiest thing in the world to me,' said Mary Anne; 'you know you must be in some sort of frame, every minute; and you must have passed a day profitably or unprofitably, or heard conversations, or sermons or prayers, edifying or unedifying. Nothing is easier than to put these down, and record a notice, thankful or humble, as may be. Then there are all the opportunities of good that occur, and which should be mentioned.'[218]

[213] A. C. Outler, *John Wesley*, p. 37.

[214] W. Haller, *The Rise of Puritanism: or the Way to the New Jerusalem as set forth in Pulpit and Press from Thomas Cartwright to John Lilburne and John Milton, 1570–1643*, (New York, 1938), p. 96. Cf. N. Gash, 'The Complexities of a crusader', *TLS* (8 Nov. 1974), p. 1245.

[215] M. M. Sherwood, *Fairchild Family*, Pt. I, 84.

[216] [C. E. Browne Phelan Tonna], 'Charlotte Elizabeth', *Personal Recollections* (1841), p. 21.

[217] *Fairy Bower*, pp. 153–4.

[218] *Lost Brooch*, ii, 184–5.

It is this disproportionate attention to the minutiae of daily experience which both makes Wilkie Collins's Miss Clack a valuable witness in *The Moonstone* and contributes to her absurdity. The comedy which Collins exploits from this diarist's pretensions and self-deceptions makes it at first glance surprising that other Victorian novelists seem to have avoided the diary as a mode of narration. Perhaps it was felt to be too nearly akin to the outmoded device of telling a tale through the means of an exchange of letters. A more likely explanation is that Victorian practitioners of the psychological novel were often too anxious to place their characters' self-analyses within the framework of the society which influenced their thought processes to allow full play to the record of a single mind, uninterrupted by a narrator's comments.

The Evangelicals themselves finally concluded that the diary was an instrument of limited value. Like the novelists who rejected it because it provided insufficient opportunity to present external relations they began to suspect that diary-keeping focuses the attention more upon the writer than on his God.[219] The diary could, however, have more than a merely personal value. The devotional literature favoured by Evangelicals was 'experimental' rather than mystical in genre, so that edited diaries provided invaluable material for memoirs and biographies. 'Without diaries there would have been no Pascal's Thoughts, no Baxter's Life, no Adam's Private Thoughts, no William's Diary, no Milner's Memoranda, no Austin's Confessions; and, I think, I may say, no Rom. vii, 14, &c. . . .'[220] Their predilection for these works was again shared by their Puritan forebears. The terms in which the seventeenth-century Puritan, Richard Baxter, had recommended these religious biographies are closely paralleled two centuries later by the publisher in *Lavengro* who remarks that the most marketable literary commodities are 'a well-written tale in the style of the "Dairyman's Daughter" '[221] or 'a compilation of Newgate lives and trials'.[222]

The report of one Souls Conversion to God, and of the Reformation of one Family, City, or Church, and of the noble Operations of the blessed Spirit, by which he brings up Souls to God, Conquereth the World, the Flesh, and the Devil; the Heavenly Communication of God unto Sinners,

[219] R. W. Dale, *The Old Evangelicalism and the New* (1889), p. 30.
[220] *Eclectic Notes*, ed. J. H. Pratt, p. 310.
[221] G. Borrow, *Lavengro: the Scholar, the Gypsy, the Priest* (3 vols., 1851), ii, 18.
[222] Ibid. ii, 49.

for their Vivification, Illumination, and holy Love to God, and to his Image, are as far better than the Stories of these grand Murderers, and Tyrants, and their great Robberies, and Murders called Conquests, as the Diagnosticks of Health are than those of Sickness.[223]

The devotional purpose of reading such documents was articulated by Thomas Scott in a sermon entitled, *The Duty and Advantage of remembering Deceased Ministers* (1808). He suggested that by recollecting the peculiar circumstances of a minister's life the Gospel truths that he had been endeavouring to teach them might also be remembered. The ease with which the 'peculiar circumstances' could in fact be divorced from the 'Gospel truths' they were intended to recall is commented on by George Eliot, as she presents Mrs. Linnet 'confiding her perusal to the purely secular portions'[224] of such works. Religious biographies, in various forms, were popular at every level of society, and read by all age groups.

Not until the second generation of Evangelicals took the lead did tracts specifically written for children appear, a phenomenon perhaps reflecting the consciousness, stimulated by the Romantic Movement, of the child as something other than a small adult.[225] As secretary of the Religious Tract Society, the Revd. Legh Richmond achieved a circulation, if not a readership, of over 1,354,000 with his tracts, *The Dairyman's Daughter*, *The Young Cottagers*, and *The Negro Servant.*[226] Armed with fictional pictures of tracts falling upon stony ground, returned unread like Miss Clack's, or thrust upon the illiterate like Mrs. Pardiggle's, one has reason to suspect that readership in no way matched circulation figures, but, even with this *caveat* in mind, a variety of repercussions from this vast dissemination of material can be observed.

Tracts such as those written by Legh Richmond were directed at winning a readership amongst those more used to the crude sensationalism of the cheap press. The novelists derived endless amusement from parodying the titles of these tracts, originally calculated to catch the eye of careless readers. Andrew Kerr has

[223] Quoted in W. Haller, *The Rise of Puritanism*, p. 101.

[224] *Scenes*, ii, 79–80.

[225] See, e.g., the tracts brought back by John Trueman, the sincere Christian servant to the Fairchild family, for the children. The one chosen for Henry, and vetted approvingly by Mr. Fairchild, strikes the modern reader as highly unsuitable, dealing, as it does, with two covetous women and childbirth. *Fairchild Family*, i, 166–77.

[226] M. J. Quinlan, *Victorian Prelude, a History of English Manners, 1700–1830* (New York, 1941), p. 124.

noticed that Hannah More adopted two contrasted prose styles, according to the class which her work was intended to reach.[227] Of her *Village Politics*, and the remark would seem to hold good for her other tracts written for the working classes, she wrote to Mrs. Boscawen, 'It is as vulgar as heart can wish; but it is only designed for the most vulgar class of readers. I heartily hope I shall not be discovered; as it is a sort of writing repugnant to my nature. . . .'[228]

When these tracts fell into the hands of a sophisticated stylist like Thackeray how could he resist the temptation to mock the simplicity, or simple-mindedness, resulting from such a self-discipline as 'Charlotte Elizabeth' openly declared that she had imposed upon herself?

> . . . I was able to adopt the suggestion of a wise Christian brother, and form a style of such homely simplicity that if, on reading a manuscript to a child of five years old, I found there was a single sentence or word above his comprehension, it was instantly corrected to suit that lowly standard. This is an attainment much to be coveted by those who write, preach or expound for general edification: no rational objection can be urged against it: vanity alone can enter a protest. Though our lettered readers or hearers may not find matter to gratify their taste or pamper the pride of intellect still they cannot fail to understand what is suited to the capacities of their children and their servants. . .[229]

Richmond's son-in-law and biographer, Grimshawe, was insistent about the distinction between these true stories recorded by his father-in-law and that 'class of publications which profess to convey religious truth under the garb of fiction'.[230] He felt the need to stress the point because Evangelicals' novels or tales so often modelled themselves upon the formula detectable in the religious biography. Just as a tacit recognition of an accepted formula has been detected in the Puritan spiritual autobiography[231] so a similar code, with

[227] 'The Literary Contribution of Hannah More to the Evangelical Movement', B. Litt. thesis, Glasgow, 1967, p. 281.

[228] W. Roberts, *Memoirs of the Life and Correspondence of Mrs. Hannah More*, 2nd. edn. (4 vols., 1834), ii, 378–9.

[229] C. E. B. P. Tonna, *Personal Recollections*, pp. 168–9.

[230] *Memoir of the Rev. Legh Richmond*, p. 316. Cf. the sub-title of *The Dairyman's Daughter:* 'An Authentic and Interesting Narrative'.

[231] See, e.g., W. Haller, *The Rise of Puritanism*, pp. 96–102; L. D. Lerner, 'Puritanism and the Spiritual Autobiography', *Hibbert Journal*, 55 (July 1957), 373–86; and John Bunyan, *Grace Abounding to the Chief of Sinners*, ed. R. Sharrock (Oxford, 1962), pp. xxvii–xxx.

significant variations, seems to have existed for the Evangelical biographer. A brief chapter was all that was necessary to fill in the subject's early childhood experiences, because from the Evangelical point of view it cannot be said to contain the meat of the matter, whatever subsequent psychological analysis may have led modern readers to assume. Similarly the Evangelical novelist does not concentrate with the loving detail of a George Eliot in *The Mill on the Floss*, or a Dickens in *David Copperfield*, on childhood memories, except in as far as they provide specific examples of natural depravity or, more rarely, early and instinctive piety. The first structural climax in novel and biography alike is the conversion to Gospel truth. The two stages of Evangelical conversion, to legalism and then to an awakened state could enable the writer to sustain the drama over a period of years. The more sensational novelists could and did exploit this for the 'popular (and quite unreligious) appeal of the suspended-conversion motif'.[232] The biographer then devoted the remainder of the work to an extensive treatment of the example provided by his subject's subsequent life. Unlike the romantic novelist, whose story came to an end when hero and heroine were united in mutually recognized love, the Evangelical novelist could continue the tale with the history of his subject's subsequent attempts to bring others, even possible lovers, to Christ.[233] Perhaps it was an adaptation of this tradition that led George Eliot to depict Dorothea going to Rosamund as the spiritual fruit of her 'conversion' experience the previous night.[234]

Religious biographies served to feed the imagination of many a child whose hunger for adventure and romance found no opportunity to quench itself on novels. The editor of the *Christian Observer* openly recognized the value of this material as a substitute in the literary diet.

We do not, however, think that those who cannot find entertainment in argument should be deprived of a reasonable share of lighter matter; and there is always one resource in particular, which all classes of persons, the

[232] K. Tillotson, *Novels of the Eighteen-Forties* (Oxford, 1954), p. 129.

[233] A device used in C. Scott, *The Old Grey Church*.

[234] An impression supported by the way in which George Eliot tries to elevate a secular and perhaps physical experience to a spiritual realm. 'In that hour she repeated what the merciful eyes of solitude have looked on for ages in the spiritual struggles of man—she besought hardness and coldness and aching weariness to bring her relief from the mysterious incorporeal might of her anguish . . .' *Middlemarch*, iii, 388.

superficial as well as the most meditative, may in common avail themselves of—namely, interesting and useful narrative, especially religious biography. . . .[235]

So staple a part of the middle-class reader's diet did religious biographies become that it taught one critic, nurtured upon them, to speak of the novel in terms of a fictional biography differing only in that, in the novel, interest was centred upon love and marriage rather than the professional life of 'a popular clergyman'.[236]

Perhaps the one truly distinguishing feature of the Evangelical biography is the care devoted to the presentation of the death-bed scene. It is difficult to distinguish the precise nature of the Evangelical contribution to the tradition of *ars moriendi*, or to explain exactly why the Evangelical theology centred so markedly on this moment of a man's life. That such a tradition had long existed can be swiftly illustrated by reference to the late medieval obsession with the macabre dance of death and to a monumental art which encouraged the contemplation of physical decay as a reminder of life's transience. Izaac Walton's account of Donne's personal mode of meditation upon death,[237] combined with the poetry of both Donne and Herbert,[238] serve to indicate the way that Protestantism was to adopt this element of Catholic tradition. F. C. Gill has listed such progenitors of the Evangelical tradition as Burton's *Anatomy of Melancholy*, Blair's *Grave*, Young's *Night Thoughts*, Addison's 'Meditations among the Tombs of Westminster Abbey', Thompson's *Sickness*, Gray's *Elegy*, and Warton's *Pleasures of Melancholy*, and has drawn attention to the way in which the cult of painful emotion linked Puritanism with Romanticism.[239] Miss M. Doody has demonstrated Samuel Richardson's awareness, and reliance on a similar awareness on the part of his audience, of Christian devotional death-bed literature from both Catholic and Anglican sources[240] in

[235] *CO* (1834), p. 732, n. Cf. *Christian Lady's Magazine* I (1834), ii. 'The impression seems also very strong, and very general, that we should not indulge in fictitious narrative: we will gladly meet this, by seeking specimens of interesting biography . . .'

[236] J. F. Stephen, 'The Relation of Novels to Life', *Cambridge Essays contributed by Members of the University* (1855), p. 160.

[237] *Izaak Walton's Lives* (1952), pp. 50–1, 68–9.

[238] For a study of the way in which their poetry draws upon this tradition see L. L. Martz, *The Poetry of Meditation* (New Haven, 1954), pp. 135–44.

[239] *The Romantic Movement and Methodism* (1937), ch. 3.

[240] 'A Comparative Study of Samuel Richardson's *Clarissa* and *Sir Charles Grandison*' D. Phil. thesis, Oxford, 1968.

presenting the death-beds scenes of Belton, Clarissa, and Sinclair.[241] Despite Richardson's indebtedness to a corpus of religious devotional literature *Clarissa* evinces a moral rather than a religious interest in the event of death. In his letters Richardson speaks of his intention to draw a series of contrasting moral tableaux where the poetic justice of the deaths corresponded with the moral judgement he had made upon the lives of his characters.[242] Though the righteous Clarissa makes brief allusion to the '*foretastes*' and '*assurances*'[243] she enjoys, her death is presented in terms of a final moment which gives symbolic expression to the life she has led up to this point. Death is not seen as an interim state on the way to final union with, or alienation from, God, but as a climax in itself. Judgement is awarded on earth rather than waiting for the final Judgement Seat. Reprobates endure the agonies of hell actually on their death-beds.

This tradition of depicting death-beds which were morally rather than religiously satisfying survived into the nineteenth century. The alleged horrors of Voltaire's death-bed continued to provide valuable ammunition for Protestant and Catholic sermons.[244] George Eliot's fiction provides fine examples. Mr. Dempster's feverish outbursts in 'Janet's Repentance' demonstrate a survival of this tradition. Where George Eliot denied immortality her moral philosophy demanded an emblematic climax to life. The dying Featherstone's struggle to exert the warped power his life has thrived upon receives a symbolic physical memorial: '. . . Peter Featherstone was dead, with his right hand clasping the keys, and his left hand lying on the heap of notes and gold'.[245] Also in this tradition is one of the most famous Evangelical warning scenes ever painted. In Mrs. Sherwood's *The History of the Fairchild Family* Mr. Fairchild discovers his children quarrelling and, anxious to offer them a cogent illustration of the probable consequence of such altercations, takes them to see a rotting corpse upon a gibbet.[246]

Of course the Evangelicals had to come to terms with the fact

[241] S. Richardson, *Clarissa Harlowe: or, the History of a Young Lady Comprehending the Most Important Concerns of a Private Life* (8 vols., Oxford, 1930), vii, 171–84, 202–10; viii, 1–7, 53–69, 275–7.

[242] *Selected Letters of Samuel Richardson*, ed. J. Carroll (Oxford, 1964), pp. 95, 118–22.

[243] *Clarissa*, viii, 3.

[244] See *CO* (1842), 668–75; and G. Flaubert, *Madame Bovary*, ed. C. Gothot-Mersch (Paris, 1971), p. 352.

[245] *Middlemarch*, ii, 72.

[246] *Fairchild Family*, i, 56.

observed by the Puritan Bunyan that notoriously wicked men occasionally died quietly in their beds. Bunyan was prepared to affirm that 'there is no surer sign of a mans [*sic*] Damnation, than to dye quietly after a sinful life; than to sin and dye with his eyes shut. . . .'[247] Patrick Brontë, in his novel *The Maid of Killarney*, dispatched his hero to attend the death-bed of a prominent local sinner so that the man's atheistical supporters should not lie about the final tortures, as he suspected the sceptical philosopher David Hume's friends to have done. This sinner satisfyingly dies in extreme torture but Patrick Brontë hedged his bets to cover all eventualities: 'Wicked men in general, die evidently under terrible apprehensions of impending judgement; and where there appears to be an exception to this rule, I believe it is owing to pride and vanity, which keep back the truth, or to death, who arrests the tongue, when it is at length inclined to make a full confession.'[248]

Initially, the eighteenth-century Evangelicals had used the materials ready to hand. Charles Wesley spoke of Young's *Night Thoughts* as more useful than anything apart from Scripture.[249] Soon, however, they made their own contributions to the genre. The immensely popular *Meditations amongst the Tombs* by James Hervey, an early Methodist, laid the evangelical seal on the tradition of graveyard moralizing. So attached to this means of instruction did they become, that Legh Richmond was accustomed to take a seat next to the churchyard when teaching children and point to the 'heaving sods' as a reminder of life's transience.[250] For those without such considerate pastors Mrs. Sherwood provided *Père la Chaise*, in which Evangelical attitudes to death are spelt out. A bereaved, but sincerely pious, mother gives her children a conducted tour of this famous French cemetery. After seating them by their father's grave to listen to a discourse upon the corruption of the body, she draws their attention to the elaborate sarcophagi around them and remarks upon the 'secret kind of infidelity, my dear children, from which proceeds the desire of raising the sculptured tomb, the marble urn, the weeping statue . . .'[250a]

A High Church tradition of death-bed literature also emerged but became clearly distinguishable from its Evangelical counterpart.

[247] *Life and Death of Mr. Badman*, ed. J. Brown (Cambridge, 1905), p. 174.
[248] *Maid of Killarney*, p. 69.
[249] G. Rowell, *Hell and the Victorians*, p. 7.
[250] T. S. Grimshawe, *Memoir of the Rev. Legh Richmond*, p. 304.
[250a] *Père La Chaise* (Wellington, 1823), p. 90.

The *Christian Observer* review of *Death-Bed Scenes and Pastoral Conversations by the late John Warton*, begins rather charmingly: 'The work before us bears an inviting title', but proceeds to warn readers of its dangerous doctrinal tendencies, manifested in 'a strong bias in favour of the Papal doctrine of the *opus operatum* of the eucharist' and the tolerance of prayers for the dead.[251] Dying heroes and heroines in the novels of the High Church Charlotte Yonge usually die having received the full benefit of the presence of the clergy who can administer the last communion and offer prayers for the departed. Perhaps this might form one line for distinguishing the High Church from the Protestant approach: the High Church tends to concentrate upon the dying person whereas Protestantism throws greater emphasis upon the effect made upon the bystanders. High church ritual came into conflict with Evangelicalism in its need for the attendance of a priest. The Tractarian novelist, F. E. Paget, specifically charged his fictional Evangelical minister with pastoral negligence. A week's attendance at the Evangelical May meetings at the Exeter Hall had prevented him from administering 'the consolations of religion' to the dying.[252] Despite the presence of this High Church tradition the emphasis on death as a centre for teaching gained recognition as a typically Evangelical concern. Mrs. Trollope, attempting to explain the Vicar of Wrexhill's initial success with his parish, made the surprising admission that the arrival of an Evangelical parson at a house where recent bereavement had occurred was a welcome relief, since he could be counted upon to break the evasive silence of other visitors with his open allusions to death.

Although the entire death-bed cult can be seen as a ritual evolved to cope with a society in which it was reasonable for a man to begin the dedication to his autobiography to his children, with the words: 'If any of you should live to manhood',[253] Evangelical doctrine gave special prominence to the event. Robert Elsmere's death, in Mrs. Humphry Ward's novel of that name, provides the moving setting for the last conflict between the old Evangelicalism of his wife and his own unorthodox religious position:

All persons of the older Christian type attribute a special importance to

[251] *CO* (1827), pp. 741–56. This pseudonymous publication of the Revd. William Wood's became the only 'story book' permitted to the hero of Froude's *Nemesis of Faith* when his family turned from their old orthodoxy to the new High Church movement.

[252] F. E. Paget, *Warden of Berkingholt*, p. 60.

[253] *The Autobiography of Isaac Williams*, ed. G. Prevost, p. vii.

the moment of death. While the man of science looks forward to his last hour as a moment of certain intellectual weakness . . . the Christian believes that on the confines of eternity the veil of flesh shrouding the soul grows thin and transparent, and that the glories and the truths of Heaven are visible with a special clearness and authority to the dying. It was for this moment, either in herself or in him, that Catherine's unconquerable faith had been patiently and dumbly waiting.[254]

The faithful were at this moment acutely conscious of their proximity to the Judgement seat. Legh Richmond's counsel: 'Let it be your *sole* business here to prepare for eternity',[255] helps to explain Simeon's life-long habit of regarding himself as a dying man: 'As for me, I have been a dying creature these fifty years, and have as on the borders of eternity sought for truth only, and that from the fountain of truth itself.'

Simeon was unusual in rejecting the ritual at his own death-bed. When his friends gathered round his bed he roused himself to offer a stern rebuke: ' "You are all on the wrong scent, and are all in a wrong spirit; you want to see what is called a dying scene. THAT I ABHOR FROM MY INMOST SOUL. I wish to be alone, with my God, and to lie before Him as a poor, wretched hell-deserving sinner—yes, as a poor, hell-deserving sinner." '[256]

This did not apparently prevent the Revd. William Carus from recording all that passed in minute detail.

Despite Anne Brontë's purgatorial beliefs, the sense of imminent judgement is strong and accounts for the apparent emotional brutality of Helen Huntingdon at her dying husband's bedside: ' ". . . I don't want to lull you to false security. If a consciousness of the uncertainty of life can dispose you to serious and useful thoughts, I would not deprive you of the benefit of such reflections, whether you do eventually recover or not." '[257]

Mrs. Oliphant drew a particularly moving picture, in *A Son of the Soil*, of the morbid fanaticism resulting from the conviction that 'the great object of our lives is to know how to die'.[258] Read against the background of her autobiography, with its account of her endless attempts to shield her ailing family from hardship and the truth of their position, one begins to understand the anxiety of Lauderdale,

[254] Mrs. Humphry Ward, *Robert Elsmere* (2 vols., 1911), ii, 548–9.
[255] T. S. Grimshawe, *Memoir of the Rev. Legh Richmond*, pp. 274–5.
[256] W. Carus, *Memoirs of the Life of Charles Simeon*, p. 810.
[257] *Tenant of Wildfell Hall*, p. 404.
[258] *Son of the Soil*, i, 281.

the travelling companion, to separate his convalescent charge from a fellow consumptive who speaks of nothing but death and is indignant that there are 'some who are shocked and frightened, as if speaking of death, would make them die the sooner'.[259] This Evangelical zealot, Meredith, is even pleased when the convalescent shows signs of a relapse, for he had 'feared that God was leaving him alone' whilst gathering the chosen to Himself.[260] Meredith then sets about arranging his own death-bed scene. He remains supremely conscious of Hannah More's dictum that 'to be strong in faith, and patient in hope, in a long and lingering sickness, is an example of more general use and ordinary application, than even the sublime heroism of the martyr'.[261] He called in his friends to witness his parting moments, 'never forgetting that he lay there before heaven and earth, a monument as he said of God's grace, and an example of how a Christian could die'.[262]

On his death-bed Meredith dictated the final chapter of his work, 'The Voice from the Grave'. In highly self-conscious fashion he is echoing the practice observed by many Evangelicals of recording a parting saint's dying words. In their eagerness to catch William Marsh's last testament his family installed his eldest daughter in the sick room, unseen by him, to record his conversation, whereupon he recovered and the entire process had to be repeated over a year later.[263]

It is the belief in the efficacy of the appeal made by a dying relative that is reflected in the letter left by Christina Pontifex for her children when she believes herself to be dying.[264] Butler transcribed this with very few alterations from a letter left by his own mother[265] and independent evidence supports his contention that the writing of such a document was a common practice. Henry Venn advised one of his female correspondents to try this measure[266] and Patrick Brontë gave fictional corroboration to the effectiveness of the device.[267]

The death-bed witness did not merely provide an example of 'a consummation devoutly to be wished', but also assured the circle of

[259] Ibid. i, 284. [260] Ibid. ii, 52. [261] *Practical Piety*, p. 402.
[262] M. O. W. Oliphant, *Son of the Soil*, ii, 83.
[263] C. Marsh, *Life of William Marsh*, pp. 465, 565.
[264] S. Butler, *Way of All Flesh*, pp. 104–6.
[265] *Family Letters of Samuel Butler*, ed. A. Silver, pp. 40–2.
[266] J. Venn, *The Life of Henry Venn*, ed. H. Venn, pp. 121–2.
[267] *Maid of Killarney*, pp. 120–3.

attendants that their departing friend was truly saved. For the Calvinist a Christian death-bed provided both an illustration and a vindication of the doctrine of Final Perseverance. It is Christina Pontifex's lack of certainty at the crucial moment that causes her misgivings about her own salvation. Theobald's feeling that hers is an unsatisfactory witness makes him tell Ernest 'that he could not wish it prolonged'.[268] Legh Richmond's conversation with the dying girl in *The Dairyman's Daughter* provides the prototype for the variety of catechetical exchange to establish the dying person's frame of mind. Indeed Conybeare was to complain that Evangelicals grew to expect the appropriate responses to be made parrot fashion by the dying man.[269] Dr. Johnson's dying frame of mind greatly exercised Evangelicals. Hannah More affirmed that he had achieved 'a simple reliance on Jesus as his Saviour',[270] but it continued to be disputed.[271] Dr. Arnold was the next greatly respected man to cause concern by his failure to use the accepted phraseology.[272] The quality of Evangelical witnessing could be just as suspect as that of Brontë's atheistical perjurers. Shaftesbury's manipulation of Palmerston's death-bed acquiescence,[273] or the badgering of William Marsh's harmlessly worldly brother into the admission, 'I am a brand plucked from the burning',[274] does much to explain the scene in Newman's *Loss and Gain* where Evangelicals discuss the death-bed conversion of the Pope reported by O'Niggins, a member of the Roman Priest Conversion Branch Tract Society.[275] Newman attacks both the stupidity of those prepared to accept clearly biased evidence and the arrogant assumption by the Evangelicals of a complete monopoly of the language of salvation. Newman was himself to offer nineteenth-century Roman Catholics their own version of the Christian death-bed in *The Dream of Gerontius* (1865).

Yet Evangelicals were, on the whole, suspicious of a sudden change of heart at this crucial moment. The *Christian Observer* reviewer of Warton's book had lamented the author's credulity and

[268] S. Butler, *Way of All Flesh*, p. 379.

[269] *Edin. Rev.* 98 (1853), 284.

[270] W. Roberts *Memoirs of the Life and Correspondence of Mrs. Hannah More*, i, 379–80.

[271] See W. H. White, *Catharine Furze*, i, 123. See also *CO* (1828), pp. 32–3.

[272] *Edin. Rev.* 98 (1853), 284. See also *Remarks upon the Record being an inquiry into the Spirit, Temper and Objects of the Newspaper bearing that Name by an incumbent of the diocese of London* (1849), p. 22.

[273] E. Hodder, *Life of Shaftesbury*, iii, 185–7.

[274] C. Marsh, *Life of William Marsh*, p. 346.

[275] *Loss and Gain*, 146–9.

reminded his readers that 'One was saved at the eleventh hour, that none might despair; and *but* one, that none might presume.'[276] For Hannah More the primary objection to 'death-bed converts' was that 'the symptoms must frequently be too equivocal to admit the positive decision of human wisdom'.[277] This did not prevent her from including a scene depicting the death-bed repentance of an Antinomian in her novel *Coelebs*,[278] presumably on the grounds that the author's omniscience enabled a positive decision to be reached. Charlotte Brontë's refusal to give us a full-dress repentance scene at Mrs. Reed's death-bed, or Anne Brontë's refusal to comfort Helen Huntingdon by allowing her husband a death-bed conversion, become less surprising when their father's teaching on the matter at the funeral sermon for the Revd. William Weightman, his curate, is considered.

> . . . I do not, and never did consider, the transactions of a dying bed as exclusively a safe criterion to judge of a man's character. If we would know whether a man has died in the Lord, we ought, in the first instance to ask, has he lived in the Lord? Some, I fear, have greatly and dangerously erred on this head, and an error here, would be as fatal as irretrievable.[279]

As is apparent from his novel, *The Maid of Killarney*, Patrick Brontë would have agreed with the Revd. H. Foster's contribution to a discussion at the Eclectic Society when he said, 'My chief hope is of bystanders.'[280]

Biographers gave fulsome accounts of the event only as a second best to attendance at the actual event. Henry Venn advised parents that the real thing 'will infinitely exceed the force of all instruction, to let them see with their own eyes, and hear with their own ears, the faithful servant of God speaking good of his name',[281] and Mrs. Sherwood's accounts of visits to dying children were an endeavour to encourage such activities as well as a record for those less fortunate in opportunities.[282]

Enterprising publishers were not long in recognizing the market that existed for series of death-bed scenes culled from biographies and such appetizing titles as *Death-Bed Triumphs of Eminent*

[276] *CO* (1827), p. 756. [277] *Practical Piety*, ii, 347n.
[278] *Coelebs*, ii, 364–73.
[279] *Brontëana: The Rev. Patrick Brontë, his collected works and life* (Bingley, 1898), p. 259. [280] *Eclectic Notes*, ed. J. H. Pratt, p. 325.
[281] *Complete Duty*, p. 240. [282] *Fairchild Family*, i, 145–60, 293–5.

*Christians*[283] appeared. Confronted with the evidence of a man like Henry Nevinson, who recalled that in his grandfather's house in the 1860s *The Family Sepulchre* was one of the few books considered acceptable Sunday reading for the children,[284] it is relevant to inquire how familiarity with this tradition affected the presentation of such scenes in the novel.

The distancing of the experience and consequent formal arrangement of the emotions which might take place when a writer was anxious to instruct is suggested by the way in which Legh Richmond, of *Dairyman's Daughter* fame, found himself unable to record the death of his own consumptive son, Wilberforce Richmond.[285] Evangelicals were themselves unhappy about the almost fictional quality that editing gave to death-bed accounts. At the beginning of the century the Revd. W. J. Abdy had confessed his concern at the ability to stage such scenes: 'Some people there are whom you may work up to say such things as would appear well in print, who yet betray in other ways that they are not right.'[286]

By mid-century the Revd. F. W. Robertson, a critic of orthodox Evangelicalism, expressed the problem in greater detail and more forcibly:

> . . . it is a Christian's privilege to have victory over the fear of death. And here it is exceedingly easy to paint what after all is only the image-picture of a dying hour. It is the easiest thing to represent the dying Christian as a man who always sinks into the grave full of hope, full of triumph, in the certain hope of a blessed resurrection. Brethren, we must paint things in the sober colours of truth; not as they might be supposed to be, but as they are. Often that is only a picture. Either very few death-beds are Christian ones, or else triumph is a very different thing from what the word generally implies. . . . Rapture is a rare thing, except in books and scenes. . . . It is on record of a minister of our own Church, that his expectation of seeing God in Christ became so intense as his last hour drew near, that his physician was compelled to bid him calm his transports, because in so excited a state he could not die.[287]

Even if novelists wrote from first-hand experience the more

[283] Jabez Burns, *Death-Bed Triumphs of Eminent Christians* (Halifax, 1855).

[284] *Between the Acts* (1904), p. 3.

[285] E. Bickersteth, *Domestic Portraiture* (1834), pp. 161–2.

[286] *Eclectic Notes*, ed. J. H. Pratt, p. 324.

[287] *Sermons, Preached at Brighton, Third Series* (1872), pp. 224–5. The Anglican minister referred to is almost certainly Henry Venn of whom this story is admiringly recounted in J. Venn, *Life of Henry Venn*, ed. H. Venn, p. 57.

commercially aware could linger on the topic secure in the knowledge that their audience brought a set of almost ritualistic responses to their reading. Ruskin followed up his attack on the morbid sensationalism of Dickens's death-bed scenes with the charge that this had taught weak writers to look to death as a marketable commodity because they recognized that 'if the description be given even with mediocre accuracy, a very large section of readers will admire its truth, and cherish its melancholy'.[288] To a breed of Victorian literary critics brought up in the Evangelical theological tradition this form of 'botanising upon one's mother's grave', as one of them expressed it,[289] was peculiarly obnoxious. James Fitzjames Stephen and his brother-in-law, 'Velvet' Cunningham's son, joined Ruskin in inveighing against the sentimental and perverted use of the death-bed tradition consequent upon the loss of perspective which religion gave to its treatment of the event. Stephen chose Dickens's treatment of Little Nell's death for especial criticism, noting how he 'touches, tastes, smells and handles as if it was a savoury dainty which could not be too fully appreciated'. He contrasted this with the modesty and restraint of a Biblical model, Ezekiel's reception of his wife's death, and concluded of Dickens's writing:

> This is but one illustration out of ten thousand, of the spirit which leads people to indulge their timidity or their love of luxury, by disregarding the essential points of observation for the sake of accessories, and instead of looking death, and grief, and pain in the face, to trifle with the dramatic incidents by which they may be attended.[290]

Stephen is outraged not just by the unreality of the picture but by the way in which Dickens deliberately uses death to set off his heroine's beauty. In Evangelical death-bed literature the link between the taint of original sin and the hope of being raised incorruptible was illustrated in the most literal manner by the appearance of the corpse, that last remnant of the old man, riddled with disease. Mr. Fairchild laboriously explains this to his children. 'As death is sent as a punishment for sin', he tells his children, '. . . it cannot but be very terrible . . .' As proof of his words he then takes them to see the corpse of their gardener. Surveying the yellowing corpse with its 'smell of corruption' he observes, 'such is the taint

[288] *Works*, xxxiv, 274.

[289] Wordsworth's phrase is used in this context by H. Cunningham, *Wheat and Tares*, p. 159.

[290] *Cambridge Essays*, pp. 175–6.

and corruption of the flesh, by reason of sin, that it must pass through the grave, and crumble to dust'.[291]

Dickens never brings himself to look death full in the face in this manner. The macabre philosophizings of Mrs. Gamp side-step the issue with a series of daring jokes which contribute to a black comedy approach to the subject of death. When Dickens has 'to compose' the limbs of his heroines 'in that last marble attitude' he stands back, like Mrs. Gamp, to survey 'a lovely corpse'.[292] He uses techniques, familiar to us from Evelyn Waugh's *The Loved One*, to deprive death of that ultimate reality and deep significance which Evangelicalism had assured it. The following paragraph from *The Old Curiosity Shop* perfectly illustrates Dickens's attempt to nullify the truth of the first sentence. 'She was dead. No sleep so beautiful and calm, so free from trace of pain, so fair to look upon. She seemed a creature fresh from the hand of God, and waiting for the breath of life; not one who had lived and suffered death.'[293]

Our uneasiness when confronted with such scenes is perhaps related to a further lack of the religious convictions which inspired the tradition that Dickens is using. Despite the strident assertions of immortality, and personal immortality at that, provided by Dickens, he is anxious to provide a terrestrial after-life and significance for his heroines which those with as little religious faith as his will be able to appreciate. The 'mighty, universal Truth', which the reader must gather from Little Nell's demise is more akin to religious humanism despite its use of orthodox vocabulary, than to Christian dogma.

When Death strikes down the innocent and young, for every fragile form from which he lets the panting spirit free, a hundred virtues rise, in shapes of mercy, charity, and love, to walk the world, and bless it. Of every tear that sorrowing mortals shed on such green graves, some good is born, some gentler nature comes. In the Destroyer's steps there spring up bright creations that defy his power, and his dark path becomes a way of light to Heaven.[294]

In direct relation to their uncertainty about immortality is the anxiety on the part of a George Eliot or a Dickens, to provide earthly assurances of a yet cruder variety. Despite George Eliot's attempts to relieve the heavy pathos of Milly Barton's closing moments by realistic observation of the children's reactions, her artistic integrity

[291] M. M. Sherwood, *Fairchild Family*, i, 147–51.
[292] *Martin Chuzzlewit*, p. 412. [293] *Old Curiosity Shop*, p. 39.
[294] Ibid., p. 544.

fails her at the last and Milly is depicted murmuring, 'Music—music—didn't you hear it?'[295]

The halo that surrounds the dying Paul Dombey has been the subject of much adverse criticism.

'Mama is like you, Floy. I know her by the face! But tell them that the print upon the stairs at school is not divine enough. The light about the head is shining on me as I go!'

The golden ripple on the wall came back again, and nothing else stirred in the room.[296]

To illustrate the precise quality of over emphasis that results from an incapacity to believe without seeing (and here Dickens's own summary of the scene is illuminating—'Oh thank God, all who see it, for that older fashion yet, of Immortality') I should like to set it beside the only comparable passage that I have discovered in Mrs. Sherwood's *Fairchild Family*.

. . . fixing his eyes on one corner of the room, the appearance of his countenance changed to a kind of heavenly and glorious expression, the like of which no one present ever before had seen; and every one looked towards the place on which his eyes were fixed, but they could see nothing extraordinary.[297]

Observing the final reticence, verging on anti-climax, of this account one is better able to appreciate the criticism of a Ruskin or a Stephen who recognized the vulgarization of the Evangelical tradition that had taken place. When Ruskin described Little Nell as 'simply killed for the market, as a butcher kills a lamb',[298] he was perhaps unfair in implying that Dickens had written merely with the financial rewards in mind. In bringing himself to relive Mary Hogarth's death[299] he sought also to provide consolation for himself and, indirectly, for many bereaved readers. The popularity of particular works by minor novelists seems to have rested upon the lingering and pious deaths of child heroes and heroines. Juliana Horatia Ewing's *The Story of a Short Life* (1885)[300] shares with

[295] *Scenes*, i, 111.

[296] C. Dickens, *Dombey and Son*, p. 226.

[297] *Fairchild Family*, i, 295.

[298] *Works*, xxxiv, 275n.

[299] E. Johnson, *Charles Dickens: His Tragedy and Triumph*, i, 201.

[300] Mrs. Ewing's biographer proudly claimed: 'It is a curious fact that, though her power of describing death-bed scenes was so vivid, I believe she never saw any one die . . .' H. K. F. Gatty, *Juliana Horatia Ewing and Her Books* (1885), p. 31.

Florence Montgomery's *Misunderstood* (1869) the desire to provide a fictional counterpart for the consolations offered in the Christian burial service. Descriptions of the children's affecting beauty are interspersed with hymns and texts from Revelation referring to the sorrowless glories of the New Jerusalem, reserved for those who have come 'out of great tribulation'.[301] Implicit too in Dickens's accounts of Little Nell's or Paul Dombey's death is the belief that by dying young a child had avoided the contamination of sin and could return to heaven still 'trailing clouds of glory'. The sentimentality of Colonel Newcome's death-bed partly derives from Thackeray's endeavour to obliterate the disillusioning years of adult experience and to substitute a picture of childlike saintliness which bears little resemblance to the refractory Tommy of the opening chapters: 'Now, as in those early days, his heart was pure; no anger remained in it; no guile tainted it; only peace and good-will dwelt in it.'[302] However satisfying to bereaved parents this Romantic doctrine of a child's innocence might be, it was totally unacceptable to the Evangelical. Lest we should be in any doubt on this point Mrs. Sherwood preceded her picture of Charles Trueman's death with the story of Augusta, a literary progenitor of Hilaire Belloc's Matilda, who perished by fire and so died insensible without a chance to repent.[303] Whether a Calvinist like Mrs. Sherwood, clinging to the doctrine of total depravity, or an Arminian, as Mrs. Worboise seems to have been, the Evangelicals were united on this point. In *The House of Bondage* Mrs. Worboise offers, in dialogue form, a stern rebuke to the sentimentally pious.

'Don't you think those whom God calls away in youth are greatly blessed?'

'All whom God calls to Himself are blessed; but it is not more blessed to go in youth than in old age.'[304]

It has often been noted that we find ourselves most remote from the attitudes and experiences of the Victorian novelist and his public in the treatment accorded to death, but to account for this merely by reference to modern reticence on the subject begs the question of the reasons for this change in sensibility. The reasons seem to be in

[301] Cf. Mrs. H. Wood, *East Lynne* (3 vols., 1861), iii, ch. xx, entitled, 'The Death-Chamber' which employs this tradition and these techniques.

[302] *The Newcomes*, p. 1005.

[303] *Fairchild Family*, i, 154–60.

[304] *House of Bondage*, p. 271.

part theological and in part demographical. As the Victorian debate began to concern itself more and more with the question of immortality, the impetus of theological controversy moved away from discussion of the fate of a man's soul, determined by its state at the moment of death, and towards the first question of proving that a man was actually possessed of an immortal soul.[305] Perhaps, too, the increased incidence of violent deaths in modern society, through war on a new scale, using the weapons of a new technology, through motor accidents and aeroplane crashes, has helped to minimize the theological importance formerly attributed to the last moments. The use of sedation has also contributed to this latter development. The absence of a climax in Mrs. Morel's long-drawn-out death is interesting in this context.[306]

In 1880 Ruskin could still claim that the death-bed scene was a temptation for weak novelists, 'because the study of it from the living—or dying—model is so easy, and to many has been the most impressive part of their own personal experience . . .'[307] Between 1880 and 1935 the annual death rate dropped from 20·5 per thousand of the population to 11·7 per thousand. The infant mortality figures remained fairly constant throughout the latter half of the nineteenth century, but dropped significantly thereafter. Out of 1,000 live births in 1840 and 1900 154 children died within their first year. Between 1900 and 1935 the figure fell to 57 out of 1,000.[308] Perhaps more important than the mere decline in annual mortality was the fact that there was less need for a family ritual to assimilate the event as hospitalization of the slowly dying became an accepted norm. In a survey carried out by Geoffrey Gorer in 1963 it was found that almost all children known to be seriously ill died away from their families in hospital. Although 44 per cent of the population still die at home, this number would seem to represent sudden deaths, or those occuring through the natural process of old age rather than through chronic lingering illnesses.[309] Personal observation on Gorer's part revealed that no one under the age of thirty had witnessed the death of a close relative, whilst no one over

[305] For a detailed account of this change in direction in theological debate see G. Rowell, *Hell and the Victorians.*

[306] D. H. Lawrence, *Sons and Lovers* (1966), Pt. II, ch. xiv.

[307] *Works*, xxxiv, 274.

[308] B. R. Mitchell, *Abstracts of British Historical Statistics* (Cambridge, 1962), pp. 36–41.

[309] G. Gorer, *Death, Grief, and Mourning in Contemporary Britain* (1965), pp. 18–19.

the age of sixty had not.[310] The rapidly developed role of the undertaker, a professional functionary, who can be employed to take over from the family the last office of preparing the body would seem to confirm the tendency to avoid death which has accompanied the growth of an increasingly secular society. For a complex variety of reasons the weaker modern novelist can no longer count upon conventional emotional responses to a domestic death-bed scene.

H. G. Wells, with his journalist's sensitivity to changes in fashion, marks for us the death of the Victorian death-bed scene at a moment when it was perhaps entering its final throes in everyday life. As Uncle Ponderevo lies awaiting death in a small French hotel, he and his nephew suffer 'a raid from a little English clergyman and his amiable, capable wife in severely Anglican black, who swooped down upon us like virtuous but resolute vultures . . .'[311] As the nephew witnesses the clergyman 'repeating over and over again—"Mr. Ponderevo, Mr. Ponderevo, it is all right. It is all right. Only believe! 'Believe on Me, and ye shall be saved'!" and 'trying to render the stock phrases of Low Church piety into French' for the benefit of the bystanders, the nephew reflects, 'I felt I was back in the eighteenth century.'[312] Together with the journalist's awareness of change went his ability to underline a point by exaggeration. Yet this scene neatly illustrates the cross-roads at which Wells himself, albeit unconsciously, stood, between Victorian preoccupations and twentieth-century manners. His pose as the modern man is reflected by the attitude that no longer criticizes an Evangelical death-bed scene as theologically misguided but as a tiresome and ineffectual anachronism. His nineteenth-century upbringing is shown in his willingness to confront death seriously and to articulate an individual response to it.

> Death!
>
> It was one of those rare seasons of relief, when for a brief time one walks a little outside of and beside life. . . .
>
> My doubts and disbeliefs slipped from me like a loosely fitting garment. I wondered quite simply what dogs bayed about the path of that other walker in the darkness, what shapes, what lights, it might be, loomed about him as he went his way from our last encounter on earth—along the paths that are real, and the way that endures for ever?[313]

[310] G. Gorer, *Death, Grief, and Mourning in Contemporary Britain*, p. 172.
[311] *Tono-Bungay* (1924), pp. 491–2. [312] Ibid. 493.
[313] *Tono-Bungay*, pp. 498–9.

## 4. *Missionary and philanthropic endeavour*

As the nickname they proudly appropriated suggests the Evangelicals laid particular stress upon the duty of preaching the Evangel, or Gospel. Although there were Evangelical Calvinists, such as the notorious Doctor Hawker at Plymouth,[314] who believed missionary endeavour to be at odds with the theory of predestination, most moderate Calvinists[315] agreed with the Arminian J. W. Cunningham. He claimed that Christ's command, 'Go ye, therefore, and teach all nations' was 'a sort of *prospective reply to all the main objections* which have been, or which perhaps can be, urged against the fulfilment of this duty'.[316]

It may seem surprising that an aspect of their practical piety in one sense so important should be so briefly treated, yet any attempt to sketch in a paragraph or two the history of Evangelical missionary endeavour would be impossibly misleading and curiously irrelevant to discussion of the novel. Despite the vast extent of the mission field and the lure which one might have expected missionary tales, broadcast by way of Exeter Hall, to have held, early and mid-nineteenth-century non-Evangelical novelists made little use of this facet of Evangelicalism in their work. India or Burma provided a useful narrative device for the disposal of an unwanted, but virtuous, male lover, in much the same way as a convent would have done for a girl in a less fanatically anti-papist age. St. John Rivers and Eustace Grey were both to take this path.[317] Their fate was perhaps inspired by the well-known history of that early romantic martyr of the Evangelical movement, Henry Martyn. In practice few of the early missionaries returned to tell of their adventures in person, and, had they done so, would have found scant welcome from crowds accustomed to hearing of the societies' achievements from the noble and famous rather than from labourers in the field.[318]

[314] E. Stock, *History of the Church Missionary Society*, i, 282.

[315] For an explanation of their position see the Rev. W. Goode's statement, *Eclectic Notes*, ed. J. H. Pratt, p. 226.

[316] *General Objections against Missions for the Conversion of the Heathen Considered* (1818), pp. 1, 3.

[317] C. Brontë, *Jane Eyre*; and C. L. Scott, *Old Grey Church*.

[318] E. Stock, *My Recollections*, p. 77, stresses that missionary speakers did not appear at meetings in mid-century. We are helped to date the change by a magazine article which refers to the presence of actual missionaries as speakers, 'Evangelical Drawing-Rooms', *Tinsley's Magazine*, 9 (1871–2), pp. 112–14.

Mrs. Sherwood published a number of works based upon her experiences in India, the most famous of which, *The History of Little Henry and His Bearer*, though primarily written for English children living in India achieved popularity in England and had the effect of familiarizing English readers with individual Evangelicals' missionary efforts amongst the Hindu.[319] The tales of Anglo-India, which Thackeray's children heard from their Evangelical grandmother, Mrs. Carmichael Smyth, were reinforced by the reading of this book.[320] The strangest of Mrs. Sherwood's many publishing exploits must have been her version of *Pilgrim's Progress* written for a Hindustani audience but finally published in England.[321] 'Charlotte Elizabeth' wrote a lengthy poem in heroic couplets entitled *Osric: A Missionary Tale* (1825) in which the hero, shipwrecked on the Canadian coast, is led to the truth by a Red Indian, himself a convert of an English missionary. The West Indies formed the background for two of her prose tales, *Perseverance; or Walter and his little school* (1826) and *The System; a Tale of the West Indies* (1827), which were designed as part of the Evangelical campaign against slavery.

Livingstone's *Missionary Travels in South Africa*, published in 1857, served to acquaint a wider audience than the Evangelical with the adventurous possibilities of missionary life. Apart, however, from children's books like R. M. Ballantyne's *The Coral Island* (1858), which paid passing tribute to missionary achievement, the broader reaches of empire did not enter the non-religious novel till the closing decades of the nineteenth century. The novelists' own travels, and therefore those of their potential readership, might take them to Europe, the Eastern Mediterranean, the United States, or even the Antipodes, but they left India and Africa to be depicted by those with first-hand experience.[322] Moreover the mid-century novelists, with whom I am mainly concerned, were for the most part content to exploit England's self-centred interest in the social

[319] *History of Little Henry and His Bearer*, 7th edn. (Wellington, 1816). This edition still bears the moral, 'Little children in India, remember Henry L—, and *go and do likewise*.' p. 138.

[320] *Thackeray Letters*, iii, 20.

[321] *The Indian Pilgrim; or, the Progress of the Pilgrim Nazarene (Formerly called Goonah Purist, or the Slave of Sin), from the City of the Wrath of God to the City of Mount Zion. Delivered under the Similitude of a Dream* (Wellington, 1818).

[322] A brief guide to this literature can be found in E. F. Oaten, 'Anglo-Indian Literature', *Cambridge History of Literature; XV The Nineteenth Century*, ed. A. W. Ward and A. R. Waller, (Cambridge, 1916).

changes which followed the Industrial Revolution and to concentrate their attention on the inadequacy of the Evangelical endeavour on the home front.

Although fair-minded ecclesiastics, and the occasional novelist, approvingly recognized the fruits of Evangelical labour in both town and country parishes,[323] the perennial accusation was made that the home mission field was neglected in favour of the welfare, spiritual and physical, of the natives of Borrioboola-Gha. Dickens re-emphasized in his letters the opinion that Mr. Weller had voiced and that Jo and Mrs. Jellyby had presented in dramatized form—[324] 'that the two works, the home and the foreign, are *not* conducted with an equal hand, and that the home claim is by far the stronger and the more pressing of the two'.[325] Many novelists missed the positive intensity of sympathy for the heathen at home which Dickens managed to combine with his destructive satire of the missionary effort. They could, however, join with him in deploring the manner in which English Evangelical audiences clasped to their bosom any foreign convert, a Kusinera[326] or a Chowbok,[327] whilst ignoring their immediate responsibilities. Mrs. Sophia Alethea Newcome employed a 'black footman (for the lashings of whose brethren she felt unaffected pity)'[328] to chastize her step-son, who is later sent away from the bosom of the family to India. Carlyle,[329] *Punch*,[330] and the novelists joined forces in calling the nation's attention to the way in which Exeter Hall's annual jamborees, the May meetings, at which reports on missionary ventures were given, attracted those who were prepared to listen, entranced, to glamourized travel and adventure stories, whilst ignoring the more immediate misery of the English working classes. The high literary quality of some of this satire has perpetuated their accusations and allowed us to forget that the leading Evangelicals themselves were often acutely aware of this phenomenon. Wilberforce, addressing a meeting anxious to improve the lot of climbing boys, urged his

[323] e.g. W. Conybeare, *Edin. Rev.* 98 (1853), 273–342; *Perversion*, i, 354–8; and [C. S. C. Bowen], 'The English Evangelical Clergy', *Macmillan's Magazine*, 3 (1860), 119.

[324] *Pickwick Papers*, p. 371; *Bleak House*.

[325] *Letters of Charles Dickens*, ed. W. Dexter, ii, 401.

[326] B. Disraeli, *Falconet*.

[327] S. Butler, *Erewhon*, and *Erewhon Revisited*.

[328] W. M. Thackeray, *The Newcomes*, p. 27.

[329] 'Occasional Discourse on the Nigger Question', *Fraser's*, 40 (1849), 670–9; and 'Shooting Niagara: and After?' *Macmillan's Magazine*, 16 (Aug. 1867), 319–36.

[330] 'Exeter Hall Pets', *Punch*, 6 (1844), 210.

listeners 'to manifest the same humanity for the sons of their own country that they had for the children of Africa'.[331] Shaftesbury, a stern critic of his Evangelical compatriots, remarked of a Reformatory project he had in hand, 'If our asylum contained dead Indians or tattoed Zealanders we should excite overwhelming interest, but because it contains only live Penitents we have scarcely any [funds]'.[332]

Yet when the Evangelical impulse manifested itself nearer home, criticism did not diminish. The strength of their convictions and their determination to preach the word both in and out of season ensured that Evangelicals could not be politely ignored since such a reception bespoke the very worldly indifference against which they had vowed to fight. Their enthusiasm for embarking upon 'serious conversation' in the most unlikely circumstances was variously interpreted. Sir Henry Cunningham characterized it as mere social maladroitness in his picture of a clergyman's wife at an evening party choosing 'the fastest man in his division', as her agent for the conversion of the army.[333] A strong sense of accountability to God for one's fellow men could lead to a deadly serious critical spirit. A bride who had married into the Thornton family at Clapham remarked that, 'If there was a spot upon the glorious Sun himself, the Thorntons would notice it.'[334] The wholly unsympathetic Wilkie Collins had no hesitation in diagnosing a positive enjoyment of 'the glorious prospect of interference'[335] offered to proselytizers.

Collins's caricature of the tract distributor, Miss Clack, is probably a product of his own annoyance and embarrassment at being persistently pursued by two pious Evangelical ladies, when on holiday with his mistress and illegitimate daughter at Broadstairs. Once aware of the nature of the relationship between the three companions, the two young women set to work to distribute tracts in the path of the sinners calling them to repentance.[336] Collins claimed that this caricature was the secret of the book's popularity. Missionary and philanthropic activities certainly provided occupation for many to whom professions were closed, notably spinsters whose energy was insufficiently tapped by domestic concerns. Thackeray's reference to Lady Emily Southdown as 'A mature

[331] Quoted by B. Harrison, 'Philanthropy and the Victorians', *VS*, 9 (1965–6), 372.
[332] E. Hodder, *Life of Shaftesbury*, ii, 417. [333] *Wheat and Tares*, p. 119.
[334] E. M. Forster, 'Battersea Rise', *Abinger Harvest* (1967), p. 242.
[335] *Moonstone*, p. 227.
[336] N. P. Davies, *The Life of Wilkie Collins* (Urbana, 1956), pp. 226–7.

spinster . . . having but faint ideas of marriage, her love for the blacks occupied almost all her feelings',[337] was one of many such cruel parodies to give readers and writers alike the chance to release their exasperation in laughter at grotesques whilst suspending human sympathy. Charlotte Brontë, herself a spinster when she wrote *Shirley*, attempted to supply a corrective to these literary stereotypes in her portrait of Miss Ainsley, whom some disparagingly called 'a saint', because 'she referred to religion often in sanctioned phrase', but whose good works proved her 'a Sister of Charity', rather than a mere 'Lady Bountiful'.[338]

These lay agents, district visitors, and Lady Bountifuls, were also vulnerable to attack on doctrinal grounds. High Church novelists claimed that their work was not sanctioned by the authority which the clergy derived from their office and so they depicted well-meaning men and women, employed by Evangelical societies, whose efforts were doomed to failure because they showed insufficient recognition of the Church's authority.[339] Such pictures, however, have less chance of gaining the attention of modern readers than the simpler satire of the secular novelists based upon the discrepancy they perceived between the concept of Christian charity and the cold, overbearingly self-righteous manner in which it was sometimes dispensed.

So far I have made no formal distinction between the missionary work directed to spiritual salvation and the philanthropic endeavour to improve material welfare. The Evangelicals did not see the relief of suffering as their main objective. Though they attempted to relieve it, suffering chiefly moved them to intensify their battle against its cause, the evil rooted in men's souls. It could be argued that Evangelicalism had unwisely resorted to propaganda which promised more than spiritual comfort, for when it attempted to fall back upon the purity of a single-minded appeal to salvation it was accused of indifference to, or harsh neglect of, man's physical needs. Sir James Stephen pinpoints the distinction between a secular and an Evangelical philanthropy in his description of Henry Thornton, Clapham's wealthy banker. He spoke of him as 'a lover of mankind, but not an enthusiast in the cause of our common humanity',[340]

[337] *Vanity Fair*, pp. 411–12. [338] *Shirley*, pp. 164–5.

[339] [W. Sewell], *Hawkstone: A Tale of and for England in 184-* (2 vols., 1845). C. M. Yonge, *Castle Builders*, and *Pillars of the House*.

[340] *Essays in Ecclesiastical Biography*, ii, 296.

because Thornton's immense charitable donations[341] were theocentrically motivated. Thornton himself, ever mindful of Christ's command, 'Seek ye first the kingdom of God and his righteousness . . .', used the story of Abraham's sacrifice to express the distinction.

Worldly men stumble at this story because they know not the value of faith. To please God is with them a small matter; to discharge, as they term it, their duty to their fellow-creature is the all in all. This story may therefore serve to prove how unscriptural is their mode of thinking. . . .[342]

Those novelists whose humanitarian consciences had led them to sympathize with the many philanthropic ventures set afoot by the Evangelicals, could not accord the same sympathy to the philosophy which considered these works as merely a by-product of missionary zeal, not their chief aim. Escott, who claimed that Trollope's 'great ground of quarrel with Evangelicalism was its tendency to divorce conduct from religion', once heard him say to an old Evangelical,

'You tell me . . . that, in effect, virtue becomes vice if its practical pursuit be not sanctified by a mystical motive not within the understanding of all. Such a theory, I retort, can in its working have only one of two results—the immorality of antinomianism, or a condition of perplexity and confusion which must drive men from religion in disgust and despair.'[343]

George Eliot, who well understood that 'the highest state of mind inculcated by the Gospel is resignation to the disposal of God's providence—"Whether we live, we live unto the Lord; whether we die, we die unto the Lord" ',[344] captured this doctrine at work in the hands of Bulstrode, a man personally predisposed to value temporal power. ' " . . . I will boldly confess to you, Mr. Lydgate, that I should have no interest in hospitals if I believed that nothing more was concerned therein than the cure of mortal diseases." '[345]

The subtle comparison of Lydgate's motives with those of Bulstrode in the plans for improving the local hospital is often missed because Bulstrode is so forthright in his declaration whilst Lydgate as yet is unaware of the extent to which he himself discounts the importance of individual human welfare in the pursuit of his

[341] Details given by E. M. Howse, *Saints in Politics*, p 126.

[342] Quoted by S. Meacham. 'The Evangelical Inheritance', *JBS* 3 (1963), 91.

[343] *Anthony Trollope*, pp. 226–7.

[344] *Essays of G. Eliot*, p. 181.

[345] *Middlemarch*, i, 191.

scientific interests. George Eliot is just enough to admit that the Bulstrodes of the world perform a valuable philanthropic function, yet she is concerned to pass on the message learnt from Feuerbach and Comte that even the most active of Evangelical social reformers, working primarily for 'the glory of God', is wasting valuable sources of natural compassion by transferring them from man to an abstract Godhead.

Dickens, whose tendency it was to discount motives in favour of action, was unable to credit the sincerity of a belief which could elevate concern above philanthropic impulse. In real life his judgement of various religious doctrines, and the men who represented them, was formed upon humanitarian principles, and in his novels this tendency results in a dismissal of doctrinal subtlety. Chadband, who retains the Evangelical tone, divorced from doctrinal content, is, for all his preaching, an avaricious, miserly hypocrite, whilst Snagsby, who sees Jo's needs entirely in terms of the odd half-crown, emerges as the good man.

Snagsby may have done nothing to ensure Jo's spiritual growth, but his charity demands no recompense. Bulstrode, on the other hand, if he took 'a great deal of pains about apprenticing Tegg the shoemaker's son . . . would watch over Tegg's church-going . . .'[346] The accusation that Evangelicals followed a sectarian policy in the distribution of their charities was frequently made. Hannah More may have approved of withholding alms from the politically subversive[347] but did not extend the policy to the theologically uncooperative. Coelebs, the eponymous hero of her novel, when confronting a woman who 'had a great dislike to relieve any but those of her own religious persuasion', 'could not forbear observing, that I did not think it demanded a combination of all the virtues to entitle a poor sick wretch to a dinner'.[348] Patrick Brontë, a working Evangelical parson, was of the opinion that 'as God causes the rain to fall on the just and the unjust, so it is our duty, whilst we are administering to the wants of the righteous, not to pass by the miserable abodes of the wicked'.[349]

The myth of the Evangelical closed system, propagated by novelists like Mrs. Trollope,[350] doubtless arose from watching Evangelicals gain control of the major societies. If conversion was at

[346] *Middlemarch*, i, 235. [347] See F. K. Brown, *Fathers of the Victorians*, p. 144.
[348] *Coelebs*, i, 67. [349] *Maid of Killarney*, p. 150.
[350] *Vicar of Wrexhill*, ii, 266–9.

least equally as important as the relief of material needs it was necessary to ensure that correct doctrine was inculcated by the officers of the society. Tractarians, indeed, complained of Evangelical permissiveness, of 'the tone of semi-dissent' which they allowed to prevail in interdenominational societies.[351] Since missionary society meetings had always provided a forum for the major theological controversies they were also used in sectarian warfare. Criticism varied from Trollope's disgust at the use of an annual meeting to discuss problems of ecclesiastical strategy on the home field, apparently unrelated to the mission in question,[352] to complaints of underhand behaviour on the mission field. *Kate Gearey: or, Irish Life in London*, a novel by Miss Mason, which was serialized in the convert catholic periodical, *The Rambler*, launched a bitter attack upon Lord Shaftesbury, thinly disguised as the Earl of Lindore, and his Ragged Schools. The Earl's niece, herself a convert Catholic, first claims that Protestant ladies are too 'delicate' to enter the slums of London's Irish quarter, and then that Protestants are bribing Irish Catholics and their children to apostasize, making callous use of harsh winters to augment their flock. Regardless of her own quite considerable efforts at detraction, she becomes incensed when she reads the anti-Papist abuse sanctioned by the Committee responsible for the Ragged School Union Annual Report. The intransigent doctrinal position maintained by Evangelical societies seems less singular when we hear this Catholic ministering angel remark of her wards, 'Better their bodies waste from want, than the soul perish eternally.'[353]

Evangelical anxiety to win Protestants from the clutches of Rome had undoubtedly led them into a number of foolish practices. Repeated missions to the Irish, and in particular the 'special fund for spiritual exigencies', inaugurated in 1846, had so frequently been denounced, both in the papers and in Parliament,[354] for employing bribery, as to merit an unannotated reference in Disraeli's novel

[351] F. E. Paget, *Warden of Berkingholt*, p. 271; W. Sewell, *Hawkstone;* and C. M. Yonge, *Gleanings from Thirty Years Intercourse with the Late Rev. John Keble*, p. xl.

[352] 'The Zulu in London', *Pall Mall Gazette* (10 May 1865), pp. 3–4.

[353] *Rambler*, 10 (1852), 102. My attention was directed to this novel by S. W. Gilley, 'Evangelical and Roman Catholic Missions to the Irish in London, 1830–1870', D. Phil. thesis, Cambridge, 1970, p. 115. The novel was published in 1853, but the British Museum's copy was destroyed during the war, and others do not seem to have survived elsewhere.

[354] T. R. Birks, *Memoir of the Rev. Edward Bickersteth*, ii, 368.

*Tancred.*[355] Mrs. Oliphant found fault with Tract societies 'more zealous than scrupulous', who were prepared to countenance lies to customs officers, if by this means Bibles could be smuggled to Roman Catholics.[356]

The social ethic implicitly accepted by the majority of the authors I discuss rendered them unsympathetic to one persistent line of attack upon the Evangelical missionary enterprise, formulated by the more radical critics. The novelists rarely accused Evangelicalism of being the linchpin of reactionary politics. Cobbett's verdict has formed the basis for a tradition of historical thought which finds Evangelicalism inimical to social progress:

> . . . it was well known, that the set of politicians, ironically called the Saints, were the main prop of the Pitt System; it was well known, that under the garb of sanctity, they aided and abetted in all the worst things that were done. The political history of the Saints, would exhibit a series of the most infamous intrigues and most rapacious plunder, that, perhaps, ever was heard of in the world. They were never found wanting at any dirty job; and invariably lent their aid in those acts, which were the most inimical to the liberty of England.[357]

Hannah More's *Village Politics*, commissioned as a counterblast to the Jacobinical works of Tom Paine, Wilberforce's close friendship with Pitt and the Sabbatical campaign which oppressed the poor rather than the rich, formed the basis for the contemporary radical attack. Yet Dickens, whose radical sympathies might have led us to expect a similar biting attack, contents himself with sporadic outbursts against particular instances of oppression or mismanagement rather than formulating an indictment of systematic bourgeois oppression by the Evangelicals. Mrs. Trollope, after a fact-finding mission, made easier for her by introductions from Lord Ashley,[358] wrote *The Life and Adventures of Michael Armstrong, the Factory Boy*, in which she spoke of factory children compelled to attend Sunday Schools, where the owners preached that 'obedience to

[355] *Tancred*, pp. 70–1. [356] *Son of the Soil*, ii, 38–40, 45.

[357] *The Autobiography of William Cobbett*, ed. W. Reitzel (1967), p. 94. Cobbett's contemporary, William Hazlitt, expressed similar views in 'Lord Eldon—Mr. Wilberforce,' *Works*, xi, 147–50. Some of the more prominent guardians of the tradition in the twentieth century have been J. L. and B. Hammond, *The Town Labourer 1760–1832: The New Civilization* (1966), pp. 233–8; J. Hart, 'Nineteenth Century Social Reform: a Tory re-interpretation of history', *Past and Present* 31 (July 1965), pp. 39–61; and E. P. Thompson, *Making of the English Working Class*, pp. 60–1, 141, 161, 442.

[358] M. Sadleir, *Trollope, a Commentary*, p. 93.

their earthly masters was the only way of saving children from the eternal burning prepared for those who were disobedient in the world to come'.[359] As in *The Vicar of Wrexhill*, however, she succeeded rather in suggesting how Evangelicalism might be harnessed to an oppressive regime than in demonstrating that it was itself the key to social tyranny. Thackeray parted company from the *Punch* editorship because of the anti-clerical turn that their radicalism had taken.[360] Mrs. Gaskell might depict a Methodist withdrawing from the fight for improvement of temporal conditions to escapist dreams of eternal bliss and equality[361] but there is no suggestion of political manipulation by evangelical teachers at the root of this error. William Sewell's picture of The Royal and National Grand African Colonization and Timbuctoo Civilization Society, which at first sight appears like an early attack upon imperialist exploitation carried on under the camouflage of missionary zeal, turns out to be illustrating the High-Churchman's belief, that inter-denominational societies are liable to corruption because their basis of religious authority is so nebulous.[362]

The English Victorian novel produced nothing comparable to Tolstoy's *Resurrection*, in which the German and English Evangelical missionaries,[363] even when apparently philanthropically concerned, are judged and found wanting in the context of a coherent ideological framework. Tolstoy mistrusted any religion that taught men to look to the Redemption, to salvation by faith rather than by the fruit of human works. The English novelists had absorbed much of the Evangelical ethic and were intent upon grafting on to this an ultimately irreconcileable humanitarian ethic. Mrs. Gaskell or George Eliot, like the Evangelicals, still looked to individual conversion rather than to legal reform to realize their humanitarian dreams. Other novelists had apparently accepted uncritically the Evangelical tendency to portray its faith as resulting in temporal as well as spiritual salvation.

[359] *Michael Armstrong*, (3 vols., 1840), ii, 306. Mrs. Trollope is here repeating a popular contemporary view. Cf. a letter from Southey to Lord Ashley, '. . . Sunday Schools have been subservient to the merciless love of gain. The manufacturers know that a cry would be raised against them if their little white slaves received no instruction; and so they have converted Sunday into a *school-day*, with what effect may be seen in the evidences.' E. Hodder, *Life of Shaftesbury*, i, 156–7.

[360] G. N. Ray, *Thackeray: The Uses of Adversity, 1811–1846* (1955), p. 370.

[361] *North and South* (1906), pp. 117–18.

[362] *Hawkstone*, i, 365–79.

[363] *Resurrection*, trans. V. Traill (1947), Pt. II, ch. xvii, and Pt. III, ch. xxvii.

Evangelicals had never been tempted to elevate poverty as a virtue, but held in curious tension the ideas of a station in life appointed by God and the Puritan work ethic, which encouraged men to see in secular success, a sign of God's favour, and, in misery or squalor, a sign of punishment for superstition or irreligion.[364] Even Anne Brontë, a member of a family usually capable of fairly sophisticated criticism of Evangelical attitudes, produces, in *Agnes Grey*, a chapter entitled 'The Cottagers', which might well have formed the substance of a tract by Hannah More. One of the cottagers goes through a period of careless indifference to household chores whilst in religious turmoil, but once firmly rooted in Gospel truths becomes a model for domestic cleanliness and suffering patience.[365]

As the nineteenth century progressed, missionary and philanthropic societies multiplied and satirical fictional comment proliferated. The novelists' grounds for abusing the societies ranged from unfortunately chosen names and activities to their competitive spirit, zealous interference and the opportunity they provided for the social adventurer to enter good society under the guise of good works. Those numerous fictional pictures of a thoughtless leisured class, diverting itself with the organization of fancy-fairs, help to explain Carlyle's savage indictment of his mid-century contemporaries as 'Sunk in deep froth-oceans of "Benevolence", "Fraternity", "Emancipation-principle", "Christian Philanthropy", and other most amiable looking, but most baseless, and in the end baleful and all-bewildering jargon . . .'[366]

## 5. *The Evangelical response to 'the world'*

> In praising culture, we have never denied that conduct, not culture, is three-fourths of human life.
>
> Only it certainly appears, when the thing is examined, that conduct comes to have relations of a very close kind with culture.[367]

[364] In an appeal for the special Irish fund (1846) Bickersteth said of the famine and illness '. . . such afflictions come from the hand of God, they are his chastisement for our sins. . . . If the appointed weeks of harvest bring no harvest, the reason is especially stated. "Your iniquities have witholden these things from you".' T. R. Birks, *Memoir of the Rev. Edward Bickersteth*, ii, 367–8.

[365] *Agnes Grey*, ch. xi.

[366] *Fraser's*, 40 (1849), 671. In his last novel *Edwin Drood* (1870) Dickens is still pursuing this line of attack.

[367] M. Arnold, *The Complete Prose Works of Matthew Arnold*, ed. R. Super (10 vols., Ann Arbor, 1960–74), vi, 407.

> 'The object of all a Christian does, should be to improve a subject, and if he can do this by any means, it matters very little whether the lines by which he accomplishes it are gracefully drawn, or the shades finely tinted.'
> '. . . your principle would lead to the disregard of all rules of taste and order, and that by such disregard, where one person is benefitted, a hundred or a thousand may learn to connect ugliness and deformity, instead of beauty and order, with religion; and so as much injury as good may be done in the end to the cause of truth.'[368]

Practical Evangelical piety was not confined to the formal acts of devotion examined in the preceding sections. Any activity not subordinated to a theocentric pattern of life must be construed as disloyalty to God. The Evangelical must live in the world, where Providence had placed him, but must not be of the world. It required a mature and sensitive intelligence to keep these ideas in permanent synthesis. In 1797 Wilberforce advised that the true Christian 'should demean himself, in all the common affairs of life, like an accountable creature', but equally be prepared to 'relax in the temperate use of all the gifts of Providence. Imagination, and taste, and genius, and the beauties of creation, and the works of art, lie open to him.'[369] A century later J. C. Ryle still felt the need to publish a tract, entitled *Worldly Conformity*, *What it is not*, *and What it is*, in which the misunderstanding of the concept of separateness current amongst some Evangelicals is reflected.

> When St. Paul says, 'Come out and be separate', he did not mean that Christians ought to take no interest in anything on earth except religion. To neglect science, art, literature, and politics,—to read nothing which is not directly spiritual,—to know nothing about what is going on among mankind, and never to look at a newspaper,—to care nothing about the government of one's country, and to be utterly indifferent to the persons who guide its counsels and make its laws,—all this may seem very right and proper in the eyes of some people. But I take leave to think that it is an idle, selfish neglect of duty.[370]

Ryle's account did not exaggerate. Even J. C. Philpot, an Evangelical of the Evangelicals, regarded his friend Tiptaft's fear of the

[368] H. Mozley, *Lost Brooch*, ii, 176–7.
[369] *Practical View*, pp. 344, 455.
[370] *Worldly Conformity* (1878), p. 23.

taint of worldliness as excessive. 'While he [Tiptaft] was with us *The Times*, *Blackwood*, and *The Quarterly*, which my father always took in, had to be put out of sight, for he dreaded lest they should draw him away from Christ.'[371]

It was all too easy for weaker brethren to regard the world as entirely given over to Satan and to retreat behind a stultifying code of rules. Of one such clergyman's wife it is reported, 'When her fine manly boys came home from their holidays, she would not allow them to stand at the windows of their father's Parsonage without making them turn their backs so as not to look at the romantic views by which the house was encircled, lest the loveliness of "Satan's earth" should alienate their affections from the world to come.'

Abner Brown, the narrator of this tale, asserted that by the 1830s 'It seemed to be a settled point that "the living God did not give us richly all things to enjoy".'[372] As Wilberforce's choice of words made clear the Evangelical reading of the text, even at its most liberal, would have supplanted the adverb 'richly' by 'temperately' or 'moderately'. The late 1820s and early 1830s mark a discernible period during which the split between the secular and religious worlds widened. It was these years that witnessed the emergence of the conservative Recordite group—men closely tied to the clergy and the Establishment on a parochial basis—and their tendency to distance themselves from the urbane, predominantly lay world of Clapham and the 'Saints'. Earlier generations of Evangelicals who had come to the Gospel via the path of the Law remained peculiarly alive to the temptation of substituting a rigid asceticism, the most subtle form of works, for total reliance upon Christ. But for later generations the clear distinction between legalism and Gospel freedom was not always a matter of personal experience, and there came a tendency to confuse sacrifices necessitated in the early stages of the crusade, the secondary products of the faith, with the faith itself. Novelists, accusing them of papistical self-persecution, demonstrated how rigid orthodoxy could become a cloak for individual fears and dislikes whilst self-mortification might be practised as a substitute for positive religious experience. The effort to maintain a favourable spiritual bank balance by acts of gratuitous self-punishment provides the common denominator in characters otherwise as diverse as Mrs. Clennam, Miss Clack, Mrs.

[371] J. H. Philpot, *The Seceders*, p. 177.
[372] *Recollections of Simeon*, pp. 79–80.

Prime and Mrs. Bolton, Christina Pontifex and Mr. Bulstrode.[373] It is easy to see how such misconceptions arose when we consider that a man like Leslie Stephen, who had seen Evangelicalism practised at its most liberal at Clapham, could remark that his father had once smoked a cigar, but had enjoyed it so much that he never smoked again.[374] In the elder Stephen's case this may well have been an example of 'the religious delicacy and profound asceticism' of which, as Matthew Arnold remarked, so few Englishmen had any comprehension. Spiritual self-discipline rather than self-indulgent attempts to prove himself righteous sound more in keeping with a man who observed, 'Saints who have mortified themselves to the quick are to be met with in every collection of ecclesiastical worthies. But how few who have enjoyed themselves to the utmost! How few elevated enough to believe that such joy would be acceptable to God!'[375]

The sacrifices made by the Evangelicals might seem like the petty austerities of a gloomy and negative religion but, as Edward Bickersteth reminded his mother, 'He that despiseth small things shall fall by little and little'.[376] Critics suggested that such a conviction paid insufficient regard to the mixed nature of human beings or the relative gravity of their failings. In Mrs. Bolton's mind, if a man drank and 'gambled' in mining speculations, it was all too probable that he had also committed bigamy.[377] Yet when they detected any tempering of these harsh standards the same critics were swift to use it as a clear indication of insincerity or Laodicean apathy. Once or twice only in the pages of a non-Evangelical novelist is a man shown sympathetically who allows greater laxity in the bosom of his family than he does in public preaching. Although not as lovable as George Eliot's Dissenter, Rufus Lyon, and with more of the taint of worldliness upon him, Trollope's Dr. Comfort, as his name suggests, is enabled to solace the troubled by virtue of the liberality with which he tempers those hard words preached from the pulpit. Critics often failed to realize that, in a theological world where

[373] To be found in the following novels: C. Dickens, *Little Dorrit*, p. 52; W. Collins, *Moonstone*, p. 206; A. Trollope, *Rachel Ray*, p. 4; *John Caldigate*, p. 429; S. Butler, *Way of All Flesh*, p. 72; G. Eliot, *Middlemarch*, ch. liii.

[374] *Life of Sir James Fitzjames Stephen*, p. 61.

[375] Entry in Journal, 28 March 1846. C. E. Stephen, *The First Sir James Stephen*, p. 108.

[376] T. R. Birks, *Memoir of the Rev. Edward Bickersteth*, i, 78.

[377] A. Trollope, *John Caldigate*.

individual judgement was a paramount responsibility, an activity which had at one time proved harmless might become a stumbling-block, and that the speed of this change might vary from one family to another, or from one generation to another.[378] Patrick Brontë might declare,

The generality of Novels are what you Englishmen say of us Irishmen, when you liken us to our own bogs—green, smooth, and tempting, on the surface, but concealing underneath the miry slough, or deadly pool. . . . But I must say of my girl, that she subsists on no such food. She reads nothing of the kind alluded to, but what first passes through my hands, and meets my approbation. And there are a few Novels which I have handed over for her perusal, which are not only harmless, but very entertaining and instructive.[379]

Yet, given his daughter's reading matter, we have to assume either that Patrick Brontë became exceedingly liberal as his family grew up, or that he was forced to recognize their ability to judge for themselves. Charlotte clearly enjoyed a greater latitude than Patrick Brontë's heroine, Flora, since she had read French novels, which she judged to be 'clever, wicked, sophistical and immoral'.[380] Yet, when it came to advising others, she adopted the same pattern of careful selection as her father. 'For fiction, read Scott alone; all novels after his are worthless',[381] she counselled a friend.

The discrepancy between spiritual ideology and its practice nowhere made itself more strongly felt in the non-Evangelical world than in the Evangelical observance of the Sabbath. The very term 'Sabbath' was offensive to non-Evangelical ears. Thackeray observed that the 'good old Saxon word, Sunday', was 'scarcely known' at Clapham.[382] Grimshaw and Henry Venn renewed the Puritan traditions,[383] making practical efforts to coerce their parishioners into church attendance. Critical novelists' comparisons with Judaic practices were well-founded. The Eclectic Society concluded that Sunday was the seventh day observed by the Jews

[378] M. Hennell, *John Venn and the Clapham Sect*, p. 158.
[379] *Maid of Killarney*, p. 60.
[380] E. C. Gaskell, *Life of Charlotte Brontë*, ed. T. Scott and B. W. Willett (Edinburgh, 1924), p. 177.
[381] E. C. Gaskell, *Life of Charlotte Bronte*, ed. T. Scott and B. W. Willett, p. 115.
[382] *The Newcomes*, p. 22. Cf. A. Trollope, *Barchester Towers*, p. 25. The implied distinction is made clear in one of George Eliot's letters, where she writes, 'Our Sunday is really a Sabbath now—a day of thorough peace'. J. W. Cross, *George Eliot's Life*, iii, 233.
[383] See P. Collinson, *The Elizabethan Puritan Movement*, pp. 436–7.

transferred to the first day of the week under the new covenant.[384] Accounts abound to confirm the picture painted by Mrs. Mozley, who speaks of an Evangelical governess who 'never does anything after seven o'clock on Saturday evening, because of Sunday'.[385] The day was to be set aside, said the *Christian Observer*, as one on which trifling bodily concerns might be dispensed with, leaving time to attend to the affairs of the soul.[386] Critics, underlining the negative quality of this approach, reminded the Evangelicals that Christ had sanctified every day of the week, not just one seventh, to God's use. The novelists frequently depicted Sunday as a day on which token atonement was made for the worldliness of one's weekdays by a period of unrelieved gloom and mortification. Mrs. Proudie atoned for 'dissipation and low dresses during the week', by 'a perfect abstinence from any cheering employment on the Sunday'.[387] Mrs. Clennam, even when she is driven by fear to destroy the will whose terms she has for so long contravened, gives strict instructions that it is not to be burned on a Sunday night.[388] The novelists' view of Sabbatarianism as a negative coercive force had some foundation. Evangelicals like Thomas Scott, convinced of total depravity, could not afford to trust in the 'Spirit of godliness' working in a man to make him an 'observer of the Lord's Day', and endeavoured to create the necessary social conditions for universal observance: 'This binds the conscience of the *believer*. I want to get a bond on the conscience of *all men*.'[389]

The Society for the Suppression of Vice, founded in 1802, had as one of its major aims the suppression of Sabbath breaking. In the first two years of the Society's existence three thousand people in London alone were given warnings about Sabbath observance while 623 convictions were obtained.[390] In 1809 this activity was considered important enough to warrant the formation of a separate society. Various other legislative endeavours to obtain 'a bond on the conscience of *all men*', followed. Wilberforce tried to get an Act prohibiting the sale of Sunday newspapers which were just coming on the market.[391] A mark of Sir Pitt Crawley's move away

[384] *Eclectic Notes*, ed. J. H. Pratt, pp. 41–7. [385] *Fairy Bower*, p. 278.
[386] *CO* (1805), pp. 401–4. [387] A. Trollope, *Barchester Towers*, p. 21.
[388] C. Dickens, *Little Dorrit*, p. 783. [389] *Eclectic Notes*, ed. J. H. Pratt, p. 43.
[390] L. Radzinowicz, *A History of English Criminal Law and its Administration from 1750*, iii, *Cross-Currents in the Movement for the Reform of the Police* (1956), pp. 168–9.
[391] For an account see I. Bradley, 'The English Sunday', *History Today*, xxii (1972), 355–63, and R. I. and S. Wilberforce, *Life of William Wilberforce*, ii, 338, 424–6.

from the friendship of Wilberforce, after he had achieved his coveted Parliamentary seat, is his purchase of the Sunday *Observer*, justified by its reports of Government news, which were, however, almost hidden behind the accounts of social and sporting events.[392] Wilberforce endeavoured to prevent Sunday travelling on government business.[393] Helen Huntingdon's request that the carriage should not be used on a Sunday first gives rise to her reprobate husband's attacks on her 'saintliness'.[394] Henry Cunningham's kindly Mrs. Ashe is prepared to welcome a French orphan to the family circle but she 'had a keen eye to the Decalogue, and an especial aversion to Sunday packets', and was therefore 'inclined at first to be a little fussy about so untimely an arrival'.[395] The concept of 'a Sabbath day's journey' was even more rigorously interpreted in some households. In the Macaulay family 'Sunday walking for walking's sake, was never allowed; and even going to a distant church was discouraged.'[396]

In the 1830s a new champion appeared who endeavoured to realize Scott's dream of universally enforceable legislation. Sir Andrew Agnew was instrumental in founding the new Society for Promoting Due Observance of the Lord's Day in 1831, and in 1833 introduced a comprehensive bill into Parliament by which fairs, hunts, lectures, drinking, hiring carriages, and any activities subsumed under the umbrella clause, 'any pastime of public indecorum, inconvenience or nuisance', would have been banned on a Sunday. The bill lost by only six votes.[397] As Dickens was at pains to point out in 'Sunday under Three Heads' this bill was mainly directed at the amusements and activities of the poor, for whom Sunday was the only free day.[398] G. K. Chesterton's description of Dickens's work as 'the last cry of Merry England against the Puritan spirit,[399]

[392] W. M. Thackeray, *Vanity Fair*, p. 679.

[393] R. I. and S. Wilberforce, op. cit. iii, 397.

[394] A. Brontë, *Tenant of Wildfell Hall*, p. 192.

[395] *Wheat and Tares*, p. 110.

[396] G. O. Trevelyan, *Life of Macaulay*, i, 119. Cf. E. J. Worboise, *Thornycroft Hall*, p. 25.

[397] For his annual attempts to reintroduce such a Bill see, E. Halévy, *The Triumph of Reform*, 163 n. 3.

[398] *Uncommercial Traveller and Reprinted Pieces*, pp. 637–63. This was to become one of the most popular lines of attack. The Evangelicals, in their turn, accused the wealthy opponents of Lord's Day Observance of masking their own interests under the guise of acting as defenders of 'the poor man's liberties and pleasures'. W. F. Wilkinson, *Rector in Search of a Curate*, p. 321.

[399] G. K. Chesterton, *Appreciation and Criticism of the Works of Charles Dickens* (1911), p. xx.

is nowhere more demonstrably true than in this series of three polemical essays. His vision of 'Sunday as it might be made', with its picture of a country parson arranging cricket matches, would have found favour neither with those who saw Charles I's 1633 instruction, for *The Book of Sports* to be read in all parish pulpits, as a gratuitous insult, nor with 'Clericus', who wrote, in great perturbation of spirit, to the *Record*, in 1828, explaining that he found it impossible to stop cricket being played in the adjoining parish on a Sunday, or to prevent his parishioners attending if they had already been to Church that day.[400] The rich did not altogether escape censure; Queen Victoria herself was privately besought to change plans that entailed Sunday travel,[401] and publicly berated by the *Christian Observer* for a lapse in this respect.[402] Sunday trains and excursion trips proved a lasting thorn in the flesh fo Evangelicals.[403]

Lord Shaftesbury earned the title 'Lord Sackcloth-and-Ashleys' from *Punch*[404] for his contribution to the next stage of the Evangelical attack. His victory in carrying a Bill that prohibited collections and deliveries of post on Sundays was short-lived but won certain rights for 'believers'. Trollope depicts in fictional terms the arguments employed by the anti-Sabbatarian *Punch.*[405] Miss Mackenzie is a day late in hearing of her brother's fatal illness because the Stumfoldians choose not to receive letters on a Sunday.[406] The next *casus belli*, the closing of parks on a Sunday,[407] is the subject of comment in *The Three Clerks*, where Undecimus Scott loses his Whip's favour by failing to prevent the passage of such a bill.

If Evangelicals had not managed to secure 'a bond on the conscience of *all men*',[408] the extent of the achievement can perhaps be gauged by the phrase to which their activities had given currency,

[400] *Record* (23 May, 1828), p. 3.

[401] G. W. E. Russell, *Victoria Buxton*, p. 7.

[402] *CO* (1844), p. 704.

[403] Slope's activities on this front (A. Trollope, *Barchester Towers*, ch. x) are merely routine in comparison with the obsessive energy expended by Sir Andrew Agnew and his supporters. See J. Bridges, *Memoir of Sir Andrew Agnew* (Edinburgh, 1849); and 'A Watchman', *Record* (29 Mar., 1866), p. 3.

[404] *Punch* 19 (1850), p. 2.

[405] *Punch*, 19 (1850), p. 8.

[406] *Miss Mackenzie*, p. 177.

[407] Details of the mid-century campaign can be found in O. Chadwick, *Victorian Church*, i, 455–68.

[408] The religious census of 1851 confirmed Dickens's predictions ('The Sunday Screw', *Household Words* (22 June 1850), 289–92), in that it showed how ineffectual legislation had been in producing working class Sabbatarianism.

'Ennui was born in London on a Sunday.'[409] For most middle-class Victorians the way in which the Sabbath was observed epitomized, as it had been intended to, the Evangelical life of practical piety. Even if, like Ruskin, one managed in later life to abandon the childhood routine, which had thrown the gloom of Sunday back as far as Friday, one was still surrounded by those whose very conformity acted as a reproach.

It is now Sunday; half past eleven in the morning. Everybody about me is gone to church except the kind cook, who is straining a point of conscience to provide me with dinner. Everybody else is gone to church to ask to be made angels of . . . And I am left alone with the cat, in the world of sin.[410]

Novelists usually shy of theological debate were sufficiently affected to provide non-fictional comment upon a practical piety which they believed to be in direct opposition to the spirit of Christ's teaching.[411] Of all the polemic that appeared on the subject the best comment upon the topic remains Dickens's imaginative re-creation of a London Sunday as seen by Arthur Clennam,[412] where he manages to combine specific criticisms of the refusal to open museums or parks and the inefficacy of such laws for the purpose of increasing church attendance, with a personally experienced sense of the horror and futility of these negative attitudes.

Ideally of course an Evangelical's weekday behaviour was utterly consistent with his Sabbath conduct. 'Tell me how a man spends his evenings,' wrote J. C. Ryle, 'and I can generally tell what his character is'.[413] The problem with this rule of thumb guide is that it cannot be applied consistently throughout the century. Smoking and drinking, for instance, passed unreproved at Clapham. George Eliot's Revd. Camden Farebrother is almost prophetic in his instinctive feeling that 'Bulstrode and Company' will object to his one luxury, a pipe.[414] By the time that Ernest Pontifex temporarily renounces his favourite habit as a symbol of Evangelicalism's harsh

[409] E. Hodder, *Life of Shaftesbury*, iii, 27.

[410] *Works*, xxxv, 25; xxviii, 51.

[411] M. O. W. Oliphant, *Sundays* (1858), pp. 1–17. A. Trollope, 'The Fourth Commandment', *Fortnightly Review*, 3 (1866), 529–38.

[412] *Little Dorrit*, Bk. I, ch. iii. His device of creating an awareness of commonplace Sabbath dreariness through the eyes of a stranger was again used by B. Disraeli, *Falconet*, pp. 479–80.

[413] *Worldly Conformity*, p. 28.

[414] *Middlemarch*, i, 261.

demands, the Anti-Tobacco Society, founded in 1853, had arrived, and met with Evangelical support.[415]

The temperance, or total abstinence movement, on the other hand was not immediately espoused by the Evangelicals. When Margaret Maison suggests that 'Janet's Repentance' is 'A story typical of the Evangelical tracts of the period (so concerned with drink, depravity, temptation, conversion and consumptives' deathbeds)',[416] we feel the need of a more specific reference to the period in question. In the 1830s of the tale's setting, Anglican Evangelical involvement with the temperance question was minimal.[417] In *The Cunning Woman's Grandson* Charlotte Yonge goes so far as to excuse Hannah More and her contemporaries for allowing men to drink ale, 'for nobody then seemed to have thought of the temptation lying in odd draughts of liquor at uncertain hours . . .'[418] Temperance rather than abstinence, was the watchword of the early Evangelicals.[419] However, 1857, the year of the composition of 'Janet's Repentance', also saw the publication of the first address by Evangelicals urging their fellow clergy to set an example by abstinence.[420] Such a well-publicized event may well have informed the part that intemperance and alcoholism played in George Eliot's reconstruction of the Buchanans' family life.[421] It is only in the second half of the century that novels start to reflect this new movement.[422]

Concerning certain amusements there arose a virtual unanimity in the decision to abstain. Hunting and field sports were anathema to men who opposed cruelty to animals.[423] Attendance at the races was deplored since racecourses encouraged gambling, an activity which

[415] *Way of All Flesh*, pp. 209–10.

[416] M. M. Maison, *Search Your Soul, Eustace*, p. 107.

[417] B. Harrison, *Drink and the Victorians* (1971), p. 179. Dickens suggests the dissenting connections and the appeal to economic self-improvement of the early stages of the movement in his picture of the Brick Lane Branch of the United Grand Junction Ebenezer Temperance Association. *Pickwick Papers*, ch. xxxiii.

[418] *Cunning Woman's Grandson*, p. 91.

[419] H. Venn, *Complete Duty*, pp. 248–54.

[420] B. Harrison, op. cit., pp. 181–2.

[421] For the theory that George Eliot considerably blackened the figure of James William Buchanan, Nuneaton lawyer, by exaggerating his drinking propensities, to produce the picture of Lawyer Dempster, see, G. S. Haight, 'George Eliot's Originals', *From Jane Austen to Joseph Conrad*, ed. R. C. Rathburn and M. Steinmann Jnr., p. 180.

[422] See below, p. 251.

[423] See *CO* (1805), pp. 473–5, 541–2, 601–6, 667–71, 737–9; and M. Hennell, 'Evangelicalism and Worldliness', *Studies in Church History*, 8, ed. G. Cuming and D. Baker (Cambridge, 1971), pp. 232–3.

was roundly condemned. Wilberforce refrained from attending his constituency's races at York despite the votes it was feared this might cost him.[424]

It was the gambling associated with card-playing that made Simeon and Wilberforce uneasy, for in Regency society the stakes were often very high,[425] but it was not until the second third of the century that the card pack came to be known as 'the Devil's prayer book'.[426] As in the case of hunting and dancing the Evangelical campaign slowly came to affect the conduct of those outside the Evangelical fold. Even Dr. Grantly, the creation of an addicted whist player, is forced to admit that he would not permit whist to be played in the Barchester Palace of the 1860s as it had been in his father's day, though, like his creator, he retains the desire to denounce the Proudies and their Evangelical colleagues as being prompted to renounce this amusement for no other reason than a desire to appear more righteous than others.[427]

Simeon and the Clapham Sect, always anxious to demonstrate that it was possible for Evangelical principles and upper class life to co-exist, could condone dancing as a form of exercise in the belief that '*dancing* is not a sin *per se*—for David danced before the ark'.[428] The attendant evils of the ballroom rather than the dancing itself worried Venn and Hannah More.[429] Removed from the strains which this society imposed, Patrick Brontë could afford a more wholehearted denunciation.

They may call it if they please a healthy exercise, the art of acquiring graceful attitudes and airs, and the school of politeness: but I call it the destroyer of constitutions, the underminer of morals, the consumer of time. Consider the dress, the heat and the bustle, the nightly air, and the trifling and giddy manners of a ball-room; justly weigh these, and many

[424] R. I. and S. Wilberforce, *Life of William Wilberforce*, i, 276; ii, 98. For fictional comment see C. L. Scott, *Old Grey Church*, ii, 127–8; and C. M. Yonge, *The Three Brides*, p. 535.

[425] A. W. Brown, *Recollections of Simeon*, p. 247; R. I. and S. Wilberforce, op. cit. v, 16.

[426] G. W. E. Russell, *A Short History of the Evangelical Movement* (1915), pp. 74–5; C. M. Yonge, *Chantry House*, i, 120.

[427] A. Trollope, *Last Chronicle of the Barset*, i, 225; ii, 37; and *Autobiography*, p. 135. See also *Miss Mackenzie*, ch. ii, and *The Bertrams*, ch. xxii.

[428] A. W. Brown, op. cit., pp. 246–7. Cf. E. M. Forster, *Marianne Thornton* (New York, 1956), 183–4.

[429] H. Venn, *The Complete Duty of Man*, p. 262; H. More, *Strictures on the Modern System of Female Education* (1830).

other necessary appendages, and when you have done, tell me, whether in your cooler moments of reflection, you would choose for your wife the heroine of such a scene?[430]

This was a lesson taken to heart by two of his daughters. For Ginevra Fanshawe the ballroom is nothing more than a display room where she can attract the attention of other worthless butterflies. Agnes Grey expresses surprise at the presence of the local clergyman at a ball and records the sad progress of a marriage made on the ballroom floor.[431] The young Mary Ann Evans seems to have typified mid-nineteenth-century middle-class views in her conviction that she 'was not in a situation to maintain the *Protestant* character of the true Christian', when she attended a dance.[432]

The reforming zeal that led Hannah More to deplore the excessive time spent by the upper classes on the cultivation of the drawing room arts[433] was in danger of totally undermining Enlightenment values. Edward Bishop Elliott was not alone in seeing culture as a dangerous, hidden mine, planted by the Roman Catholics, whose cause was helped by, 'romances, and novels, and works on poetry, history, music, architecture'.[434] Yet these remarks were made by men and women of considerable education and culture reacting against a society that had, as they believed, got its priorities wrong. Their flocks were less often in a position to savour the joys of education and cultivated society before rejecting its snares. The Evangelical backlash against the fine arts that set in between the 1820s and late 1850s perfectly illustrates Mark Antony's contention —'The evil that men do lives after them; / The good is oft interred with their bones.'

The visual arts, if not actively fostered by the Evangelicals, passed without much criticism. The correspondent who wrote to the *Record* under the pseudonym, 'FLAG OF DISTRESS', 'I rejoice that you are going to censure our exhibitions of paintings, through which we cannot imagine Christ, or even Paul, to have passed without a frown, or a sigh, or uttering a rebuke',[435] was scarcely representative.

[430] *The Maid of Killarney*, p. 53.
[431] C. Brontë, *Villette;* A. Brontë, *Agnes Grey.*
[432] *G. Eliot Letters*, i, 41.
[433] *Strictures on the Modern Female System of Education* (1830), 43–59.
[434] *Horae Apocalypticae* (3 vols., 1844), iii, 1221.
[435] *Record* (5 July, 1838), p. 3.

In 1855 Evangelicals flocked to the exhibition of John Martin's three Judgement pictures, which had long been favourites with them.[436] Perhaps in these they found an answer to the question Canon Butler posed his son, Samuel, 'Pray what more good are you to effect for your generation in drawing?'[437] The young Ruskin and his father came from the Evangelical middle classes and, despite the enthusiasm with which they had started to explore the world of English art, they experienced something of that cultural shock that 'the weight of unintelligible Rome' had made upon Dorothea Brooke, 'a girl who had been brought up in English and Swiss Puritanism, fed on meagre Protestant histories and on art chiefly of the hand-screen sort'.[438] In the architectural sphere the Cambridge Camden Society affair ensured that an Evangelical subsequently saw only thinly disguised Tractarianism in antiquarian interest or artistic enthusiasm.[439]

Music, an art whose allurements and uses the Evangelicals were more alive to, as their adoption of hymn-singing showed, was a more contentious subject. For home music-making favourite tunes could be salvaged from Satan's grasp by supplying new words.[440] Public performances of oratorios were more problematic.[441] The practice of interspersing selections from sacred music with secular works was one cause of distress. A correspondent of the *Record* reminded readers that Mrs. Hemans had said, 'when I see the position of The Messiah on the placards thus,

MISCELLANEOUS CONCERT,

MESSIAH

FANCY DRESS BALL

I always think of the two malefactors!'[442] The foundation of the Sacred Harmonic Society, in 1832, and the possibility of using the Exeter Hall for performances brought about a gradual change in

[436] G. Rowell, *Hell and the Victorians*, p. 10. Martin's pictures were keenly admired in the Brontë household. W. Gerin, *Charlotte Brontë: The Evolution of Genius* (1967), p. 42. Branwell Brontë, moreover, found paternal backing for his ventures into the art world.

[437] *Family Letters of Samuel Butler*, ed. A. Silver, pp. 80–1.

[438] G. Eliot, *Middlemarch*, i, 296. Cf. J. Ruskin, *Works*, xxxv, 267.

[439] For details see W. H. B. Proby, *Annals of the Low Church Party*, i, 467–83, and *CO* (1848), 104–7.

[440] A habit denounced by Mrs. Trollope as 'a jest, and a very indecent one too . . .' *Vicar of Wrexhill*, i, 317.

[441] T. R. Birks, *Memoir of the Rev. Edward Bickersteth*, ii, 187.

[442] *Record* (5 June, 1837), p. 4.

opinion,[443] but in mid-century any vacillation on this point could still be taken as a weakness of commitment to Evangelicalism itself.[444] Unfortunately Samuel Butler, with his passion for Handel, was to meet, at Cambridge, one of the most passionate opponents of choral festivals, the Revd. Charles Clayton.[445] Attachment to music, particularly the organ and choral works of Handel, therefore became a touchstone by which to judge the characters presented in *The Way of All Flesh.*

Oratorios had also been the subject of controversy because of the frequent employment of professional operatic stars—whose name was a by-word for the immorality of the theatre. *Daniel Deronda*, with its portrait of Mirah Cohen, and Klesmer's advice to Gwendolen, indicates how unsavoury the career of an opera singer was felt to be even in the 1870s. Lest the wave of liberalism in the last quarter of the century should create any doubt in the Evangelical mind about the compatibility of the profession of Christian with a career on the stage, Emma Jane Worboise undertook to dramatize the choice. Margaret Torrington rejects the quick wealth to be gained by an engagement with a theatre for the humble drudgery of teaching.

> My place, as a Christian, was not upon the stage. There would be no harm in singing in public, I knew; but how could I tell what I might be called upon to sing? What companionship could I ensure? What life but one of glare, and vanity, and excitement could I expect? And this taking the very fairest view of the profession. I could not place myself in such a position and then kneel down and say, 'Lead me not into temptation.'[446]

In the eighteenth century, Henry Venn, taking his cue from William Law, had had no hesitation in telling the Evangelicals that the theatre was 'riddled with profanity',[447] and the next generation saw no reason to dissent from this view. This was the period at which Sarah Dunkirk would have been disinherited by her family for becoming an actress.[448] The members of the Eclectic Society agreed that attendance at the theatre was not conducive to 'redeeming the

[443] F. M. Holmes, *Exeter Hall and its Associations* (1881), ch. xvi.

[444] e.g. cf. *G. Eliot Letters*, i, 9 and i, 68. See also W. M. Thackeray, *Vanity Fair*, pp. 568–71.

[445] In 1865 Clayton was still conducting rear-guard action, *Record* (24 May 1865), p. 4.

[446] *Margaret Torrington*, p. 360.

[447] *Complete Duty*, p. 262.

[448] G. Eliot, *Middlemarch.*

time', and were clearly embarrassed by the existence of Mrs. Hannah More's *Sacred Dramas*, *The Search for Happiness* and three other secular plays. The Revd. Basil Woodd voiced their unease: 'Mrs. More's sacred dramas have done injury. They have associated an idea of innocence with the drama. I know two young men now on the stage in consequence of being taught to act Mrs. M.'s sacred dramas.'[449]

Hannah More's post-conversion repentance is seen in the preface to her tragedies in the *Collected Works*, where she describes the essentially anti-Christian morality of such drama as '. . . a dazzling system of worldly morality in direct contradistinction to the spirit of that religion whose characteristics are "charity, meekness, peaceableness, long-suffering, gentleness, forgiveness" '.[450]

By attending the theatre one was also likely to be responsible for the corruption of servants and to 'encourage the actors and actresses in a course of life extremely unfavourable to their immortal interests'.[451] Though excessively paternalistic to the modern ear, these fears receive some corroboration from an independent source. Sir Walter Scott vouchsafed it as his opinion that theatres were 'destined to company so scandalous, that persons not very nice in their taste of society, must yet exclaim against the abuse as a national nuisance' —'prostitutes and their admirers usually' forming 'the principal part of the audience'.[452] The turn of the eighteenth century probably witnessed the nadir of British theatrical life and writing. The comedy of manners was still seen in such plays as Shadwell's, Wycherley's, and Congreve's, but increasingly the sentimental moralizing plays of authors like Hannah More gained popularity in the patented playhouses. The new larger theatres were poorly designed acoustically and so were given over to the production of brash spectaculars. These productions were possibly in Pratt's mind when he gave vent to the most splendid *non sequitur* in the records of the Eclectic Society's debating history, 'A sermon is the essence of dulness after a play: this shews the evil of the play-house.'[453] Occasional preachers, such as Francis Close at Cheltenham, were fortunate enough to ensure the cessation of unfair competition. So

[449] *Eclectic Notes*, ed. J. H. Pratt, pp. 159–63.

[450] *Poems-Tragedies* (1830), p. 135.

[451] *CO* (1809), p. 296.

[452] Quoted by Allardyce Nicoll, *A History of the English Drama 1660–1900* (6 vols., 1955–9), iv, 10.

[453] *Eclectic Notes*, ed. J. H. Pratt, p. 162.

strong had 'the Parish Pope's' preaching against the Theatre Royal been that when it was burnt down in 1839 it was not rebuilt.[454] The *Record* noted with ill-concealed glee the depressed state of many provincial theatres.[455] From the comically aggrieved tones of novelist and dramatist, Wilkie Collins, one might gather that some preachers had decided to adopt the wisdom of the children of this world.

> The last time I was in London, my mistress gave me two treats. She sent me to the theatre to see a dancing woman who was all the rage; and she sent me to Exeter Hall to hear Mr. Godfrey. The lady did it, with a band of music. The gentleman did it, with a handkerchief and a glass of water. Crowds at the performance with the legs. Ditto at the performance with the tongue.[456]

Shakespeare, admitted to be part of the national heritage, was often exempted from the general condemnation. Pendennis's Evangelical tutor, Mr. Smirke, clearly feels that his proposed lapse may be partially mitigated by the particular dramatist in question.

> Helen, in her good humour, asked Mr. Smirke to be of the party. That ecclesiastic had been bred up by a fond parent at Clapham, who had an objection to dramatic entertainments, and he had never yet seen a play. But, Shakespere!—but to go with Mrs. Pendennis in her carriage, and sit a whole night by her side!—he could not resist the idea of so much pleasure, and made a feeble speech, in which, he spoke of temptation and gratitude, and finally accepted Mrs. Pendennis's most kind offer.[457]

Some Evangelicals who refrained from going to the theatre because of its attendant evils, saw the amusement to be gained from reading Shakespeare at home or allowing the performance of charades, but the *Christian Observer* for 1808, in a review of Thomas Bowdler's *Family Shakespeare*, undertook to consider the question, '. . . if you condemn the theatre, can you persistently permit us to *read* the drama?'[458] The reviewer concluded that *Robinson Crusoe* was less dangerous than Shakespeare for 'the young person under twenty-one' because less realistic, and that it would have

[454] G. Berwick, 'Close of Cheltenham: Parish Pope', *Theology*, 39 (1939), 194.

[455] *Record* (18 Oct. 1832), p. 3.

[456] *Moonstone*, p. 51. For further indications of professional rivalry see W. Collins and C. Dickens, 'The Lazy Tour of Two Idle Apprentices' reprinted in C. Dickens, *Christmas Stories*, p. 747; and C. Dickens, *The Mystery of Edwin Drood*, ch. xvii.

[457] W. M. Thackeray, *The History of Pendennis*, p. 71.

[458] *CO* (1808), p. 326.

been better to leave the flaws, in the plays selected, unaltered so that the 'vulgarity and absurdities of style and morality' might act 'as an antidote to his seductions'. Although contested by some readers we have confirmation that this continued to be representative of the moderate Evangelical view in an 1860 review of a new edition of Thomas Bowdler's *Family Shakespeare*[459] and in Samuel Butler's uncomprehending amazement at his father's attitudes.

My father is one of the few men I know who say they do not like Shakespeare. I could forgive my father for not liking Shakespeare if it was only because Shakespeare wrote poetry; but this is not the reason. He dislikes Shakespeare because he finds him so very coarse.[460]

Fears for the 'young person under twenty-one' could hardly have been quieted by reading the memoirs of that most widely read of our nineteenth-century Evangelical authors, Charlotte Elizabeth. Her views upon the provision of suitable reading matter for the young were dramatically, not to say hysterically, affected by reading *The Merchant of Venice* at the tender age of seven.

. . . I drank a cup of intoxication under which my brain reeled for many a year—. . . I revelled in the terrible excitement that it gave rise to; page after page was stereotyped upon a most retentive memory, without an effort, and during a sleepless night I feasted on the pernicious sweets thus hoarded in my brain. . . . Reality became insipid, almost hateful to me; conversation, except that of the literary men . . . a burden: I imbibed a thorough contempt for women, children, and household affairs, entrenching myself behind invisible barriers that few, very few, could pass. Oh, how many wasted hours, how much of unprofitable labour, what wrong to my fellow-creatures, what robbery of God, must I refer to this ensnaring book! My mind became unnerved, my judgement perverted, my estimate of people and things wholly falsified, and my soul wrapped in the vain solace of unsubstantial enjoyments during years of after sorrow, when but for this I might have early sought the consolations of the gospel.[461]

The fear of unduly exciting the imaginative faculties of the young was nowhere more apparent than in the Evangelical attitude to the reading of fiction. A movement anxious to preserve itself from the charges of 'enthusiasm' and emotional hysteria inevitably exercised

[459] Ibid. (1860), pp. 360–1.
[460] *Notebooks*, p. 182.
[461] *Personal Recollections*, pp. 24–5.

excessive precautions which resulted, in many cases, in an inability to recognize that the exercise of the imagination might be spiritually profitable. The effort to persuade a generation, educated in such a manner, of the spiritual advantages to be derived from novel reading nowhere manifested itself more strongly than in the writing of those educated in the Evangelical school, who in later life adopted a more liberal outlook. In a later chapter I shall show how three such writers, Ruskin, James Fitzjames Stephen, and George Eliot, were prompted by this early contact with Evangelicalism to lay great stress upon realism as a means of producing sympathy.

Only Trollope, amongst the major novelists who had always been hostile to Evangelicalism, articulated the step from condemning the Evangelicals' opposition as blind prejudice to considering how the novel might encourage a profitable exercise of the imagination. In his autobiography he tells us how, as a novelist, he has ever thought of himself 'as a preacher of sermons'[462] because he is aware of the dangers and benefits which can arise from a novel 'which appeals especially to the imagination and solicits the sympathy of the young'.[463] These reflections brought him to see the novel as a potential instrument for moral education and a conviction that the teaching of the young 'might best be done by representing characters like themselves'—two tenets that go far in accounting for the great esteem in which George Eliot held him.

The spread of the novel-reading habit, without an accompanying growing conviction of its moral value, was a topic that greatly interested Trollope. In 1879 he had written an article on this subject much of which was reproduced in his autobiography.[464] His account serves to remind us that there were others apart from the Evangelicals who frowned upon novel-reading as a frivolous, time-wasting occupation. This is the advice proffered on the subject by Benson, Headmaster of Wellington College, to his fourteen-year-old son as late as 1874.

Novel-reading is a great cause of dreaminess. The characters and situations rise up between you and your work—and then also they awaken ideas which have no reality and you feel as if the real world was duller. . . . Also

[462] *An Autobiography* (1968), p. 126.

[463] Ibid., p. 188.

[464] Cf. A. Trollope, 'Novel-Reading: The Works of Charles Dickens, The Works of William Makepeace Thackeray', *Nineteenth Century*, 5 (1879), 38–43 with A. Trollope, *An Autobiography*, pp. 186–96.

the reading of novels is as tiring to the head as any other reading—(perhaps more, because of the excitement)—and so you come with tired powers to your work.[465]

Utilitarians too deplored the useless stimulation of the feelings aroused by such an occupation and the energy consequently wasted.[466]

In the dissenting world Dr. V. Cunningham has managed to trace the appearance of Unitarian writers in the 1830s followed by Congregationalists at the close of that decade,[467] but it is not easy to detect a comparable linear pattern of liberalization in the emergence of Evangelical novelists. The opening years of the nineteenth century saw a number of Evangelical novels appear: Hannah More's *Coelebs in Search of a Wife* (1808), the Revd. J. W. Cunningham's *The Velvet Cushion* (1814), Patrick Brontë's *The Maid of Killarney* (1818), but enthusiasm for such performances flagged. The composition of two early contributors, Mrs. Sherwood and 'Charlotte Elizabeth' Browne Phelan Tonna, continued to be popular partly because of the dearth of competitive material. The next group of Evangelical novelists. Lady Catherine Long, Ann Howard, Anne Flinders, and the Revd. C. B. Tayler, appeared in response to the need to combat Tractarianism with its own weapons. Such writers, however, could not be certain of a unanimous welcome from an Evangelical audience when even Bible stories retold by the faithful could receive the harsh treatment accorded to them by Henry Venn Elliott, the close friend of William Carus Wilson: 'He was very jealous of transgressing the boundary of facts, and took the "Peep of Day", and "Agathos" away from his children, because the one added to the history of Jonah, and the other spoke of beautiful carriages and horses, as exhibited by Satan at the third temptation.'[468]

It is not difficult to produce individual examples of extreme bigotry or astounding liberalism but the finest indicator of the changing *mores* and spectrum of opinion embraced by Evangelicalism is to be found in the reviewing habits of the party's periodicals and newspapers. They provide a particularly useful source in this respect because in an over-populated and competitive market, changes of

[465] Quoted by D. Newsome, *Godliness and Good Learning* (1961), p. 173.

[466] Though, to judge by J. S. Mill's account of his father borrowing 'books of amusement' for his children, as with the Evangelicals, private practice was not always in line with public pronouncements. *Autobiography*, ed. J. Stillinger (1971), p. 8.

[467] *Everywhere Spoken Against*, pp. 48–62.

[468] J. Bateman, *Life of Henry Venn Elliott*, p. 206.

opinion seem more often to reflect wishes of sponsors and readers than the whim of any individual editor. Detailed study of the policy adopted towards the reviewing of fiction by the *Christian Observer* (1802–77), the *Christian Guardian* (1802–53), the *Christian Lady's Magazine* (1834–46), the *Record* (1828–1948), and the *Rock* (1868–1905) served to corroborate Mrs. Tillotson's assertion that 'a warning is necessary against the popular foreshortening of the Victorian age, against confusing the eighteen-forties with the sixties or seventies, or eighties, or on the other hand with the strictness of Evangelicals in the early years of the century'.[469] The publication of *Coelebs* led the *Christian Observer* in 1809 to take the considered step of reviewing the occasional novel.[470] Although this measure did not gain the support of all readers, reviews continued until 1826. Between 1826 and 1844 no notices or reviews of even religious fiction appeared since, it was considered, 'silence in these matters is better than refutation'.[471] This period of almost twenty years self-imposed restraint is important because it fell within the formative years of interested observers of the religious scene such as George Eliot and Trollope.

The millenial teaching of the late 1820s had given rise to a sense of impending judgement and a frenzied search for apostolic purity which could tolerate no intercourse with the devil as represented by the 'silver-fork' school of novelists. The appearance of the *Record* in 1828, in itself a symbol of Evangelical concern for 'the Church in danger', may have caused the *Christian Observer* some reluctance to display a liberality which might so easily be interpreted as unsoundness. An interesting example of the obeisance formally paid to the reading public at this period is shown by the *Christian Lady's Magazine*. Edited though it was by 'Charlotte Elizabeth', the first volume, published at the height of 'the repression', contained the following editorial declaration: 'The impression seems also very strong, and very general, that we should not indulge in fictitious narrative: we will gladly meet this, by seeking specimens of interesting biography, preserving the charm of originality as much as possible.'[472]

Without further comment 'Charlotte Elizabeth' then proceeded

[469] *Novels of the Eighteenth-Forties*, p. 54.
[470] *CO* (1809), pp. 109–21.
[471] Ibid. (1834), p. 731.
[472] *Christian Lady's Magazine*, i (1834), ii.

in the first six months of the periodical's publication to serialize 'Berenger and Emilie', a tale by the author of 'Little Henry and His Bearer' (Mrs. Sherwood).

Always less inclined to apocalyptic fervour or prophetical speculation the *Christian Observer* was the first to recognize the metamorphosis of the novel from idle plaything to *roman-à-thèse*. The desire to warn parents and teachers of the lurking dangers of Tractarianism forced the *Christian Observer* to break its self-imposed restraint in 1844.[473] Even though reviews continued to concentrate upon doctrine to the virtual exclusion of aesthetic criteria, their very existence amounted to a clear recognition of the fact that a policy which ignored the novel had not been effective in diminishing its popularity.

The *Christian Guardian*, also a monthly periodical, directed to a readership 'whose necessary engagements in worldly business deprives them of leisure for the perusal of larger compositions; or whose pecuniary resources are inadequate to their purchase',[474] assumed that fiction would not be a major concern to its buyers, but at no point did it declare firm opposition.

The *Record* was far more forthright in its condemnation of fiction. Instead of adopting the discreet but ineffectual silence of its ecclesiastical colleagues, it was roused to fight a curious battle on behalf of its readers. The review of Mrs. Trollope's *Vicar of Wrexhill* is a masterpiece of its kind. The reviewer assumes throughout that his readers will not have read this scurrilous tale and just to ensure that none succumb to his titillating references contrives never to name the book or its publisher.[475] By the 1860s the *Record* had belatedly joined the *Christian Observer* in reviewing the occasional religious novel favourably. Yet this concession entailed even more stringent

[473] *Christian Observer* (1844), pp. 503–10. [474] *Christian Guardian* (1802), p. 3.

[475] Evidence to suggest that the *Record* rated the restraint of its potential readership too highly can be found in *Romilly's Cambridge Diary 1832–1842* ed. J. P. T. Bury (Cambridge, 1967), pp. 153–4. The Revd. Joseph Romilly, an attender at Cambridge's leading Evangelical church, read the 'infamous' work through to the end, although he 'thought it (with all skipping & alterations made by me) utterly unfit to read loud'. Neverthless he continued to read Mrs. Trollope's novels. See 'Romilly Diaries', 3 July, 18 July, 1848 (MS. held by Cambridge University Library, Add. 6804–42. 1791–1864). The sample year 1847 reveals that the fictional diet with which he regaled his sisters included not only the standard works acceptable to most Evangelicals, such as *Coelebs*, *The Arabian Nights* and Scott, but the new numbers of *Dombey and Son* as they appeared, also works by B. Disraeli, Elizabeth Sewell, Captain Marryatt, Theodore Hook, Mrs. Gore, and many other contemporary minor novelists. Sunday evenings were reserved for religious biographies.

responsibilities to guard the faithful. In 1863 the *Record* launched a series of vehement attacks upon rivals in the religious press, such as *Good Words*, who pandered to the public by praising, or worse still, employing popular secular writers.

It had taken the new rash of sensational literature to awaken the die-hards to the need to harness the forces of imagination for religious profit. The weekly newspaper, the *Rock*, started in 1868 as other Evangelical papers were beginning to emerge from thirty years or so in the fictional wilderness. Its editors consciously aimed, 'with the blessing of God, at adopting the policy of the children of this world, who "in their generation, are wiser than the children of light" ',[476] and by 1875 had resolved to publish their own serial, 'A Convent Mystery', allegedly recounting the true story of a Miss Weppner's experiences, but making its appeal by the sensational nature of its revelations.

Meanwhile those opposed to such flirtation with the enemy had not been idle. The year 1854 saw the inauguration, under Lord Shaftesbury's leadership and with the membership of three archbishops and sixteen bishops, of the Pure Literature Society. This society endeavoured to get *Good Words* blacklisted,[477] a potentially effective form of blackmail when one realizes that the society was 'actively engaged in promoting the circulation of pure and interesting literature', by two means. By 1886 it had distributed £57,000 worth of books at half price to working men's libraries and schools, whilst it also dispatched over 1,000 parcels a month of 'selected periodicals', to 100 or more of its 'Magazine Associations'.[478] The Religious Tract Society, begun in 1799 under Evangelical and Dissenting auspices, published a new paper, *Leisure Hour*, on 1 January 1852, in which, with apologies to its stricter subscribers, stories began to appear. Stimulated no doubt by the controversy over the policy of *Good Words* the Society laid down moral rules for the choice of fiction in 1863. The tales they published were to be '*moral* . . . *natural* . . . and *unexciting* . . .'[479] In the 1870s the society, employing authors like Henty, Verne, and Conan Doyle, began a vigorous warfare with the penny-dreadful market. The last decades of the century provided triumphant vindication of their policy with

[476] *Rock*, 17 Jan. 1868, p. 2.
[477] R. D. Altick, *The English Common Reader*, p. 125.
[478] *The Official Year-Book of the Church of England, 1886* (London, 1887), p. 179.
[479] M. Maison, *Search Your Soul, Eustace*, p. 111.

the appearance of juvenile best-sellers such as *Christie's Old Organ*, or *Jessica's First Prayer*.[480] The latter tale was first serialized in the Society's magazine, *The Sunday at Home*, and in book form was to sell over 1,500,000 copies.[481] Such societies proliferated, and novelists may well have had cause to prefer the days of Evangelical abstension from fiction to the days when the Church of England Book Society (founded 1881) existed to 'pass through its crucible secular and religious works selected from the whole range of the publishing world . . .' in an effort to 'exclude all that are inconsistent with the Evangelical and Protestant principles of the Church of England, or any with Rationalistic tendencies'.[482] The Society for Promoting Christian Knowledge, who had long been anxious to provide 'Literature for the Working Classes',[483] in 1888 launched an immensely successful 'Penny Library of Fiction', in response to the demands of 'a large number of the parochial clergy, who have endeavoured to meet the wants of the people by the establishment of libraries and the circulation of a monthly magazine'.[484] Independent evidence of clerical involvement with the use of their congregations' recently acquired literacy exists. The Visitation Returns for the Diocese of Canterbury in 1872 included the question, 'Is there any Parochial Library?' About three-quarters of the parishes already possessed one but the Revd. G. J. Blomfield, incumbent of Aldington's, answer gives some indication of the kind of impact made and the control exerted on a parish's reading when these societies were responsible for the provision of the only readily available literature. '*No*. I propose to begin a Parochial Library—in connection with S.P.C.K.—R.T.S. & The Pure Literature Society.'[485]

Something of the importance which educating men into correct reading habits achieved in Evangelical concern, combined with a dim perception of the unequal battle being waged, glimmers

[480] G. Hewitt, *Let the people Read: A Short History of the United Society for Christian Literature* (*1949*), pp. 50, 62–4.

[481] R. D. Altick, *The English Common Reader*, p. 389.

[482] *Official Year-Book of the Church of England*, *1885*, p. 163.

[483] The Revd. Erskine Clarke, whose efforts in this direction are particularly applauded by the Society for Promoting Christian Knowledge (*Official Year-Book of the Church of England*, *1894*, p. 192), had tried to persuade George Eliot to compose tracts. J. W. Cross, *George Eliot's Life*, ii, 132.

[484] *Official Year-Book of the Church of England*, *1888*, pp. 209–10.

[485] The Diocese of Canterbury Visitation Returns, 1872, deposited in Lambeth Palace Library. Answer to Question 35 d.

through the reply of the Revd. Francis Storr, Evangelical incumbent of Brenchley, to the question, 'Can you mention anything which specially impedes your own Ministery, or the welfare of the Church around you? Can you suggest any remedies?' 'Public houses, Beershops, Sunday Newspapers and Sensational Publications. Remedies Difficult. Rooms opened for reading, Chess, Drafts, good fire, easy access, not too much controlled. I have long thought that a weekly newspaper should be published by the Christian Knowledge and Religious Tract Society—news in Common, in other respects matters special to each society.'[486]

Since a serious practitioner of the novel form, like Trollope, openly avowed that, 'by the common consent of all mankind who have read, poetry takes the highest place in literature',[487] one might expect to find that nineteenth-century Evangelicals were prepared to extend a more cordial welcome to the imagination in its poetic guise. Bagehot, no doubt thinking of the old description of Evangelicalism as a 'one book religion', was unjust in referring to Cowper as 'the one poet of a class which have no poets'.[488] Cowper's poetry and hymns did much to recommend to Evangelicals the practice of reading and writing devotional poetry. Men like Legh Richmond, whose contempt for, and fear of, the evils of prose fiction knew no bounds, readily turned to verse. During the 1820s and 1830s Mrs. Hemans continued to be popular whilst poets like Pollok and Montgomery reflected the apocalyptic interests of the period and more specifically of Evangelical circles. The poetry of Frances Ridley Havergal and Roden Wriothesley Noel, born respectively in 1834 and 1836, both the offspring of Evangelical parents, gained a wide readership despite Noel's increasing unorthodoxy. By the 1880s, however, such poetry tended to be confined for its potential readership to Evangelical circles and consequently increasingly attracted religious versifiers. Such poetry had rarely produced more than minor talents of whose work their most widely read critic, Hoxie Neale Fairchild, wrote, 'In their writings the puritan's dread of images and the poet's sensuousness usually cancel out, leaving them with nothing but a pious sense of obligation to versify the stock ideas and sentiments of their religion.'[489]

[486] Ibid., Answer to Question 25. [487] *An Autobiography*, p. 186.

[488] *Literary Studies by the Late Walter Bagehot*, ed. R. H. Hutton (2 vols., 1879), i, 296.

[489] *Religious trends in English Poetry*, iv, *1830–1880; Christianity and Romanticism in the Victorian Era* (New York, 1957), p. 25.

Justification for this, at first sight, easy dismissal by generalization comes from a contemporary critic with intimate knowledge of Evangelical patterns of thought. Of the most ardent of Mrs. Mozley's Evangelical characters it is observed, ' "... Constance says that there is no poetry in the New Testament; she thinks that Christianity is essentially a revelation of truth, and that it was intended to abolish all imagery of mind, as well as ceremonies and types." '[490]

Grace Leslie, a Christian, but not of the Evangelically earnest variety, with great daring admits, 'I do not like the Paradise Lost, and I admire some parts of Lord Byron!'[491] With unerring accuracy Mrs. Mozley has pinpointed the test cases of Evangelical poetic appreciation. Milton was known, if not loved, even in the strictest of households, but more as a formative member of the Puritan tradition than as a literary genius. For Alice Meredith, Mrs. Oliphant's Evangelical emotional innocent, the 'knowledge of poetry was confined to hymns, over which hung an awful shadow from the "Paradise Lost".'[492] For Overton and Ernest Pontifex a slighting joke at the expense of *Paradise Lost* gives them the *frisson* often sought in blasphemy.[493] Milton, 'sweet Cowper', Goldsmith and extracts of pre-nineteenth-century poets found their way even to Constance Duff's bookshelves,[494] but nineteenth-century secular poets were the subject of dispute. The *Christian Observer* devoted reviewing space to Crabbe, Scott, and Byron in its early years, even receiving grateful tribute for its 'just criticism' of the 'Giaour' from Byron.[495] 'Excubitor's' voice, however, sounded a warning cry against the 'romances in rhyme' of Scott and Byron.[496] In the year after Byron's death the reviewing space of four numbers was devoted to an examination of the character and opinions of this poet.[497] Though the review concentrated upon illustrating the 'miseries of sinful courses', its very existence reflects an attention accorded to secular poets, not shared at this time by secular novelists.[498] The first edition of the *Record*, which announced an intention to accept only advertisements in keeping with its general character,

[490] *Lost Brooch*, ii, 86. [491] *Lost Brooch*, ii, 89. [492] *Son of the Soil*, ii, 60.

[493] S. Butler, *Way of All Flesh*, p. 362. [494] H. Mozley, *Fairy Bower*, p. 288.

[495] *CO* (1813), pp. 731–7. [496] Ibid. (1817), p. 374.

[497] *CO* (1825), pp. 79–87, 151–8, 214–22, 281–8.

[498] A list of books, compiled by C. Partridge, demonstrates that, in one Evangelical home, whilst Scott's poetry appeared there, his novels, other eighteenth-century novels and nineteenth-century secular novels did not appear until the second half of the century. 'Evangelical Children's Books', *N & Q* 195 (1950), 56–8.

evidently did not consider that Murray's notice of *The Poetical Works of Lord Byron* infringed their rule.[499] As usual, the non-Evangelical world expected the Evangelicals to be more scandalized than they were by anything which disturbed the secular moral sensibility. After the Harrow vestry meeting at which it was decided to refuse permission for a headstone to Byron's natural daughter by Claire Clairmont, Allegra, the Vicar, 'Velvet' Cunningham, wrote a letter to Byron in which he remarked that he had 'on reading *Cain*, which was then scandalizing the world, felt a profound admiration for the genius of the author'.[500] Cunningham, a practising and published poet himself,[501] may well have been able to appreciate Byron's poetic gift whilst deploring the poet's manner of life—a position perfectly compatible with the *Christian Observer* editorial line—but by Mrs. Trollope and her friends the Drurys it was seen as a clear assertion of his 'innate and invincible flunkeyism'. The incident itself is only of literary interest because it provided Mrs. Trollope with material for a long satirical poem, since lost, but the way in which her latest biographer has uncritically retailed the judgement of Cunningham's adversaries,[502] without troubling herself to examine the background for his attitudes, is indicative of the manner in which the historical myth of nineteenth-century Evangelicalism has grown up. Even in 1838, at the peak of Evangelical cultural depression, the *Record*'s leader column acknowledged 'the unhappy Byron to be the greatest poet of his day', though feeling a duty to speak out against a proposed memorial in Westminster Abbey as an unsuitable tribute to so irreligious a man.[503] Poetry, like fiction, tended to receive close doctrinal scrutiny and little aesthetic appreciation in the Evangelical newspapers. The reviewer of Wordsworth's poetry in the *Christian Observer* for 1850 prefaced his remarks with an allusion to the apparent absurdity of a Puritan judging poetry and an announcement of his intention to confine himself to 'the religion of Wordsworth's poetry'.[504] In the same year Browning's *Christmas Eve and Easter Day* was accorded qualified approval, although the reviewer felt that the poet might have found

[499] *Record* (1 Jan. 1828), p. 1. [500] T. A. Trollope, *What I Remember*, i, 91–2.

[501] J. W. Cunningham, *De Rancé* (1815), has a lengthy preface defending the practice of writing poetry.

[502] E. Bigland, *The Indomitable Mrs. Trollope*, pp. 39–40, where the author sees fit to give us a modern translation of the insult—'Cunningham, a toady to his backbone'.

[503] *Record* (16 Aug. 1838), p. 4. [504] *CO* (1850), pp. 307–20.

a service more to his liking had he entered an Anglican Church.[505] Tennyson, as Poet Laureate, needed careful watching over. His *Gareth and Lynette* (1873) was rebuked for its subject matter, adultery.

> There are those who seem to delight in the exquisite skill and the delicate ingenuity with which they can gild corruption and enlist sympathy with sin.
>
> We wish we could wholly exempt the Poet Laureate from this charge, but we cannot honestly do so.[506]

Two years later the paper was pleased to notice that his play *Queen Mary* manifested the increasing orthodoxy of Tennyson's 'evening hours'.[507]

Standards of judgement which paid so little attention to aesthetic values help to explain the picture of Evangelicalism we may derive from the novel. The numerous pictures of an Evangelical childhood, where the imagination was starved or forced to find strange and pathetic outlets, were often drawn by those who had only been spurred on to unleash their creative faculties by a resentment of the Evangelical system. Others remained uncritical adherents of a faith which concentrated its energies upon conduct so earnestly as to exclude culture and, in process of time, became the imaginatively stunted tutors of a new generation. It was to these that Matthew Arnold addressed his pleas for the education of the whole man and his warnings of the corruption of conduct itself, which would result from a refusal to take into account man's wider nature and needs.[508]

[505] Ibid. (1850), pp. 872–4.
[506] Ibid. (1873), p. 70.
[507] *Christian Observer and Advocate* (1875), pp. 761–4.
[508] *Culture and Anarchy* (1869) and *Literature and Dogma* (1873).

# PART TWO

## CHAPTER IV

# George Eliot

I have heard him say that it was his custom at this period to walk almost every evening in the cloisters of Trinity College during the time that the great bell of St. Mary's was tolling at nine o'clock; and, amidst the solemn tones and pauses of the bell, and the stillness and darkness of the night, he would indulge in impressive and awful reflections on Death and Judgement, on Heaven and Hell.

John Venn of his father Henry Venn (1725–97). J. Venn, *Annals of a Clerical Family* (1904), p. 71.

I remember how, at Cambridge, I walked with her once in the Fellows' Garden of Trinity, on an evening of rainy May; and she, stirred somewhat beyond her wont, and taking as her text the three words which have been used so often as the inspiring trumpet-calls of men,—the words *God*, *Immortality*, *Duty*,—pronounced, with terrible earnestness, how inconceivable was the *first*, how unbelievable the *second*, and yet how peremptory and absolute the *third*. Never, perhaps, have sterner accents affirmed the sovereignty of impersonal and unrecompensing Law. I listened, and night fell; her grave, majestic countenance turned toward me like a sibyl's in the gloom; it was as though she withdrew from my grasp, one by one, the two scrolls of promise, and left me the third scroll only, awful with inevitable fates. And when we stood at length and parted, amid that columnar circuit of the forest-trees, beneath the last twilight of starless skies, I seemed to be gazing, like Titus at Jerusalem, on vacant seats and empty halls,—on a sanctuary with no Presence to hallow it, and heaven left lonely of a God.

F. W. H. Myers, 'George Eliot', *Century Magazine*, N.S.I. (Nov. 1881), 62.

THROUGHOUT the first section of this book George Eliot has repeatedly emerged as paramount amongst major novelists in the accuracy and subtlety with which she used her experience of Evangelicalism. In a study which presumes to lay historical and literary evidence side by side lurks the ever-present danger of praising mere accuracy of reproduction at the expense of literary inventiveness. However unjust Dickens's caricatures, Stiggins and Chadband, as pictures of Dissenting ministers, or Collins's Miss Clack as a protrait of an Evangelical spinster, the critical reaction which finds in them only stereotypes unworthy of a mature response to the claims of Nonconformity or Evangelicalism is indicative of a certain partiality.[1] Indignation on behalf of people and beliefs thus travestied should not blind the literary critic to the generations of readers who have been roused to laughter by these caricatures. Nineteenth-century readers sympathetic to Evangelicalism were sometimes able both to recognize the injustices perpetrated and honestly to admit the amusement they derived from these distortions of the truth. One such reader, the Revd. Joseph Romilly, the Cambridge Registrar, who attended Charles Simeon's old church with his Evangelical sister Lucy, committed to his diary this final response to Mrs. Trollope's novel. 'Finished Mrs. Trollope's Vicar of Wrexhill: think it an infamous book tho full of talent:—it is coming it rather strong to make Mr. Cartwright the Vicar have a child by Widow Simpson & his cousin Stephen Corbold attempt a rape on Miss Mowbray . . .'[2]

Equally a recognition of George Eliot's seriousness of purpose in endeavouring to expose and explore these familiar stereotypes should not preclude the literary judgement that had she been authoress of *Scenes of Clerical Life* alone she would have been even less likely to

[1] A partiality which V. Cunningham falls prey to in his otherwise estimable book, *Everywhere Spoken Against: Dissent in the Victorian Novel.* See particularly ch. viii.

[2] *Romilly's Cambridge Diary 1832–1842*, ed. J. P. T. Bury (Cambridge, 1967), p. 154.

have earned herself a lasting reputation than would Dickens had he written nothing after *Pickwick Papers*.

Her claim in this book to detailed study as perhaps the one major novelist to portray Evangelicalism with detailed fidelity and imaginative sympathy is obvious. Less obvious, perhaps, is the manner in which Evangelicalism not only provided her with a subject, but itself contributed to her view of the role and responsibilities of the novelist. It is to this aspect that I should first like to direct attention before considering the discrepancy between George Eliot's most savage attacks in a review upon the religion she had discarded and the attitudes apparent in the novels themselves which are then examined.

### 1. '*Realism*', '*sympathy*', *and the Evangelical heritage*

The precise nature of George Eliot's doctrine of realism in fiction owed more to her Evangelical background than has previously been suggested. Although one should not discount the influence of her favourite poet Wordsworth, nor overlook her knowledge of the eighteenth-century tradition of fictional realism as seen in Fielding, Richardson, and Jane Austen, too much has been made of her debt to George Henry Lewes. Alice R. Kaminsky's article, 'George Eliot, George Henry Lewes, and the Novel', explored their common interest in the doctrine of realism but failed, I think, to support her thesis that George Eliot's interest in realism was 'due to the influence of Lewes who constantly emphasised the need for realism and the need for the avoidance of falsism'.[3] She attributes 'the highly self-conscious discussion of realism in Chapter XVII' of *Adam Bede* directly to Lewes's *Westminster Review* article, 'Realism in Art: Recent German Fiction'. 'He had demanded, "Either give us true peasants or leave them untouched; either paint no drapery at all, or paint it with the utmost fidelity; either keep your people silent, or make them speak the idiom of their class". And she gave us true peasants in her first novel.'[4]

But these principles, though not so clearly applied to the peasant class, had been in operation in the *Scenes of Clerical Life*, published in 1857, and had been apparent in her article, 'The Natural History of German Life', published in July 1856. 'Opera peasants, whose

[3] A. R. Kaminsky, 'George Eliot, George Henry Lewes, and the Novel', *PMLA* 70 (2) (1955), 997–1013. [4] Ibid., p. 1009.

unreality excites Mr. Ruskin's indignation, are surely too frank an idealisation to be misleading . . . But our social novels profess to represent the people as they are, and the unreality of their representations is a grave evil.'[5]

The reference to Ruskin in this context is significant. George Eliot had reviewed the third volume of Ruskin's *Modern Painters* for the April issue of the *Westminster Review* that year and had shown appreciative interest in his distinction between the False and the True Ideal in art with its corollary that falsity becomes pernicious if it is likely to be accepted as a representation of fact.[6] Lewes reviewed the fourth volume for the *Leader* in May 1856[7] and had clearly discussed the work with George Eliot who had been reading it aloud to him in February of that year,[8] but George Eliot would, I think, have recognized Ruskin's work as a sympathetic critical philosophy without Lewes as intermediary. Indeed the echoes from Ruskin's work are clearer than Lewes's influence in Chapter xvii of *Adam Bede*. The illustration that she chose to illuminate her contention that in art, verbal or pictorial, 'Falsehood is so easy, truth so difficult', must have been suggested by her reading of Ruskin. In his attempt to distinguish between true and false art Ruskin discusses two plates depicting a Lombard-Gothic and a classical griffin.[9] George Eliot's illustration runs as follows:

> The pencil is conscious of a delightful facility in drawing a griffin—the longer the claws, and the larger the wings, the better; but that marvellous facility which we mistook for genius is apt to forsake us when we want to draw a real unexaggerated lion.[10]

This passage rather curiously introduced in a paragraph that leads to an expression of her delight in the 'rare, precious quality of truthfulness' that she found in Dutch paintings, would suggest that Ruskin's critical writings had made a deep impression on her. They articulated moral demands on art and a justification of the artist's work which had appeared in fragmentary form in her very earliest letters. This affinity for Ruskin's critical philosophy stems, I would suggest, from the one common inheritance they shared, Evangelicalism. It was in response to Evangelical attitudes that they formulated their literary philosophies.

[5] *Essays of George Eliot*, p. 270. [6] 'Belles Lettres', *WR*, N.S. 9 (1856), 625–37.
[7] *Leader*, 7 (1856), 497–8. This review makes no mention of Ruskin's attitudes to Realism and Idealism. [8] *G. Eliot Letters*, ii, 228.
[9] J. Ruskin, *Works*, v, 140–7. [10] *Adam Bede*, i, 268.

Ruskin's childhood reading had been carefully, though not prudishly, selected by his Evangelical mother; a comparatively liberal Evangelical upbringing enabled the seventeen-year-old Ruskin to defend the practice of novel-reading in moderation, against the arguments for total abstinence deployed by many a prominent Evangelical of the day. It was in response to the Evangelical claim that fiction, being 'a continual tissue of falsehoods', is necessarily evil that Ruskin started to formulate his distinction between falsehood and the true imagination.[11]

George Eliot's childhood reading had been determined at first by her father's chance selection, then by Miss Franklin's relatively liberal hand, and finally by her own rigid standards.[12] Her pronouncements upon the expedience of reading works of fiction, given in a letter to her ex-teacher, now confidante, Maria Lewis, reflect very closely the editorial policy of the *Christian Observer* at this period of maximum repression. She excepted from her censorship,

> . . . standard works whose contents are matter of constant reference, and the names of whose heroes and heroines briefly and therefore conveniently describe characters and ideas. Such are Don Quixote, Butler's Hudibras, Robinson Crusoe, Gil Blas, Byron's Poetical romances, Southey's do. etc. Such too are Walter Scott's novels and poems. . . . Shakespeare has a higher claim than this on our attention but we have need of as nice a power of distillation as the bee to suck nothing but honey from his pages.

This list had been legitimated for Evangelical readers by reviews or honourable mention in the pages of the *Christian Observer*. Her letter continues,

> I am I confess not an impartial member of a jury in this case for I owe the culprits a grudge for injuries inflicted on myself. I shall carry to my grave the mental diseases with which they have contaminated me. When I was quite a little child I could not be satisfied with the things around me; I was constantly living in a world of my own creation, and was quite contented to have no companions that I might be left to my own musings and imagine scenes in which I was chief actress. Conceive what a character novels would give to these Utopias.[13]

When this quite specific account of the positive evils fostered by

[11] 'Essay on Literature; 1836: Does the Persual of Works of Fiction act Favourably or Unfavourably on the Moral Character?' *Works*, i, 357–75.

[12] The common erroneous assumption that George Eliot's family were Evangelical is repeated in M. N. Cutt, *Mrs. Sherwood and Her Books for Children*, p. 75.

[13] *G. Eliot Letters*, i, 21–2.

the novel-reading habit is compared with the over-simplification of Evangelical attitudes presented to us by the critical theorist, Richard Stang, we begin to see how the Evangelical impetus behind prominent literary critics of the nineteenth century has been undervalued. 'The evangelical wing of the church and most of the dissenters strongly disapproved of all imaginative literature as mere entertainment, as a waste of time that should be spent praising God or making money.'[14]

In *The Mill on the Floss* George Eliot portrays for us something of her own experience in coming to terms with the realization that the imagination might be employed in a way that was spiritually profitable.[15] As a small child Maggie Tulliver had received great pleasure from books both because the pictures and stories had stimulated her imagination and because her fondness for them represented the cleverness in which her father took such amazed pride. Her childish apprehensions made no distinction between fiction and reality. *Pilgrim's Progress* was accommodated to the familiar landscape of the Floss,[16] whilst the book provided her with archetypes through which to express her own experience. Her sense of fear and acute danger led her to see a 'fierce-eyed' old gipsy as Apollyon,[17] for, as she explained to Riley, the auctioneer, 'the devil takes the shape of wicked men, and walks about and sets people doing wicked things, and he's oftener in the shape of a bad man than any other, because, you know, if people saw he was the devil, and he roared at 'em, they'd run away, and he couldn't make 'em do what he pleased'.[18] It is the disappearance of the books when the Tullivers are sold up that brings home to Maggie the reality of the change in their circumstances and the prospect of a life devoid of the pleasures of the imagination.[19]

Only when the books have been removed does Maggie realize the extent of her dependence upon them, and her craving for them become a moral weakness. A similar sense of deprivation must have hit Mary Ann Evans when her Evangelical convictions led her to restrict her novel reading activities, for she had been one of those 'omnivorous' readers for whom 'we cannot legislate'.[20] Her consequent discontent led her to express her condemnation of this

[14] R. Stang, *The Theory of the Novel in England 1850–1870* (1959), p. 5.

[15] Ruskin's dismissal of this novel, partly because of the very commonplace nature of the heroine's trials, is interesting. *Works*, xxxiv, 377.

[16] *Mill on the Floss*, i, 57. [17] Ibid. i, 171–3. [18] *Mill on the Floss*, i, 21.

[19] Ibid. i, 375–6. [20] *G. Eliot Letters*, i, 21.

activity as a sin in strong terms. Maggie's craving for escapist fiction and her subsequent behaviour could stand as an exemplar for *Christian Observer* articles on the injurious effects of novel reading. One review in the *Christian Observer* for 1822 is particularly interesting in this context. Noting 'that the modified character of the Waverley Novels has gained access for them into many families in which general novel-reading has been strictly interdicted',[21] it was decided to devote a review, over two issues, to Scott's *The Pirate*, pointing out the dangers of reading even the least offensive novels. The similarities between this review, Maggie's predicament, and the wording of George Eliot's early letters lead one to wonder if Mary Ann could have read this particular review; in 1832, the *Christian Observer* specifically referred younger readers back to it for an expression of the periodical's views on novel-reading.[22] George Eliot's subsequent choice of the *Christian Observer* as the periodical in which to publish her poem, 'Farewell', indicates her sympathy with its contents and tone.[23] A further small indication that this review may have remained at the back of George Eliot's mind when writing *The Mill on the Floss* is the way in which *The Pirate*[24] is substituted as the partially read novel for the copy of *Waverley* which had to be returned to a neighbour in 1827 before Mary Ann had finished reading it.[25]

The school books which remained for Maggie gave no emotional satisfaction, 'without the indirect charm of school-emulation'.

Sometimes Maggie thought she could have been contented with absorbing fancies; if she could have had all Scott's novels and all Byron's poems!—

[21] *CO* (1822), p. 158.

[22] *CO* (1832), p. 814. If Maria Lewis, who was about twenty-two in 1822, had bought a copy of the original number she would probably have kept it, since the purchase of this periodical would represent a significant expenditure for an impoverished governess.

[23] It is apposite to recall the seventh verse of this poem,

> Books, that have been to me as chests of gold,
> Which, miser-like, I secretly have told,
> And for you love, health, friendship, peace, have sold
>
> *Farewell! CO* (1840), p. 38.

[24] *Mill on the Floss*, ii, 59. The substitution cannot altogether be explained by George Eliot's frequent habit of choosing for her characters books which had been published very recently before the date of the novel's setting (e.g. in *Middlemarch* Mary Garth is reading Scott's *Anne of Geierstein* (1829), whilst in *Adam Bede* Arthur Donnithorne receives *The Lyrical Ballads* (1798) from his bookseller). Since Maggie refers to reading the first volume of the novel as a child there is no specific merit in referring to *The Pirate* (1821) in preference to *Waverley* (1814).

[25] J. W. Cross, *George Eliot's Life*, i, 22.

then, perhaps, she might have found happiness enough to dull her sensibility to her actual daily life. And yet . . . they were hardly what she wanted. She could make dream-worlds of her own—but no dream-world would satisfy her now. She wanted some explanation of this hard, real life. . . .[26]

Of the escapist element in contemporary fiction the *Christian Observer* left its readers in little doubt. 'He [the author] wishes his spell to be inextricable: his ideal world is to cast into the shade all tame realities of this visible sphere: joy and sorrow, health and duty, are all to be forgotten . . .'[27]

A desire for understanding and a wish to excel in the masculine fields of learning led Maggie to take temporary consolation from school-books but her mind soon reverted to the thoughts implanted there by eager novel-reading.

She rebelled against her lot. . . . Then her brain would be busy with wild romances of a flight from home in search of something less sordid and dreary: she would go to some great man—Walter Scott, perhaps—and tell him how wretched and how clever she was, and he would surely do something for her. But, in the middle of her vision, her father would perhaps enter the room for the evening, and, surprised that she sat still without noticing him, would say complainingly, 'Come, am I to fetch my slippers myself?' The voice pierced through Maggie like a sword. There was another sadness besides her own, and she had been thinking of turning her back on it and forsaking it.[28]

The memories of 'wild romances' exacerbated her misery as the reviewer had suggested they would.

It is a prime secret for happiness to learn the art of lowering our expectations; to be satisfied with a little; to be content with the state of life in which we are placed; to improve, and thus to enjoy, the present hour, and to look for no perfection either in men or things. But how different the lessons taught by the bulk of poets and novelists![29]

It was indeed a constant plaint of Evangelicals that emotion and sympathy upon fictional characters inevitably deadened or dissipated one's love and sympathy for fellow creatures in distress, a warning that George Eliot carefully heeded when composing her own novels. It is not by chance that Maggie thinks of Sir Walter Scott in her egoistic fantasies. George Eliot remembered only too clearly the

[26] *Mill on the Floss*, ii, 28.
[27] *CO* (1822), p. 237.
[28] *Mill on the Floss*, ii, 30–1.
[29] *CO* (1822), pp. 240–1.

effect of those novels which had 'gained access into many families in which general novel-reading [had] been strictly interdicted'. After reading Lockhart's *Life of Scott* she had written to Maria Lewis, 'The spiritual sleep of that man was awful . . . Sir W. S. himself is the best commentary on the effect of romances and novels. He sacrificed almost his integrity for the sake of acting out the character of the Scotch Laird, which he had so often depicted.'[30]

Many years later, when Mrs. Congreve asked her what influence had first shaken her Evangelical orthodoxy, she replied unhesitatingly, 'Oh, Sir Walter Scott's.'[31]

When we next see Maggie she seems to have heeded some such warning as the *Christian Observer's*. 'Surely nothing can be more ensnaring to ardent and youthful minds, or more calculated to destroy that tranquil acquiescence in the allotments of Providence which forms a grand constituent in human happiness, than such highly wrought exhibitions of ideal scenes and characters.'[32]

She has given up books, 'except a very, very few',[33] 'Yet one has a sense of uneasiness in looking at her—a sense of opposing elements, of which a fierce collision is imminent . . .'[34]

She rejects Philip's proffered loan of the second volume of *The Pirate* from a fear that it would make her 'long to see and know many things'—a tacit admission that fiction could fulfil some positive role. Philip describes her stand as 'narrow asceticism' and affirms that 'Poetry and art and knowledge are sacred and pure.'[35] It was her struggle with this same 'narrow asceticism' that led George Eliot to 'an appreciation of the sacredness of the writers' art', and to her insistence on 'those moral qualities that contribute to literary excellence'.[36]

At their next meeting in the Red Deeps Philip sets out to justify his assertion. Maggie defines the philosophy upon which she has been acting: 'Is it not right to resign ourselves entirely, whatever may be denied us? I have found great peace in that for the last two or three years—even joy in subduing my will.'[37]

How familiar this philosophy was to George Eliot may be judged by a letter of the young Mary Ann Evans to Martha Jackson.

[30] *G. Eliot Letters*, i, 24.
[31] Quoted by G. S. Haight, *George Eliot: A Biography* (1969), p. 39.
[32] *CO* (1822), p. 241. [33] *Mill on the Floss*, ii, 59.
[34] Ibid. ii, 49. [35] *Mill on the Floss*, ii, 60.
[36] *Essays of G. Eliot*, p. 323. [37] *Mill on the Floss*, ii, 94.

My imagination is an enemy that must be cast down ere I can enjoy peace or exhibit uniformity of character. I know not which of its caprices I have most to dread—that which incites it to spread sackcloth 'above, below, around', or that which makes it 'cheat my eye with blear illusion, and beget strange dreams' of excellence and beauty in beings and things of only 'working day' price.[38]

Philip totally rejects 'this narrow self-delusive fanaticism, which is only a way of escaping pain by starving into dulness all the highest powers of your nature'.

'Joy and peace are not resignation: resignation is the willing endurance of a pain that is not allayed—that you don't expect to be allayed. Stupefaction is not resignation: and it is stupefaction to remain in ignorance—to shut up all the avenues by which the life of your fellow-men might become known to you.'[39]

It is from arriving at a position like Philip's that George Eliot begins to think of fiction as an avenue 'by which the life of your fellow-men might become known to you', and it is such a conviction that lies behind the defence of her art in *Scenes of Clerical Life* and *Adam Bede*. The approximation of Maggie's feelings and experiences with those of her author is further authenticated for us by Maggie's words after a year of reading Philip's books.

'I'm determined to read no more books where the blond-haired women carry away all the happiness. I should begin to have a prejudice against them. If you could give me some story, now, where the dark woman triumphs, it would restore the balance. I want to avenge Rebecca, and Flora MacIvor, and Minna and all the rest of the dark unhappy ones.'[40]

Since Philip, and popular authors of the day, failed to supply such a story George Eliot embarked upon a career as a novelist in which she was to give us the story of Dorothea and Rosamund.

In her first two fictional works George Eliot was still fighting Philip's battle with Maggie directly with her reader, endeavouring to show how her concept of fiction differed from that of the majority of contemporary novelists. It was as if her works were intended to illuminate Ruskins' distinction.

Now *nearly* all artistical and poetical seeking after the ideal is only one branch of this base habit—the abuse of the imagination in allowing it to

[38] *G. Eliot Letters*, i, 65–6. [39] *Mill on the Floss*, ii, 94. [40] Ibid. ii, 102.

find its whole delight in the impossible and untrue; while the faithful pursuit of the ideal is an honest use of the imagination, giving full power and presence to the possible and true.[41]

It was easy to differentiate her works from the merely sensational novel and, incidentally, to administer a firm rebuff to the reader who was unwilling to take an interest in his commonplace fellow men.

As it is, you can if you please, decline to pursue my story farther; and you will easily find reading more to your taste, since I learn from the newspapers that many remarkable novels, full of striking situations, thrilling incidents, and eloquent writing, have appeared only within the last season.[42]

More important, however, was the distinction between realism and falsification in the 'social' novel. If *The Pirate* produced from the reviewer the reaction that,

. . . we cannot but feel that we have been, if not absolutely in an ideal world, yet in a still more perplexing scene, compounded so indiscriminately of truth and fable, that no beneficial moral impression, nor any valuable lesson of experience, much less any certain matter of fact, is gained from the narrative.[43]

then Mary Ann exhibited truly Evangelical concern when she wrote, 'The weapons of the Christian warfare were never sharpened at the forge of romance. Domestic fictions as they come more within the range of imitation seem more dangerous.'[44] This was a sentiment that she was to retain when she lost her Evangelical beliefs, rephrasing it, 'But our social novels profess to represent the people as they are, and the unreality of their representations is a grave evil.'[45]

The Evangelicals were far from undervaluing the power of literary examples of moral goodness, but if they were to provide a useful incentive or guide to the Christian life, the situations and people they described must be realistically presented so as to prove imitable. Once a man of Evangelical background, aware of the efficacy of practical Evangelical literature, had become convinced of the positive values of the imagination, it was natural to justify the use of fiction in the terms of the old Evangelical arguments. It is in their desire to defend realism on moral rather than aesthetic grounds

[41] *Works*, v, 71–2. [42] *Scenes*, i, 68. [43] *CO* (1822), p. 242.
[44] *G. Eliot Letters*, i, 23. [45] *Essays of G. Eliot*, p. 270.

that one can detect the affinity, the common heritage, of Ruskin, Sir James Fitzjames Stephen, and George Eliot.

Although Stephen was becoming increasingly Broad Church in his sympathies (he was to conduct the legal defence for Dr. Rowland Williams)[46] the very title of the essay he published in 1855, 'The Relation of Novels to Life', illustrates the way that his criteria for literary judgement had been influenced by his Evangelical upbringing. He argued that since novels are '. . . read as commentaries upon the life which is just opening before the reader, and as food for passions which are lately awakened but have not yet settled down to definite objects', then it was important for the young reader to be aware of the distortions of reality necessitated by the genre and to be able to differentiate these from the 'false morality' of individual authors.[47] Stephen's demonstration of the manner in which *suppressio veri* can easily become *suggestio falsi* recalls Mary Ann's observations on her childhood reading.[48]

The absence of any evidence to suggest that George Eliot had read Stephen's essay makes the similarity of his views with those expressed in George Eliot's most famous statement on realism in the novel all the more interesting as support for the hypothesis of Evangelicalism as the common denominator.[49] Stephen's conviction that the enlargement of the reader's knowledge of the world and the excitement of the feelings constituted the major moral effects of novel-reading makes us realize that the way in which George Eliot linked her appeal for realism with her 'doctrine of sympathy' was by no means unique. Stephen states that this knowledge of the world 'consists not in mere acquaintance with maxims about life, but in applying appropriate ideas to clear facts'. The novel, he insists, affords material for self-examination and moral probing. 'To produce or to stimulate self-consciousness by such means, may not be altogether a healthy process, but it is unquestionably one which has powerful effects.'

[46] L. Stephen, *Life of Sir James Fitzjames Stephen*, pp. 127–9, 184. For Sir James's slow progress to scepticism whilst retaining the moral convictions of an Evangelical see J. C. Livingston, 'The Religious Creed and Criticism of Sir James Fitzjames Stephen', *VS* 17 (1974), 279–300.

[47] *Cambridge Essays* (1855), p. 151.

[48] See above p. 4.

[49] There is a passage in Leslie Stephen's *George Eliot* (1902), p. 18 which suggests that he recognized the element of continuity between Evangelical literary criticism and exposition of 'the true relations of art and morality' propagated by 'aesthetic prophets' later in the century.

Stephen then takes on, by implication, his Evangelical opponents. He notes that with some people emotion is more readily aroused by fiction than by history, and then pauses to parry the anticipated blow. 'It is sometimes broadly stated that emotion produced by fiction is an evil, and tends to harden the heart. This statement goes further than its authors suppose. The parables are fictions . . .'[50]

These are the ideas which recur in George Eliot's 'The Natural History of German Life', although in this case more succinctly expressed.

The greatest benefit we owe to the artist, whether painter, poet, or novelist, is the extension of our sympathies. Appeals founded on generalizations and statistics require a sympathy ready-made, a moral sentiment already in activity; but a picture of human life such as a great artist can give, surprises even the trivial and the selfish into that attention to what is apart from themselves, which may be called the raw material of moral sentiment.[51]

A glancing blow is once again struck at that same shadowy adversary, the Evangelical denigrator of the imagination. 'When Scott takes us into Luckie Mucklebackit's cottage . . . more is done towards linking the higher classes with the lower, towards obliterating the vulgarity of exclusiveness, than by hundreds of sermons and philosophical dissertations.'[52]

The urge to wrestle with, or enlighten, those still in the grips of a rigidly orthodox Evangelicalism never left those who had once experienced it in an ardent and sincere form. Ruskin too felt impelled to address an aside to the Evangelicals in his chapter on 'The False Ideal'.

The group calling themselves Evangelical ought no longer to render their religion an offence to men of the world by associating it only with the most vulgar forms of art. It is not necessary that they should admit either music or painting into religious service; but if they admit either the one or the other, let it not be bad music nor bad painting. . . .[53]

The literary criticism of these writers showed a desire to account for Evangelical prejudices and to build upon the best of the heritage they had enjoyed. Stephen, lamenting both the novelists' tendency to smooth out inconsistencies in the characters they depicted and the

[50] *Cambridge Essays*, pp. 152–4. [51] *Essays of G. Eliot*, p. 270.
[52] Ibid., pp. 270–1. [53] *Works*, v, 88.

difficulty of showing great men doing great things in the novel, appealed to that literary genre he knew best as an example of the portrayal of the commonplace business of life which he believed to be the province of the novel. 'If any one of the numerous biographies of popular clergymen which are so common in the present day were from beginning to end an entire fiction, it would be no doubt the most extraordinary feat of imagination ever performed.'[54]

One wonders whether he recognized George Eliot's *Scenes of Clerical Life*, or more especially 'Amos Barton' and 'Janet's Repentance', as the fulfilment of his fantastic hypothesis.

## 2. *A changing perspective*

The seeming paradox of the *Scenes of Clerical Life* appearing only two years after the swingeing attack on Evangelicalism in 'Evangelical Teaching: Dr. Cumming', has frequently been remarked. The apparent *volte face* is partly explained by the difference of genre and of subject matter. For her publisher she carefully spelt out the centre of interest in 'Janet's Repentance'. 'My irony, so far as I understand myself, is not directed against opinions—against any class of religious views—but against the vices and weaknesses that belong to human nature in every sort of clothing. . . . I should like *not* to be offensive . . .',[55] whereas in her article, although admitting the personal idiosyncrasies of Dr. Cumming's position, George Eliot is aiming a broadside against a certain class of religious views.

In writing for the *Westminster Review* George Eliot could be fairly confident of not offending a readership to whom the free-thinking editorial policy was known. Her fiction, on the other hand, might well, and occasionally did, fall into the hands of firm believers.[56] In her essay on 'Antigone and its Moral', published six months after her review of Dr. Cumming's works, she showed herself alive to the dangers of aggressive proselytizing: '. . . preach against false doctrines, and you disturb feeble minds and send them adrift on a sea of doubt . . .';[57] and in 1862 she wrote to Barbara Bodichon:

Pray don't ever ask me again not to rob a man of his religious belief, as if you thought my mind tended towards such robbery. I have too profound

[54] *Cambridge Essays*, p. 160.
[55] *G. Eliot Letters*, ii, 347–8.
[56] *Silas Marner*, for instance, was considered suitable reading in a parsonage to which one of C. M. Yonge's characters is taken to regain her faith. *Clever Woman of the Family*, pp. 346–7.
[57] *Essays of G. Eliot*, pp. 264–5.

a conviction of the efficacy that lies in all sincere faith, and the spiritual blight that comes with No-faith, to have any negative propagandism in me. In fact, I have very little sympathy with Free-thinkers as a class, and have lost all interest in mere antagonism to religious doctrines.[58]

The word 'lost' implies a previous conviction in the validity of polemics employed against orthodox religion, and a former feeling of 'mere antagonism'. Her letters from Switzerland, immediately after her father's death, reflect a little of the newly converted agnostic's mocking spirit directed at her former associates. She fell in at her pension in Geneva with the Forbeses, a 'very evangelical' family, who lent her a religious novel concerned with the fate of a fearful infidel. Anxious that she was enjoying their surprising friendliness under false pretences she decides to tell them that she is no longer an Evangelical. 'I quite expected from their manner and character that they would forsake me in horror, but they are as kind as ever.'[59]

She has clearly erected a set of stereotype reactions for Evangelicals which are the very ones she endeavours to disprove in her fiction, where we are shown a Jerome or a Mrs. Pettifer who welcome Janet, despite her errors and previous hostility, or a Mrs. Bulstrode who stands by her husband after his downfall. Evident in her essay on Dr. Cumming are the desires to articulate her own reasons for abandoning Evangelical belief and to indulge in 'negative propaganda'. 'One more characteristic of Dr. Cumming's writings, and we have done. This is the *perverted moral judgement* that everywhere reigns in them. Not that this perversion is peculiar to Dr. Cumming: it belongs to the dogmatic system which he shares with all evangelical believers.'[60]

It is in her fiction that she first gives tribute to her early religious life as something other than totally morally enervating. Together with her admission that,

. . . Evangelicalism had brought into palpable existence and operation in Milby society that idea of duty, that recognition of something to be lived for beyond the mere satisfaction of self, which is to the moral life what the addition of a great central ganglion is to animal life.[61]

She administers what could be seen as self reproach for the violence of her own reactions to a discarded faith.

[58] *G. Eliot Letters*, iv, 64–5.
[59] *G. Eliot Letters*, i, 308–9.
[60] *Essays of G. Eliot*, p. 184.
[61] *Scenes*, ii, 162–3.

Yes, the movement was good, though it had that mixture of folly and evil which often makes what is good an offence to feeble and fastidious minds, who want human actions and characters riddled through the sieve of their own ideas, before they can accord their sympathy or admiration.[62]

By the time of *Adam Bede* her nostalgic affection and recognition of a debt to her early religious experiences even embraces the forms of that religion.

And to Adam the church service was the best channel he could have found for his mingled regret, yearning, and resignation; its interchange of beseeching cries for help, with outbursts of faith and praise—its recurrent responses and the familiar rhythm of its collects, seemed to speak for him as no other form of worship could have done. . . . The secret of our emotions never lies in the bare object, but in its subtle relations to our own past: no wonder the secret escapes the unsympathising observer, who might as well put on his spectacles to discern odours.[63]

These reflections are clearly related to the Victorian agnostic's Religion of Humanity and not to the conscious response to his father's funeral of even an educated village carpenter at the turn of the eighteenth century. That they represent George Eliot's own maturing response to the experiences of her youth can be confirmed by referring to a direct statement in a letter of 1875 to Mrs. Ponsonby in which she wrote, 'I should urge you to consider your early religious experience as a portion of valid knowledge, and to cherish its emotional results in relation to objects and ideas which are either substitutes or metamorphoses of the earlier.'[64]

The date of this statement is interesting when read in conjunction with the correspondence the following year between George Eliot and Elizabeth Stuart Phelps. Miss Phelps had written, 'Knowing me to be a believing Christian, you will foresee the points in which I should mourn over your later works.'

In response George Eliot asserted the continuity of her approach.

It is perhaps less irrelevant to say à-propos of a distinction you seem to make between my earlier and later works, that though I trust there is some growth in my appreciation of others and in my self-distrust, there has been no change in the point of view from which I regard our life since I wrote my first fiction—the 'Scenes of Clerical Life'. Any apparent change of spirit must be due to something of which I am unconscious.[65]

[62] Ibid. ii. 164. [63] *Adam Bede*, i, 300.
[64] *G. Eliot Letters*, vi, 120. [65] Ibid. vi, 318.

One instance of a 'change in the point of view' which would have aroused Miss Phelps's regret would be the way in which George Eliot had removed the morally perverse Evangelical from the side-lines, where he had stood in previous novels, and placed him in a position of central importance, subject to the full light of her penetrating analysis. The 'something' of which she was momentarily unconscious was perhaps the complex part played by her memory as a source of creative inspiration, a role she acknowledges elsewhere: '. . . at present my mind works with the most freedom and the keenest sense of poetry in my remotest past, and there are many strata to be worked through before I can begin to use *artistically* any material I may gather in the present.'[66]

Only after she had attempted to enter the Evangelical world of her own early days upon its own terms, depicting characters true to the spirit of the movement as she had known it, could she then permit herself to dramatize her fundamental objections to Evangelicalism as a dogmatic system, without the danger of becoming consciously 'offensive'.

### 3. *Scenes of Clerical Life* to *Middlemarch*

The Evangelical movement provided the backdrop for two of the *Scenes of Clerical Life*, 'Amos Barton', and 'Janet's Repentance'. A polemical intention and a recognition of a descriptive talent led to the choice, but these two sources of inspiration did not always sit at ease with one another.

The Evangelicals, whose quirks were known with irritating familiarity, presented perhaps the most effective test case, in personal terms, for the exercise of George Eliot's 'doctrine of sympathy'. An obituary notice in the *Contemporary Review*, written by Julia Wedgwood, confirms this impression. 'She once said to the writer that in conversation with the narrowest and least cultivated Evangelical she could feel more sympathy than divergence . . .'[67]

George Eliot's reviewing work had enabled her to perceive the potential of this sphere as material for fiction. Only a year before embarking on fiction herself she had written,

[66] *G. Eliot Letters*, iii, 128–9.

[67] [J. Wedgwood], 'The Moral Influence of George Eliot', *Contemporary Review*, 39 (1881), 181.

The real drama of Evangelicalism—and it has abundance of fine drama for anyone who has genius enough to discern and reproduce it—lies among the middle and lower classes; and are not Evangelical opinions understood to give an especial interest in the weak things of the earth, rather than in the mighty?[68]

Furthermore the study of Evangelicalism presented her with a perfect opportunity to demonstrate how the religion of humanity secularized the best elements of orthodox religion. By choosing to write about Evangelicals, George Eliot could appropriate the terminology of the Christian religion to present the quasi-religious humanism she had adopted from Feuerbach and Comte. From Feuerbach she had learnt to see the Incarnation as man's dream of becoming God and the perception that man's only chance of realizing this desire lay in transcendent love of one's fellow man. Her desire to preach this new gospel in a manner inoffensive to orthodox readers resulted in passages, such as the following comment on Mr. Tryan's influence on Janet Dempster, where the central issue—the presence or absence of a God—remains blurred.

Blessed influence of one true loving human soul on another! Not calculable by algebra, not deducible by logic, but mysterious, effectual, mighty as the hidden process by which the tiny seed is quickened, and bursts forth into tall stem and broad leaf, and glowing tasselled flower. Ideas are often poor ghosts; our sun-filled eyes cannot discern them; they pass athwart us in thin vapour, and cannot make themselves felt. But sometimes they are made flesh; they breathe upon us with warm breath, they touch us with soft responsive hands, they look at us with sad sincere eyes, and speak to us in appealing tones; they are clothed in a living human soul, with all its conflicts, its faith, and its love.[69]

Finally, Evangelicalism, as a background to her earliest fiction, appealed because her acquaintance with it lay in just that 'remotest past' in which her imagination moved with most ease. Since she had always thought herself 'deficient in dramatic power, both of construction and dialogue', and feeling that she would be at ease 'in the descriptive parts of a novel',[70] Evangelicalism provided the sphere for the sociological exactitude of external detail which she had so warmly recommended to novelists like Holme Lee as a means of making melodramatic incidents acceptable.[71]

[68] *Essays of G. Eliot*, p. 318.
[69] *Scenes*, ii, 36.
[70] *G. Eliot Letters*, ii, 406.
[71] 'Belles Lettres', *WR*, N.S. 11 (1857), 321.

The extraordinarily retentive quality of George Eliot's memory for the books she had read has, I think, often been underestimated. Although she confessed to reading little contemporary fiction[72] after her own career as a novelist began, apart from the odd novel by her friends Miss Thackeray and Anthony Trollope,[73] she had spent two years as writer for the 'Belles Lettres' section of the *Westminster Review* and had always been a voracious reader. A very real fear of unconscious plagiarism is suggested by this remark, 'But when I am writing, or only thinking of writing fiction of my own, I cannot risk the reading of other English fiction.'[74]

The format of *Scenes of Clerical Life* may well have been suggested to her by her earlier reading. In 1840 she had recommended to Maria Lewis a book by Erskine Neale entitled, *The Life-Book of a Labourer; or, The Curate with his Trials, Sorrows, Checks and Triumphs* (1839).[75] In this book the author gives a number of reminiscences of parishes and parsons he has known, in the form of a series of short stories. As with George Eliot the author's own reflective stance forms the major element of continuity, although George Eliot in addition employs some degree of geographical proximity to link the stories. Neale frequently reminds the reader that 'the tenure of a curacy is painfully uncertain',[76] and of the hardships that this entails; this may well have recalled the book's title to George Eliot when she came to write her first story, 'The Sad Fortunes of the Rev. Amos Barton'. Several incidents and characters in *Scenes of Clerical Life* suggest that a recollection of the work lingered in George Eliot's mind.[77] Above all the motto, printed on the first page, would have ensured that George Eliot still remembered it favourably in days when her agreement with its specific religious message had ceased. 'We are all eagle-eyed in discerning points of difference; slow in admitting points of union. Our journey is, at best, a short one; why mark its stages by distrust and division?'[78]

[72] *G. Eliot Letters*, iv, 123, 377 [73] Ibid. vi, 123.
[74] *G. Eliot Letters*, vi, 199. [75] Ibid. i, 78.
[76] *Life-Book of A Labourer* (George Eliot read the first edition of the work. My references are to the second edition (1850), which had been slightly emended), p. 12.
[77] Cf. the variety of clerical practice and character at the Milby Clerical Meeting with 'A Fastidious Parish', *Life-Book of a Labourer*, pp. 54–74; the character of Mr. Gilfil with 'The Rough Clergyman', ibid. pp. 113–34; Caterina's removal of the dagger from the cabinet in the gallery at Cheverel Manor with ibid., pp. 31–2.
[78] Ibid., p. 1.

Although Mary Ann seems not herself to have enjoyed access to a lending library the *Christian Observer* would have provided her both with the idea of such an institution[79] and with suggestions for the books she ordered from her bookseller. *Father Clement: A Roman Catholic Story* (1823) by Miss Grace Kennedy had been censured as polemical writing by the *Christian Observer* in 1837. The editor had spoken out against the unfair and dangerous practice of condemning one's opponents in works of fiction.[80] Perhaps George Eliot, recalling this, made a reference to the work the excuse for Miss Pratt to defend her own conduct. 'This story of "Father Clement" is a library in itself on the errors of Romanism. I have ever considered fiction as a suitable form for conveying moral and religious instruction, as I have shown in my little work "De Courcy" . . .'[81]

The *Christian Observer's* lengthy review of the Revd. T. S. Grimshawe's *A Memoir of the Rev. Legh Richmond* (1828), contained a warning which may well have provided the germ of George Eliot's picture of Mrs. Linnet's reading habits:

> We fear that a large class of readers are in the habit of passing over such remarks and disquisitions, and fixing their attention, solely upon the narrative; but if they can be induced to forego [*sic*] this perfunctory practice . . . they will find abundant matter to instruct and benefit, as well as to interest them.[82]

George Eliot dramatizes this fear for us.

> She then glanced over the letters and diary, and wherever there was a predominance of Zion, the River of Life, and notes of exclamation, she turned over to the next page; but any passage in which she saw such promising nouns as 'small-pox', 'pony', or 'boots and shoes', at once arrested her.[83]

Other library tales mentioned suggest that George Eliot relied on memory rather than fresh research in constructing these episodes.[84]

[79] *CO* (1822), p. 699; (1829), p. 228; (1830), p. 94; (1837), p. 742.
[80] *CO* (1837), p. 307. [81] *Scenes*, ii, 78.
[82] *CO* (1828), p. 665. [83] *Scenes*, ii, 80.
[84] *Memoirs of Felix Neff* (*Scenes*, ii, 77) and *Life of Henry Martyn* (*Scenes*, ii, 262). Both titles are incorrectly quoted. The first was probably an allusion to *A Memoir of Felix Neff* (1832) by the Anglican Revd. W. S. Gilly, rather than to *Memorials of Felix Neff the Alpine Pastor* (1833) by T. S. Ellerby, a Dissenter. The second was presumably a reference to J. Sargent, *Memoir of the Rev. Henry Martyn* (1819).

Perhaps an excessive reliance upon her experience as a comparatively isolated Evangelical, relying upon the *Christian Observer* for information, was responsible for the historical insensitivity of her assertion in 'Amos Barton' that 'by this time the effect of the Tractarian agitation was beginning to be felt in backward provincial regions'.[85] Although Newman and the editor of the *Christian Observer* conducted a lengthy debate in the paper's columns in March 1837[86] widespread Evangelical opposition to Tractarianism was much slower to gain impetus.[87] Mary Ann, whose zealous fervour in pursuing newly published, controversial literature must have made her one of the more up-to-date Evangelicals in the provinces,[88] does not mention the Oxford Movement and its repercussions on her letters until 1839.[89] It is, therefore, unlikely that the 'vibration' of this movement had reached Milby by 1837.

Despite George Eliot's rebuff to hunters of 'originals' for the characters and incidents in *Scenes of Clerical Life*,[90] her defensive letters[91] leave little doubt that she had used two clergymen of her acquaintance, the Revd. John Gwyther and the Revd. John Edmund Jones, as models for Mr. Barton and Mr. Tryan.

It seems probable in the case of both of these clerical portraits that George Eliot confined herself in the main to reproducing the circumstances of her 'originals' ' lives rather than creating characters that would be instantly recognizable as fictional replicas of Gwyther and Jones. Yet, as she well knew, character and circumstance are not totally separable phenomena. Even if she claimed that her Amos Barton was a better man than Gwyther[92] she retained identifying

[85] *Scenes*, i, 44. [86] *CO* (1837), pp. 141–98.

[87] Not until 1838 did J. B. Sumner, Evangelical Bishop of Chester, whom George Eliot heard at the Bible Society meeting that year, warn against Tractarianism in his charge. G. Berwick, 'Close of Cheltenham: Parish Pope', *Theology*, 39 (1939), 197.

[88] I take her reading of books such as Leveson Vernon Harcourt, *The Doctrine of the Deluge* (2 vols., 1838) to be an indication of how closely she followed all sides of the various contemporary debates publicized in the *Christian Observer*, rather than the surprising exception that G. S. Haight would make it out to be when he writes, 'Along with the usual lives of missionaries and pious devotional tracts there are occasional references to new books like Vernon Harcourt's . . .' *G. Eliot Letters*, vol. i, xliii. Indeed his remark is further misleading in that it suggests that the lives and tracts she read were old books. I have cross-checked the books mentioned in her early letters with reviews and advertisements in the *Christian Observer* and have found that in no case does she allow more than a year to elapse before obtaining an important work through her local bookseller.

[89] *G. Eliot Letters*, i, 25, where she alludes to the controversy 'on the nature of the *visible* church'.

[90] Ibid. iii, 156. [91] Ibid. ii, 375–6; iii, 156–7. [92] Ibid. iii, 156.

features because they made for herself a comprehensible and real personage. Barton's grammatical lapses, also discernible in an extant letter of Gwyther's,[93] 'surprised the young ladies of his parish extremely',[94] and so of course assisted in undermining the social respect usually accorded to a clergyman. This loss of prestige and the admiration of young, zealous women, like Mary Ann Evans, prepared the way for Barton to be overwhelmed by the flattery, interest, and companionship offered him by the Countess.

There was, however, another determining factor in the character presentation of these two men. George Eliot consciously set out to challenge the literary stereotypes of the Evangelical minister. In drawing Amos Barton, George Eliot took on the literary caricatures beloved by Dickens, Mrs. Trollope or Thackeray, made her hero ill-educated, self-important, and ugly, and then determined to demonstrate to her readers that these flaws did not make a hypocrite and were indeed compatible with 'poetry and pathos'.[95] George Eliot's own experiences made her aware of the temptation to brand Evangelicalism with the stigma of greasy hypocrisy. In the letter from Geneva in 1849 in which she had described the 'very evangelical' Forbes family she also told the Brays of another visit she had received: 'He [Mr. Sibree] introduced a vulgar-looking man, exceedingly oily, pitted with the small-pox as "My brother from Birmingham".'[96]

Amos Barton shares the physical affliction of smallpox scars with Mr. Peter Sibree the Independent Chaplain of the Birmingham General Cemetery, but in Amos's case George Eliot challenges us to separate the physical deformity from deformity of soul.

In her letters she was not always careful to avoid the easily damning epithet. In recommending the publications of the Society for the Promotion of Christian Knowledge she compared it with the works of another religious society. 'This Society brings out some excellent books, and has not the stamp of slimy evangelicalism which belongs to the Religious Tract Society.'[97]

This popular image is also taken up and subjected to a subtle commentary in *Scenes of Clerical Life*. The anomaly of an Evangelical clergyman who was also a gentleman had surprised the people of Laxeter:

[93] Ibid. iii, 83–4. [94] *Scenes*, i, 32. [95] *Scenes* i, 67.
[96] *G. Eliot Letters*, i, 309. [97] *G. Eliot Letters*, v, 443.

... for of the two other Low Church clergymen in the neighbourhood, one was a Welshman of globose figure and unctuous complexion, and the other a man of atrabiliar aspect, with lank black hair, and a redundance of limp cravat—in fact, the sort of thing you might expect in men who distributed the publications of the Religious Tract Society, and introduced Dissenting hymns into the Church.[98]

Readers of the earlier 'Amos Barton' might be expected to associate the last reference with Amos himself and also to remember that when the 'Tract Society' was first mentioned it was seen as an instrument of social utility. The rich farmer's wife, Mrs. Hackit, vouches for its fringe benefits. ' ". . . I've seen more o' the poor people with going tracking, than all the time I've lived in the parish before. And there'd need be something done among 'em; for the drinking at them Benefit Clubs is shameful." '[99]

In order to dissociate Amos Barton from the 'slimy evangelicalism' of literary tradition George Eliot provides a control figure, the Revd. Archibald Duke. Duke is a gloomy bigot. He is also a glutton, and his greed recalls the secret gourmandizings of a Mrs. Clennam or a Mr. Prong, the open gluttony of a Chuzzlewit or a Chadband, or the taunts at the 'savoury fleshpots' of Clapham.[100] Gluttony, the most comically debased of the seven deadly sins, was frequently used as a means of satirical attack; for what simpler device could there be for showing the gap between a man's spiritual pretensions and his physical weaknesses? Duke's greed and excessive expenditure on himself are then unfavourably compared with Amos's honest poverty, incurred in bringing up a large family on too small an income. Amos's healthy appetite and fondness for 'a glass, or even two glasses, of brandy-and-water' are stimulated by his hard work and relieved by his parishioners rather than by the scanty housekeeping his home affords, so he gains an unjustified reputation for succumbing 'to the things of the flesh',[101] and men find it easy to believe in his intimacy with a man of the Stiggins or Chadband school—'a fellow who soaked himself with spirits, and talked of the Gospel through an inflamed nose'.[102]

In her portrait of the Revd. Edgar Tryan George Eliot attempted to undermine two popular images. She wanted to suggest that

[98] *Scenes*, ii, 90–1. [99] *Scenes*, i, 18.

[100] C. Dickens, *Little Dorrit;* A. Trollope, *Rachel Ray;* C. Dickens, *Martin Chuzzlewit; Bleak House;* W. M. Thackeray, *The Newcomes.*

[101] *Scenes*, i, 73. [102] Ibid. i, 91.

Evangelicalism was consistent with a good education and gentlemanly manners and also to offer an example of 'the real drama of Evangelicalism' to novelists of 'the *white neck-cloth* species'.[103] Unfortunately these aims conflict. In her desire to satirize the school and save the hero she creates a pasteboard character, whose faults are either so literary in origin as to be unbelievable or as soon as they are admitted are qualified so as to save his image from being tarnished. How closely Mr. Tryan and his adherents at Milby approximate to the circle usually depicted by Evangelical lady novelists may be judged by reading 'Janet's Repentance' against the background of George Eliot's critical essay, 'Silly Novels by Lady Novelists'.

> The Orlando of Evangelical literature is the young curate, looked at from the point of view of the middle class, where cambric bands are understood to have as thrilling an effect on the hearts of young ladies as epaulettes have in the classes above and below it. . . . The young curate always has a background of well-dressed and wealthy, if not fashionable society. . . .[104]

Mr. Tryan's social respectability is vouched for by his 'very fine cambric handkerchiefs'[105] and by the existence of two off-stage characters, his father and sister, who are ready to urge him to give up his curacy and take him to a southern climate for the good of his health.[106] Yet Tryan's saintliness is increased by his rejection of the escape his wealthy relatives offer him. By making Tryan choose to live in Mrs. Wagstaff's miserable lodgings at Paddiford George Eliot is challenging the image propagated in Conybeare's article, 'Church Parties'.[107] This accommodation lends plausibility to references to his work amongst the lower classes,[108] whilst allowing the drama to remain firmly anchored in middle-class Evangelicalism. Tryan is never really in danger of losing social caste by living in the poorer area of his parish. The comment made upon the respectability lent to Evangelicalism by Janet's adherence to it as a wealthy widow applies even more closely to Tryan, whose position can profitably be compared to Barton's in this respect: 'Errors look so very ugly in persons of small means—one feels they are taking quite a liberty in

[103] *Essays of G. Eliot*, p. 317. [104] Ibid. p. 318.

[105] *Scenes*, ii, 81. [106] Ibid. ii, 302.

[107] *Edin. Rev.* 98 (1853), 273–342. Also see above p. 42. A letter to Charles Bray suggests that George Eliot expected many of her readers to recognize the subject of her attack. 'Everybody is talking of the article on the Church in the Edinbro' Review'. *G. Eliot Letters*, ii, 121. [108] *Scenes*, ii, 52, 180–2.

going astray; whereas people of fortune may naturally indulge in a few delinquencies.'[109]

Unfortunately, having done comic justice to the mixture of romance and religion in the hearts of Tryan's female followers, George Eliot loses control of the lightly mocking tone when she introduces 'the Orlando of Evangelical literature':

> Even in these enlightened days, many a curate who, considered abstractedly, is nothing more than a sleek bimanous animal in a white neckcloth, with views more or less Anglican, and furtively addicted to the flute, is adored by a girl who has coarse brothers, or by a solitary woman who would like to be a helpmate in good works beyond her means. . . .
>
> But Mr. Tryan has entered the room, and the strange light from the golden-sky falling on his light-brown hair, which is brushed high up round his head, makes it look almost like an aureole. His grey eyes, too, shine with unwonted brilliancy this evening.[110]

The transition to the present tense, often a danger signal in George Eliot's early writing, heralds a passage hinting at unknown depths, sufferings, and secrets, which is snatched back from the realms of melodrama by the anti-climactic phrase: '[M]r. Tryan's face in repose was that of an ordinary whiskerless blond.' Tryan remains too closely related to the Eustace Grey type curate whom George Eliot had dismissed with such fine scorn when reviewing *The Old Grey Church*.[111] His days of 'thoughtless self-indulgence' are related in more detail than those of Eustace but his confession has the ring of a set-piece about it. George Eliot never allows us to see Tryan from the inside to understand his 'fluctuating faith and courage' or that strange combination of self-mortification with true resignation. Had she stuck a little closer to her 'original', her character portrayal might have been more convincing. The writer of an unpublished diary, unearthed by Professor Haight, wrote on Jones's death that he 'was of the Evangelical School in Religion and had caused more divisions and quarrels on a religious score in the Town among the Church people and Dissenters than had taken place during the last ½ century'.[112] Even though George Eliot tells us that Tryan's conduct on the Sunday of the march to the Evening Lecture might be seen by the timid as 'rather defiant than wise' the

[109] Ibid. ii, 283. [110] Ibid. ii, 88. [111] *Essays of G. Eliot*, pp. 318–20.

[112] Quoted by T. A. Noble, *George Eliot's 'Scenes of Clerical Life'* (New Haven and London, 1965), p. 14n.

chapter ends with a reminder of his physical frailty and it is as Janet's consumptive friend and counsellor that he remains in our minds.[113]

The inability to adopt any consistently critical stance where Tryan is concerned is part of a more fundamental uneasiness in this tale. Since she has chosen to place 'morality 'and 'religion' firmly on the side of Evangelicalism in 'Janet's Repentance', there is little opportunity for the author to stand outside the tradition. 'Amos Barton' had not posed this problem for her because in that tale 'the educating of men's souls',[114] the highest function of the Christian religion for George Eliot, takes place despite the doctrinally rigid Evangelical system to which Amos clings. Amos's sermon to the inmates of the workhouse indicates how easily the biblical language and symbols favoured by the Evangelicals could become divorced from the spiritual truths they were originally employed to convey. 'He talked of Israel and its sins, of chosen vessels, of the Paschal lamb, of blood as a medium of reconciliation; and he strove in this way to convey religious truth within reach of the Fodge and Fitchett mind.'[115]

Having established for herself and her readers a critical awareness of the weaknesses to which Evangelical terminology is susceptible she can make subtly ironic use of it herself. The Countess, for instance, finds no difficulty in acquiring the right turn of phrase with which to ingratiate herself with the Bartons, and in turn her lack of real vice or indeed any depth of spiritual character is underlined by the way she begins to adopt Evangelical attitudes at their most shallow level. 'She had serious intentions of becoming *quite* pious—without any reserves—when she had once got her carriage and settlement.'[116]

In this shallow, selfish woman her 'uneasy sense that she was not altogether safe' in the spiritual world led not to being a 'serious Christian' but to possessing 'serious intentions', a difference that any reader acquainted with the writings of Hannah More or Wilberforce would be quick to discern.

This quality of understatement and this knowledge that George Eliot's views of the speaker's words are different from those of the speaker are absent from the Evangelical language used in 'Janet's Repentance'. We see only a hackneyed attempt at revitalizing the

[113] *Scenes*, ii, ch. ix. [114] *Essays of G. Eliot*, p. 181.
[115] *Scenes*, i, 40; Cf. 'Our Parish', *Sketches by Boz*, p. 39. [116] *Scenes*, i, 64.

language of Evangelical autobiography and tract in a fictional context. In her occasionally facile adoption of Evangelical phraseology and imagery there is something of that '*radical insincerity*'[117] of which she accused the poet Young. The strangely inappropriate laboured imagery used by Tryan in his advice to Janet leads us away from the issue at stake, and, consequently, the desired emotional intensity behind the scene which leads to Janet's desire for prayer ebbs away too.

'But as soon as we lay ourselves entirely at his feet, we have enough light given us to guide our own steps; as the foot-soldier who hears nothing of the councils that determine the course of the great battle he is in, hears plainly enough the word of command which he must himself obey.'[118]

On other occasions the desire to give a religious quality to what had become for George Eliot an essentially secular experience led to the use of a Bunyanesque violence of language employed without the vital simplicity that inspired his writings.

She wanted to summon up the vision of the past; she wanted to lash the demon out of her soul with the stinging memories of the bygone misery; she wanted to renew the old horror and the old anguish, that she might throw herself with the more desperate clinging energy at the foot of the cross, where the Divine Sufferer would impart divine strength.[119]

We can feel George Eliot straining to whip up this feeling of moral revulsion into an expression of the orthodox literary Evangelical response to temptation. There is a lack of artistic delicacy and perception in the way that she tries to create a fever pitch of emotion by embroidering those direct expressions of religious anguish that she had borrowed. To repeat the word 'divine', to add 'with the more desperate clinging energy' only diminishes the force of the whole. It is not that Evangelicals *could* not have written like this but that they would not have needed to. In arguing for the retention of the language of the Authorized Version of the Bible, Ian Robinson maintained that modern English provided no equivalent substitute for the 'language of due seriousness' and to illustrate his remarks compared the Authorized Version's rendering of miracles with the translation provided in the New English Bible, to the detriment of the latter. 'The difference between frivolously lying tales and stories with a real significance—a truth—becomes here almost wholly a

[117] *Essays of G. Eliot*, p. 366. [118] *Scenes*, ii, 233. [119] *Scenes*, ii, 290.

question of style: as they convince, or fail to convince, so they are true or false.'[120]

It is precisely in this question of style that one detects the difference between the first-hand Evangelical experience George Eliot purports to be representing and the contrived nature of the reproductions she achieves.

With her portrait of Dorothea Brooke George Eliot put behind her the attempt to graft an ultimately irreconcileable Religion of Humanity on to an Evangelical framework and determined to illuminate the transition from a religious allegiance, denominated 'Methodistical' by Mrs. Cadwallader, to a devotional life centred on man rather than God.

One immediately noticeable difference between the treatment of Evangelicalism in *Scenes of Clerical Life* and in *Middlemarch* is the comparative absence of documentary material in the later work. George Eliot was by now writing for an audience amongst whom would be many too young to have been touched by the Evangelical Movement during the period she saw as the turning point in its career, and for whom the name of the books she had cited in *Scenes of Clerical Life* would awaken no immediate response, or carry no particular nuance. The primary reason, however, for this change of presentation is her concern with the moral effects of the doctrine on the individual rather than on society at large. This closer focusing of the artistic lens perhaps denotes, too, a development in her theory, indicated in her essay of 1868, 'Notes on Form in Art', where she writes,

> . . . things must be recognised as separate wholes before they can be recognised as wholes composed of parts, or before these wholes again can be regarded as relatively parts of a larger whole.
>
> Form, then, as distinguished from merely massive impression, must first depend on the discrimination of wholes & then on the discrimination of parts.[121]

Once she had worked through the stratum of her earliest memories, setting out in detail the 'massive impression' of a society coming to terms with the Evangelical Movement, then she could start to 'use artistically' the kind of discrimination between dogma and morality, doctrine and the individual interpretation of that

[120] 'Religious English', *Cambridge Quarterly*, 2 (1967), 314.
[121] *Essays of G. Eliot*, p. 432.

belief that had led to her rejection of Evangelicalism. In 'Janet's Repentance' she had warned the reader of judging the doctrine by the people who practised it. 'Religious ideas have the fate of melodies, which, once set afloat in the world, are taken up by all sorts of instruments, some of them woefully coarse, feeble or out of tune, until people are in danger of crying out that the melody itself is detestable.'[122]

Such coarse and feeble instruments are fleetingly alluded to in previous novels. Amongst the Anglican fraternity we see the Revd. Archibald Duke or hear, from Adam Bede, of Mr. Irwine's successor, Mr. Ryde. *Silas Marner*, *Romola*, and *Felix Holt* offer further examples. In *Silas Marner* George Eliot presents a thoroughgoing religious hypocrite. William Dane is swiftly sketched in the prelude to the main story. Perhaps George Eliot came to realize that it would have been impossible to develop his character at any length because his hypocrisy would only become credible if one could analyse the reasons for which he wished to achieve distinction and power in that small community at Lantern Yard. Were she to become involved in recording the subtle interplay between individual motivation and social circumstances the bald hypocrite would disappear and a far more complex character rise to the surface. In the greater breadth of *Middlemarch* George Eliot was able to present two variations of her belief that the Evangelical creed was peculiarly susceptible to being played out of tune if there were any flaw in the individual instrument.

Analysis of George Eliot's portrayal of Evangelicalism in *Middlemarch* tends to centre upon the character of Bulstrode, but the commentary begins much earlier in the initial chapters on Dorothea. Dorothea's ardent, serious nature inclined her to sympathize with a doctrine which stressed accountability for every action, decision and pastime to God. 'She could not reconcile the anxieties of a spiritual life involving eternal consequences, with a keen interest in guimp and artificial protrusions of drapery. Her mind was theoretic, and yearned by its nature after some lofty conception of the world . . .'[123]

It was a condition of mind that George Eliot remembered only too well, and in her letters she recorded the sudden sense of freedom that she momentarily found when she put Evangelicalism behind her.

I confess to you that I feel it an inexpressible relief to be freed from the apprehension of what Finney well describes, that at each moment I tread

[122] *Scenes*, ii, 162. [123] *Middlemarch*, i, 8–9.

on chords that will vibrate for weal or woe to all eternity. I could shed tears of joy to believe that in this lovely world I may lie on the grass and ruminate on possibilities without dreading lest my conclusions should be everlastingly fatal.[124]

The doctrine appealed to Dorothea both because she saw in it a chance to fulfil her personality and ambitions and because it encouraged the exercise of personal judgement. Dorothea takes delight in explaining to Casaubon her belief in the 'secondary importance of ecclesiastical forms and articles of belief compared with . . . spiritual religion'.[125] It is the very flexibility of such a creed in the hands of a dominant personality that George Eliot finds alarming. Dorothea's processes of self-justification are treated with more tolerant criticism than Bulstrode's, but in her decision to retain the emeralds the same mental acts are taking place. 'All the while her thought was trying to justify her delight in the colours by merging them in her mystic religious joy.'[126]

The consequent ability to interpret one's decisions and desires as God's will is shown to be reprehensible in as far as it leads to defining any person opposed to that will as unregenerate. Celia's quiet criticism evokes just such a response.

She was disposed rather to accuse the intolerable narrowness and the purblind conscience of the society around her: and Celia was no longer the eternal cherub, but a thorn in her spirit, a pink-and-white nullifidian, worse than any discouraging presence in the 'Pilgrim's Progress'.[127]

Mrs. Cadwallader's complaint that Dorothea has 'a flighty sort of Methodistical stuff' in her and Sir James's 'fear lest Miss Brooke should have run away to join the Moravian Brethren, or some preposterous sect unknown to good society', though comical exaggerations, are both indicative of the zealous 'enthusiasm' and absolute confidence in the rightness of her own standards that ally Dorothea with the spirit of the sectarians.[128]

Slowly Dorothea is brought to extend her sympathies, to realize that another point of view may be as morally valid as her own. This growth is accompanied by a change in the form in which her

[124] *G. Eliot Letters*, i, 143–4.

[125] *Middlemarch*, i, 34. The unconscious irony of Dorothea's remark works, as so often in this novel, both against Dorothea and her husband.

[126] Ibid. i, 17. [127] *Middlemarch*, i, 52. [128] Ibid. i, 83.

devotional piety expresses itself. When she had received Casaubon's letter of proposal she had 'cast herself, with a childlike sense of reclining, in the lap of a divine consciousness which sustained her own'.[129] Her 'religion' retains its mystic quality but she no longer sees the divine power as a bolster to her own desires. ' "I have always been finding out my religion since I was a little girl. I used to pray so much—now I hardly ever pray. I try not to have desires merely for myself, because they may not be good for others, and I have too much already." '[130]

Bulstrode, however, never achieves this spiritual development. Even after his public downfall his religion, such as it is, remains unchanged. 'His equivocations with himself about the death of Raffles had sustained the conception of an Omniscience whom he prayed to, yet he had a terror upon him which would not let him expose them to judgement by a full confession to his wife . . .'[131]

His 'god' remains an elevation of self, but real religious absolution, George Eliot suggests, could only be obtained by self-abasement and confession to a fellow sympathizing human being. Only by this means would Bulstrode be enabled to perceive in Feuerbachian terms that 'Such as are a man's thoughts and dispositions, such is his God; so much worth as a man has, so much and no more has his God. Consciousness of God is self-consciousness, knowledge of God is self-knowledge.'[132]

It is not by chance that Bulstrode is depicted as a Calvinist rather than an Arminian Evangelical.[133] George Eliot never makes the crude mistake of affirming that Calvinism is directly responsible for Bulstrode's perverted moral perceptions but she does draw attention to tendencies inherent in a doctrine which she believes to be peculiarly dangerous. This interpretation is supported by reference to the strength of her immediate revulsion for the doctrinal bent of her own Evangelical years. Mary Sibree gives the following record of this stage in her development. 'Last week mother and I spent an evening with Miss Evans. She seems more settled in her views than ever, and rests her objections to Christianity on this ground, that

[129] Ibid. i, 62. [130] *Middlemarch*, ii, 180. [131] Ibid. iii, 444.

[132] L. Feuerbach, *The Essence of Christianity*, trans. from 2nd. German edn. by M. Evans (1854), p. 12.

[133] M. Svaglic's assertion that 'Mr. Bulstrode could hardly have been a Wesleyan for instance, since such a religion offers insufficient gratification to his kind of nature', mistates the case because he ignores the pitfalls offered by Assurance and Perfectionism to Wesleyans. *JEGP* 53 (1954), 154.

Calvinism is Christianity, and this granted, that it is a religion based on pure selfishness.'[134]

Mrs. Bulstrode's combination of simple admiration for her husband's religious professions and anxious love for her brother's family serves to show up the 'pure selfishness' of which rigid orthodoxy is capable. She suggests that at least they should 'pray for that thoughtless girl', Rosamond.

'Truly, my dear', said Mr. Bulstrode, assentingly. 'Those who are not of this world can do little else to arrest the errors of the obstinately worldly. That is what we must accustom ourselves to recognise with regard to your brother's family. I could have wished that Mr. Lydgate had not entered into such a union; but my relations with him are limited to that use of his gifts for God's purposes which is taught us by the divine government under each dispensation.'

Mrs. Bulstrode said no more, attributing some dissatisfaction which she felt to her own want of spirituality. She believed that her husband was one of those men whose memoirs should be written when they died.[135]

The callous indifference to the fate of the non-elect displayed by those who believed in a predestined Particular Redemption sharply divided Calvinism from Arminianism in George Eliot's mind. In a letter to Sarah Hennell she spoke of the impression made upon her by her aunt, Elizabeth Evans, who had left the Wesleyans to join the Arminian Methodists. 'I had never talked with a Wesleyan before, and we used to have little debates about predestination, for I was then a strong Calvinist.'

She remembered being especially shocked by the Universalism embraced by her aunt but later described her aunt's hope that a certain minister might reach heaven despite the tippling habits he had succumbed to[136] as 'the spirit of love which clings to the bad logic of Arminianism'. It was precisely this 'spirit of love' which drew the Revd. Rufus Lyon away from the practical consequences of strict Calvinist doctrine and resulted in his care for the unregenerate Catholic, Annette Ledru.[137] George Eliot most admired him when he was furthest from the Calvinist standpoint that he recognized as true.

The second area, George Eliot believed, in which Calvinism was

[134] J. W. Cross, *George Eliot's Life as Related in Her Letters and Journals*, New edn. (1 vol., Edinburgh, 1887), p. 51.

[135] *Middlemarch*, ii, 112–13.

[136] *G. Eliot Letters*, iii, 175.

[137] *Felix Holt*, ch. vi.

peculiarly susceptible to 'pure selfishness' was in the strange combination of a conviction of Total Depravity with a knowledge of predestined Election.

He [Mr. Bulstrode] was doctrinally convinced that there was a total absence of merit in himself; but that doctrinal conviction may be held without pain when the sense of demerit does not take a distinct shape in memory and revive the tingling of shame or the pang of remorse. Nay, it may be held with intense satisfaction when the depth of our sinning is but a measure for the depth of forgiveness, and a clenching proof that we are peculiar instruments of the divine intention.[138]

The subtlety of George Eliot's portrait of Bulstrode lies in the way that she avoids the Antinomianism attributed to the High Calvinists by many another novelist. At each stage Bulstrode is anxious to set himself right with God. He never entertains the idea of a complete superiority to the moral law. His sins initially incline to being sins of omission rather than commission. '. . . Mr. Bulstrode shrank from the direct falsehood of denying true statements. It was one thing to look back on forgiven sins, nay, to explain questionable conformity to lax customs, and another to enter deliberately on the necessity of falsehood.'[139]

A real desire for humiliation and pardon leads Bulstrode to request an interview with Ladislaw, the man he had wronged, but the God he worships is essentially a pagan deity who needs to be appeased. Bulstrode thinks of a device by which he can obtain God's forgiveness, but leaves room for an envisaged process of self-congratulation, totally alien to the Christian's humble acceptance of the fruits of the Redemption. His attitude leads him to adopt the character of Spenlow whilst reducing the Lord to the position of Jorkins. God has become a sleeping partner when Bulstrode takes it upon himself to act as an arbiter of man's spiritual fate, telling Mr. Vincy that to help Fred, in the manner requested, 'will not tend to your son's welfare or to the glory of God'.[140] By the time that Bulstrode takes over Stone Court he and the divinity whom he worships have become inseparable, and his dwelling place is described in terms of a church: '. . . he had bought the excellent

[138] *Middlemarch*, ii, 379. [139] Ibid. ii, 389.

[140] Ibid. i, 195. George Eliot's essay on Dr. Cumming had shown her to be particularly suspicious of references to 'the glory of God' as a justification for a course of action. *Essays of G. Eliot*, pp. 186–7.

farm and fine homestead simply as a retreat which he might gradually enlarge as to the land and beautify as to the dwelling, until it should be conducive to the divine glory that he should enter on it as a residence . . .'[141]

Bulstrode gradually ceases to be an instrument for God's exclusive use, and begins to use God as an instrument for his own aggrandizement. This becomes apparent in his manipulation of the concept of Providence, a secondary Evangelical doctrine for which George Eliot displayed increasing dislike.

In the *Mill on the Floss* George Eliot, as narrator, expresses her objections to a doctrine upon whose interpretation many Evangelicals disagreed.

> If we only look far enough off for the consequences of our actions, we can always find some point in the combination of results by which those actions can be justified: by adopting the point of view of a Providence who arranges results, or of a philosopher who traces them, we shall find it possible to obtain perfect complacency in choosing to do what is most agreeable to us in the present moment.[142]

At one level, that of the weak but warm-hearted Mr. Vincy, Providence is little more than an expression for good luck. His phrase, '. . . one must trust a little to Providence and be generous',[143] represents 'the shallow immorality of believing that all things would turn out for the best', against which George Eliot warned Oscar Browning.[144] Her next allusion to Providence in *Middlemarch* takes the form of a comic anecdote related by Mr. Brooke, who tells how Flavell, a local Methodist preacher, had been brought before him on a charge of poaching: ' "Well, now, Flavell in his shabby black gaiters, pleading that he thought the Lord had sent him and his wife a good dinner, and he had a right to knock it down, though not a mighty hunter before the Lord, as Nimrod was—I assure you it was rather comic . . ." '[145]

Although the charge of hypocrisy is easily levelled here the story also serves to underline the more serious point that an implicit belief in Special Providences may encourage one to ignore the more obvious moral codes. In her choice of the name Flavell, George Eliot may well have been thinking of *Divine Conduct: or, The*

[141] *Middlemarch*, ii, 375.
[142] *Mill on the Floss*, ii, 98.
[143] *Middlemarch*, i, 193.
[144] Quoted by G. S. Haight, *George Eliot: A Biography*, p. 408.
[145] *Middlemarch*, ii, 181.

*Mysterie of Providence*, a much-read book by the seventeenth-century minister John Flavel—a work of which Simeon had remarked, ' "Flavel on Providence" is a favourite author of mine, only I grieve for his credulity.'[146]

The doctrine of Providence, George Eliot underlines, has serious logical flaws. Bulstrode taught himself to see his purchase of Stone Court 'as a cheering dispensation conveying perhaps a sanction to a purpose which he had for some time entertained without external encouragement'.

His doubts did not arise from the possible relations of the event to Joshua Rigg's destiny, which belonged to the unmapped regions not taken under the providential government, except perhaps in an imperfect colonial way; but they arose from reflecting that this dispensation too might be chastisement for himself, as Mr. Farebrother's induction to the living clearly was.[147]

Either Providence takes no account of the distinction between regenerate and unregenerate, or, its operations seem to involve serious harm to the unregenerate in the pursuit of vindicating the superior righteousness of the regenerate. As Bulstrode reflects upon the career which has led him from an orphanage to prominence in Middlemarch he notes particularly the way in which his course had 'been sanctioned by remarkable providences'.

Death and other striking dispositions, such as feminine trustfulness, had come, and Bulstrode would have adopted Cromwell's words—'Do you call these bare events? The Lord pity you!' The events were comparatively small, but the essential condition was there—namely, that they were in favour of his own ends. It was easy for him to settle what was due from him to others by inquiring what were God's intentions with regard to himself.[148]

The Providence which had called him to wealth had deprived a mother of her daughter and the true heirs of their inheritance. Similarly Bulstrode manages to convince himself that Raffles, far from being an instrument for his chastizement, is an obstacle that Providence might do well to remove from Bulstrode's path of usefulness: '. . . he felt a cold certainty at his heart that Raffles—

[146] A. W. Brown, *Recollections of Simeon*, p. 328.
[147] *Middlemarch*, ii, 377–8.
[148] *Middlemarch*, iii, 130–1.

unless providence sent death to hinder him—would come back to Middlemarch before long.'[149]

Once the hypothesis as to the desires of Providence has presented itself to him in this form acts such as giving Raffles money to spend on drinking bouts, which shatter his health,[150] can be rationalized into co-operation with the ways of the Almighty.[151] Indeed in his prayers, as he nurses Raffles, Bulstrode finds a kind of temporary palliative for his own fevered condition in anticipating the workings of Providence. 'Should Providence in this case award death, there was no sin in contemplating death as the desirable issue—if he kept his hands from hastening it—if he scrupulously did what was prescribed.'[152]

His desires serve to create the shape of his beliefs until he feels 'that he could go to bed and sleep in gratitude to Providence', only 'if Raffles were really getting worse, and slowly dying'.[153]

When Bulstrode hands over the key of the wine-cooler to Mrs. Abel he surrenders the mental initiative which has produced his power. The silence behind the door represents a mental collapse. He is 'at rest' because his will no longer makes the effort to accommodate itself to his doctrinal professions.

He had been a man 'giving out as the Ten Commandments are not enough for him, and all the while he's worse than half the men at the tread-mill'.[154] Bulstrode had overshot the Evangelical position by moving from the proposition that 'legalism' was insufficient to the act which indicated that he had jettisoned the entire moral foundation of Christianity. George Eliot has left it to the corrosive tongue of characters, whose partiality can be weighed by the reader, to caricature Bulstrode and Evangelicalism. The prejudice which lay behind so many of the caricatures of Evangelicalism seen in the work of other novelists is neatly captured in the growth of the belief that a man whose social origins were obscure, and whose philosophy of life not easily comprehensible, might well be capable of secret, and therefore disreputable, actions.

. . . Mrs. Taft, who was always counting stitches and gathered information in misleading fragments caught between the rows of her knitting, had got

[149] Ibid. iii, 125. [150] Ibid. iii, 237–8.

[151] By tracing the slow convolutions of Bulstrode's thoughts George Eliot dramatizes for us Feuerbach's remarks upon 'the Idea of Providence'. 'Human need is the necessity of the Divine Will. In prayer man is the active, the determining, God the passive, the determined. God does the will of man.' *Essence of Christianity*, trans. M. Evans, p. 300.

[152] *Middlemarch*, iii, 262–3. [153] Ibid. iii, 269. [154] Ibid. iii, 289.

it into her head that Mr. Lydgate was a natural son of Bulstrode's, a fact which seemed to justify her suspicions of evangelical laymen.

Mrs. Farebrother, aware of Bulstrode's enmity towards her son, is prepared to clear Lydgate of the imputation, 'But as to Bulstrode —the report may be true of some other son.'[155]

George Eliot herself does not totally abandon Bulstrode. By staying with the loyal but mourning Mrs. Bulstrode she remains 'wedded' to even this man, one of the least lovable of her creations. Moreover, by showing the capacity for love and sympathy in this honest, simple woman, George Eliot affirms that an unintellectual, imitative piety is entirely compatible with humanitarian concern. Thesiger and Tyke may desert Bulstrode in his hour of need but Mrs. Bulstrode is prepared to share the humiliation with her husband. If nothing else, Evangelicalism has provided her with a mode of expression, a method of witness by which she may demonstrate to her husband and others her willingness to embrace this new life. Her 'little acts which might seem mere folly to a hard onlooker'[156] are not dismissed from a 'bird's-eye station'. In *Middlemarch* George Eliot goes beyond mere doctrinal critique or the recreation of a period flavour to explore the emotional needs which draw men to Evangelicalism and the weaknesses of such a simple creed when exposed to the deviousness of ingenious logic. She had in this work measured up to her own critical yardstick provided fourteen years before. 'Our subtlest analysis of schools and sects must miss the essential truth, unless it be lit up by the love that sees in all forms of human thought and work, the life and death struggles of separate human beings.'[157]

[155] *Middlemarch*, i, 401–2. [156] Ibid. iii, 334. [157] *Scenes*, ii, 166.

CHAPTER V

# *Thornycroft Hall:* An Evangelical Answer to *Jane Eyre*

> They [her novels] did not outrage probability. They revealed scenes of family life such as not only well might be, but such as actually were taking place in many English homes.
>
> *Literary World* (2 Sept. 1887), p. 209. Speaking of Mrs. Worboise.

> . . . her picture is that of a morbid fancy, mixing up fiction with fact, and traducing, with a random pen, an Institution to which she and her family were wholesale debtors.
>
> *Christian Observer* (1857), p. 428. Speaking of Charlotte Brontë's *Jane Eyre*.

MRS. GUYTON, or Emma Jane Worboise as she was professionally known, combined an Evangelical conscience with a shrewd commercial instinct. Her publishing career began in 1846, at the age of twenty-one, and ended with her death in 1887. During those years she produced about fifty works, occasionally publishing as many as three in one year. So popular were her novels that a collected edition appeared during her own lifetime. Her publishers, James Clarke and Company, recognizing her skill at judging the market, asked her to edit a new venture, *The Christian World Magazine*, in the first edition of which she pledged herself to 'provide something purer' to replace the condemned popular literature of the day.[1]

Her business acumen was reflected not only in her capacity as editress but in her own writing. The titles of her novels occasionally reflect a willingness to capitalize upon the success of others that, in one less spiritually minded, might be described as sharp practice.

[1] *Christian World* (Jan. 1866), pp. 1–3.

The choice of a name familiar to novel-readers might well encourage the prospective purchaser to select her novel in preference to the welter of fiction emerging from the religious press at the same time. *Helen Bury: or the Errors of My Early Life* (1852) recalls the name of Jane Eyre's schoolgirl companion. *Overdale: or the Story of a Pervert: A Tale for the Times* (1869) might hope to capture those who had eagerly read Conybeare's *Perversion: or, the Causes and Consequences of Infidelity: A Tale for the Times* (1856). *Heart's-Ease in the Family* (1874) might well prove to be an Evangelical version of or even a sequel to C. M. Yonge's *Heartsease, or the Brother's Wife* (1854). Any one of these derivative titles might have been coincidental, but, taken in conjunction, a certain forethought is suggested.

Nor was she any less hesitant in appropriating successful themes, incidents and characters. In *Margaret Torrington* Gilbert Tredgold's tale of shipwreck bears striking resemblances to that of Harry May in Charlotte Yonge's *Daisy Chain.*[2] In *Heart's-Ease*, *Overdale*, *Margaret Torrington*, and *Thornycroft Hall* an orphan child of good Christian parents, is consigned to cruel or indifferent guardians, who endeavour to make her remember her station in life and prepare her for the status of governess, in true Jane Eyre mould. Not only had this formula attested its success in Charlotte Brontë's work but it possessed clear advantages for an authoress anxious to isolate the Evangelical experience in life and stress the compelling need for total dependence on the Divine Friend and Counsellor. The governess in *Margaret Torrington* perfectly expresses the situation Mrs. Worboise was so keen to create :

'Remember, Margaret, that I am more than twenty years your senior; I know the troubles of early womanhood. Oh, my dear, a girl of eighteen, spirited, impulsive, and orphaned as you are, with no father to protect, no mother to guide, no home to which you really have a claim, is placed in a position where she may be assailed by countless dangers to which girls more happily situated are strangers. I know what it is to fight my own way in the world; I know what it is to be wilfully misconstrued, to be causelessly, cruelly suspected: and I feel for you, Margaret, and I fear for you? —for your nature is a more daring one than mine; and you do not make God your guide, your ruler—you do not commit your way to Him. Very soon you will have no friend in this house save Gussie, a child who cannot help you; for I shall soon be gone.'[3]

[2] Cf. *Margaret Torrington*, ch. xliii, and *Daisy Chain*, Pt. II, ch. xvii.
[3] *Margaret Torrington*, p. 240.

In the light of her literary borrowings[4] it is interesting to observe how, when Emma Jane Worboise came to write a literary apologia for her old school, Carus Wilson's Casterton, she adopted the framework of *Jane Eyre*, the novel whose allegations she was endeavouring to combat. The title of her novel, *Thornycroft Hall: Its Owners and Heirs*, is, as it were, a declaration of intent. In its adaptation of Charlotte Brontë's Thornfield Hall and the way that it is used as the name for the equivalent of Gateshead Hall rather than the Rochester residence Mrs. Worboise indicates the extent of the liberties she will take in reinterpreting her source material.

There were many similarities between Mrs. Worboise and Charlotte Brontë. Both came from Evangelical backgrounds, both attended Carus Wilson's school, both spent a period of time teaching, but preferred to make their living from literary work.[5] Mrs. Worboise, however, if her fictional persona's career is any guide, attended the school at a later age when she was capable of appreciating the different facets of Carus Wilson's teaching. Like Charlotte Brontë she strongly disapproved of rigid Calvinism, as she showed in her novel *The House of Bondage* (1872), but she saw Carus Wilson, not as an exponent of this doctrine, but as a kindly 'second father' whose personal and theoretic charity she admired. It is for Carus Wilson's acceptance of the universal Church, proclaimed in pamphlets such as *Thoughts on the Times: with reference to the Present Position of the Church of England* (1842) that Mrs. Worboise especially solicits our admiration.[6] Although the majority of her novels concentrate upon the Anglican Evangelicalism in which she had been brought up the pattern detectable in her novels suggest that she became, possibly on her marriage, a Nonconformist, thus earning the sobriquet, awarded to her by the obituary writer, of 'the novelist of Evangelical Dissent'.[7]

In Charlotte Brontë's eyes, however, this very tolerance of Dissent on Carus Wilson's part may have served to discredit him yet further. Mrs. Gaskell had 'heard her condemn Socinianism,

[4] The vehemence with which she refuted the charge of literary plagiarism is significant. *House of Bondage*, p. 521.

[5] 'She had been a teacher in earlier years, and hence, perhaps, it came about that a governess was one of the common characters in her works.' *Literary World* (2 Sept. 1887), p. 210. Charlotte Brontë's desire to find an occupation which permitted her to live at home is too well known to require further documentation.

[6] *Thornycroft Hall*, pp. 248, 267, 273–4.

[7] *Literary World* (2 Sept. 1887), p. 209.

Calvinism, and many other "isms" inconsistent with Church of Englandism',[8] and Charlotte's letters underline the contempt that her early work and her novels displayed for much Dissenting practice. 'I consider Methodism, Quakerism, and the extremes of High and Low Churchism foolish, but Roman Catholicism beats them all.'[9]

In their opposition to religious bigotry or convention masquerading as morality the two authors were in agreement. Charlotte Brontë's Preface to the second edition of *Jane Eyre* addressed to 'the timorous or carping few . . . in whose eyes whatever is unusual is wrong'[10] could equally well have served as an introduction to *Thornycroft Hall.* It is a mark of Mrs. Worboise's Christian integrity that she dared to pillory certain Evangelical attitudes prevalent in the very classes for whom she was writing. She offers no overt criticism of *Jane Eyre* but the way in which she tells her story shows why she felt it needed retelling. Mrs. Worboise is always first and foremost a didactic writer; at each stage of her tale moral judgements are passed upon the behaviour of individual characters. Her readers must be enabled to apply the lessons learnt from fiction to their daily lives, and how were they to do this if her stories 'outraged probability'? No one who remembered Thackeray's feeling that Charlotte Brontë was 'rebuking our easy lives, our easy morals',[11] or who recognized the extremely literal manner in which Rochester meets the penalty sanctioned by Scripture for his attempted adultery[12] could question her innate concern with moral issues. Yet Charlotte Brontë makes no pretence to be depicting a representative experience. She presents instead the romance of a highly individualized character, made ordinary only by her physical dissimilarity to the heroines of romance.

The reasons, then, for the muting of tone and incident in Mrs. Worboise's novel are twofold. Firstly Mrs. Worboise genuinely tries to apply the process of self-discipline that Jane Eyre speaks of striving for but never really attains. '. . . I reviewed the information I had got; looked into my heart, examined its thoughts and feelings, and endeavoured to bring back with a strict hand such as had been

[8] E. C. Gaskell, *Life of Charlotte Bronte*, p. 126.
[9] Ibid., pp. 214–5. [10] *Jane Eyre*, p. xxx.
[11] Quoted by W. Gérin, *Charlotte Brontë: the Evolution of Genius*, p. 405.
[12] See editorial footnote by J. Jack and M. Smith, *Jane Eyre*, p. 602, which is based upon an article by J. Prescott, *Letterature Moderne* (Bologna; 9 Dec. 1959).

straying through imagination's boundless and trackless waste, into the safe fold of common sense.'[13]

Secondly, in reading her work we are conscious of being in the presence of the Coleridgean Fancy, where the raw material of memory is manipulated by the will, whereas *Jane Eyre* brings us into contact with the 'secondary imagination' which 'dissolves, diffuses, dissipates, in order to re-create; or where this process is rendered impossible, yet still, at all events, it struggles to idealise and to unify'.[14]

The plot of *Thornycroft Hall* bears certain striking similarities to *Jane Eyre*, especially in its opening stages. Ellen Threlkeld is the daughter of a clergyman who made a poor marriage, and by 1842 both her parents are dead. She is then sent to live with the wealthy Wards, Mrs. Ward being her father's half-sister. Although Mr. Ward, unlike Mr. Reed, is still alive, he is little more than a cipher in the house, which his wife, a powerful but foolish woman, rules. Mrs. Worboise transfers the denunciatory, rigid Evangelicalism of Brocklehurst to Mrs. Ward, who sets herself up to judge the preaching of local ministers and at home imposes a severe regime of negative formalism. Her rules are ineffective, her children read the proscribed fairy-tales, romances, and Circulating Library Books in the seclusion of the nursery. When the children escape from the schoolroom tyranny they are quick to see that more worldly standards operate in the drawing-room. Mrs. Ward is again linked to Mrs. Reed in the part she plays in attempting to deprive one of the characters of his rightful inheritance. Yet Mrs. Reed's capricious spite in telling Jane's uncle that she is dead rings truer than Mrs. Ward's careful concealment of her father-in-law's will, which would have given the property out of the family to a cousin, whom Ellen finally marries. Both twists of the plot derive from the world of romance but Mrs. Reed's fitful humour is convincing in a way that Mrs. Ward's fails to be when the author constantly stresses that her character is not a hypocrite.

As Ellen grows up in this household she meets with some of the treatment meted out by the children of the Reed family to Jane, but true to her softening of the picture Mrs. Worboise provides Ellen with one friend, the youngest of the family, Julia. The incident

[13] *Jane Eyre*, p. 200.

[14] S. T. Coleridge, *Biographia Literaria*, ed. G. Watson (1967), p. 167.

which results in Jane being sent to school is again carefully paralleled. The enmity and spite of the oldest child, Maria, get Ellen into trouble. Like Jane, Ellen is caught hiding; she is trapped behind an oak-tree and afraid to reveal herself when Maria and her suitor decide to take a walk that way. Unlike Jane, however, Ellen's conduct is commented on reprovingly by Mrs. Worboise, who has created a situation in which Ellen should have had the moral courage to reveal herself. Mrs. Worboise strives to paint a scene, from which young readers might draw a moral lesson, whilst still maintaining that Ellen, like Jane, was more sinned against than sinning. Ellen, when cornered, responds, like Jane, with a passionate outburst against her cousin and her aunt, who then appears on the scene and sends Ellen to her room. Ellen does not suffer the spectral terrors of the Red Room, but the far more natural punishment of being sent to Coventry and deprived of all outings with the family. Maria continues her persecution by ensuring that Ellen is sent coarse and unattractive food, the kindly Bessie's place is taken by a less individualized servant, Kitty, and by Maria's suitor who gives Ellen comfort and improving advice. Even after removing the Red Room Mrs. Worboise could not resist the temptation to provide some event which should have comparable consequences. Maria, incensed by her suitor's sympathy for Ellen, shakes and beats her young cousin, but of course, when reporting the incident, says that Ellen struck the first blow. Although Mrs. Ward takes her daughter's side, like Mrs. Reed, she is frightened by the effect of the drubbing Ellen has received and recognizes that Ellen is really ill.

Ellen is not allowed to nurse her passionate defiance as Jane is. A new arrival, Mrs. Cleaton, the mother of Maria's suitor Marshall Cleaton, makes it her business to find out the truth about the incidents with Maria. Nor is Ellen left to discover for herself that a spirit of vengeful anger is a corrosive force. A child whose 'natural' reactions would incline her to harbour a grudge must instantly be shown a higher way. Ellen's guidance is not left to a chance encounter at school with Helen Burns but to the mature, and certainly more orthodox, Mrs. Cleaton:

'. . . . remember what the Bible says:- "For what glory is it, if, when ye be buffetted for your faults, ye shall take it patiently? but if, when ye do well, and suffer for it, ye take it patiently, this is acceptable with God." '[15]

[15] *Thornycroft Hall*, p. 131.

Meanwhile, Ellen's aunt, who graciously accepts her apology but unwisely makes it the excuse for another long lecture, has arranged for her to be sent away to be tamed at the Clergy Daughters' School at Casterton. Mrs. Cleaton takes Ellen to the school and warns her, ' "Of course you will find trouble there, as everywhere else; and in so large an establishment there must be errors and abuses, of which the principals are probably not cognizant." '[16]

At this point in the book Mrs. Worboise abandons all semblance of consistent characterization. We hear nothing of a young child's reaction to this new environment, but instead we are treated to a picture of William Carus Wilson, 'the kind, the good, the laborious, the eminently pious',[17] and then given a detailed account of the daily timetable, which answers point by point the accusations made in Jane Eyre's account of Lowood. As I shall show later, to make her account carry conviction Mrs. Worboise deflates Charlotte Brontë's picture by suggesting that whilst it might accurately describe a child's vision, tinged as it would be with emotion, the mature eye could recognize the immense exaggeration of the occasional errors of judgement made by those in authority.

With the exception of her second summer holidays, which she is invited to spend at Thornycroft Hall, Ellen spends five whole years at the school. Just before her seventeenth birthday she is summoned back to Thornycroft Hall, where her uncle is dying, and told that she can be of use as a finishing governess for her cousin Julia who is a year her junior. From this point in the story the direct parallel to *Jane Eyre* ceases to exist. Ellen herself does not become involved with a Rochester, but Mrs. Worboise carefully reworks characters and situations so that she can present an effective answer to the moral problems that Jane encounters. She even makes an attempt at creating a dramatic, but less shocking parallel to the scene where Jane discovers that Rochester is already married. After Marshall Cleaton has turned down the fortune he stands to inherit by fulfilling his childhood betrothal to the vixenish Maria, he becomes secretly engaged to Ellen. The enmity of Ellen's cousin Arabella leads to her inserting a notice of Marshall's marriage to another in a national paper, but Arabella's subterfuge is discovered and all ends happily.

Arabella's character bears a strong resemblance to Georgiana Reed's. She is a feeble-minded voluptuary, has also enjoyed a

[16] *Thornycroft Hall*, p. 135. [17] Ibid., p. 147.

secret romance, which was stopped by her family, and now idles her time away in reading fashionable, sensational novels, and in constant eating and drinking. Arabella unites John Reed's fondness for drink with Georgiana's selfishness. Jane can tolerate her cousin's behaviour for a brief time, inwardly thinking, 'If you and I were destined to live always together, cousin, we would commence matters on a different footing.'[18] Ellen finds that she is forced to live with her cousin and takes appropriate action, forcing her cousin to sign a pledge, and recommending her aunt to forbid sensational novels within the house and to take out a subscription at Mudie's.

Like Mrs. Reed, Ellen's aunt confesses her great sin on her deathbed, having kept her secret to the very last from a similar reluctance to humiliate herself before those whom she has wronged.

By oblique references Mrs. Worboise makes clear the fate Jane Eyre should have anticipated in agreeing to marry the strong and healthy Rochester in the days before he had worked out his expiation and admitted himself 'a brand plucked from the burning'. Ellen's cousin Julia marries a young man whom she adores, although, as she tells Ellen, Horace Stansfield is not 'the sort that insists upon being "born again"; the sort that counts nothing you can do of any avail, and yet holds it an inalienable duty to do everything that can be done . . .'[19] Before the marriage Ellen hears rumours of Horace's past life which are similar to those of Rochester's, though nothing as shocking as Rochester's affair with Céline Varens, the French opera-dancer, is related. Julia marries Horace, so strong is her infatuation, only to find on their honeymoon that a leopard cannot change his spots. Horace deserts her, pursues a married woman whom he had previously known, and is only brought back in time for Julia to forgive him on her deathbed.

Meanwhile Ellen gets St. John Rivers in the person of the Revd. Marshall Cleaton. He is of course endowed with some of Rochester's romantic appeal; it is probably not a coincidence that their first meeting, when Ellen is still a child, takes place when Ellen has been frightened by the appearance of his massive hound, Gelert, a substitute for the 'Gytrash' which appears to Jane. Marshall is cleared of the cold-heartedness of St. John in refusing to marry his cousin Maria, though he too sacrifices wealth in the process, but like St John, his vocation as a minister overrides all other considerations. When he has the chance of regaining the property of

[18] *Jane Eyre*, p. 302. [19] *Thornycroft Hall*, p. 309.

which he has been unjustly deprived, he burns the newly discovered will, and when finally he and Ellen inherit the fortune of another relative, like St. John he refuses to allow the money to make any difference to his status, and continues to work as a Baptist minister. In this he of course goes one better than St. John, because ambition and ability do not tempt him to leave his obscure country ministry.

I have already briefly indicated Mrs. Worboise's favourable opinion of Carus Wilson, but he was only human, and Mrs. Worboise would have been failing in her loyalty to Evangelical doctrine if she did not present him as subject to the weaknesses tainting post-lapsarian man.

> He was, as Jane Eyre tells us, a very tall man. When I first saw him he was already grey and looking elderly; he must have been fifty years of age. He was not an eloquent preacher, nor an erudite divine; his writings were always simple, but sound; he was, perhaps, not singularly large-minded, and he certainly held some peculiar views; he attached great importance to trifles, and was in some degree self-opinionated, and inclined to arbitrary action.[20]

When she closes her character-study with the words, 'Let none presume to descant upon the trivial failings of the holy dead',[21] we are tempted to feel that none need bother to add to her already extensive list. The admissions, which are meant to be engagingly honest and preserve Carus Wilson from further vilification, effectively substantiate Charlotte Brontë's picture, when one considers that she saw him with a small child's eye at a particularly bad time in the school's history. Against his petty tyrannies, Mrs. Worboise counterpoints examples of his personal kindness in arranging outings for girls stranded at the school during the holidays, in an attempt to convey to us the sociable, hospitable nature of the man whose ever open house caused Edward Bickersteth to refer to Casterton Hall as 'the Evangelical hotel'.[22]

Yet even his Evangelical friends sometimes found his 'peculiar views' unacceptable. The *Christian Observer*'s obituary mentions that Carus Wilson was initially rejected for ordination on account of his 'Calvinistic opinions' and later, referring to his teaching, remarks that 'the principles of evangelical truth were far more

[20] *Thornycroft Hall*, p. 144.

[21] *Thornycroft Hall*, p. 147.

[22] Mrs. [F. B.] Meyer, *The Author of the Peep of Day, being the Life Story of Mrs. Mortimer* (1901), p. 93.

singular, even thirty years ago, than happily they have become since . . .'[23]

Mrs. Worboise and Shepheard's *Vindication* alike refer to Carus Wilson's protracted illness during which his close contact with the direct management of the school was given up to a committee selected by himself but both remain silent about the nature of his illness.[24] In the *Christian Observer* obituary the cryptic remark is made that 'Mr. Carus Wilson was assailed at various times in various ways' and throughout the article many physical causes are put forward, ranging from indigestion caused by eating too fast in an endeavour to save time for his evangelical work, to a brain tumour, to account for 'all his morbid symptoms, which had long perplexed the various medical men whom he had consulted'.[25]

Did Carus Wilson's gloomy Calvinistic predictions become too overpowering for him to retain his sanity? Perhaps he finally succumbed to those morbid fears that Charlotte Brontë described: 'longing for holiness, which I shall *never*, *never* obtain—smitten at times to the heart with the conviction that ——'s ghastly convictions are true—darkened, in short, by the very shadows of spiritual death'.[26] We shall never know, for those who could have told us, like Shepheard or Mrs. Worboise, had reasons for not doing so and the obituary writer was too tactful to specify the exact nature of these 'singular principles' and 'morbid symptoms'. Shepheard would have been unwilling to broadcast his father-in-law's misfortune especially since he shared the Calvinist views that may have led to such a state.[27]

As a reply to Charlotte Brontë's picture of 'Lowood', Mrs. Worboise's novel has one fundamental drawback, shared with many of the letters produced in defence of the original institution; Charlotte Brontë had described the early years at Cowan Bridge, Mrs. Worboise wrote of a more settled period in the school's history after

[23] *CO* (1860), pp. 145–56.

[24] *Thornycroft Hall*, p. 436. H. Shepheard, *A Vindication of the Clergy Daughters' School and of Rev. W. Carus Wilson from the remarks in 'The Life of Charlotte Brontë'* (Kirkby Lonsdale, 1857), p. 10.

[25] *CO* (1860), pp. 145–56.

[26] *The Brontës, Their Lives, etc.*, ed., T. J. Wise and J. A. Symington, i, 147.

[27] As a deputation speaker for the Church Missionary Society Shepheard had 'stated more than once, without the least reserve or qualification', that the heathen who had not yet heard God's word 'would all be damned'. C. C. Lowndes, *Unevangelized Heathen, Everlasting Torments, and Church Missions: A Correspondence between the Rev. H. Shepheard, M.A. and the Rev. C. C. Lowndes* (1866), p. 5.

the move to Casterton. In view of the changes that must have taken place between 1825, when Charlotte left the school, and 1844 when Ellen Threkeld begins her school career, the desire to answer the accusations in detail shows a misplaced sense of devotion. Mrs. Worboise painstakingly rehearses the old ground covered in letters in the *Halifax Guardian*[28] and in the first edition of Mrs. Gaskell's *Life of Charlotte Brontë* (March 1857). Her writing assumes the style of a legal deposition, echoing closely the evidence of the much maligned Sarah Baldwin, the clergyman's wife who had declared, 'I solemnly affirm that our food was uniformly abundant, good, and generally well cooked; but no reasonable person could expect that in a large establishment like that, any more than in a private family, a failure in cooking should not sometimes happen.'[29]

> And it was no 'Do-the-girls Hall', as some people have asserted: I here solemnly declare that during the whole of my residence—nearly five years —I never saw the table otherwise than plentifully and wholesomely supplied. Of course, there were accidents in the cooking department sometimes; disasters that interfered with our comfort occasionally occurred....[30]

We are treated to an account of the diet at Casterton with acknowledgements that the porridge was sometimes burnt, that butter was a rare commodity but that bread was served not in small half-slices but in inelegantly thick 'planks'. So eager is Mrs. Worboise to impress upon the readers the virtue of this diet that she introduces a scene where Marshall Cleaton makes a surprise visit to Ellen after she has been at Casterton for three years. The resulting conversation reads like a 'before' and 'after' advertisement campaign. Having commented flatteringly upon her change from a puny, sallow child to her present bloom, Marshall inquires to what she owes this change. Ellen gives full praise to their starch diet. ' "I suppose it cannot be much plainer; but it is always good, and plenty of it. The new girls sometimes make complaints, but they soon grow accustomed to our table, and enjoy their meals as heartily as the rest." '[31] Ellen is also enabled to achieve a valuable triumph over her temper when her cousin Maria repeats Augusta Brocklehurst's taunts about the pauperish appearance of the school uniform.[32] These efforts to accommodate Charlotte Brontë's accusations, whilst deflating the

[28] Reprinted in *The Brontës, Their Lives, etc.*, ed. T. J. Wise and J. A. Symington, iv, Appendix I.

[29] Ibid. iv, 304.

[30] *Thornycroft Hall*, p. 143.

[31] *Thornycroft Hall*, p. 177.

[32] Ibid., p. 152. *Jane Eyre*, p. 36.

imaginative impressions of the small child's view, repeatedly led Mrs. Worboise into conceding the essential truth behind the picture of 'Lowood'.

The combination of her devotion to fact and the paramount desire to provide an Evangelical witness were Mrs. Worboise's downfall.

To this end Mrs. Worboise is prepared to sacrifice psychological plausibility and to shed the illusion of a first person narrator. She is prepared to litter her novels with corpses if only her readers can be brought to recognize the blessing and peace of a truly Christian death. For one who is doctrinally indisposed to accept the ideal of Eternal Damnation, Mrs. Worboise is extremely anxious that even the worst of her characters shall accept the Gospel truths before they actually die. Mrs. Cleaton, the hero's mother, summons her oldest relative to her death-bed and enquires in true 'tract' fashion, '. . . I am almost at my journey's end: are you coming my way, dear Aunt Isabella?'[33] Should this be insufficient to move our hardened hearts, Julia's harrowing death is painted in full and loving detail. Ellen wrestles with her cousin's soul that she may be brought to perceive that a personal relation with the Saviour is required, not merely intellectual assent to Christian tenets. Julia's weak physical state and bouts of delirium are used as a moral tableau under which Mrs. Worboise can pen the caption of 'the terrible danger, the suicidal folly, the utter madness of putting off to the last the great, the awfully great question of one's eternal salvation!'[34]

The Brontë sisters did not look with favour upon the 'serious conversation' in which many Evangelicals delighted, preferring to keep their religion a matter for private contemplation. In her account of the first meeting between Jane Eyre and Mrs. Brocklehurst, Charlotte Brontë indicated her suspicion of the absence of imaginative sympathy with one's audience that might lie behind the easy use of religious argot. The occasion of their second meeting at Lowood provided her with an opportunity to illustrate the blind illogicality behind many Evangelical prejudices which were elevated, by the use of misapplied theological vocabulary, into moral condemnations. ' "Julia's hair curls naturally", returned Miss Temple, still more quietly. "Naturally! Yes, but we are not to conform to nature. I wish these girls to be the children of Grace . . ." '[35]

[33] *Thornycroft Hall*, p. 259. [34] Ibid., p. 397. [35] *Jane Eyre*, p. 73.

Where it is permissible to laugh with Miss Temple at the absurdity of Brocklehurst's position it is inappropriate to sneer at the misguided sincerity of St. John Rivers. The dangers implicit in the use of conventional imagery and rhetoric to describe a personal conversion experience are fully explored in St. John Rivers's account of his own calling. A description of the symptoms often accompanying conversion, garbed in biblical phrases, may serve to convince a man that he has experienced the thing itself. St. John describes his period of intense misery and revolt. 'I considered my life was so wretched, it must be changed, or I must die. After a season of darkness and struggling, light broke and relief fell . . . my powers heard a call from heaven to rise, gather their full strength, spread their wings and mount beyond ken.'[36]

St. John's rational decision to seek another sphere in which to fulfil himself, and his effort of will (note the repetition of 'must' in the first line), are transformed to a sense of particular redemption. The note of self-abnegation before his Saviour is, however, altogether missing. In case the reader is tempted to ascribe the self-delusion merely to St. John's peculiar temperament Charlotte Brontë shows the similar appeal that such suggestive vocabulary can have on a character of totally dissimilar emotional make-up.

> The Impossible—*i.e.* my marriage with St. John—was fast becoming the Possible. All was changing utterly, with a sudden sweep. Religion called—Angels beckoned—God commanded—life rolled together like a scroll—death's gates opening, shewed eternity beyond: it seemed, that for safety and bliss there, all here might be sacrificed in a second. The dim room was full of visions.[37]

Jane, who recognized with her creator that, 'The right path is that which necessitates the greatest sacrifice of self-interest . . .',[38] was tempted to sacrifice her soul rather than her 'self-interest'.

In view of the amply underlined dangers in the use of the traditional language of Evangelical conversion it comes as something of a surprise to hear Rochester's account of his change of heart in the penultimate chapter of the book. As an author of a tract on conversion Patrick Brontë would have had occasion to be proud of his daughter's skill at the genre.[39] Rochester recounts how in his 'stiff-necked rebellion' he fought against God's decrees: 'Divine

[36] Ibid., p. 462.
[37] *Jane Eyre*, p. 534.
[38] E. C. Gaskell, *Life of Charlotte Brontë*, p. 276.
[39] See above, p. 62.

justice pursued its course; disasters came thick on me: I was forced to pass through the valley of the shadow of death. *His* chastisements are mighty; and one smote me which has humbled me for ever.'

Rochester is amongst those for whom the nature and the symptoms of their conversion are so strong that they can 'name the day': ' "Some days since: nay, I can number them—four: it was last Monday night—a singular mood came over me: one in which grief replaced frenzy—sorrow, sullenness. I had long had the impression that since I could nowhere find you, you must be dead." '

Yet the object of his search and of his prayers oscillates between God, with whom he wishes to be reconciled, and Jane. At each stage of his spiritual and emotional crisis, the vocabulary and phrases employed lead us to anticipate the culmination of a soul's unity with its Creator, only to find that this has been but a step on the way to that final union with Jane which forms his chief desire.

> 'Oh, I longed for thee both with soul and flesh! I asked of God, at once in anguish and humility, if I had not been long enough desolate, afflicted, tormented; and might not soon taste bliss and peace once more. That I merited all I endured, I acknowledged—that I could scarcely endure more, I pleaded; and the alpha and omega of my heart's wishes broke involuntarily from my lips, in the words—"Jane! Jane! Jane!" '[40]

Once Jane has been restored to him he is also capable of recognizing his new relation with God: ' "I thank my Maker, that in the midst of judgement he has remembered mercy. I humbly entreat my Reedemer to give me strength to lead henceforth a purer life than I have done hitherto!" '[41]

This progression underlines the book's rejection of a Calvinistic God of judgement untempered by mercy and love, the God whom St. John Rivers worshipped. More than this it indicates the way in which Rochester, in many respects so closely allied to the Byronic heroes of Angrian stories, attains 'true' greatness only when he recognizes the necessity of 'religion and principles'.[42] The language employed has thematic and moral significance, but its debt to the heightened rhetoric characterizing many accounts of conversion

[40] *Jane Eyre*, pp. 571–2. [41] Ibid., p. 573.

[42] This development was perhaps prompted by watching Branwell's slow deterioration for it was of him that she wrote, '. . . I seemed to receive an oppressive revelation of the feebleness of humanity—of the inadequacy of even genius to lead to true greatness if unaided by religion and principle . . .' Quoted by W. Gérin, *Charlotte Brontë: the Evolution of Genius*, p. 373.

shows Charlotte, like her sister Emily, resorting to the highest emotional register she knew, the language of religious devotion, to portray the intensity of human passion.

This brief analysis of one aspect of Charlotte Brontë's attitude to the Evangelical world, shown in her approach to and use of its particular religious diction, illustrates the nature of the division between the major novelist and the vastly more prolific, yet minor, novelist who attempted to challenge her on her own terms. Mrs. Worboise was capable of appreciating the laughter at Brocklehurst's expense. She never, however, achieved the same lightness of touch. Her satire is heavily laboured, relying on repetition rather than on Charlotte Brontë's quick thrust, which telescoped lengthy and serious criticism into memorable flashes of wit. The complexity of St. John Rivers's character would have been beyond Mrs. Worboise and she would not have risked the scene in which he described his call to missionary life. At least, her novels produce no evidence for such a capacity, for she was always aware of, and always catered for, her audience's possibly limited comprehension—this in itself the sign of a minor novelist. The reader is not expected to distinguish for himself between true conversion and a sincere but mistaken belief in conversion, nor would he have to rely upon a sensitivity to verbal innuendo to discover such an occurrence. 'Nominal' Christians, however rigorous in their observance of the externals of the faith, may have mistaken their election but are never left in any doubt of the moment of their true conversion in her works. Once their conversion has taken place, Mrs. Worboise makes their new status crystal clear by allowing them to explain in some detail the way in which they had formerly relied on upbringing or works for the assurance of their faith. On the other hand, for precisely this reason, Mrs. Worboise would not have made the error which perhaps accounted for Thackeray remarking, 'St. John the Missionary is a failure I think but a good failure . . .'[43] For the final tribute made by Jane to St. John seems to me strangely out of keeping with her previous critical attitude. She still recognizes his sternness and ambition, but these have acquired a certain grandeur in his life of action. He has now become one of God's saints, assured of his reward in heaven. It is as if she finally comes to accept St. John's own assessment of himself. It is only when St. John is in conflict with Jane that he comes alive as a figure; when he ceases to be a potential

[43] *Thackeray Letters*, ii, 319.

threat to her, he ceases to be sharply delineated. Charlotte Brontë treated him as one would a powerful enemy in whom one's interest fades once he has been overcome.

Mrs. Worboise never becomes so involved with her main character as to lose interest in the spiritual state of the other major characters. If St. John had appeared in one of her novels the last chapter would have made his position clear. Although all her characters must necessarily be tainted with the greyness of original sin, they are quite recognizably predominantly black or predominantly white by the close of the book. In order for St. John to have been numbered amongst the saints he would have to have experienced an observable change of heart and had he experienced this Mrs. Worboise would not have neglected to have shown this to the reader. Mrs. Ward's fate is a fine example of this trait in her writing. She is treated to a melodramatic death-bed confession scene and then allowed to recover so that she may prove her change of heart in the time given her for amendment of life.

Rochester's testimony lies totally outside the range of Mrs. Worboise's writing. More than any other passage it illuminates the factors that divided these two authors. There is no indication that Mrs. Worboise found this transposition of the religious metaphor into the expression of human passion offensive; possibly she was so grateful for Rochester's reformation that she did not pause to analyse its nature. The distinction lies partly in the nature of their inspiration. Charlotte Brontë had clearly imbibed much of the Evangelical ethic and recognized it as a fruitful source on which her creative imagination could feed. Mrs. Worboise harnessed her creative abilities to provide as powerful a vehicle as she might for the propagation of the Gospel. Charlotte Brontë was unhampered by the consciously doctrinal interest of a George Eliot or the obsessively antagonistic approach of a Samuel Butler in using this strand of her experience. She did not strive for a detailed realism, not considering it the province of fiction 'to state every particular with the impartiality that might be required in a court of justice'.[44] It is of interest to the critic to analyse the way in which she achieved her effects, but an ignorance of Evangelical conversion literature does not impair the quality or the intensity of the feeling that Charlotte Brontë wished to convey to her reader. Mrs. Worboise's novels were admired by her contemporaries, as the quotation that heads

[44] E. C. Gaskell, *Life of Charlotte Brontë*, p. 51.

this chapter indicates, for their domestic realism. This critical approbation neglected to mention the melodramatic props of plot and character that she used, with far less skill than Charlotte Brontë, to twist the tale for the better enunciation of her message. Yet her very strength, the revelation of 'scenes of family life such as not only might be, but such as actually were taking place in many English homes', seems to 'date' her work in a manner that better novels avoid. When, with the decline of Evangelicalism as a dominant influence in society, the agonizings of the specifically Evangelical conscience ceased to be of interest because of their very typicality, then her work lost its appeal, except for those interested in its period flavour or those easily gripped by the melodramatic machinery, rather than the message behind her novels.

CHAPTER VI

# Samuel Butler

JUST as Samuel Butler's perverse obstinacy prevented him from recognizing his talent as a novelist and led him to pose as philosopher, scientist, and littérateur in turn, so it prompted him to dismiss George Eliot's work, although the strength of *The Way of All Flesh* lies in its development of a strain of social history first exploited in *Scenes of Clerical Life*. Theobald Pontifex is the Amos Barton of mid-Victorian England. There is no evidence to suggest that Butler ever read George Eliot's first work, but Miss Savage's persistence brought him to read *Middlemarch*.

I am reading *Middlemarch* and have got through two-thirds. I call it bad and not interesting: there is no sweetness in the whole book, and, though it is stuffed full of epigrams, one feels that they are lugged in to show the writer off. The book seems to me to be a long-winded piece of studied brag, clever enough I daresay, but to me at any rate singularly unattractive.[1]

Even Butler was forced to recognize its 'cleverness' and the presence of the 'epigrams' to which his own writing was so addicted. The 'sweetness' he misses is not Arnold's 'sweetness and light' but the bitter-sweet quality of the mocking wit which pervaded his own writings. He could not forgive George Eliot for her high-minded seriousness which smacked to him of 'studied brag'. His distrust of moral earnestness,[2] whether Evangelical or high agnostic, forced him to be continually on the defensive, puncturing the ideals of others, and left him with little creative strength to give life to his own evolutionary religion. Whereas in her portrait of Bulstrode George Eliot had said the worst that could be said of the Evangelicals, but subordinated this to her picture of the growth of a new

[1] H. F. Jones, *Samuel Butler: Author of Erewhon*, i, 184.

[2] Significantly it is George Pontifex who chooses his grandson's name on the grounds that 'the word "earnest" was just beginning to come into fashion'. The hypocrisy of many of the advocates of moral earnestness is thus suggested by presenting as advocate a man who has made his fortune by accommodating himself to the previously fashionable Evangelicalism and now pays lip service to the new mode.

religious humanism, the real centre of *The Way of All Flesh* lies in the attack on Battersby and all that it stands for, not in the schematized portrayal of Butler's theory of the Continuous Personality. Butler never managed to rid himself of his obsessive desire to ridicule and parody the old religion. The Sunchild Evidence Society in *Erewhon Revisited*[3] is proof of the compulsive way in which Butler continued to read and hoard information, keeping himself abreast of the habits and concerns of a religious group, whose activities he had supposedly put behind him, when his life received that necessary external impetus for change, which alone could effect a variation in the hereditary line.

Like some Evangelicals Butler could name the day of his conversion.

Prayers are to men as dolls are to children. They are not without use and comfort, but it is not easy to take them very seriously. I dropped saying mine suddenly once for all without *malice prepense*, on the night of the 29th of September 1859, when I went on board the *Roman Emperor* to sail for New Zealand. I had said them the night before and doubted not that I was always going to say them as I always had done hitherto. That night, I suppose, the sense of change was so great that it shook them quietly off.[4]

The Evangelicals, however, would have warned him that the effectiveness of his conversion was not to be judged by its suddenness but by the rejection of all that characterized his 'unregenerate' life. Butler's life was to be one of continual 'backsliding' in this respect. Ernest Pontifex's attitude to the Simeonites represents one of Butler's endearing flashes of self-knowledge. 'They had a repellent attraction for him; he disliked them, but he could not bring himself to leave them alone.'[5]

Butler's satirical writings show his conviction that truth was for him stranger and more amusing than fiction. His unholy glee at the elaborate confidence trick he had managed to perpetrate in *The*

[3] As Butler tells us in his Notebooks, '. . . all the part of Hanky's sermon dealing with the Sunchild evidences is taken almost word for word from a letter in the *Times*, December 8th, 1892, written by Sir. G. Gabriel Stokes and Lord Halsbury and asking for money on behalf of the Christian Evidence Society.' *Further Extracts from the Note-Books of Samuel Butler*, ed. A. J. Bartholomew, pp. 343–4. Butler must have kept the cuttings for their personal curiosity value, since this appeared in 1892 and the first mention of a definite intention to write a sequal to *Erewhon* does not occur until 1896. H. F. Jones, op. cit. ii, 251.

[4] *The Notebooks of Samuel Butler*, p. 213.

[5] *The Way of All Flesh*, p. 208.

*Fair Haven* might have been diminished had he realized how some readers came to regard it as a distasteful ebullition of personal rancour.[6] Apart from the introductory Memoir the book is little more than a private joke. The arguments in favour of the retention of 'the Christ-Ideal', which to Butler were so palpably absurd, cannot be infallibly detected as satiric in intention without the aid of his preface to the second edition.[7] The same belief, that the truth about the religion of his upbringing was far more ludicrous and appalling than any disguised parody could be, led Butler, albeit unconsciously, to write a history of Evangelicalism, practised at the domestic and parochial level, for which a social historian might have cause to be grateful.

Graham Hough's praise of Butler's realistic treatment of 'the Victorian ecclesiastical garden'[8] should be endorsed with one important qualification. It was only the Evangelical corner of the garden Butler could paint with any fidelity. The High Church party as represented by Pryer, in *The Way of All Flesh*, or the ritualist that Professor Hanky becomes, at the end of *Erewhon Revisited*, is allowed no integrity. The Broad Church, for whose position he finally shows a measure of sympathy[9], is described as intellectually disreputable, but no attempt is made to describe the flavour and texture of these principles as practised at the domestic level.

Dr. Samuel Butler, the author's grandfather, seems to have been of the old High and Dry school, unattracted by the 'enthusiasm' of the Evangelicals or the new conservatism of the Tractarians. His letters as Archdeacon show the skill with which he managed to sit on the ecclesiastical fence. Although he refrained from taking the chair at a newly formed clerical society, which, it emerged, was to be a weapon of the Evangelicals rather than the forum for discussion of parochial difficulties he had initially envisaged, he refused to respond to pressing invitations of the old guard to head an attack upon this movement.[10] He managed simultaneously to retain the respect of

[6] For this view see Edmund Gosse, *Aspects and Impressions* (1922), p. 208.

[7] See A. O. J. Cockshut, *The Unbelievers: English Agnostic Thought 1840–1890* (1964), pp. 108–9.

[8] G. Hough, 'The Aura of the Victorian Vicarage', *Listener*, 47 (19 June 1952), 995.

[9] Dr. Downie, who is directly equated with a Broad Churchman, is finally seen as the safest guardian of Butler's belief 'that beyond the kingdoms of this world there is another, within which the writs of this world's kingdom do not run'. *Erewhon Revisited*, pp. 221, 227–9.

[10] *The Life and Letters of Dr. Samuel Butler*, i, ch. xx.

the Evangelicals, a Tractarian such as W. F. Hook,[11] and the friendship of Mrs. Trollope's intimates, the Drurys of Harrow.[12] The undistinguished orthodoxy of his grandfather's theological position may explain the rather vague and slightly confusing portrait of George Pontifex. The career of religious publisher is briefly alluded to and we are encouraged to assume that George has Evangelical leanings.[13] Apart from the matter of the 'will-shaking' George's endeavour to impose himself as the head of a 'happy, united, God-fearing family' is very similar to Theobald's. So similar, in fact, that the repetition seems to owe more to a blurring of information about George than to the desire to show how the offspring must resemble the parent. When called upon to illustrate the means by which a George Pontifex might achieve 'moral influence' over his family, Butler cites a book popular in his own childhood, *Agathos and Other Sunday Stories*, published in 1839.[14] The impression that lack of knowledge about an earlier generation of Evangelicals lies behind the sketchy portrait of George is reinforced when we see how Samuel Butler uses letters from his own father to express George's disapproval at Theobald's attempt to avoid ordination.[15] Had Thomas Butler's reputed desire to enter the Navy[16] been countered by the current Evangelical arguments against the moral dangers of the Services for young men, Butler would not have been able to refrain from a further chance to parody Evangelicalism. George Pontifex's character, then, can be resolved into its constituent parts—anecdotes of Dr. Butler's behaviour[17] blended uneasily with the views of an Evangelical of Theobald's generation.

With Theobald we reach the motivating force of the novel. Ernest is, by contrast, merely a passive agent, manipulated in turn by his parents, his Aunt Alethea and Overton. When he *is* roused to independent action it is frequently to spite Theobald or as a reaction against all that his father's teaching stood for. At the turning point

[11] Ibid. ii, 89. [12] Ibid., *passim*. [13] *Way of All Flesh*, pp. 18–19.

[14] S. Wilberforce, *Agathos and other Sunday Stories* (1839). First alluded to in *The Way of All Flesh*, p. 27. The second allusion (p. 127) is to the story, 'The Children and the Lion'.

[15] The letter from George Pontifex to his son in which he warns, 'You shall not receive a single sixpence from me till you come to your sense', and reminds him of his other children (*The Way of All Flesh*, p. 35) is closely based on one from Canon Butler to his son of 9 May 1859. *The Family Letters of Samuel Butler 1841–1886*, ed. A. Silver, pp. 74–5.

[16] R. S. Garnett, *Samuel Butler and his Family Relations*, p. 13.

[17] H. F. Jones, op. cit. i, 18–19.

of Ernest's career, when he decides to emulate Towneley, it is not Pryer's way of life that he is rejecting but Theobald's. Butler continually finds it necessary to assert Ernest's growing strength and freedom by asserting Theobald's impotence. Theobald's very first friendships at University, which he might have used to escape the home influence, are made with 'staid and prim' men 'of evangelical tendencies'. His introduction to the Cowey set is effected through his father, Professor Cowey's publisher. In fact Theobald's prototype, Canon Butler, probably moved, under his own impulse and with ease, from the High and Dry orthodoxy of the home atmosphere to the periphery of the Evangelical circle in Cambridge. During Thomas Butler's days at Cambridge Simeon was still running his popular meetings for ordinands. Samuel Butler wisely refrained from depicting the, by then famous, gathering[18] with which he was himself unfamiliar. He substituted instead one mode of Evangelical activity popular in his own period at Cambridge. Edwin Guest was Master of Caius College from 1852 to 1880 and secured the college as a centre for Evangelicalism in the University. His wife's influence, though less academic, was more wide-reaching.[19] Like her opposite number at Oxford, Mrs. Symons of 'tea and hassocks'[20] fame, Mrs. Guest ran prayer meetings, or as Butler unkindly remarked, 'She gave evening parties once a fortnight at which prayer was part of the entertainment.'[21]

Butler, as we might expect from his scientific interests, is precise in his allusions to the Evangelical battle with geology. Theobald's early 'Liberalism' reflects the best of the Evangelical response to the challenge of the geologists. He is anxious to show himself intellectually open enough to recognize this new threat, and his views, though palpably absurd to the modern reader, as to Butler, on this occasion, follow the much respected line taken by men like the Revd. J. Pratt, secretary of the Eclectic Society, who felt that the historical interpretation of the Biblical account of Creation was inherently more probable than the allegorical.[22] Once ensconced at Battersby Theobald beats a hasty retreat from the intellectual fray; but his

[18] Although he could have turned to William Carus or Abner Brown's account as J. H. Shorthouse did. The opening chapters of *Sir Percival: A Story of the Past and Present* (1886) make verbatim use of W. Carus, *Memoirs of the life of Charles Simeon.*

[19] For this reference, and for much of the subsequent information on Evangelicals in Cambridge in Butler's day, I am indebted to B. E. Hardman, op. cit., p. 405.

[20] J. S. Reynolds, *The Evangelicals at Oxford*, p. 104.

[21] *The Way of All Flesh*, p. 38.

[22] *Eclectic Notes*, ed. J. H. Pratt, p. 47.

earlier pretensions make him unprepared to uphold, without the semblance of investigation, the fully integrated doctrine of biblical authority that was emerging in Evangelical circles by mid-century. He enters instead a world of second hand commentary as worthless as Mr. Casaubon's, 'making a Harmony of the Old and New Testaments'.[23] The scorn with which this activity is treated is interesting given the contents of a letter Samuel Butler wrote to the Revd. Frederick Gard Fleay, who, before relinquishing his orders in 1884,[24] had written an orthodox book in 1864 entitled, *The Book of Revelations*. 'I will gladly and thankfully have your pasted extracts from the gospels, if you can easily find them; if not I can soon cut them out. It certainly should be done. I am going to devote myself to doing this thing as well as ever I can.'[25]

The spirit with which the enterprise was undertaken and the purpose would appear to make the operations entirely dissimilar in Butler's mind. Yet even here he displays a faithfulness to the tradition he is portraying. 'Alongside the extracts', Theobald 'copies in the very perfection of handwriting extracts from Mede (the only other man, according to Theobald, who really understood the Book of Revelation).'[26] Joseph Mede (1585–1638) was one of the originators of the Evangelical mode of eschatology.[27] Had Theobald held fast to the tradition of Biblical literalism, embraced by Christina, he would have found a position with sufficient internal logic to present a stone-wall defence to neologists and evolutionists alike, but he drifts instead into an intellectual vacuum. He is forced to retreat behind Christina's skirts, virtually admitting in the process that he can envisage no defence adequate to combat the doubt from which he shrinks.

Theobald settles down to the pattern of life of the 'clergyman of moderate views, but inclining rather to Evangelicalism', so often advertised for in the pages of the *Ecclesiastical Gazette*, the only religious paper to which he subscribes. This is another of Butler's allusions which serve to authenticate the picture he is drawing. *The Ecclesiastical Gazette; or, Monthly Register of the Affairs of the Church of England and of its Religious Societies and Institutions* was first published on 10 July 1838. It was circulated free to all parochial

[23] *The Way of All Flesh*, pp. 67–8. [24] *DNB*.

[25] A. J. Hoppé, *A Bibliography of the Writings of Samuel Butler . . . with some letters from Samuel Butler to the Rev. F. G. Fleay* (1925), p. 169.

[26] *The Way of All Flesh*, p. 68.

[27] For this information I am indebted to S. C. Orchard, op. cit., pp. 1–3.

incumbents, who were then invited to become regular subscribers. On the front page of the thirteenth number under the list of subscribers appears the entry, 'Butler, Rev. T., Langar, Notts.'[28] The lukewarm nature of Theobald's Evangelicalism can be gauged by the fact that he does not take the *Record*, the chief organ of the more vehement of the Evangelical party. Theobald employs himself otherwise with the characteristic occupations of the Evangelical parson, church-building, visiting the sick and dying, and combating dissent. His parishioners being stolid farmers or hard-working agricultural labourers, Theobald deploys the remainder of his time in teaching his children, and 'collecting a *hortus siccus*'.

The perfunctory quality of Theobald's practical Evangelical piety is indicated by the fact that family prayers took only ten minutes. It is therefore totally in keeping that Theobald should, as Butler put it, have been 'frightened out of his wits' by the 'gushing impulsive letter' written by Ernest to announce his conversion, for 'he smelt mischief in this sudden conversion of one who had never yet shown any inclination towards religion'.[29] Ernest appears to have been caught up by the wave of Revivalism that hit Cambridge in 1858 and Theobald's reaction to this new phase of Evangelicalism is typical of many of his generation. Chary of undue emotionalism and suspicious as always of sudden conversions this type of Evangelical is best represented by Nathaniel Dimock, a leading Evangelical theologian who wrote, in 1860, a pamphlet entitled, *A Word about Revivals: A Clergyman's Address to His Parishioners.* He counselled them thus:

> . . . it is no mere animal excitement, no being 'struck' with strange sensations or peculiar kinds of fits, that we are seeking . . . we must seek a reality quite distinct from these things. If these things follow—well: but if not—perhaps far better. These things may accompany true conversion—but these things may come and go without conversion, and the peace of God may come and abide without any 'strikings'.[30]

This caution became coupled with a desire to prove true affection for the Church. The chronology of Butler's account of Theobald's progress towards 'Popish' practices is interesting because it ceases to be an accurate representation of general Evangelical trends. Samuel's own mother died in 1873 at Mentone; in the novel he

[28] *Ecclesiastical Gazette*, 2 (9 July 1839), 1. [29] *The Way of All Flesh*, p 227.
[30] *A Word About Revivals*, 2nd. edn (1860), pp. 7–8.

backdates the event by a decade and makes it the excuse for Ernest to pay a visit to Battersby. That Butler included the episode of Ernest's attendance at Battersby Church from a desire to portray the death throes of 'the ever receding tide of Evangelicalism'[31] is indicated by the Appendix for the chronology of the book, made when he was rewriting, where he gives this reference. 'Bishop Ellicot on y$^{e}$ furtive progress o' high churchism—see *Times* Jan. 17 1885 (for note to y$^{e}$ episode re this in the deathbed o' Xtina chapters).'[32]

The report of Bishop Ellicot's pastoral letter does not in fact specify the practices which Butler concentrates upon, but deals with the practices of extreme ritualists.[33] Theobald's services now partake of the nature of what C. M. Davies described as 'Transitional Evangelicalism'.[34] Davies, however, took his sample of Church practices in the 1870s. If by 1863 Canon Butler had taken to wearing a surplice, permitting his congregation to turn East during the repetition of the Belief, now called Creed, using *Hymns Ancient and Modern*[35] and allowing the psalms to be chanted, he would have been well in advance of even the most advanced of liberal Evangelicals. Most clergy only felt obliged to allow some of these innovations after the celebrated Purchas Judgement of 1871. It is just conceivable that Samuel Butler had found these changes when he returned home from New Zealand in 1865 but more likely that he consciously ante-dated this period of change in the Evangelical world. After all, he could expect his few contemporary readers like Miss Savage, once governess to the Evangelical Archbishop Sumner's grandchildren, to be alive to the distortion he perpetrated here, especially after the careful realism of his earlier accounts. Why then did he do it? I think there are two reasons. Firstly there was the need to reassure himself that the Evangelicalism he had, or thought he had, suffered from so greatly was in its death throes and if the symptoms

[31] *The Way of All Flesh*, p. 381. [32] H. F. Jones, op. cit. ii, 470.

[33] 'Referring to extreme practices in the Church, the Bishop regrets that they are on the increase. "Practices are now being quietly introduced compared with which lights and vestments are innocence itself", and he specifies reservation of the Sacrament, celebrations of the Eucharist that are repulsive even to advanced High Churchmen, studied avoidance of the use of the New Testament in the religious teaching in the parish schools, careful exclusion of the diocesan inspector, and admissions to confirmations only on conditions of regular and periodical confession. These practices, Bishop Ellicot contends, are "furtively increasing." ' *The Times* (17 Jan. 1885), p. 6.

[34] *Orthodox London*, pp. 35–48.

[35] Especially as *Hymns Ancient and Modern* was first published in 1861.

had been manifest twenty years before he wrote this piece, rather than ten years before, the diagnosis became that much more convincing. Secondly it contributed to the literary torture and murder of Theobald. Ernest's vulgar financial triumph over his father is reinforced by his ability to celebrate Theobald's impotence as religious leader and patriarch. The extent of the collapse of this Pontifex, or high-priest, can be estimated by the unprecedented swiftness with which Charlotte and Christina had overthrown the old order.

In a strange way Butler's writing can again be compared to George Eliot's in its desire to do justice to the variety to be found within the Evangelical fold. The enthusiasm displayed by Christina and her literary predecessor, Mrs. Owen, in their pietistic devotions and in the emotional zeal with which they pursue prophetical speculations indicates a strain of fervour unknown to the Laodicean Theobald. Speaking of Mrs. Owen, her second son, William Bickersteth Owen, describes her as a proponent of the 'lowest school of Evangelical literalism': 'Whatever she believed she believed literally, and, if I may say so, with a harshness of realization which left little scope for imagination and mystery.'[36] This is precisely the type of criticism made by the Revd. T. R. Birks when talking of his father-in-law's increasing interest in prophetical studies: 'His occupation, and the peculiar character of his mind, which was practical and earnest, but not imaginative, seemed likely to confirm him in the view he had so early embraced.'[37]

Edward Bickersteth's name had become an eponym for Evangelical millenarian study, and it is surely this to which William Owen's second name refers, not, as previously suggested, to 'the famous Bickerstaff in the paper war carried on by Swift against Partridge, the almanac maker'.[38] Bickersteth's *A Practical Guide to*

[36] *The Fair Haven*, p. 3.

[37] *Memoir of the Rev. Edward Bickersteth*, ii, 42.

[38] W. G. Bekker, *An Historical and Critical Review of Samuel Butler's Literary Works* (Rotterdam, 1925), p. 160. Butler clearly had some specific purpose in the choice of the brothers' names since he changed them from Richard Purdoe Davies and Hesketh Davies (H. F. Jones, op. cit. i, 162) to John Pickard Owen and William Bickersteth Owen. The significance of Pickard escapes me but the name John Owen was closely bound up with the Evangelical heritage. John Owen D.D. (1616–83) had been one of the most eminent of the Calvinist puritan divines and his works were standard reading amongst the early Evangelicals. A second John Owen (1766–1822) fulfilled the promise of his name by becoming the principal unpaid secretary of the British and Foreign Bible Society, entered the lively pamphlet warfare in its defence and wrote the society's first history.

*the Prophecies, with reference to their interpretation and fulfilment, and to personal edification*, a work enthusiastically acclaimed by the young Mary Ann Evans,[39] and his prominent part in founding a Prophetical society and annual series of lectures, marked him as the leader of the pre-millenial school of Anglican eschatologists. Bickersteth himself refrained from giving a precise date[40] for Christ's Second Advent, the restoration of the Jews and the resurrection of the saints, but others were less cautious and mentioned specific dates. Edward Bishop Elliott and John Cumming 'risked the credibility and authority of the millenarian movement on the fulfilment of their predictions for 1866–67'.[41] Mrs. Owen's and Christina's prediction of 1866[42] had been falsified by the time of *Fair Haven's* publication, 1873. In these portraits Butler presents the central paradoxes of this mode of Christianity. He points to the strange way in which extremely literal reading of the Bible can co-exist with, or even give birth to, the most exotic of day-dreams. The 'personal edification', to which the title of Bickersteth's book refers, could easily be transformed from an injunction to prepare for the imminent event to an anticipation of it in which self-praise and self-reward were allowed full range. The literalism with which Christina, in a moment of self-doubt, decides to interpret the dietary laws advocated in Acts 15: 29, was apparently taken from an incident in the life of Mrs. Butler,[43] yet her abstension from black puddings seems far more of a satirical exaggeration to the modern reader than her fantasizing. Butler, Overton, and Ernest, if the three are strictly divisible, all find Christina's brand of 'religious romanticism' preferable to Theobald's cold dogmatism. This is because Butler was his mother's son, just as Ernest is most clearly Christina's son when he allows his head to be turned by the success of his first publication.[44] The way in which, in their dreams, Christina and Mrs. Owen attain pre-eminence through martyrdom, preferably vicariously experienced, suggest what this novel was for Butler. Struggling always for recognition both from Langar and the outside world Butler realized his dreams in a literary fantasy in which Ernest achieves a victory over his past and, finally, the freedom Butler never achieved, a complete indifference to worldly fame. Ironically

[39] *G. Eliot Letters*, i, 48.

[40] *A Practical Guide to the Prophecies*, 4th edn. (1835), p. 84.

[41] E. R. Sandeen, *The Roots of Fundamentalism* (Chicago, 1970), p. 83.

[42] *Fair Haven*, p. 12, and *The Way of All Flesh*, p. 89.

[43] H. F. Jones, op. cit. i, 24.

[44] *The Way of All Flesh*, p. 396.

it was to be through *The Way of All Flesh* that Butler achieved that posthumous recognition which was the temporal equivalent of these women's religious visions.

Despite the emotional basis of her religion 'Even Christina refrained from ecstasy over her son's having discovered the power of Christ's word'.[45] The form of Evangelicalism Ernest encountered at Cambridge was something quite different from anything his parents had experienced. Since the day when Simeon, the only Evangelical parochial minister in Cambridge, had encountered hostility Evangelicalism had flourished with the result that more churches were now under Evangelical control and their ministry reflected the diversity of Evangelical practice current in mid-century. Within the colleges there were still groups which reflected the hall-mark of Simeon's social background and it was from this 'evening party' type, conducted by leaders of academic and social distinction, that Butler took his framework for the Evangelical Cambridge of Theobald's day. The leader, Charles Clayton,[46] who had succeeded Simeon in his ministry at Holy Trinity, in 1851, and attracted sons of Evangelical clergy to Gonville and Caius where he was senior tutor, exercised broader influence than his predecessor but at a less personal level. In consequence, although groups might 'place themselves under the guidance of a few well-known tutors',[47] junior members began to organize themselves increasingly without consulting senior members of the University. This desire for autonomous organizations was acceptable neither to Senior members who feared misdirected 'enthusiasm' nor to the Theobalds and Christinas to whom it was doubly obnoxious in presenting some kind of threat to patriarchal authority. The knowledge that authority did not look favourably upon some of the Simeonite activity of his day probably made the young Samuel Butler feel free to mock them

[45] Ibid., p. 227.

[46] Charles Clayton is mentioned by name both in *The Way of All Flesh*, p. 206, and in Butler's parody of a Simeonite Tract, *A First Year in Canterbury and other Early Essays*, p. 58. This tract further illustrates Butler's knowledge of the Cambridge Evangelical scene. Without any apparent source in the pamphlet he was parodying he referred to 'Barnwell' as 'one of the descents into the infernal regions'. J. H. Titcomb, the moderate Calvinist Vicar of Barnwell, conducted open-air ministries in his 'downtown' parish (1845-59) and ran the Jesus Lane Sunday School. He also employed as curate (1849–59) the Revd. S. B. Sealy, described by Joseph Romilly as 'the hideous Mr. Sealy' (Romilly Diaries, 16 Nov. 1856). Such noted deformity might have been sufficient for Butler to create Badcock as a product of Evangelicalism.

[47] *The Way of All Flesh*, pp. 207–8.

and yet stimulated his interest in them. He seems at this stage of his career to have been orthodox in his practice and outlook, attending chapel and communicating as often as, but no more frequently than, the rules dictated.[48] His objections to Evangelicalism in this guise, as revealed in a parody of a Simeonite tract written in his second term, would not serve to differentiate him from many a novelist of orthodox Christian belief who disliked the interfering nature of their proselytizing, their self-righteousness and the foolish pomposity with which they proclaimed a message better confined to the sphere of private devotion. The final paragraph of this parody reveals a seriousness of approach which the later Butler glosses over.

A child will often eat of itself what no compulsion can induce it to touch. Men are disgusted with religion if it is placed before them at unseasonable times, in unseasonable places, and clothed in a most unseemly dress. Let them alone, and many will perhaps seek it for themselves, whom the world suspects not. A whited sepulchre is a very picturesque object, and I like it immensely, and I like a Sim too. But the whited sepulchre is an acknowledged humbug, and most of the Sims are not, in my opinion, very far different.[49]

The tract does display the epigrammatic wit of the later Butler but this is about the only similarity between this and the tract on 'Personal Cleanliness' as a subject intimately related with godliness, written by Ernest.[50] The later Butler was less ashamed to admit to tasteless persecution than to a detailed response to a Simeonite tract. By the time of writing *The Way of All Flesh* Butler attributes his dislike of the Simeonites to the fact that they had offended against

[48] Despite his recognition that the Badcock set were not particularly acceptable in University circles Butler also manifested a lively awareness of the advantages to be gained by assuming a mask of piety. In a poem entitled *The Two Deans*, two Deans, who meet on their way to Sunday morning chapel, in the Court of St. John's College, are willing to account for Butler's absence from chapel on the assumption that his piety prefers to display itself in a less formal manner; an impression dispelled by the sight of Butler rushing past with his arms full of the ingredients for a punch.

> He never comes to Sunday morning chapel.
> Methinks he teacheth in some Sunday-School.
> Feeding the poor and starveling intellect
> With wholesome knowledge, or on the Sabbath morn
> He loves the country and the neighbouring spire
> Of Madingley or Coton, or perchance
> Amid some humble poor he spends the day . . .

*A First Year in the Canterbury Settlement*, p. 48.

[49] *A First Year in the Canterbury Settlement*, p. 59.

[50] *The Way of All Flesh*, p. 208.

his moral code—an admiration of the handsome, wealthy, self-possessed English gentleman. Just as Badcock, 'one of the most notorious of all the Simeonites',[51] is made to sum up Butler's repulsion for Evangelicals in his poverty, ugliness and deformity, so Butler tries to account for the Revd. Gideon Hawke's appeal in terms of his appearance and social adroitness. 'The virtue lay in the man more than in what he said',[52] and therefore when his presence is removed the temporary cachet he had lent to Badcock and his set and the sense of being specially selected by this admirable man are quickly dissipated. Even if Ernest's admiration was momentarily won, because he 'felt instinctively that the "Sims" were after all much more like the early Christians than he was himself',[53] Butler's was not. A passage from *Fair Haven* serves to illustrate Butler's ironic intention.

> How infinitely nobler and more soul-satisfying is the ideal of the Christian saint with wasted limbs, and clothed in the garb of poverty—his upturned eyes piercing the very heavens in the ecstasy of a divine despair —than any of the fleshly ideals of gross human conception such as have already been alluded to.[54]

On the surface there is little to distinguish Badcock and his companions from the grotesque caricatures of Dickens or Trollope, who disguise the absence of intellectual analysis behind their dislike, by producing figures whose aesthetic repulsiveness will serve as a deterrent. In Butler's case, however, these grotesques are created as a result of his intellectual convictions. They represent a code or philosophy whose ideal runs counter to the qualities which had most chance of survival in the breeding of the best Continuous Personality possible. Their deformity is a natural consequence of their deviation from all that contributes to the life force. Such mutants should be left to die. Mr. Hawke is redeemed from the general condemnation because of his vital energy, which is capable of arousing others and stimulating them to a change in their life, however temporary.[55]

The Revd. Gideon Hawke represents the last lease of life in the ebbing tide of Evangelicalism. The Cambridge Prayer Union,

[51] Ibid., p. 217. The name Badcock may have been suggested by an Evangelical character in Mrs. H. Mozley's popular anti-Evangelical, children's novel, *The Lost Brooch*.

[52] *The Way of All Flesh*, p. 223.

[53] Ibid., p. 218.

[54] *Fair Haven*, p. 230.

[55] *The Way of All Flesh*, p. 251.

founded in 1847 as a movement to encourage private prayer, had soon developed a corporate nature, meeting in members' rooms on the first Saturday of every month and producing a quarterly prayer circular. Ernest's introduction to the group coincides with, or is a direct result of, the new spirit of revivalism whose effect was evidenced in Cambridge by the rapid growth of the Prayer group and the decision in 1858 to hold the prayer covenant every Saturday. Mr. Hawke's sermon, which Butler reproduces as a piece of period history, is a finely judged appeal for conversion. He induces a sense of guilt in those to whom his attention is directed, then assumes their assent to the 'legal' stage of Christianity, implying, by his offer to deal with them separately, that doubters are in some sense extraordinary. A straight choice is then presented to them in practical terms, 'as a plain matter of business'. The appeal to reason is swiftly followed by an emotional conclusion which confirms the preacher's status as a chosen vessel and offers them a similar assurance.[56] Ernest reacts appropriately with the ardour of the new convert to 'give up all for Christ'. His subsequent 'snipe-like flights' in fact confirm both Butler's and Ernest's parents' suspicion of emotional conversions.

Minor dating errors do occur in *The Way of All Flesh*. *Essays and Reviews* appeared in 1860, not 1859;[57] Evangelical contempt for the doctrine of priestly absolution reached its main expression in the late 1860s, after the two-part publication of *The Priest in Absolution* by the Society of the Holy Cross, not in 1858, as indicated by Butler, to fit in with his further antedating of events.[58] Yet in general terms Butler has produced a well-documented history of the Evangelical movement in the middle third of the nineteenth century. The secondary characteristics are faithfully described, both because Butler had intimate knowledge of the scene he described and because he hoped that this would lend credence to his account of the flavour and texture of Evangelical life and thought as he saw it.

It is in his presentation of Evangelical attitudes and beliefs that we see how deeply Butler had been affected by his contact with Evangelicalism and how this personal involvement impaired his judgement and his artistry.

I have drawn attention to Butler's account of family life in an earlier chapter, but here I must make brief mention of the paradox

[56] *The Way of All Flesh*, pp. 219–23. [57] Ibid., p. 205. [58] Ibid., p. 228.

that underlies his treatment of the subject. It results in an ambiguity of attitude which is not artistically enriching since Butler himself never fully recognized it. At Heatherley's School of Art Butler won the nickname, 'The Incarnate Bachelor',[59] yet, although he fought off any association which might have led to conventional family ties,[60] he tried, first with Pauli, and then with Henry Festing Jones, to establish a type of friendship which could replace the emotional ties he so badly needed, having cut himself off from his own family. In *Erewhon Revisited* he tried to re-create the emotional ties which bind a family together, freed from the context of the patriarch-ridden hierarchy which he had grown to hate and fear. The years spent in England by Higgs and Arowhena as a conventionally married couple are swiftly passed over, albeit with strange hints of mutual suffering. Higgs, after his wife's death, returns to Erewhon and soon meets his son George, whose existence had hitherto been unsuspected.

He had the greatest difficulty in hiding his emotion, for the lad was indeed one of whom any father might be proud. He longed to be able to embrace him and claim him for what he was, but this, as he well knew, might not be. The tears again welled into his eyes when he told me of the struggle with himself that he had then had.[61]

The sentimentality of the writing here is a product of Butler reflecting on the warmth and paternal pride which he sought throughout life to elicit from his father, who had no such reason for hiding them. When they finally part by the statues it is George's turn to burst into tears, so quickly has the emotional bond between the two grown in Higgs's brief stay.[62] The strength and nature of their mutual affection remains unconvincing however physically demonstrative Butler makes the scene. Even after we have been repulsed by the extraordinary rationale of the Mayor—that his marriage to an already pregnant Yram will only prove happy if he too is allowed to consummate their marriage before its formal celebration—we still feel that the Mayor has become the proxy father to whom George owes his first allegiance. Instead we are treated to the sight of George lavishing affection on the father who

[59] H. F. Jones, op. cit. i, 140.

[60] The nature of his relationships with Miss Savage or with Lucie Dumas, from whom he kept his name and address a secret for fifteen years, illustrates his fear of marriage. H. F. Jones, op. cit. ii, 128.

[61] *Erewhon Revisited*, p. 49.

[62] *Erewhon Revisited*, p. 233.

has done nothing to earn it, and, more importantly, has had no chance to disappoint his son.

The young Owens' admiration for their father is aided by his early death. Ernest Pontifex provides his children with foster parents and only retains any link with them by a system of liberal tipping. Although Ernest truimphs over his father, in a way that Samuel never did, surprisingly he feels a sense of bitterness at his father's death, 'not because of anything his father had done to him—these grievances were too old to be remembered now—but because he would never allow him to feel towards him as he was always trying to feel'.[63] Finally he comes close to admitting a basic incompatibility of temperament as the source of friction between father and son, but throughout his works Butler persisted in shifting the blame from the harshness of the individual to the dogma and tradition of family life, perhaps because this theory always left hope that his father might be jolted into some show of admiration for his son's achievement. That he clearly did transfer the blame in this manner can be seen both in his direct statement in *The Way of All Flesh* about the change effected in family relations by the advent of Puritanism,[64] and by the way in which he removes the fathers from the equation in other instances. In a series of letters published in the *Examiner* Butler opens the fictitious correspondence, about the choices before an impoverished clergyman who has lost an orthodox faith, with a letter signed 'An Earnest Clergyman.' The clergyman was an orphan, raised by his aunt, and he describes the influences she brought to bear on him as,

> . . . the same, I imagine—*mutatis mutandis*—as those brought to bear on nine out of every ten readers of my own age and in the middle class of life. My aunt had been brought up during the height of the Evangelical movement, and never lost the impressions that had been made upon her in her youth. She believed indulgence to be a bad thing for children, and though I well know she loved me tenderly, she seldom showed it.[65]

Butler seems to be willing himself, and us, to realize that, if the father's personality and any question of want of affection are removed, and harshness still remains this must then be attributable to the teaching of the Evangelical movement.

When Butler has once made such strong efforts to exonerate Theobald from personal culpability, the taunts, which he finds he cannot

[63] *The Way of All Flesh*, p. 403.
[64] *The Way of All Flesh*, pp. 21–2.
[65] *Collected Essays*, i, 54.

refrain from making, emerge as the bitter products of a personal feud which embarrass the reader. In the scenes where Theobald administers consolation to Mrs. Thompson, Butler produces artistry comparable with George Eliot's treatment of Amos Barton and Mrs. Brick at the workhouse. The scene is credible because Butler fully admits the material aid which Theobald liberally dispenses and the concept of duty which forces him to perform rites for which he is so unsuited. 'Poor fellow! He has done his best, but what does a fish's best come to when the fish is out of water?'[66] The very success of this episode serves to highlight the cheapness of the insult Butler is offering when he describes Theobald's reaction to Christina's death. ' "She has been the comfort and mainstay of my life for more than thirty years," said Theobald as soon as all was over, "but one could not wish it prolonged", and he buried his face in his handkerchief to conceal his want of emotion.'[67]

The pawn of fate, in the form of hereditary characteristics reinforced by the environmental force of Puritan tradition, is transformed into a monster of hypocrisy.

Butler's weakness as an artist is his inability to maintain a consistent pose. Dickens's caricatures, though unfair if judged in the context of an historical appreciation of the Evangelical movement, are artistically successful because he never supplies that frame of reference. Butler hovers between a desire to give us an historical analysis of the movement and the inclination to caricature it. This instability of purpose is also reflected in the breakdown of the distinction between Overton, Ernest, and the author. Presumably Overton was created as a commentator on Ernest's progress in escaping the toils of home influences. An attempt is made to establish his impartiality by depicting him as personally unaffected by Evangelical religion and as a potential friend of Theobald's. Yet his justifiable dislike for Theobald's domestic tyranny does not account for his sudden transformation into professional ridiculer of the Puritan tradition. Overton has become Butler the rebel against Evangelicalism when he appears as the author of a pantomine version of *The Pilgrim's Progress*[68], or when he says of the payment

[66] *The Way of All Flesh*, p. 66. [67] Ibid., p. 385.

[68] *The Way of All Flesh*, p. 112. An entry in Butler's *Notebooks* makes it clear that Bunyan's work troubled him, for, while he could condemn its message out of hand, he recognized the gripping power of its narrative. *Notebooks*, pp. 188–90. His own fondness for music-halls and pantomines doubtless suggested this particular mode of deflating Bunyan's serious intent.

Milton received for *Paradise Lost*, '. . . a great deal too much . . . I would have given him twice as much myself not to have written it at all'.[69] It is not a Swiftian change of persona that we are witnessing here but the slow collapse of independent characterization as the mask falls off to reveal Butler himself. Miss Savage, Butler's most perceptive critic, tried to make this flaw clear to him while he was writing but her repeated cautions bore no fruit.[70]

Inconsistency of characterization, whether in depicting Theobald, or Overton and Ernest, sprang from a divided vision incompatible with the demands of satire. His writing betrays his real inability to decide whether Evangelicals were hypocrites capable of any enormity or merely pathetically deluded. He would have preferred it had they been the former. Pauli, the man by whom he had been defrauded, he could forgive; Canon Butler, whose way of life he could never really fathom, he could not. For much of the time Butler reacted like the young John Pickard Owen, who wanted everything 'to be perfectly consistent, and all premises to be carried with extremest rigour to their legitimate conclusions',[71] and yet a lurking suspicion that Evangelicalism and all it stood for might not be totally hollow led him to approve of Ernest when he remarked, 'no man's opinions . . . can be worth holding unless he knows how to deny them easily and gracefully upon occasion in the cause of charity'.[72]

The inability to escape from his heritage however hard he mocked is reflected also in his language. Like Higgs, Butler as a boy 'had had his Bible well drilled into him, and never forgot it. Hence Biblical passages and expressions had been often in his mouth, as the effect of mere unconscious cerebration'.[73] The Notebooks are full of Butler's attempts to stand biblical sayings and stories on their heads in pursuit of epigrammatic wit, but finally Butler's rhetoric of emotion is the same as Christina or Theobald's because he turned naturally to what he knew best, just as Theobald most truly expresses himself by his choice of Bible readings appropriate to his mood that day. The problem then arose, when Butler used biblical language as a vehicle for his emotion, that only by hearing his inflexion could one judge the meaning Butler intended it to convey. Once again in language as well as content his writing becomes obscure if we

[69] *The Way of All Flesh*, p. 362. [70] H. F. Jones, op. cit. i, 204–5.
[71] *Fair Haven*, p. 7. [72] *The Way of All Flesh*, p. 410.
[73] *Erewhon Revisited*, p. 35.

attempt to interpret it in autonomous terms. Butler wrote a poem, *In Memoriam H.R.F.*, as a valedictory tribute to a young friend, Hans Rudolf Faesch, which ended in the lines, 'So take him into thy holy keeping, O Lord, / And guide him and guard him ever, and fare him well!'[74]

Faesch was not unnaturally 'puzzled that Butler should use such expressions', so the poet wrote to explain himself.

You must not think that I am becoming more a believer in prayer and all that nonsense than I was. We think exactly the same, but I know no words that express a very deeply felt hope so well as those I have used, and the fact that others make money by prostituting them shall not stop me from using them when I am in the humour for doing so.[75]

In his fictional writing the reader sometimes experiences a similar bewilderment to Faesch's. What, for instance, are we to make of the passage where Theobald consults Overton on the composition of Christina's epitaph?

'I would say', said he, 'as little as possible; eulogies of the departed are in most cases both unnecessary and untrue. Christina's epitaph shall contain nothing which shall be either the one or the other. I should give her name, the dates of her birth and death, and of course say she was my wife, and then I think I should wind up with a simple text—her favourite one for example, none indeed could be more appropriate, "Blessed are the pure in heart for they shall see God." '

I said I thought this would be very nice, and it was settled.[76]

Read at face value Theobald's remarks seem to embody perfectly unexceptionable sentiments, yet Overton's acquiescence with Theobald, which usually betokens thinly veiled sarcasm, makes us uneasy. We then reread the passage in search of hidden indications which will make the authorial stance clear and show where the joke lies. Clearly the calmness with which Theobald discusses the topic reflects his unemotional character and perhaps the epitaph is an ironic reference to the concern displayed by Christina on her death-bed that, 'she had not been so spiritually minded as she ought to have been. If she had, she should probably have been favoured with some direct vision or communication'.[77] In the latter case, is the irony directed against Theobald's incapacity to appreciate Christina's pathetic doubts at the end, or merely a restatement of dogged

[74] H. F. Jones, op. cit. ii, 202. [75] Ibid. ii, 205.
[76] *The Way of All Flesh*, p. 386. [77] Ibid., p. 379.

and unquestioning acceptance that orthodox Christians will meet their just rewards in the afterlife? Perhaps Overton's agreement springs in this case from a genuine impulse to accord Christina her due merits, for he had always entertained a liking for her; yet by this stage in the book it is almost impossible for the reader to take a biblical reference at face value, and especially when it appears in epitaph form. The previous lapidary inscriptions chosen to commemorate the Pontifex family have all had a double-edged quality about them that tended to reflect the character of the inscriber as much as the commemorated.

Given Butler's radical weaknesses as an artist, his inconsistent vision, his reliance as 'an unimaginative person'[78] upon a detailed observation of real life, a fidelity to the truth which only underlines the uncontrolled bitterness of his highly personal accusations, why does his work demand individual treatment in this book? The part played, particularly by *The Way of All Flesh*, in the tradition of portraying the Anglican Evangelical heritage, would suffice to secure attention for Butler.

In this novel Butler had called upon the various traditions portraying Evangelicalism and interwoven them in such a way as to make their separate use again unlikely. He had united the caricaturing stance of Dickens or Wilkie Collins with the personal knowledge of his subject of George Eliot or Charlotte Brontë. Yet Butler's realism sprang from different origins from George Eliot's, from a desire to substantiate accusations not as a basis for a plea for sympathy. Again he adopts the method favoured by Charlotte Brontë in *Jane Eyre* or Dickens in *David Copperfield* to show up the cold, stifling cruelty of such a religion by presenting it through the eyes of a child, a symbol of the romantic desire for the free development of the individual. But Dickens and Charlotte Brontë achieved some measure of distance from their first-person narrators' childhood experience by recalling intense visual memories, so that the thing seen and the seer form a tableau, in which the self-observed can attain identity separate from his or her creator. In the endeavour to avoid the pitfall of authorial loss of control in depicting his own childhood, Butler chose an adult narrator to distance himself from the child's suffering. We have already seen how the narrator becomes a partial witness, but more than that he becomes an outside voice, with adult perceptions, corroborating the appalling injustices which

[78] H. F. Jones, op. cit. ii, 354.

Ernest suffered. Dickens and Charlotte Brontë are at pains to remind the reader that childhood impressions, though real to the child, are frequently coloured by an imagination which does not always distinguish between the villains peopling the world of fictional romance and the real adults whom they meet and find antipathetic: '. . . I looked up at—a black pillar!—such, at least, appeared to me, at first sight, the straight, narrow, sable-clad shape standing erect on the rug: the grim face at the top was like a carved mask, placed above the shaft by way of capital.'[79]

It is curious to me how I could ever have consoled myself under my small troubles (which were great troubles to me), by impersonating my favourite characters in them—as I did—and by putting Mr. and Miss Murdstone into all the bad ones—which I did too.[80]

Very occasionally Butler employs the same technique, or reminds his reader that Ernest was a young prig, but more often Butler uses Ernest as an object for voicing his self-pity for his own childhood suffering, so that scenes, nominally about Ernest, become opportunities to launch attacks on parents who are at least as bad, if not worse, says Butler, than the young Ernest realized.

How could any later author hope to expand upon this well-documented attack on Victorian Evangelicalism, or indeed was there any need to? E. M. Forster, who repeatedly acknowledged his debt as a writer to Samuel Butler, recognized him as a sympathetic author precisely because Butler had voiced his own predicament:

. . . what he had to say was congenial, and I lapped it up. It was the food for which I was waiting. And this brings me to my next point. I suggest that the only books that influence us are those for which we are ready, and which have gone a little farther down our particular path than we have yet got ourselves.[81]

Given Forster's own close acquaintance with Evangelical ways, and his adherence to the tradition of the Victorian novel of social criticism, it may at first sight seem surprising that he did not re-explore the same ground as Butler in his novels. Instead he uses

[79] C. Brontë, *Jane Eyre*, p. 33.

[80] C. Dickens, *David Copperfield*, p. 56.

[81] E. M. Forster, 'A Book that Influenced Me', *Two Cheers for Democracy* (1951), p. 227. Cf. 'He, Jane Austen, and Marcel Proust are the three authors who have helped me most over my writing, and he did more than either of the other two to help me to look at life the way I do.' 'The Legacy of Samuel Butler', *Listener*, 47 (12 June 1952), 955.

Butler as a stepping-stone to enable him to get to the subjects he really wants to discuss. A knowledge of Butler and *The Way of All Flesh* is assumed as background reading to *A Room with a View*. Lee Elbert Holt has stressed the link between Mr. Emerson and Butler, instancing in particular Mr. Emerson's objection to the baptism of his son George.[82] *The Way of All Flesh* is specifically mentioned as part of Mr. Emerson's library. The choice of the name Charlotte for that trying spinster, Miss Bartlett, is perhaps a further allusion to Butler's influence. By the specific acknowledgement of a literary debt, Forster is relieved of the necessity of explaining the anti-clericalism pervading this book. Not until 1958, with the publication of *Marianne Thornton*, does Forster finally make the attempt to deal with his Evangelical forbears on their own terms and shake off Butler's mantle, which fell too easily upon him.

Other post-Butlerian writers who alluded, however briefly, to Anglican Evangelicalism showed their debt, even if unconsciously. The hero's mother in H. G. Wells's *The New Machiavelli* is a portrait of the author's own mother, but the last phrase of the ensuing description makes her also a literary daughter to Christina: 'Perhaps she dreamt gently of much-belaced babies and an interestingly pious (but not too dissenting or fanatical) little girl or boy or so, also angel-haunted.'[83]

The only field left open was that of Dissent, and even here Butler's influence percolated, either as an example for a mode of treatment, or as an attitude and manner towards one's subject to be consciously rejected. Edmund Gosse's *Father and Son* is in a sense a rebuttal of Butler's approach in its critical, but fundamentally affectionate, appraisal of his father's life and views. His disapproval of Butler's attitude found expression in a review of Festing Jones's *Memoir*.

He [Butler] disliked excessively the atmosphere of middle-class Evangelicalism in which he had been brought up, and we must dislike it too, but we need not dislike the persons involved so bitterly as Butler did. It was narrow, sterile and cruel, and it deserved no doubt the irony which Butler expended upon it. So long as we regard *The Way of All Flesh* as a story, invented with the help of recollections which the novelist was at liberty to modify in any way he thought desirable, there is no quarrel to be picked with any part of it. But when we are led, as we have been, to take it as a

[82] L. E. Holt, 'E. M. Forster: Samuel Butler', *PMLA* 61 (1946), 804–19.
[83] *The New Machiavelli*, p. 56.

full and true record of Butler's own life, with nothing changed but the names of the persons, we see by the light of Mr. Festing Jones that this is an absolutely untenable position. *The Way of All Flesh* is not an autobiography, but a romance founded on recollection.[84]

Although Arnold Bennett's attention to detailed realism in *Clayhanger* owed more to the French realists' influence than to any kinship with Butler, yet Book One of this novel betrays a curious similarity of approach to Butler's. Not only is there the obvious resemblance of theme, the study of a boy slowly beginning to question and suffer from the rigid tyranny of his father's philosophy, but Edwin Clayhanger shares Ernest's ingenuousness. Like Ernest, or John Owen, he is dismayed when he first discovers inconsistency in the advocates of religion, and Bennett, like Butler, allows the reader to identify with the boy in his feeling that such illogicality and insincerity may well pervade the entire system to which his allegiance is demanded. Were the names Edwin and Mrs. Hamps replaced by Ernest and Christina, the following passage might well have been taken from the 'sofa' scene in *The Way of All Flesh.*

Edwin was dashed. His faith in humanity was dashed. These elders were not sincere. And as Mrs. Hamps continued to embroider the original theme of her exhortation about the Bible, Edwin looked at her stealthily, and the doubt crossed his mind . . . whether the whole of her daily existence, from her getting-up to her lying-down, was not a grandiose pretence.[85]

Butler had drawn upon the various tools of the anti-Evangelical Victorian novelists and fashioned a myth which gained not only literary transmission but the status of historical evidence. As Compton Mackenzie phrased it, '. . . there is no doubt that the younger generation did find in *The Way of All Flesh* a point of concentration for their ideas of the Victorian age which was of inestimable benefit for putting those ideas in order.'[86]

His observation is interesting in that it indicates the semi-conscious desire of a new generation to confirm the sense of change provided by arbitrary chronological divisions. Butler's work served

[84] *Aspects and Impressions*, (1922) p. 63.

[85] *Clayhanger* (1910), p. 58. Bennett's letters provide evidence of his appreciation of Butler's work and opinions. *The Way of All Flesh* he described as having 'the severity & austerity of a classic', and later wrote 'I solace myself with the "Notebooks" of Samuel Butler.' *The Letters of Arnold Bennett*, ed. J. Hepburn (3 vols., 1966–70), ii, 344; iii, 40.

[86] *My Life and Times: Octave III, 1900–1907*, p. 127.

this need, helping men to regard the nineteenth century from which they had just emerged as a closed chapter. He depicted a hero who had apparently managed to free himself from his past and whose progressive modernity was symbolized by his insistence 'on addressing the next generation rather than his own'.[87] The real tension of the novel lay in the conflict between Ernest and Theobald which had been waged in mid-century, and the retrospective mode in which the work was written served to confirm for a new generation the remoteness of Evangelicalism as a dominant force.

Although Virginia Woolf may seem wilfully apocalyptic in her claim that '. . . in or about December, 1910, human character changed . . . All human relations have shifted—those between masters and servants, husbands and wives, parents and children. And when human relations change there is at the same time a change in religion, conduct, politics, and literature',[88] the new century undoubtedly witnessed a change in the artist's response to his times. Though the Edwardians continued to produce descendants of the Victorian novel, pre-eminently concerned with man as a social animal involved in personal relations, the Modernist note had been struck. An art which reflected scepticism of traditional religious and social values, a sense of man's isolation in the universe, and turned in upon itself to find expression in a concern with style and form found no room to rework the theme of Evangelical piety as practised in family life.

As the last in the long line of novelists to have portrayed Evangelicalism, however perversely, as a central concern of his society, the extent of Butler's achievement can best be gauged by the necessity his work creates to emphasize the singularity of an experience which has become widely and misleadingly accepted as a representative account of Evangelical life in Victorian England.

[87] *The Way of All Flesh*, p. 140.
[88] *Collected Essays* (4 vols., 1966–7), pp. 321–2.

# Select Book-list

This book-list makes no attempt to duplicate the detailed referencing of sources, both published and unpublished, to be found in the footnotes, nor to list the novelists and fiction under discussion, which can easily be identified by turning to the index. In the interests of brevity I have also omitted references to standard biographies of major novelists, familiar bibliographies, and works of reference.

*General Background*

M. Maison's *Search Your Soul, Eustace : a survey of the religious novel in the Victorian age* (1961) and R. L. Wolff's *Gains and Losses: Novels of Faith and Doubt in Victorian England* (New York, 1977) prove useful reference guides to the general field of the Victorian religious novel, although the first suffers from its brevity and inaccuracy, whilst the second is more valuable as a plot guide than as a work of criticism.

O. Chadwick's *The Victorian Church*, 2nd edn. (2 vols., 1970, 1972) provides an indispensable account of the controversies afflicting the Established Church. Also useful are the *Official Year-Book of the Church of England* (1883– ), H. Davies, *Worship and Theology in England*, iii, *From Watts and Wesley to Maurice, 1690–1850*, iv, *From Newman to Martineau, 1850–1900* (1961, 1962), and L. E. Elliott-Binns, *Religion in the Victorian Era*, 2nd edn. (1964).

Anglican Evangelicalism has been poorly served by Church historians. Four essayists attempted nineteenth-century surveys of the party: [C. S. C. Bowen] 'The English Evangelical Clergy', *Macmillan's Magazine*, 3 (1860), 113–21; [W. J. Conybeare], 'Church Parties', *Edin. Rev.* 98 (1853), 273–342; W. E. Gladstone, 'The Evangelical Movement: its Parentage, Progress, and Issue', *Gleanings of Past Years* 1875–8, 7 (1879), 201–41; and J. Stephen, *Essays in Ecclesiastical Biography* (2 vols., 1849). At the close of the century E. Stock's *The history of the Church Missionary Society, its environment, its men and its work* (3 vols., and Supplement, 1899–1916) is more comprehensive in its account of the party than its title would suggest and serves as a useful corrective to the High Church W. H. B. Proby's *Annals of the 'Low Church' Party in England down to the death of Archbishop Tait* (2 vols., 1888). In similar vein one may read the Evangelical G. R. Balleine's *A history of the Evangelical party in the Church of England* (1908; 1951) against the briefer sketch offered by G. W. E. Russell in *A Short History of the Evangelical Movement* (1915), the work of a High Churchman of Evangelical parentage. Of more recent date are F. K. Brown's *Fathers of the Victorians* (Cambridge, 1961), a work of immense but misapplied scholarship, useful for its detailed accounts of various Evangelical controversies but vitiated by the Calvinist witch-hunt in which it indulges; and J. S. Reynolds's, *The Evangelicals at Oxford, 1735–1871: with the record extended to 1905* (Oxford, 1975), which provides comprehensive lists of party support at all levels within the University.

Much valuable information remains largely unpublished in the form of theses: J. D. Walsh, 'The Yorkshire Evangelicals in the Eighteenth Century with Especial Reference to Methodism', D.Phil. thesis (Cambridge, 1956); I. C. Bradley, 'The Politics of Godliness: Evangelicals in Parliament 1784–1832', D. Phil. thesis (Oxford, 1974); H. Willmer, 'Evangelicalism 1785–1835', Hulsean Prize Essay (Cambridge, 1962); S. C. Orchard, 'English Evangelical Eschatology 1790–1850', D.Phil. thesis (Cambridge, 1968); B. E. Hardman, 'The Evangelical Party in the Church of England, 1855–1865', D.Phil. thesis (Cambridge, 1963); and A. Bentley, 'The Transformation of the Evangelical Party in the Church of England in the later Nineteenth Century', D.Phil. thesis (Durham, 1971).

### THE EVANGELICAL WAY OF LIFE

Three types of source emerged:

(a) *Doctrinal* In addition to the numerous sermons, tracts and pamphlets on specific issues the following were particularly useful in offering views on a wide range of matters over the span of a century and a half: H. Venn, *The Complete Duty of Man: or a System of Doctrinal and Practical Christianity* (1763; new revised edn. 1841); W. Wilberforce, *A Practical View of the Prevailing Religious System of Professed Christians, in the Higher and Middle Classes in this country, contrasted with real Christianity* (2nd edn., 1797); [J. Bean], *Zeal without Innovation* (1808); *The Works of Hannah More* (revised edn. 11 vols., 1830); J. H. Pratt, ed. *Eclectic Notes or, Notes of Discussions on Religious Topics at the Meetings of the Eclectic Society London* (2nd edn. 1865); and J. C. Ryle, *Knots Untied* (1871).

(b) *Newspapers and Periodicals*

The following nineteenth-century organs provided a spectrum of Anglican Evangelical opinion:

*Christian Guardian* (1802-53)
*Christian Lady's Magazine* (1834–46)
*Christian Observer* (1802–75)
*Christian Observer and Advocate* (1875–7)
*Record* (1828–1948)
*Rock* (1868–1905)

(c) *Biographies, Autobiographies, Diaries, and Reminiscences*

BATEMAN, J. *The Life of the Rev. Henry Venn Elliott* (1868).

BICKERSTETH, E. *Domestic Portraiture, or the successful application of Religious Principle in the education of a family, exemplified in the memoirs of three of the deceased children of the Rev. Legh Richmond* (1834).

BICKERSTETH, M. C. B. *A Sketch of the Life and Episcopate of the Right Reverend Robert Bickersteth* (1887).

BIRKS, T. R. *A Memoir of the Rev. Edward Bickersteth*, 3rd edn. (2 vols., 1852).

BROWN, A. W. *Recollections of the Conversation Parties of the Rev. Charles Simeon* (1863).

CARUS, W. *Memoirs of the life of Charles Simeon* (1847).

FORSTER, E. M. *Marianne Thornton* (New York, 1956).

GRIMSHAWE, T. S. *A Memoir of the Rev. Legh Richmond*, 3rd edn. (1828).

HENNELL, M. *John Venn and the Clapham Sect* (1958).

HODDER, E. *The Life and Work of the Seventh Earl of Shaftesbury* (3 vols., 1886).

JONES, M. G. *Hannah More* (Cambridge, 1952).

LOCK, J. and DIXON, W. T. *A Man of Sorrow: The Life, Letters and Times of the Rev. Patrick Brontë* (1965).

[MARSH, C.] *The Life of William Marsh* (1867).

*Journals and Letters of the Rev. Henry Martyn*, ed. S. Wilberforce (2 vols., 1837).

MEACHAM, S. *Henry Thornton of Clapham 1760–1815* (Cambridge, Mass., 1964).

MEYER, MRS. [F.B.] *The Author of the Peep of Day, being the Life Story of Mrs. Mortimer* (1901).

MORGAN, W. *The Parish Priest, Pourtrayed in the Life, Character, and Ministry of the Rev. John Crosse* (1841).

MOULE, H. C. G. *Memories of a Vicarage* (1913).

MOZLEY, T. *Reminiscences chiefly of Oriel College and the Oxford Movement* (2 vols., 1882).

NEWSOME, D. *The Parting of Friends: A Study of the Wilberforces and Henry Manning* (1966).

PHILPOTT, J. H. *The Seceders: The Story of J. C. Philpot and William Tiptaft* (1964).

ROBERTS, W. *Memoirs of the Life and Correspondence of Mrs. Hannah More* 2nd edn. (4 vols., 1834).

——. *Romilly's Cambridge Diary 1832–1842*, ed. J. P. T. Bury (Cambridge, 1967).

RUSKIN, J. *Praeterita and Dilecta*, ed. E. T. Cook and A. Wedderburn (1908).

RUSSELL, G. W. E. *Lady Victoria Buxton* (1919).

SARGENT, J. *Memoir of the Rev. Henry Martyn* (1819).

SCOTT, T. *The Force of Truth: an Authentic Narrative* (1779).

*The Life of Mrs. Sherwood (chiefly autobiographical) with extracts from Mr. Sherwood's Journal, edited by her daughter.*

*The Life and Times of Mrs. Sherwood 1775–1851 from the Diaries of Captain and Mrs. Sherwood*, ed. F. J. H. Darton (1910).

STEPHEN, C. E. *The First Sir James Stephen, Letters with Biographical Notes* (Gloucester, 1906).

STEPHEN, L. *The Life of Sir J. F. Stephen* (1895).

STOCK, E. *My Recollections* (1909).

[TONNA, C. E. B. P.] 'Charlotte Elizabeth', *Personal Recollections* (1841).

TREVELYAN, G. O. *The Life and Letters of Lord Macaulay* (2 vols., Oxford. 1932).

TURNER, J. H. *Brontëana: the Rev. Patrick Brontë, his collected works and life* (Bingley, 1898).

VENN, J. *The Life and Selection from the Letters of the late Rev. Henry Venn*, ed. H. Venn (1834).

VENN, J. *Annals of a Clerical Family* (1904).

WILBERFORCE, R. I. and S. *The Life of William Wilberforce* (5 vols., 1838).

# Index